BAD IN THE BLOOD

ALSO BY MATTEO L. CERILLI

Lockjaw

BAD IN THE BLOOD

MATTEO L. CERILLI

tundra

Text copyright © 2025 by Matteo L. Cerilli
Cover art copyright © 2025 by Evangeline Gallagher

Tundra Books, an imprint of Tundra Book Group, a division of Penguin Random House Canada Ltd., 320 Front Street West, Suite 1400, Toronto, Ontario, M5V 3B8, Canada
penguinrandomhouse.ca

Published simultaneously in the United States of America by Tundra Books of Northern New York, an imprint of Tundra Book Group, a division of Penguin Random House Canada Ltd., P.O. Box 2040, Plattsburgh, NY 12901, USA

Tundra with colophon is a registered trademark of Penguin Random House Canada Ltd.

All rights reserved. No part of this book may be reproduced, scanned, transmitted, or distributed in any form or by any electronic or mechanical means, including information storage and retrieval systems, without permission in writing from the publisher, except by a reviewer, who may quote brief passages in a review. No part of this book may be used or reproduced in any manner for the purpose of training artificial intelligence technologies or systems.

The authorized representative in the EU for product safety and compliance is Penguin Random House Ireland, Morrison Chambers, 32 Nassau Street, Dublin D02 YH68, Ireland, https://eu-contact.penguin.ie

Publisher's note: This book is a work of fiction. Names, characters, places and incidents either are the product of the author's imagination or are used fictitiously, and any resemblance to actual persons living or dead, events, or locales is entirely coincidental.

Library and Archives Canada Cataloguing in Publication

Title: Bad in the blood / Matteo L. Cerilli.
Names: Cerilli, Matteo L., author.
Identifiers: Canadiana (print) 20240524640 | Canadiana (ebook) 20240524659 | ISBN 9781774882337 (hardcover) | ISBN 9781774882344 (EPUB)
Subjects: LCGFT: Detective and mystery fiction. | LCGFT: Fantasy fiction. | LCGFT: Queer fiction. | LCGFT: Novels.
Classification: LCC PS8605.E75 B33 2025 | DDC jC813/.6—dc23

Library of Congress Control Number: 2024949715

Edited by Peter Phillips
Cover designed by Matthew Flute
Interior images: Adobe Stock, RawPixel, and supplied by the author
Typeset by Erin Cooper
The text was set in Minion Pro.

Printed in Canada

1 2 3 4 5   29 28 27 26 25

To my partner, for encouraging me to write.
And to my sister, for giving me so much to write about.

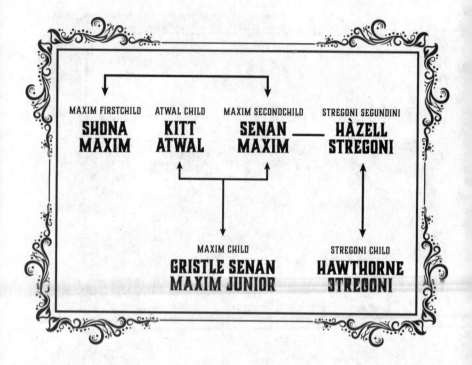

NOTE:
Due to the addictive properties of fey symptoms, overreliance on symptoms as a coping mechanism will begin to erode rational thinking, resulting in increasingly dangerous and erratic behavior. A stress test can then be performed to determine if a fey's symptoms have escalated to become harmful to themself or others, thus constituting madness.

PROLOGUE

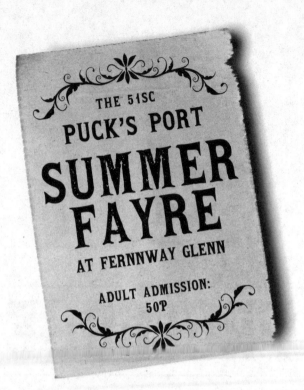

STREGONI CHILD IN
"MIDWAY MONSTERS"

Now that all my feyness is coming in, I think I oughta get involved in the family business, even if I gotta eavesdrop to do it.

I'm still only eleven this cycle, which is plenty small enough to hide under one of the painted carnie wagons in the back lot of the Summer Fayre. The wheel spokes split the world up into sections of bright summer sun and pretty carved shadows. I skim my eyes across the wooden bumps and loops, every little nick and swirl. The pattern hums down into my bones like a tuning fork when you smack it. It twines up in harmony with the smell of dust and animals and bedstraw-and-daisy-and-ribbon wreaths on every post out here, and the slapping of canvas fayre flags high above, and even the faraway sound of the bandstand keys and horns and the midway rattle.

Last cycle, I wouldn't have been able to hear it all so well. Now, I'm growing into myself, just like Mum says.

Ahead, in the back lot, one of the carnival barkers is sitting on an upside-down wash bucket and reading a pink pamphlet, with a droopy-eyed hound dog nosing at her hand. The gems on her vest glint so sharp and hot that my teeth grit.

I let the singing up to my hands. When I shake out both wrists, tiny sparkles ride the heat up and disappear, taking all my tension with them.

Maxim crouches next to me, careful enough to keep the hem of their Solstice dress out of the dirt. "Is she fey?" they ask me as they watch the barker. "I can't see anything fey on them."

Their voice whips down into my stomach, builds impulsive pressure, and before I can stop it, "People don't always *look* fey, Maxim," I snap. A blast of hot air rushes over them, wilting the daisy behind their ear and gusting their fluffy black hair from their face.

The last bit of energy's gone now. In the silence, Maxim just blinks at me with their lips wrinkling up. They've got a wide brown face and wide green eyes, real open and honest in a way that always makes me feel a bit rotten getting mad at.

"Shoot," I mutter. Mum says that by the time I'm picking my name and deciding who I'm gonna be as a grown-up, I'll have enough practice to keep from snapping like that. But for now, I gotta be careful. I flex my hands a bit. "I didn't mean that."

Maxim's too good. "S'okay," they say, just as quiet. Maxim's not a smiling sort, but I see how clear their eyes are and I know we're alright.

I lean sideways so our shoulders bump each other. Maxim's mortal and born in Dale, where they don't much talk about fey out loud, and had five whole cycles without me. I know I oughta catch them up. I point between the spokes, dragging my sharp nail through the air. "She's got her dog. See how she keeps petting at it? It's gotta be a familiar."

"That makes sense," they say, both of us squishing warm and tight to watch.

"I heard about all this—fey mortal hold-hands-around-the-fire hoopla," the worker in the lot says. Her dog noses at her knee, she takes a long, deep breath, and she sets the pamphlet on her lap. She turns her face away from us. "So, before I say anything more, I oughta know if you're the Maxim twin with the good sense to stay in midtown, or the one that's always picking fights on the docks."

She's talking to Maxim's daddy leaned against another wagon nearby, the painting on the side putting him in a frame like he's a pretty curiosity. His hat is low on his white-pale face, cutting a big, black shadow across his eyes.

When he speaks, a cloud of cigar smoke washes around him. "For the record, we were *born* on the docks, so I figure it's my fight to pick," he says, looking all wiry and wily like only dockside folk can, mouth grim and serious in the smoke. Maxim and I both peer closer. I gotta say, Senan Maxim might be the coolest person we both know. "If you're worried we'll tell any cops about what you say here, trust me when I tell you that they'd kick my stomach in before I could get anything out."

"I don't chum with mortals," the barker says. So she *is* a fey.

"And I'm sure the folks eating caviar on 1st Street are glad for that," he says, shoulders tense and ready. "I understand the reservations, miss, but I come from the poor yards too. I think us down here eating gristle ought to remember what we have in common."

Maxim squints. "Gristle," they say quietly, and then twice more even quieter. "What's that mean?" they ask me, turning like I got all the answers. I shrug. I'm not any older than they are—we've got different parents and still we were born on the same day. Real fated like that.

The back of the barker's candy-striped uniform shifts, like she's grown something along her spine. Feathers, maybe, or crystals. The dog senses her energy's up—it starts to growl, lips wrinkled back from its teeth. I take my hands off the spokes to flick sparkles from my nervous fingers.

"Well, then, I don't want trouble," she says, in a voice that makes Maxim shuffle closer to me. "And trouble seems to follow you."

The corners of Senan's mouth twist up. He turns his head to the third person in the back lot, just out of our sight.

"I'd argue that a private investigator is following the trouble," Mum says, from the shadow off the huge circus tent. Her voice swings with a thick Verdossi accent, all calm like a slow river twisting through mountains I barely remember now. Even the dog's snarling stills. It creeps back toward its owner, beady eyes still on Senan. "But I think we can make better use of our time than by interrogating his credentials. Rest assured that I keep my mortal man in check where he needs it."

The barker's knees relax as Mum steps forward, in a Verdossi dress and sash that she brought on the boat when I was small, the hems bordered with embroidered flowers and the same style covering the kerchief holding back her thick, dark curls. In the light, with my senses all sharp, I notice how we look so damn similar, down to the tanned skin and the arch of our noses. Except Mum's older than me, her power so much stronger: she's grown a band of opal-shining scales from nose to cheekbone. One of my eyes is that same color, the first thing I changed before I much knew how to control this.

"The carnival owners can pay us fey half of what they'd pay men like my husband. It drives down the price of his labor, endangers newcomers to this country who don't care how the coin comes in, keeps us all begging for scraps," Mum says. The barker must be cooling off—the back of her uniform smooths. "I see no downside to a fair wage for all of us, do you?"

Maxim and I press our shoulders together, watching close to see how the barker reacts. She don't look worried no more.

Instead, she tilts her head, like she's sizing up the argument. "Legally," the barker says, crossing her arms, "they ain't under no obligation to pay me full. Never finished school. Had to leave when the condition got too strong."

Me too. As soon as I started spitting out sparkles whenever the math problems were too hard, and my teachers wanted to put me in classes by myself, Mum and Senan knew regular school wasn't gonna help me much. I swallow the prickly feeling in my throat, try to listen to what the barker is saying through the searing sunshine, but I hear "—gave in to the impulse and ended up on the ground with my stomach unzipped from navel to neck. I wasn't old enough to stress-test, so they just expelled me—" and I have to close my eyes tight.

I hate hearing about what happens when the power gets too big and you ain't ready for it. I hate knowing about the stress-tests, and the madhouses.

"Stregoni," Maxim whispers, putting their hand careful over mine. It's grounding, and stops my pointy nails from glowing orange. I crack my eyes open just a tiny bit, enough to see Maxim looking at me with those big, sincere, mortal eyes. "We can go get popcorn? I still have tickets."

I press my lips together. I know I oughta leave, but the temptation to keep listening is too damn strong, like it's got its claw on my chin to make me watch. I snap my fingers to let piddly sparkles off, and it's enough. But this is small power, new and learning to grow stronger and smarter . . .

If my body asked me to unzip myself to make the bad feelings go away, would I catch the thought before it was too late? If it asked me to hurt someone, could I stop it?

The question pushes up behind my already-sharp teeth, building pressure in my veins until my ears ring. I stare at Maxim so close I can see every pore and the flecks of coal dust and dirt still clinging there even out here in the sunshine-y country where birds are chirping just nearby. I want to ask "Would you still love me if I hurt someone, Maxim?" but I don't want to say it out loud. Because, just for today, we're out where the sun is shining like the bad things can't get us. I know we'll hop back on the trolley in only a few bells, and fade back into the smoky city of Puck's Port, where things don't feel perfect at all.

"I got you, Stregoni," Maxim says, 'cause they can read my mind like a blood twin. Like we're Maxim & Maxim, the dockyard duo, heroes and geniuses fit for radio plays. "Things are changing, right? I bet you . . ." They swallow, because they can't make promises, but they try anyway. "I bet you there won't even *be* madhouses once we're named. And you'll be all powerful like your mum, keeping things real controlled."

It's that last part that makes the tension flood out of my feet to parch the dirt. It's a nice thought, but Maxim's only mortal. I squint back between the spokes, to where Mum's standing in the light with her pearly scales. "The world isn't made for us," she says. Two tiny horns sprout from just above her hairline. "The uptown folks can pretend Dale has changed since the pyre-burning days, but they built a world without us while we rotted out of reach of it. We can make something better, all of us."

Between the tents, dark laneways lead back to the carnival rows screaming out for us, and back to the city that can't stand us.

"You talk like a radical," the barker says. She stands up, but she don't look scared one bit. She's smiling, with all her teeth just barely pointed so I only notice now that I'm looking. "Careful with that talk, miss. They save cells for folks like that."

And if they take Mum away? What then? I press my hands together, breath held tight, tight, tight.

"I dare them to try," Mum says. "Until then, we're happy to be in contact with you."

The barker eyes Senan a bit, but he's got his sights on the lanes. "Charmed," the barker agrees. She steps forward, extends her hand. "Can I have your name?"

Mum grins. She claps their palms together in a sturdy shake. The air pauses like the *clack* of a radio shutting off, like all the singing auras are quiet to hear the fey.

"Hàzell Stregoni," Mum says, and proves just how strong she is.

A ripple sprints through the air, smelling like green and dew. Maxim and I, wide-eyed, press forward between the spokes to watch vines bloom from Mum's clasped palm, looping over the barker's hand and wrapping tight at their wrists like handfasting cords. Pink specks grow from the green, twisting into foxgloves that move and sway to their own little songs, the petals falling and regrowing and falling again, whipping around Mum and the worker while the dog barks happily. The petals climb in a torrent of wind the color of pink pearls, kicking up sparkling dust. Beside me, Maxim reaches one clay-brown hand out for them. Through the storm, Senan looks to Mum and sweeps his hat back to watch. His eyes are wide as Maxim's, awestruck and sparkling above his straight mouth.

And Mum in the middle, she doesn't even blink, doesn't even shake, don't lose breath or control of the power rushing out of her like a smooth wave. I get that feeling like a cherry pit in my heart, that ache of loving someone so much you think you might choke on it. Love you'd die for.

Looking at Mum, I know that being a fey doesn't mean you're destined to be destroyed by the thing in your blood. You *are* that thing, Mum says, and madness is a mortal word for something they don't understand.

"Keep your eye on us," Mum says. I hum, bringing heat into my throat and purring under my skin, letting out all that love in tiny rays of light that make Maxim gasp. They're brighter than they were yesterday. "I promise that change is coming far sooner than you think."

I'm changing too, and this rotten world better be ready.

Property of the
PUCK'S PORT POLICE DEPARTMENT

Article A-52 in the case of
Maxim versus Stregoni

The Diary of Hàzell Stregoni,
"Radical Fey"

42 SC, 6 Summer Moons, Summer Solstice

The decision to cart myself away from my homeland and toward Dale has not been an easy one, especially with a child not yet three cycles old who already has a pale eye to proclaim their feyism. Perhaps that is why I took the trip as we churn toward the darkest days. Our village in Verdessa was an idyllic place to raise a fey child, where poor farmers need us to scent the earth and the air, where cycles run slow enough to accommodate time to calm ourselves, where we are not suppressed but embraced. Still, I can in fact scent the wind as well as any other. Once, Dale was seen as a faraway problem, something we were simply glad not to be born into, a country whose pyres and later their madhouses were nothing more than ghost stories. We were foolish.

As Dale builds its industrial wealth, as even Verdessi officials begin changing our calendars to mark cycles "Since [Dale's] Confederacy," as our city centers sprout iron smithies and telephone lines and push fast-moving factories into our slow villages to make even time unaffordable, we must act. If our country builds itself according to Dale, so many of us will starve beyond the walls of this "new world." The fey struggle is the same as that of the poor, the worker, the very old, and the very young: we are not the sorts who make political decisions, and thus we are not the sorts this new world is being built for.

I refuse the notion that our power is a curse and liability. I refuse to think myself more dangerous than the madhouses where so many of our own disappear into themselves, collapsing under their distress like dying stars. That is pain and destruction, but where is the outcry for justice in their names? The world sits by quietly while we burn.

This is why I have come to Dale. Because Verdossa will not stay safe forever, and I will not sit in wait. Call me impulsive or mad, discredit my name, but my fear is still real: Dale's capital, Puck's Port, is where real evil could occur. But (take peace and warning, both) it is also where change can spark. I will not let the world watch in silence.

Tonight, I am in Puck's Port, in a shanty apartment with walls so thin I can hear the children crying four doors down, and a radio from four floors up. Incessant trains cart autos and coal and iron day and night above our heads, and the air smells of fish screaming for their last breath before they drown on land. During the day, beggars—so many of them fey—ask for coins I do not have. Tonight, I am in Dale. Tomorrow, I will be in Dale still, because our suffering will only be temporary.

I'm not sure of how I can change anything, only that I must try, despite the perils. Change is coming to Dale, and soon the entire world. I will show them their own horrors reflected back. I will not be afraid.

After that perfect summer day, Maxim Child would be orphaned, and would spend the next cycle attempting to explain how one moment turned to the next. It was, frankly, impossible to articulate. Each time they tried, the whole mess seemed more mythical than real.

Things had started rather ordinarily, including when Stregoni had begged them to listen in on the barker. Maxim only began to mark a strangeness in the day after Stregoni and Hàzell had run off to buy popcorn, leaving Maxim's daddy to step into the cold shadows of a public phone booth with Maxim clinging close beside him. Senan Maxim kept one hand on the back of his child's head while he wrestled for a tarnished pix in his pocket.

"You . . . you know, when I was your age," he started, which was how most adults did in a country so rapidly changing. But from below, Maxim could see under the shadow of his hat—his milk-white face seemed gray amidst smoky clouds, his mouth crooked to keep the cigar between his teeth, and yet still wrinkled more than usual.

He'd been "chain-smoking" all day, a phrase Maxim had learned from his aunt when she'd playfully scolded him. "We had to send letters," Senan went on, feeding in the rattling coin and snatching up the phone piece. "'Course, we couldn't afford postage, either. I'd write to your mum on the back of newspapers, leave 'em on her sill."

Maxim nodded. They never much knew how to respond to stories about their mother, who had died when Maxim was still a toddler and left their daddy nearly catatonically devastated on his sister's doorstep. Maxim couldn't recall who had told them this, or if they'd just gleaned it from tone and subtext, its own sort of private detective mystery. Growing up with a daddy and an aunt who hunted robbers and murderers and who knew better than to share too many details, Maxim had gotten good at patterning out evidence, at least enough to know when to stay unseen and quiet.

The phone crackled on in a garble of operator chatter. Senan tapped his fingers against the phone box. "Send me to Rory, will you?" he asked. Puff, puff, puff went the cigar, burning down faster. More clicks, and another chatter on the end. "Morning, Rory," he breathed, almost like a gasp. Rory Gattano was the only switchboarder that Senan Maxim trusted.

"Hello, Mx Gattano," Maxim offered quietly.

There was a snarl of chatter. Senan's fingers tapped a bit harder against the cold iron box. "No, Vic told me it would print this morning. What's done is done," he said. Miss Victory Eze was a journalist; again, the only one Senan Maxim trusted to break bad news. He closed his eyes and swallowed. "I need you to patch me to Shona," he said, almost a whisper. The tone made Maxim's blood go icy. The carnival was reaching its mid-day rush, and yet Maxim couldn't hear or see it from the isolation of that little phone booth. "She left me a letter—I know she's pissed with me—but I need to try. Be quick." Senan looked back out to the dusty path, as if someone might be watching. "Hàzell didn't really want me calling today."

A mumble of agreement, and then the muffled tolling of the phone. Senan Maxim stared into the voice funnel with his eyes shining. Were there tears? Upon later recollection, Maxim couldn't be sure.

Maxim debated if they should say anything. The line tolled and tolled. Shona Maxim did not answer.

"Maybe she's out?" Maxim suggested.

No answer. Maxim pressed their lips together, debated again, and lightly tapped their shoe into their daddy's.

Senan blinked hard, as if surprised, but turned his head enough to see Maxim staring up at him. Had he wiped his eyes then on the rough sleeve of his suit jacket?

"Maybe she's out?" Maxim tried again.

Senan's lips pressed tight together. Maxim would later learn that she was out, on the trolley heading back from the police precinct where she'd had to do some "capital-A ass kissing" to patch up what Miss Eze had printed. Maxim & Maxim were on the outs, and everyone knew it, aside from little Maxim Child, who could only sense the unease.

The tolling stopped. Maxim craned up a bit higher.

"Sorry, Senan," Rory Gattano said in their soft, reedy voice with Verdosso still twisted onto the edges. "She's not picking up. I can call the diner under her? Midge can head up to check?"

Senan Maxim rubbed a thumb along the edge of his button-small nose. "No," he said, voice empty. "Just keep me through."

"Senan," Rory said. "I'm sure she'll cool off—"

"Put me through, Gattano," Senan Maxim snapped, so loud that Maxim flinched. "I *need* to talk to her. *Now.*"

"I . . ." Rory paused. "Patching you through, *amico*. Are we still on for Cat's tonight?"

Senan Maxim closed his eyes tight. "Maybe," he said.

Maybe, like he knew something bad was coming. In that flash-moment of understanding, one that wouldn't sink in longer than the sparked second, Maxim noticed how their daddy's slacks seemed too big now, and that he was missing a star-shaped button on his vest, that his orange hair was slipping from the silk ribbon that held it in a long tail down his back.

Maxim's pulse beat thicker, as if they understood that Senan Maxim would not survive until nightfall, and that he may well have known this too. That he wanted to get out one last "I love you," with either an "I understand what I'm walking into" or even an "I messed up, Shona. I'm scared and I need you to save me."

The line tolled and tolled, and Shona couldn't answer in time. Her twin was going to die, because she wasn't there to save him from his own mistakes.

"Maxim!" someone shouted.

Maxim Child jumped, their thoughts already evaporated to leave behind only a heavy sediment of dread. Still, they turned to see Stregoni come sprinting up to the open phone booth, framed by the hanging flower garlands over the arch, shoulders heaving from the ecstatic sprint. Maxim felt immediately better, happier and lighter just to see them with untangling braids trailing ribbons, and a wrinkled old work shirt hanging over bony limbs, and sharp teeth under mismatched eyes all alight in the sunshine beyond the phone booth.

Stregoni grabbed Maxim's wrist, yanking them out in a rush of fey-made sparkles swirling around them both like fireflies. Maxim had only a moment to look over their shoulder.

Senan Maxim stood ahead of the tolling phone, light through the top of the warped booth coming down in streams through the lingering smoke. Maxim was possessed with the unexplainable, infantile urge to cling to their daddy.

But that was the last thing Maxim Child remembered clearly. What would follow would be glimpsed only in faint memories burnt through by concussion and trauma, brief flashes like movie stills, and it was this:

Stregoni's gold-green hand yanking them down the path. Saying they were going to the carousel, leading them. The feeling of how their palms fit well into each other.

Looking back to see Hàzell standing outside the phone booth, grim-faced, snapping her fingers carefully at her side. With each pronounced click, a dusting of pollen sprinkled down around her. But when Senan hung up the phone, every flower on the booth's draped garland wilted at once. The taste of sour earth flooded through Maxim's mouth. Hàzell put her hand on her husband's arm, leading him twitchy and nervous back into the light. She looped her arm through his, tight as confinement.

Staring down the people they passed with rapt attention. The baggy flashes of trouser legs, the floral patterns on waistcoats and dresses, the silky ribbons and feathers and stuffed birds on straw hats, the lace on parasols, everyone's shoes dusted up the same so the rich people looked like the poor people. Like everyone was just people.

A barker in front of the carousel: a fey with long, thin horns who pretended not to see the suspicious glares of the mortals, and who winked at Stregoni in a rush of pearly sparkles but didn't seem to see Maxim. The monstrous faces of the carousel ponies, grinning and sneering through the blur of Maxim's aching stomach. Maxim saw themselves in those swirly mirrors on the inner post—they looked so small.

On the carousel, the soothing up and down. Watching for the post sprouted just beside the ride, where a single brass prize ring spun like a planet, and making sure to tell Stregoni when to lunge out for it, in case they were distracted. The sky was brilliantly blue.

Hàzell and their daddy, waiting so far back in the sea of parents that they were just two solitary pillars against a painfully vibrant tent. But they had their heads together, mouths sharp and quick in the bright light that hid Senan Maxim's eyes. They were arguing, Maxim realized, Hàzell's hands flying quick and Senan speaking fast, shoulders tight. Something was wrong, on a day when nothing should be. They couldn't hear through the crowd's rumbling and the calliope music.

Hàzell's hands ripped through the air like a scythe—all around her feet, the pastel grass began to wilt. Maxim held their breath, terrified that the mortals nearby might see and report her. That cops could arrive and order a stress-test to coax some truth out. But Hàzell would pass, yes? She could stay composed even as the shocks grew worse and worse, could choose to fall unconscious with the pain rather than follow the impulse to lash out mad? If anyone could, it was her. And the day would pass, and they would visit Auntie Shona, and everything would be alright.

From the outside pony, Stregoni was watching their mother too. Maxim became certain that, whatever was being said, Stregoni was hearing it. And letting in all that sound wasn't good for them: silhouetted against the sun-struck world beyond, Stregoni's fingernails had begun to glow, color leaking up their arms along the veins like bad blood, singing through the rough weave of their shirt. It wasn't dangerous, but it was obvious.

"Ring," Maxim muttered, which pulled Stregoni's focus fast. Over the crowd, Maxim watched in horror as Hàzell continued to whip through words so fast that Senan Maxim recoiled slightly, sweat beading from under the shadows of his hat. Two little specks sprouted from Hàzell's forehead, black as jet. They grew into antlers clawing up for the blue sky, sparkling with glints like stars. Hàzell knew better than to do something so powerful in public: nearby, a woman gasped and took two steps away. Hàzell shot her an angry glare, teeth snarling sharp.

Stregoni Child kept one hand gripped on their pony's post and lunged out into the light, fingers swinging toward the shiny brass ring just beyond easy grasp. Half-desperate, Senan Maxim jolted forward.

Stregoni Child's pointy-nailed finger looped through the ring and plucked away the prize.

Hàzell Stregoni's wrist was suddenly grabbed in the cold, mortal claw of her husband.

It would not stop the massacre that followed.

This concluded what Maxim understood with certainty. What they wouldn't ever know was if the next part had been a tragic accident, one last gram of gravity to collapse a titanic star in on itself, or a long-calculated choice to set this horrible, awful, rotten world ablaze.

◆

Everything following was patched together by Stregoni's account, and their aunt's, and the dozens of newspaper reports that hashed and rehashed the event until any possible recollection was overwritten by someone else's pen. As far as Maxim remembered, they were suddenly off the carousel, blinking in the white sunlight. Stregoni clutched their hand on one side and the carousel's brass ring on the other. Maxim understood that, following this moment, nothing would be the same.

"Stregoni," Maxim mumbled, blinking to stop the waning image of their sibling's face from fraying about the edges and mixing into the muddled background. Something wet was dripping from Maxim's ears. The liquid was deep gray, nearly black, so viscous it seemed unreal. Maxim could see it, somehow, as if watching the scene from a picture-show seat.

Maxim's mouth opened. The voice that came out seemed too young: "Where's my daddy?"

Stregoni's eyes stared ahead, mouth and eyes wide as a gasping fish's. Maxim found themself incapable of turning to see what Stregoni was fixated on. The air smelled like ash and smoke, but beneath that, dew and flowers. Maxim screwed up their face, trying to force out proper words. And yet there came that impossibly young, impossibly *childish* voice: "Where's my daddy?"

It startled them, because that wasn't what they'd meant to say. This was of course related to the concussion, and so too was the gray color of Stregoni's face, which was not just sick-gray but gray-gray. Maxim was increasingly aware that everything was colored like a photograph. The sky was no longer blue, Stregoni's skin was no longer green-gold, and the stitches of their kerchief were only gray on black.

"Maxim," Stregoni choked out, blinking hard like the *pop-cough* of a portrait camera. "Look."

Maxim finally turned.

What they found was devastation worse than any dockyard row fire, or even their own mother's blue-drowned body. The fayre was gone. Maxim and Stregoni stared at the great gap in the grass where the carousel had been, where there was instead nothing but gray dirt, as if someone had plucked it from this plane. The carousel was still there, simply tipped on its side, where roughly two dozen children lay dead beneath it like dropped apples. This included four children from the Tanner family, who later became the epitome of tragedy, while Maxim and Stregoni became a symbol of freakish serendipity. Because though the rest of the fayre around them in great circles was reduced to matchsticks and loose canvas, dead horses and dead elephants and dead people, Maxim and Stregoni remained virtually unharmed. It would be called either the last pure intentions of a mad radical, or a miracle.

Maxim still isn't sure.

Beside the carousel, just ten steps away from the two children, the ground was scorched blacker than pitch, still burning. Maxim knew that was where Hàzell and their daddy had stood moments ago. Where their feet had been, something sprouted into the silent air. Even from a distance, Maxim knew what it was. They found themself standing next to it, but couldn't remember walking over. Only Stregoni could tell the color of the sprouted thing, so only they could confirm what Maxim already assumed.

"It's a foxglove," Stregoni said, hollowly. But Maxim didn't care much about the flower: they were looking at the white bits near it, which they wanted to believe were just rocks. Law enforcement would later confirm them to be teeth, specifically, the teeth of controversial dockyard detective Senan Maxim, may he walk the good path.

"Mum gave in," Stregoni breathed.

Perhaps this had always been the plan. Did their daddy know? Was he arguing because he wanted it to stop? Had he willfully put his children in the blast zone, believing this could usher in a new and better age? The ringing air whistled around the two of them. All that silence. All that ash raining down.

Stregoni's voice tightened, from shock to terror. "Mum did it. Mum blew up. Maxim—"

They didn't want to hear it, and so they didn't. The day faded into gray nothingness.

Shona Maxim received tear-filled, wall-shaking, screaming custody of her brother's children. Maxim Child never recovered the ability to see color. The story goes on, the day is put in the past. As far as Maxim Child is concerned, it oughta stay there.

After all this heartache, the least the world can do is let them forget.

"THIS IS FOR FAMILY."

SHONA MAXIM PUTS HAT IN THE RING FOR 57SC PRESIDENTIAL ELECTION

Since my brother was murdered exactly two cycles ago, all I can see in this city, this country, is how we've failed to help the most vulnerable. My sister-in-law's madness has been used to push further anti-fey sentiment that worsens conditions for every fey, and only paves a stronger path toward increased violence. This vicious cycle must be stopped. Harsher fines will not solve madness, nor will fiercer police patrols. We remain the country that invented the automobile, put electricity in the wires, and still we think it fair to create second-class citizens of people afflicted with a disease. This cannot stand.

There is no candidate who represents my interests, or the interests of anyone with a fey child. That is why, today, I am officially entering the 57SC presidential race, with the support of the University of Stoutshire's Department of Fey Studies.

It may be a long shot, but I'm willing to try. This is for my brother's children, so they will not suffer as we have.

Vote Maxim. Vote for science, for progress, and for the future.

—Shona Maxim, 53SC/SS

PART ONE

"A Family Affair"

MAXIM CLIMBS THE POLLS JUST IN TIME FOR HER TWINS' NAMING CEREMONY!

3RD WINTER MOON, 57SC

One septennial ago, the name "Maxim" would have conjured up the infamous image of two handsome, red-haired detectives with a nose for clues and an eye for justice: Puck's Port's very own Shona and Senan Maxim, of Maxim & Maxim Private Detectives. But today, the name has become synonymous with a new wave in "pro-fey" justice, a phrase that would have inspired quite a few sour looks back then.

Since the loss of the youngest Maxim twin in the horrific 51SC Summer Fayre Massacre, Faerie Disorder has become a source of both fear and fascination, with Shona Maxim and her wards in the eye of this storm. They've not only braved these changes, but turned tragedy to triumph.

From her 6th Street office, Maxim stands in a well-cut suit, her brother's hat on the mantle behind her, his now seventeen-cycle-old children helping her stack posters.

"It's a family affair," says Maxim Child, in shirtsleeves and jaunty hat, with severity not unlike their aunt's. "My aunt and I just got back from the campaign trail. Stregoni and I hang posters when I walk them to school."

Shona Maxim, homegrown on the western docks like no politician this city has seen, boasts a campaign of increased wages for workers, additional international trade, a more rigorous welfare system, and something new: funding for fey-centered schools, which specialize in teaching fey children how to control their symptoms to better integrate into society, before they're old enough to be subjected to stress-tests and madhouses. Currently, Daleish fey have been expected to swim in mortal schools, or sink; increased pressures are linked to "madness," wherein repetitive exercise of fey symptoms erodes rational thought and leads to erratic behavior and dangerous power flares. If left unchecked, a fey's madness will escalate to violent self-implosion. As their disorder becomes more prominent, 30 percent of fey leave school before the age of 10 to avoid worsening their condition, and an astounding 65 percent leave by the age of 17. The remaining 5 percent exhibit only mild symptoms.

"I was pulled out of mortal school at 11," Stregoni Child says. "My Faerie Disorder came in quick—I was having flares at home, just small things when I was overwhelmed. But the more you flare, the worse they are the next time, and the harder it is to fight the impulse. I thought I'd have to hide away forever to keep it from getting dangerous."

But at the Senan Maxim School for Fey, sponsored by the University of Stoutshire and operating since 52SC, Stregoni and roughly a dozen other children are taught to control and mitigate their traits through cognitive training, while learning basic trade work that prepares them for manual labor jobs. Now, Stregoni is proud to say that they haven't had a power flare in well over three cycles. Approaching 18, the legal age to be stress-tested for madness, their benign symptoms are well within the range of sanity. Doctors have called this "a miracle" and suggested that Stregoni will soon be ready to graduate safely into the mortal workforce as the school's first success case.

With more funding, even more fey children can expect the same smooth transition into adulthood. Shona Maxim's plans for building more of these centers may seem far-fetched but have been generally well-received. While sitting president Dermott Ashley III is rewarding factory automation and productivity, reducing job opportunities for Daleish workers, a new branch of education centers would bring plentiful hiring

---

GOODFELLOWS' TAILOR

Near the corner of 8th and 2nd

Only until the 4th moon...
MID-WINTER SALE
Suits only 10R

---

opportunities for cleaners, teachers, cooks, groundskeepers, and guards.

President Ashley is facing scrutiny for refusing to visit the Senan Maxim School for Fey. When asked publicly about his thoughts on the fey, he says he "believe[s] in equality, not hand-holding," and has suggested that educating fey would oversaturate the job market rather than save it. As for his thoughts on Maxim, he claims that her platform "spits in the face of everyone who lost a loved one in the Summer Fayre Massacre," especially the Tanner family, who have publicly voiced their support for Ashley's expansion of prisons and fey-related correctional institutions.

Maxim isn't deterred by this. "It's a sensitive time," she says. "The world is changing. I hope we change with it and build a new future, one where fey children have as many opportunities as mortals. My sister-in-law was a warning shot: we can't be sure how many other fey are rotting away in this city, left without hope, with only dangerous options to choose from. I want better for her child, for my brother's child. We need to work together."

In just three days, the second generation of "Maxim cuidna" will be named, signaling a new era in this ongoing story of destruction and rebirth. When asked if they have any ideas for name and path, Stregoni proudly announces they'll be going by "Hawthorne Stregoni" along the path of their aunt (she/her). Maxim says they plan to take the name and path of their late father (he/him), who they describe only as "a kind man who did his best."

"We're going nowhere but up," Shona Maxim says, holding the shoulders of both her nearly grown wards, ready to tackle an ever-changing city and a country in the height of its boom time. "These schools work, and we're bringing change to the country, with your votes."

THE MAN FORMERLY KNOWN AS MAXIM CHILD IS...
GRISTLE SENAN MAXIM JUNIOR
IN
"DEATH AT THE DOCKS"

Senan Maxim's newly named son woke just shy of midnight, mouth dry and still whiskey-tinged. At first, he was only aware of the streetlamp glow coming through the straight-barred blinds behind him, drifting traffic-line light across his desk, and some distant ringing. Everything else was a soupy, gray-on-black mess, prickly with dusty distortion like a film reel.

The world took a second to clear, like a camera lens focusing in on him, collapsed over his usually orderly desk strewn with an offset slide of election posters and yesterday's *Dolly Day* magazine. Just in front, beside his banker's lamp and the bottle he'd polished off after a fine celebration dinner uptown with his aunt and sister, the phone was rattling up on its spindly cradle.

He stared at it cut out against the darkness behind. The past moon had been a campaign trail whirlwind, and while it was a well-earned treat to sling down in rat-hole little pubs to talk election strategy with his aunt, it was damned nice to be back to business as usual.

He swung a heavy hand out to snatch the phone from its cradle, and slouched back to stare up at the stamped-metal ceiling. "Maxim & Maxim," he croaked out. "Evidence collection and professional opinion."

"Sorry, Ace. It's the first one tonight," his aunt's voice said. From the typing clatter in the background and the slight garble of a cigar in her mouth, he was certain she was still at her campaign office. "Rory Gattano switchboarded an anonymous tip from the docks."

"I didn't know the Gattanos were still dancing with us," he rasped. Not that they needed that sort of business: everyone knew most of the Gattanos were Verdo mob hit men hiding behind the not-so-subtle front of their garage. His daddy had been chummy with the lot of them, mostly through Hàzell . . . "I thought you said they were all snakes."

"Even snakes have a price point, and a use," she told him, one of her kernels of detective wisdom that hadn't yet rotted away. "If it's another bust-in, then they'll need a photographer, and you know the cops' gal always sleeps through her calls. Let's lend a hand."

Sure thing. A hangover was nothing, and he'd never needed much sleep. Senan Maxim's son grabbed his wide-brimmed hat from where it was perched on the whiskey bottle and flipped it on at a careful jaunty angle that slid half his face into comfortable shadows. "I'm on the ball," he said.

"Rain-right. I've got meetings all day tomorrow and I'm doing lunch with your sister, but let's do dinner," she told him while he pulled on his stamped-leather camera bag. The word "sister" made him pause for a moment—he'd only ever had a "sibling." It was hard to adjust to their new names and paths. Not bad, just . . . *different*. But his aunt was a solid constant, like the sun. "Rory put Cat's on my mind. Could bring V.P. Egghead out too."

The Cat's Cantina was on the same block as the Gattano garage.

He suspected she wanted to keep an eye on the less savory Gattano siblings. You could take the detective out of the office and put her on posters, but she'd always be a dockyard gossip with an ear to the pavement strong enough to hear bad news from uptown to southside, and a mouth fit to fix it.

"And check on your sister before you go, and when you're back," she said. Because she sure did know where the trouble was. "Call me so I know not to worry."

"Rain-right." He put his phone in the stand, dried the greasy iron smell off his palm and onto his slacks, slipped his arms into the sleeves of his heavy duster, adjusted the high collar close to his ears, and marched forward. Light bled faintly from the single sconce in the hallway through the door's frosted window.

He slowed, feeling the beginnings of some distant emotion trying to crawl for him. The louder, more practical part of himself was reminded that they ought to scrape those second and third lines away to get them painted proper. They weren't what they used to be.

Maxim & Maxim
PRIVATE DETECTIVES
SHONA AND SENAN

The newly named man meant to be called Senan Maxim Junior pulled the door open. His father's name stared out from the pale glass, catching all that glow even as he kept his eyes down. He knew most kids spent the better part of eighteen cycles choosing what they'd be called. He'd dropped out of school at sixteen to help around the office, but before then, he'd hardly been able to go a sun without hearing someone fantasizing about the future. Even his *sister* had decided on "Hawthorne Stregoni" cycles ago. He'd never really cared or wanted a new name, had assumed he'd just keep trucking with "Maxim Child"—plenty of folks kept their names, proud "traditionalists."

And then there'd come that day on the election circuit in one of those rat-hole public houses so far out in the countryside they hadn't even switched to electric lights, where his aunt had turned to him over their whiskey. In the smoky moment when she was barely holding back the tears that always came around that two-drink mark, she grabbed his shoulder tight and gave him a firm little shake. It was a gesture more friend-like than maternal, bold and full of trust. He was her right hand; she was the woman who had lifted him from the ashes of Senan Maxim murdered.

"I know it's asking a lot," she'd said to him through the smoke and the slurring of the half-drunk pub band, "but have you ever considered doing your daddy's name and path some better justice?" He must have taken a second too long to answer, because her eyebrows buckled in, carving dark shadows across her face. "Saints, Ace, you're just the best parts of him. He always said that. Said that you were the one mistake he never regretted. You make me damn proud."

The ache and the compliment were dull, distant feelings, as most were. But it was still enough to convince him. And so he'd said yes and smoked his first cigar that night, slouched to savor the spices and bitter burn while she told him another story about the recklessly loving man who tied them together. He drank it down as easy as the whiskey.

Senan Maxim's child had no qualms checking himself off as a man in the city records, that was dandy enough. He'd written *Senan Maxim Junior* while flashbulbs popped to catch the "Vote Maxim" buttons on his and Hawthorne's chests, and he'd almost been alright with it. But there was a moment when he pulled the pen up, when the name seemed to scream from the glow-white page. It burned through his head, painful as a lightning strike. What sort of curse was it to be named after a man too daft to realize the danger he was waltzing them all into? Was *he* meant to fix that? Rewrite it?

The registrar reached for the book and he didn't know what to do. Nothing in life or in his father's death had prepared him for this moment. He'd felt *fine* in the past few cycles, had learned to live with this weight, but the reminder would be too much.

So he'd scribbled another word at the front, the first impulsive thing that came to mind when he thought of Senan Maxim. When they announced him and Hawthorne to the courtroom, his aunt's pale face stared stark in the crowd. She still shook his hand and bought him dinner, seeming more confused than upset.

That night, ignoring his hangover, he was so-called *Gristle* Senan Maxim Junior. He'd never gotten to ask his daddy what that word meant, and had only managed to properly look it up in a dictionary *after* it was steadfastly penned in the city records. It fit, he decided. It was a tough name, for a tough jack who had learned how to do a tough job in a tough city, and would just keep on doing it. Because everything was good now . . . had been *made* good.

If he kept up the same pattern, he'd never have to be that confused and terrified child again.

Gristle Senan Maxim Junior crept down the hall now to put his ear to Hawthorne's door. Though muffled, he could hear the faintest creak of her breath. She sounded asleep. Ordinary. Good. Fine.

Gristle turned for the stairs, the sconce light flickering as he went.

♦

Two trolleys passed Gristle, which was typical but not at all appreciated. With the Summer Solstice far behind him and the Winter Moon nights settling in deeper and longer, their modest midtown neighborhood sat cloaked in a low, dark chill that weaseled into his bones. The boutiques and diners and grocers and druggists had all flipped their painted signs to closed, and the apartments tucked up top had pulled their blinds. Even the usual pigeons that flocked the cornices were asleep. Gristle enjoyed the stillness.

He heard another trolley coming out of the gloom and knee-high fog, so he lifted his hand. This one managed to see him; it slowed, stopped, and clunked open in a bright wash of white-gray light. The hunched-over driver stared out at him from the picture frame of the open doors. Their eyes reflected light like a cat's, subtle, but Gristle was no stranger to spotting a fey. He took a slow breath.

"Evening," the driver said, ordinary enough despite a flat, vacant voice. When they tapped their fingers on the steering wheel, Gristle felt a thin wall of aural unease move through him before it crept off like a cat. "Where are you heading?"

Gristle strode up the steps, making a quick assessment of who else was in the trolley. He caught one dame sitting somewhere in the middle, absorbed in her paper. She didn't look like much trouble. "The docks," he said, dropping five bronze pix into the box. He thought to add a few more, but wondered if the fey was trying to bury that thought in his head. So he skipped that and just made sure to add an "If you'd be so kind" from under the brim of his shadowy hat.

"Right." The fey clunked the doors shut and twisted their head, sending another strange ripple under Gristle's skin. Gristle just turned with a whirl of his duster tails and marched to stand in the middle of the empty car as they chugged on.

The lone passenger was wearing a bell-shaped hat over fashionably short hair and reading the evening news. Gristle could spot himself and Hawthorne on the back page (above the obits, below the births, with two others named that day) and the most recent polls. He squinted—Ashley was still winning with decent margins, but his aunt was up a few spots. They still had nearly two moons to close the gap.

Gristle took to staring out the dark windows while they puttered west. The storefronts faded into a blur. When the car lurched to a stop, Gristle nearly stumbled into the lady as she stood.

"Oh!" she said suddenly, clutching her newspaper to her chest. She gave him a quick look. "I must have been off in my own little world—I didn't even notice you."

Gristle was tall and broad-shouldered and deep in the belly, but a good evidence collector was easy to overlook. The overhead lights slipped under his hat when he lifted his chin, slicing across his eyes. "It's alright," he said, polite enough.

"I believe this is your stop," the driver called to the woman. They flicked out their hand, just one twitch, but every hair on Gristle's body went straight up without him asking it to. The lights flickered in response.

The dame narrowed her eyes. She gave Gristle a conspiratorial eye roll. Gristle felt his temples tighten. He tried to dig in his head for a bold response, something his aunt might say about tolerance, but before he could pluck it out or else shuffle his collar to properly show that "Vote Maxim" button, she was already strutting to the front. Gristle held his breath, hoping this would at least be quick.

It was. She said nothing to the driver and left, whistling to herself at a shrill pitch.

Gristle swallowed. He watched her as far as he could, to make sure she didn't turn back to get the trolley's number. Dale may have been a place of science now, "the future" that said it was past the days it burned fey on pyres, but that didn't mean people weren't keen to call the cops for a check-in. Even those little tricks were a slippery slope, Gristle had heard. Next thing you know, the power grows bigger. Next thing you know, they can't fight the impulse. Next thing you know, they're maniacally, gleefully convincing you to hand over the keys to your bank vault.

Next thing you know, little things become big things, and big things choose to explode like a bomb, destroying everything in a three-hundred-person radius.

Gristle caught the driver's eye in the reflection of the front window. He'd learned to just let the panic dim, look away, and fade out until his stop.

Gristle didn't make it a habit to come to the western dockyards and factory sprawl, despite having spent six chaotic cycles of his life living there. Probably *because* he'd spent six chaotic cycles of his life living there, until his aunt carried them to cleaner midtown skies. But with a job to do, he waited until the trolley slipped into the swarming fog beneath the raised railroad tracks, and stepped off onto the poorly-paved streetside where everything smelled like fish left out to rot.

The trolley chugged away, and then it was just him alone, two blocks from where he'd once lived.

Gristle Senan Maxim Junior walked off quickly, scattering mist around his baggy trouser cuffs and shined-up shoes. The buildings were all close and high and dark, built for factory folk with thirteen kids and a spouse who works three jobs just to keep shoes on the First. Overhead bridges connected the tenement houses right to their factories, striking rifts of shadows across Gristle's path. Still, in the past few septennials, the economy had boomed around the iron trade, putting planter boxes beneath the sealed shutters and a few just-closed pubs on the corners. That was progress, slow but easily calculated.

He passed silent warehouses where his shadow sank in and out of door recesses, gaining on him with each wooden lamppost and then retreating. There was possibly movement in the pitch-dark alleys, waiting eyes and hands. Gristle couldn't quite tell: complete and total color-blindness did a number on his low-light vision, and so the moving shadows could have been anything. Mundane, surely. Nightmarish, possibly.

The last dockyard street opened like a gasp, releasing Gristle right to the water's edge where the waning moon shone over a sea exceedingly calm. Down the narrow street boxed in by cliff-high factories, a telephone booth formed one solitary rectangle of light. Two black shadows were cut from it, with round hats and tight-waisted tunics. The police.

Gristle crossed to their side and strode toward them, his footsteps slashing through the silence. He was so close he could have touched them before one officer lazily turned her head.

Her eyes widened, wet and open enough to catch all the light from within the shadows of her face. "Saints," she snapped in a soupy, Northern Daleish accent. She lowered her hand from the ash-wood-and-iron grip sticking from her belt. "A little dark to be sneaking up on folks with guns."

A little dark to be so trigger-happy. "I brought a camera," Gristle said blithely. "My aunt sent me to help, on behalf of Maxim & Maxim."

The second officer leaned forward. Both gave him a painfully unsubtle sweep, from jaunty hat, to baggy, out-of-fashion suit, to camera bag, and right back up. The first one took her cigarette out of her mouth to breathe a slow puddle into the fog. "If it ain't the baby Maxim," she said. The ocean sucked all the sound out to sea, letting every word land close. "Beat it, jack. I know your daddy was a yappy little thorn and I'm not fixing to work with the next generation of that."

Gristle was an expert at moving seamlessly past hurtful condescension. The key was to just keep on saying what you would have said anyway, an easy script. "My aunt and I have built a legitimate business in evidence collection and professional opinion," he droned. "We're happy to offer this service. Is your crime scene photographer on the way?"

The second cop (a folk with eyebrows so heavy their eyes were shadowed in black) tilted their head. "Can't reach her."

"There's your answer, jack," Gristle said. The other cop almost choked on her cigarette in a short snort of laughter. Gristle hadn't meant for it to be a joke, but he flipped open his bag all the same. He took out his collapsing strut camera and gently plucked up a flashbulb. "Where's the break-in?"

They both huffed. Gristle felt his skin tighten.

"This ain't no break-in," one said. Her hand reached up through the gloom like the Reaper's, pointing a bony finger back toward the towering wall of the smithy. A faint breeze whistled its way down the narrow path, smelling of clean sea brine and thick iron, but when it passed, the lack felt loud: not fish now, but closer to smoke, with a bitter, bilious reek beneath it.

For a moment, Gristle wasn't sure where it was coming from. As he took one step back across the street, parting the mist into whorls, he saw an odd, dark lump curled against the wall. Someone sleeping on the curb? No, the cops would have shooed them along already. He tilted his head, trying to gauge the shape properly. Another step closer, and he was convinced that the thing collapsed there was a clothing mannequin.

But when he drifted within a single pace of it and could stare down, with his shadow folding along the black-and-gray crevices of the thing, he didn't have to be any fine detective to know what he was looking at.

Gristle's stomach lurched like a hairpin turn. He smelled the Summer Fayre six cycles ago. His mind was wrenching against him, trying to pull him back toward the smell of popcorn and ash, and the pain of some other kid asking, asking, asking. But the dockyard was silent; even the water made no sound.

This was clearly no mannequin at all.

Splayed on the ground, incinerated to a blistered shine, was the charred husk of a person. Their skin was crisped to black, all their clothes seared away except for the melted soles of work boots. It wasn't just some easy cooking—they'd been blasted with fire so violently Gristle could see spots that went right down to the pale, cracked bone. And the smell . . . of something burnt through to the oozing organs.

Gristle couldn't find anything to say. He could only remember how this same smell had stayed in that old dress that had to be thrown away, and in his hair for nearly a cycle despite cutting it down to the scalp. The memories hooked into him, weighed him down into the sinking pain.

He was shocked from it by a voice from just beside him. "Probably some bum got in to keep warm and tried to light the stove," the cop with the bushy eyebrows said. It was enough to get Gristle's feet back to earth, forcing his eyes to look at the dead body in front of him.

He needed to do his job here. "This is the iron smithy," he forced out, more to himself. He ran through a mental catalogue of stories. He'd heard about unruly stove equipment, cases his daddy and aunt investigated against crooked bosses eons ago. "They put regulations in . . . fire's not strong enough for that," he muttered. Below him, the corpse was burned down to the bone. "If it was, they couldn't have run out here in time . . ." The streetlight gave a few flickers. This wasn't right.

"I thought you were here to take pictures," one of the cops said.

Yes. Right. He wasn't a detective. That sort of business was ugly, and the Maxims were out of it now.

Gristle slowly raised his camera up to his eye.

Pop! A blinding flash, and a moment of clarity that faded before the shadows closed in again. He could hardly feel the heat of the spent bulb when he twisted it out and returned it to its spot in his bag. He fitted the next in, crouched for a closer view, even if that smell seared through his sinuses. *Pop*, flash.

Somewhere in the back of his skull, the picture show played: "They were at a *fayre!*" he remembered his aunt wailing, in the hallway outside his hospital room. She was with the police, who his daddy had always said *never* to talk to without him and a lawyer. He'd gotten so paranoid in the end. "How could you let this happen—my brother—you knew she was dangerous and you didn't do *anything!*"

"Auntie," he'd whispered, because his voice couldn't become any louder. "Where's my daddy?"

It had happened to someone else, too long ago to hurt. Gristle stood up again. The streetlamp behind him pushed his shadow against the wall. Out in the bay, a cargo ship was lugging down the coastline, lowing its horn without late-night remorse. The sweeping light sent Gristle's shadow sprinting along the bricks.

But even when his shape fled the crime scene, a shadow still stared back at him. Not his own, fat and broad with a jaunty hat and the flowing tails of his duster. It was the shadow of a person with their hands up to block themselves against the scorch of black that surrounded them in a feathery spray.

Gristle stared at the negative image of a person cut out by fire. The leads converged. He wished they wouldn't, but they did.

"They weren't burned in the smithy," Gristle muttered. He pointed with his chin, still clutching his camera. "See the soot?"

"Leave that to the professionals, kid," one cop said.

Frustration bubbled in his throat, but Gristle let the condescension wash over him. Photos of the wall now. *Pop*, flash. Should he say it? Would his aunt want him to? He wondered, in the same way he felt responsible to stop trolley passengers from saying something cruel.

"This wasn't any ordinary fire," Gristle said. Shivers rippled down his body, but he pressed forward. "A fey did this."

The terrible power asked to be let out, and the rotted mind allowed it.

"Madness," one of the cops said, voice low. For the first time, they sounded as concerned as they should have been to start. "Call the patrols. Get a perimeter."

A train roared over the track a few blocks down, so loud Gristle thought the world would shatter around him. A mad fey was out there, could be anywhere by now, with the same rage that killed his daddy.

He couldn't let anything else be torn from the Maxim family, not after so many cycles of peace.

Hawthorne, Gristle thought suddenly, and begged her to be safe where he'd left her.

TRAGEDY AT THE SUMMER FAYRE

300 KILLED BY MAD FEY

While details are still forthcoming, and police urge the pu
due to unnatural excess stimuli, the fey brain is impulsive
ead to irrational and often violent decisions. Therefore, it i
that fey should refrain from using "power" as a coping mec

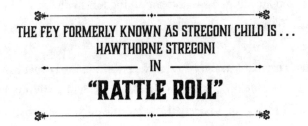

"RATTLE ROLL"

I sit on the fire escape with my legs hanging down the stair gap, still and quiet. Mist tickles into the striped shirt I stole out the bottom of Gristle's wardrobe, but it don't bother me any 'cause I've got a bottle of gin in my lap, catching the streetlights worming down the alley and lighting it up every color. I bought that myself, after Gristle slipped out. No kid can buy gin, I tell myself.

Things are changing around here.

There's a crunching from the street. I stop dead to stare out at the sliver I can see down the alley, to where the high moon shines blue on the dark boutique across the way. The sound starts coming together: tires on pavement.

My aunt's car? Gristle taking a taxi home? I snatch the gin up by the neck like a hunted goose and swing to my feet, ready to run, with all the hair on my arms standing sharp in the cold air.

Ahead, a powder-blue roadster with big yellow lights on the front grille pulls up to the curb. The driver's this pretty Ileian dame with her thick curls coaxed into glossy finger waves, one arm thrown over the side door, the top down so the moon makes her fluffy white coat glow like fresh country snow.

"I'm looking for someone," she calls. It's just barely quiet enough for this time of night. Under that coat, her dress is all fringe and flower-shaped paste-gems—not something for mediocre midtown. "But you look way too grown to be her."

You bet.

I smack my cap on over my hair tied into a curly mess in the back and go racing down the fire escape so fast it's like flying. I toss Fionne the bottle—she's barely shifted to the passenger side in time to catch it. I put both hands on the top of the door and swing myself into the driver's seat, leaning over to kiss her on the cheek.

"Thanks for the ride, Feenee," I say.

"Well, I'm not leaving my girl cooped up on her birthday," she says. My cheeks burn so I dip my chin and get to setting my feet on the pedals like I learned in school. Maybe I'm still in when everyone else my age is already graduated, but at least trade class keeps me up to speed.

Fionne checks the gin label, pursing her lips. "This is expensive stuff, H," she says, impressed. "You put it on Gristle's tab?"

"He won't squeal," I say. The only person he could tell would be our aunt, and then he'd have to admit he let me sneak out. That's our little game, me and him: I sneak out, he brings me back, I smile and he grits his teeth and we pretend it never happened. "I figure we've got three bells until he starts looking."

Fionne sighs, but she's already cracking the cap off the gin. "My little jailbird," she says, sort of wistful. "Did you ask your aunt? Like you said?"

I duck my chin even further. At a fresh-and-dandy eighteen, I thought maybe I'd finally get permission for a night out so I wouldn't feel like a sneaky kid. And yet? "Tried," I say, toeing at the clutch with my hands deep in my pockets. "She said I can go out when I graduate."

Fionne groans, overdramatic as ever. "I haven't seen you go off once," she says, waving her fingers through the air in a gesture that I guess is supposed to represent sparkles or something. I've known Fionne almost as long as I've known Gristle, but she only ever saw the fey stuff when the symptoms were small. And then . . . well, Mum happened, and I moved away, and we were only pen pals when I was at my worst. By the time she got her license and drove her baba's pretty car up to the curb, and I kissed her like I'd wanted to do forever, school had taught me how to keep myself in check.

She doesn't know what I'm actually like.

"Stow the sad face," Fionne suddenly says, snapping me from the ramble in my head to realize I really am frowning, and that a few nerves are building in my chest. The moon makes her face more indigo than brown-black, her eyelashes long and the light tracing down her smooth forehead and her round little nose. Even her teeth are pretty, like square pearls. "I'll sneak you anywhere you want, Hawthorne," she says. My heart jolts—that's the first time she's said my new name out loud. Everything's changing, in a damn good way. "No more serious talk. We're too young for it."

I agree. She's got ink under her fingernails from working all day, but she's shining in the moonlight in her baba's car, with her real-fine coat that's right on fashion. Some day, and soon, we'll have full-grown things to worry about, jobs and rent and mortgage and whatever. For now, she's here, and real.

"I'm taking you out," I tell her. She cheers, throwing her hands up into the cold mist as I rev us southbound.

◆

Midtown's all grocers and druggists, stores that sell clothes you ain't meant to sweat in or take off easy, trolley stops to take me to school and back again, and windows that say "Vote Maxim." Getting her elected is important, I know that. 'Cause I want other kids to have what I'm getting, and I want what I'm getting to keep coming. But while midtown reminds me how far our family's made it and how much farther we can still go, it ain't no place to be eighteen.

Fionne and I sip the gin while we drive south. Off in the distance, the dark clouds are diced up by roving lights. The road rumbles like a stampede on the way. I've been to the south side before, but only when the sun was up. I ain't never been sure enough about myself to go there properly, until tonight.

The rumbling morphs into music until the lights are bright like daytime and the jazz pours red-hot out of every open door, crashing together and raging fierce. The huge buildings shine in a gin-drowned way that's better than ritzy uptown, with glowing marquees out over the sidewalks that flash like Solstice fireworks. Picture houses with signs saying they got the newest films, got the biggest bands. Stagehouses with famous actors. All new stuff made in the furnaces of Puck's Port, where everyone's come to get a taste of the electric future. The sidewalks are full of people racing through the lights, tugging the hands of their friends and sweethearts into doorways or into alleys.

The traffic's thicker now, from fancy roadsters down to boxy autos that already look outdated. Fionne's standing with her hands on the top of the windshield, staring up at the signs that paint rainbows across her skin and smiling teeth. Everything's so loud and quick that my stomach's buzzing, but I breathe deep and keep it calm. We squeeze toward the good time we've been eyeing since *Dolly Day* wrote about it moons ago. Every folk our age has been craning for a look, some of 'em with a morbid sort of curiosity, and Fionne never misses a fashion.

She's been waiting on me so we can check it out proper. I'm ready.

Fionne doesn't even have to tell me which building. I suppose it don't look any different than any other club up the strip; it's got the same tall windows nearly to the top, the same blinking lights and humming sign. But it's the people I see stumbling in and out that let me know where we are. I don't realize I'm holding my breath until I pull the car to the curb and punch it to an idling park.

The infamous Dogfoot Club looms like a mountain. It makes my skin prickle in a good way.

Fionne's voice is light and thin, as excited as I am. Everything flashes in her eyes. "And we ain't even seen the inside yet," she says, waving down one of the maroon-vested valets smoking by the door. They come weaving over while Fionne pops the door open. She grabs my arm, pulling me out onto the sidewalk with her.

The valet gives me a nod, but even when they don't make any eye contact I see that both their irises are a color so confusing I can't even say what it is. When they swing over the door into the car, a faint blur bleeds behind them like a photo taken too fast.

They're fey. The other valet smoking by the door has tiny spikes up their nose like a lizard, muttering something under their breath while they wait. I almost stare, but Fionne grabs my hand and pulls me into the tight wedge of the revolving door.

We ain't at the Dog 'cause it has the best party; we're at the Dog 'cause the owner's a fey, and so's the staff. Puck's Port's changing enough for a place like this to be the talk of the town, even for mortal girls like Fionne Eze, who always knows a party when she sees one.

We spill into the gold-and-marble lobby. I'm a little drunk or maybe just reeling from all the shine off the chandelier, all the people, all the movement, all the power that reminds me why we used to call it magic before we called it science. Two folks standing next to a huge painting on the wall are waving their hands in a silent language, their fingers embedded with gems they must have grown themselves. I look up to see some man sitting on the balcony of the second level, wearing a long dress and a hat dripping dew-round beads off the brim, with a half dozen folks all big-eyed around in a gawking circle. I swear some of them are mortal. He must be setting off some pretty strong aura, 'cause even *I* can admit how fine he looks.

I keep jumping my eyes around, trying to see everything. The coat-check folk is tapping their fingers and sending off clouds of lavender-purple smoke each time. Another customer cheers and makes the air ring with the taste of gunpowder. It rushes into me, singing into my stomach and buzzing in my skin. I know fey, sure, but I know the little kids at school with their power still fresh and squirmy.

"Howdee," I hear myself saying. Fionne's looking up too, eyeing in on a fey pacing the balcony while their monstrous shadow twists and grows behind them. I wonder if she's gonna be scared, or even just nervous and too tense to have a good time like she wants. But she's awestruck like I remember Senan used to be, staring up at petals Mum sent whirling through the air.

Maybe he ain't the best person to start comparing Fionne to, considering how bright Mum burned. Some stern part of my brain tries to remind me about feeding the symptoms, letting it degrade my impulses with that chemical high until everything's too big to stop. Reminds me that these folks are playing with fire. But ain't gin a fire already? Ain't there so many things that degrade us but we do them because it's fun or it feels right?

For one night, maybe I can cut a bit loose too.

Fionne's already tossing her coat to be checked. She grabs my hand and pulls me to the batwing doors into the barroom, holding two gold roundels from her coat pocket.

"Birthday treat," she says, dropping them into the cashbox next to a doorman with a slinky cat hanging around his neck like a scarf; they both have the same thin-pupiled eyes and yellow-orange hair. The cat reaches one fuzzy paw out to bat at me. I ain't never met no familiar pet up close. I want to touch my finger to its paw, but also keep looking around the busy lobby where everyone's milling around, but also we get the nod to go in.

"Come on, H," Fionne says. She grabs my hands, backing up through the batwings while the music blares behind her. She's so damn pretty. "Show me a good time?"

Every singing little impulse in me says *yes*.

The Dogfoot Club's barroom and dance hall is just as grand. The walls are all dark velvet sparkling with fancy gold designs, spiraling off in diamonds and fans. The horseshoe bar ahead glows with lights hanging out over the mirror-backed liquor wall, the barkeeps all slinging drinks for folks stumbling up before they stumble off to the few dozen tables ahead of us, where bus-kids zip like gnats to put plates of food down for people trying to shout over the music and see each other through just one little lamp between them. In the swirling gloom, I can't much tell who's mortal and who's fey.

Fionne and I go weaving off through the tables to where the inlaid wood of the dance floor spills out like an ocean, polished so smooth you can see all the people dancing in it. There's mirrors on the ceiling too. Everything's washed in the huge, gold glow of the lights on the six-foot-tall stage. The big band's roaring loud and everyone smells like something. Booze or perfume.

It's so much, but it's so right after cycles of white-brick walls and bland meals that prepared me for this. My doctors say I could graduate soon. It means I'm ready. *I'm ready.*

"Good, H?" Fionne asks me.

"Dandy," I say, and then grab her hands. She shrieks with giggles. We collapse into all the dancing people.

"My name's Cab Kazah Junior and these are *your* Dogfoot dancers," the singer calls over the snare drumbeat. "Give 'em a hand, folks, and see if you can keep up!"

I swing, or I try. Spirits know, I got those fey rattles, that feeling like you gotta move or you'll break, and that's close enough to dancing. I'm laughing even if I can't hear it. Fionne's smiling in all the flashing lights, pulling me close and fumbling along because I don't think either of us is any good at dancing, and I know both of us are pretty drunk. That Cab fella, an Ileian man who'd look mortal if not for the otherworldly way his body seems to move, sings better than anyone I've heard. It's a voice so pretty and strange that I think most folks would walk into the woods for it.

I remember my mum used to say that people were scared of fey because they didn't understand us, yeah, but also because we can be damn powerful when we want to be, and that power's strange enough to remind mortals that anything's possible. Science and logic are well and good, but there's something magical about things you can't see coming. Call it superstition, or call it chaos, or call it wonderment. Every time you feed it, it grows more beautiful.

Fionne says something to me. She feels miles away. "What?" I ask her.

"Can you do that now?" she asks me. Up on the stage, some glamor-girl fey is changing her hair all different colors, her dress nothing more than gauze and a bodice so everyone can see the alligator scales up her leg. "I don't think you could before, but I heard fey can learn new tricks."

My skull fills with humming whispers I'd have to strain to understand. "I shouldn't," I say. I can't much tell how far my voice is going in all the sound. "It ain't good to feed it that much—you can start losing control." Go mad.

She stares so close at me as we turn and kick and grin. I'm seeing every speck of makeup on her face. I feel all my cells singing for her, singing *with* her. For the way her hands are on my shoulders, the sparkles in her eyes, the river-rock feel of her dress under my palms. She pulls me in, chest to chest, her lips by my ear and my eyes unfocusing.

Over her shoulder, the crowd swims and spills. I see horns and scales and feathers, grinning mouths and shocks of bright hair, bright eyes. If everyone else can be themselves, why shouldn't I? Ain't I more prepared than any of them, with my diploma practically printed?

"You're so serious, H," Fionne says. All the hair on my body is up now—I feel each pore straining. Cab sings like the devil. "You don't gotta hide from me."

Her voice pours right down into my whole body, warmer than gin. The trumpet screams into my bones.

Just a bit. A bit won't ruin me. And then she can love all of me, not just the nice parts.

I open the gates in my head, just the tiniest crack. Faint tingles trickle up to my skin like a barely turned tap, and yet the feeling is better than sugar and gin and screaming until your lungs are empty. I pull back from Fionne with our hands locked tight together. In her eyes, I see myself:

Tiny sparkles are zipping through my hair under my cap, floating off me as we spin. They leave a ghost behind me, a shine all gold and red and orange. My nails glow with the same color, tracing bad-blood lines up my veins that bleed through my striped sleeves.

Fionne's smile fades from ecstatic glee into something more awestruck.

"Saints," she breathes, watching the sparkles ride up on the heat off everyone. *They're brighter than when I was a kid, more real.* "How come you never showed me before?"

Because I spent my childhood feeding this power every day, like Mum taught me with her hands cradling mine. And now it's huge, star-bright.

I shrug; my shirt rubs bad against my ribs, a shearing pain that hurts ten times worse when I'm amped like this. Gotta let the feeling off—the sparks turn red as an arterial bleed. One pops loud enough that the person beside us flinches back. It's a shot of delicious relief while my body's rumbling louder. I feel my cheeks twitching, almost a grin. Another sparkle busts apart, shattering down to singe the floor. My body's still aching, pressure-built like a boiler. I stare up at all of the little lights dancing above us. *What if I made them all go off? What if . . . ?*

That'd be pretty, wouldn't it?

My cells are splitting and compounding and rushing. The mirrors above us double it all. The floor triples it and then spits it back at the mirrors. It's the best sort of pain. *They say fey have a moral deficiency, that we're too selfish to stop when we start.*

"H," Fionne says, grabbing my hands tighter.

Even if Mum let this rot grow huge inside me, I won't let it win.

I fall back on a school technique: I tighten every muscle in my body until they're damn near ready to shake apart. The sparkles all freeze in midair, bobbing slightly. "Outside," I choke.

Fionne takes the hint. She takes one last tight-lip look at the crowd then lets me grab her wrist and pulls me through all the people bashing into me. The sparkles follow like swarming flies. My stomach sends a wave up through me that crests hard against my skin, shaking it like a sandbag barrier. It whispers to just let it out, just do it.

We spill out into the alley, where the cold air sweeps smooth over my arms and face. The door closes with a heavy *whumpf*, but at least it blocks out the band and scatters the sparkles away. My skin is so tight I think it'll crack, fault lines shattering across me until whatever's inside busts out. I back up into the rough bricks.

"H," Fionne's saying, but I can't answer her. I gulp down the garbage-smelling air while my stomach's still flipping and spitting.

But I've read through all the university papers, memorized leaflets and dog-eared journals. I've been going to school since I was thirteen, been pulling myself off the ledge ever since. I know how to calm down.

I shut my eyes to be mindful. Inside I can almost see the power, like a pyre in the middle of so much blackness. It's rearing and puffing like someone threw in pine knots that smell like Verdosso. I know that ain't anything fantastical or spiritual, just an image in my hopped-up mind where all the chemicals are moving too fast. I imagine I'm backing away from it, farther and farther, watching the orange light turn to a greasy brown stain, and then not even that. I'm closing off all the little tubes that bring the singing up into my palms or my cheeks or my feet. And all the rest that's still in me, I put it into my lungs. My hands itch.

I keep them still. Quiet hands, quiet mind.

I breathe in slow through my nose to douse the energy, and breathe out until my lungs crackle like dry reeds. This time, when Fionne says, "Hawthorne?" I feel good enough to slide my back down the wall until I'm sitting. Then I can look over to her.

We're in a tight alley outside the Dog where they take the trash, I suppose, 'cause the dumpster's right there next to us, and Fionne's sitting on some empty carboard box just in front of me. Only a bit of light drifts down from the signs on the rooftops or creeps in from the street. Her eyes are wide, but calm. I can't read that expression.

I sit with my back straight like we learn at school. "Sorry," I say. Guilt tries to well up in me, but I can't even have that. I keep my head blank. "I didn't mean to scare you."

She doesn't respond for a second. "You didn't," she finally says, waving her hand. "I needed the air too."

Well . . . alright? I'm not gonna sit here and tell her that she *should* be afraid of me. "Tired?" I ask her.

"Nah. Work was just a bore. I really did need this party," she says, hiking her dress up to pull her long cigarette holder from her stocking. I fish in my pocket for the tin case she bought me last cycle, to hand over my last cigarette and my lighter. "I've been at it all week getting my *Dolly Day* portfolio finished. Last cycle they just wanted fashion articles—"

"You can write 'em in your sleep." I light the cigarette for her.

"Don't I know it," she says, batting her eyelashes, but she ain't really able to slip the annoyance out of her tone. "Now they're asking for *three* op-eds. I've got less than a moon to make that happen."

My skin prickles. I wonder if I should mention it, if that'll remind her that the party can't rage forever. "I thought your mum said internships didn't pay enough anyway," I say, careful as I sit back. Having a political family means I'm always hearing about the job market, how rough it is to find anything reliable. Maybe we're in midtown now, but I still remember those dockyards. "Maybe you let it pass? You don't like op-eds anyway. Stick it out at the *Herald* and wait for something more sure."

She scoffs and takes a long drag. "If Ma and Baba had it their way, I'd be at the *Herald* forever. And considering Ify's *still* haunting the house after . . ." She counts on her fingers. I don't know exacts, but I know Fionne's biggest sibling is bigger by a while. Old enough to sit at the grown-up table at Cat's, last time her parents and mine were all together before . . .

"Saints, he's been out of school for five cycles now," Fionne says, shuddering and rubbing at her arms. "I'll bet pix to primrose that Third is in my closet right now, stealing all my good makeup. I love them all, but if I stay at the *Herald*, I'm never having my own life."

I get that. But wanting something and getting it are two different things. She's the youngest front-page typesetter the *Herald*'s ever had, and could ride that for a while. It's a lot to throw away on a dream shared by most every fashionable folk with their nose in a *Dolly Day*. But that's Fionne, with the big dreams.

I've always had to be realistic, even when I hate it. I shuffle my knees up. I don't know if my worry for her is just jealousy that she can take big risks, so I keep my mouth shut.

Her voice creeps out quiet against the rushing of cars in the street and the muffled jazz of the south side. "I know money'll be tight," she says, almost a whisper with the ends flipping up like questions. "It'd be easier with a roommate, H."

A strike of strange annoyance lights up my bones. "You know other folks," I say, almost snapping. I see the hurt flinch across her face, and try to soften mine. I remind myself that I ain't angry, just nervous. "I mean . . . other folks are a surer bet, you know? I'm just . . ." I pull my legs up tight.

She swallows, shrugs. "You're not 'just,'" she says, tapping off her cigarette ash. "I don't want to live with other people. I want to live with you and do stuff like this every night until we can't stand it."

I want that too. It seems impossible, but when she says it, a hard pang surges up through my chest. Somehow, it's a good feeling. In all that slamming, I can imagine what that'd be like, even the boring things that'll feel so much better when I'm doing them for us.

Making breakfast, and fixing radiators, and linking arms to go laughing out to jobs we feel good about, and doing what we want to do every single night. I know I ain't perfect, but she saw that back there and loves me still. I don't wanna keep holding her up.

She can love all of me, I know it. We can grow up past the kids we were.

"I'm gonna graduate," I tell her, because I've got to. And with how well I'm going and how old I am, it's gotta be soon. And I'll leave with a good foundation from all my trade courses—maybe I'll work at *Dolly Day* too, something rougher and more my speed like fixing the presses or loading the trucks or anything. I can do *anything*. "Soon, I swear. You get that portfolio done and I'll be right there too."

And then we're smiling again, maybe because we're excited to be thinking we've got a future of big dreams, or maybe because we don't want to be all serious all night. I lean up to kiss her, and put my hands on her waist over all the smooth beads and jewels. She leaves her cigarette on the cardboard box and swings up to stand, and then we're back in the good times, giggling into each other's lips—spirits, we're still drunk, but who cares? It's my right to be fancy-free when I ain't working hard in school. Tomorrow, I'll tell the docs that I have a plan, some goals, that I want that diploma right now. And my aunt will be damn proud and know she shouldn't worry. I oughta get a say in things, shouldn't I?

But when I open my eyes just barely, sluggish and grinning with her lips on my neck and her hand low on my stomach, I see the shadows thrown into the front of the alley, of people stumbling in the light of passing cars. We're too far back to see or care about, at least when you're focused in on the next doorway. But the shadow I see getting bigger, with a wide-brimmed hat and tailed duster . . . I know that one ain't on the street for the party. I barely hear him coming. Half the time, he could sneak up on a ghost.

I groan, a little more anguished than Fionne's expecting, I guess, 'cause she pulls back.

"Guess you're gonna see the lug after all," I say, and try to grab her hand and duck inside to maybe give him the slip.

But newly named Gristle Senan Maxim Junior never gets the slip, always gives it, so I hear, "Hawthorne, I can't believe you made me take a cab all the way out to this side of town," which I know means the side of town he don't think's respectable. I turn to see my mortal brother with his freckled face all flat and severe. "We're going home. *Now*."

Like hell. We're both adults now, and he better learn that quick.

University of Stoutshire
Treatments related to
Faerie Disorder (aka "the Fey Condition")

COGNITIVE TRAINING

Using techniques such as meditation, journaling, breathing exercises, and thought experiments, patients are encouraged to slow down their thinking in order to catch impulsive desires before they escalate.

This is considered the most accessible mode of treatment, though it must be started early for best results. This treatment has very little effect on fey with dangerous symptoms (aka "madness").

TRADE SKILLS/ MANUAL LABOR

Since fey symptoms fulfill a desire for stimulation, redirecting this impulse into useful work provides a necessary distraction from dangerous thought spirals or impulses.

While not every fey is the same, many excel at repetitive or detail-oriented tasks, such as factory work. Nurturing this desire also prepares patients for independent living.

Provided a fey's symptoms are not yet dangerous to themselves or others (aka "madness"), this is the most recommended form of treatment.

SPECIALIZED CARE FACILITY

When a fey is considered a danger to themself or others (aka "madness"), doctors and care providers are legally mandated to report this to the proper authorities in order to provide necessary care. Once a stress-test[1] has confirmed madness, fey will be safely transported to low-stimulation care facilities.

---

[1] A test that includes a series of increasingly powerful electric shocks, in order to stimulate the fey brain to its furthest point of tension. The test is concluded when the fey a) exhibits symptoms that could harm themself or others, thus constituting "madness," OR b) reaches syncope for more than thirty seconds, confirming the full threshold of possible symptoms.

Note that as of 41SC, a stress-test can be performed only by court order. For minors, a stress-test will be ordered only if a crime has been committed. For adults, a stress-test will be ordered when there is sufficient evidence of potential harm or harm caused <u>after</u> 18 cycles of age.

A stress-test can only be repeated based on evidence occurring since the previous test. A stress-test cannot be ordered more than once every two moons.

GRISTLE SENAN MAXIM JUNIOR
IN
"PYRE BURNING"

Gristle Senan Maxim Junior had stood in that dockyard phone booth hearing the line ring, ring, ring. The iron smell of the phone swam in his head. Saints, he could understand why Hawthorne said it burned.

The call had rung out. He'd told the operator (not Rory, thank the saints) to call again and hoped Hawthorne was just sleeping through the ringing, but if she wasn't? If his aunt heard that there was someone out there cooking folks, and then heard he'd let Hawthorne sneak out of the apartment while a person like that crept around? She wasn't even allowed to walk home from *school* by herself, let alone slip out as much as she did. He'd always thought it would be more trouble to stop the sneaking than to just let her get away with it . . . at least until this horrible moment. Gristle could fend for himself, but Hawthorne was vulnerable.

And, just like his daddy, he'd been too soft to notice the growing threat.

Ring . . . ring . . .

Gristle had looked at the phone box again, and then up at all the cards and posters slapped onto the wooden wall behind it. Mechanics, job listings, one lost dog, and a card he recognized faintly. He only read *Dolly Day* when his name was in it, but, socially ambivalent though he was, he was an alright enough evidence collector to know this would be a hell of a place to spend an eighteenth birthday, especially for a fey, and especially for a fey like Hawthorne with the common sense of a newborn rabbit and a fashionable girlfriend always talking her into trouble.

It was a long shot, a "hunch," as they say.

The operator came on again. "Your party is not an—"
"Do you know the number of the Dogfoot Club?"
"I do."
"Give them a ring for me." Outside the booth, police sirens had been screaming closer. He needed to be gone before they shut the

perimeter, and back at the apartment with Hawthorne in tow before any of his aunt's moles slipped word to her. "Put me on with whoever's been checking the dancehall doors."

◆

Despite burning a hole in his wallet for the taxi, Gristle's hunch panned out, because even Hawthorne had a predictable pattern.

"We're going home," he said, *finally*, at the Dogfoot. He strode toward her in the cramped alley, his hands still smelling like fish and burnt bodies and maybe somehow, after all this time, still like Summer Fayre popcorn. He shut his memory off.

In the dark that made everything impossible to tell apart, and under the shadows of her cap, Hawthorne's lips curled back from her sharp teeth.

"Why?" she asked him, thumbs hooked in her suspenders and Fionne clinging on her arm. Fionne always got Hawthorne puffed up even more, but she just needed a few solid prods before she'd follow on home. "I'm an adult and I ain't hurting anyone. Matter of fact, maybe you should stay. Dancing wouldn't kill you."

"She's got a point," Fionne said. Her nose wrinkled. "Then we can talk about getting you a suit that doesn't swallow you whole."

Gristle didn't mind Fionne personally, but he resented how casual she could be about this. "Go home, Eze," he said, without looking at her. He knew better than to let civilians in on Maxim & Maxim business. Once he got Hawthorne out of earshot, he could explain everything. "Come on. I've got a cab waiting."

"Pah!" Hawthorne laughed. "Want me to go home *and* in a lousy old cab?"

Quiet threats first. "Auntie's going to be swinging by soon. We oughta be back."

"Tell her to come," Fionne said, turning for the door. Hawthorne barked out a laugh and started following.

"Hawthorne," he tried to say, sterner. The name was still jagged on his tongue. They were older. The world was changing past the patterns he knew. And here was the reminder:

"*Gristle*," she said back, crinkled cheeks turning her face into a mar of shadows. She stepped from Fionne and closer to him, straining up to be just as tall in clothes she'd clearly stolen from his wardrobe. He swore he smelled flint and steel. "*Senan Maxim Junior.* Figure out what you're doing with yourself, lug, but I'm not going home."

And then she turned from him completely. Just turned, so easy, like she'd never done before. Gristle had spent so many years treading the line with Hawthorne, knowing exactly how far he could push, what fights to let go, when to fold. But things were different now, and he wasn't sure how to cope when her back was to him like he wasn't a friend, or a threat, or anything at all.

Gristle knew he shouldn't have done it the second he started, but the impossibly frustrated impulse caught him like fey whispers. His hand lunged out. As if on a movie screen rather than through his own two eyes, he watched his grip surging for her, shining in the dim glow of the signs high above. His palm, still iron-soaked from the phone, caught hers, fit perfectly unperfect. He knew that contact alone was surprising and upsetting, but the smell was worse.

In school since she was thirteen, practically in remission and ready to graduate, a miracle case. Hàzell Stregoni had seemed miraculous too. And Gristle, perhaps like his daddy, was the reason the wire had been pulled on this human pipe bomb.

Hawthorne's hand flashed red-hot in his. Her voice launched free in a shattering scream: "DON'T TOUCH ME!"

The words hit him like a wall of sparks, stinging into his pores. Hawthorne wrenched sideways to send him stumbling forward toward the garbage cans. He scrambled to turn back to her, breath sour.

"Hawthorne?" Fionne squeaked.

Now they'd done it.

Hawthorne looked over her shoulder. Her sharp teeth were clenched shut. Gristle hoped she was just angry, a dull, mortal emotion as pure as her school claimed. But he'd pushed too far this time. Something in her head had said it had to defend itself.

So, here it was, in all its terrifying madness. Under the bill of her cap, Hawthorne's eyes had turned to a churning glow, like magma. Before he could do anything (and what could he do?), she whirled around with her fist sailing toward his upper chest. Blinding light speared from the middle of her hand. It formed into tongues and spires. Fire sped up her arm like it was an ash-wood pyre, chasing the veins.

The alley was alight, not with anything logical, but with mad flames that poured from Hawthorne's skin. Her knuckles slammed into him, sending the taste of burning copper soaking through his mouth.

The windows above them all rattled. The lights blipped off and came back on. Fionne nearly screamed Hawthorne's name but caught her hands over her mouth, her eyes fantastically wide. Gristle fell backward with his tie half-melted into a fizzing, shallow burn that filled his head with clicking and rustling like crackling kindling. He hit the garbage-splattered ground beneath the dumpster. His camera bag crashed and scuffed. He managed to roll to his knees, scraping his hat on firm, trying to stand.

But over him, Hawthorne loomed like those old pyres, fire soaking her arm. Her black curls were spilling loose into burning waves glowing like embers under her fireproof cap. Flames whipped around her in a storm, reared up like wings, seared at her clothes in patches. Gristle was frozen on the cold ground. He wanted to run. Her face was all sneering shadows.

Madness, he thought, and couldn't recognize her.

He tried to get to his feet but she ran at him again, opening her mouth in a roar that sounded like a housefire; in that close moment, he swore he saw light burning up from her throat, and sharp protrusions of teeth going straight down like a sea creature's. She smelled like the end of the world.

Hawthorne threw left and he ducked the punch, but saw her light up her other arm in one simple impulse to send it hurtling into his gut. Gristle tried to jolt backward but his back crashed into the dumpster and her fist sank *in* a good inch. The pain was like a distant carousel tune—if he just ignored it, he could be fine. He wouldn't scream, wouldn't call pedestrians to see a fey gone mad, wouldn't give her more fuel to burn hotter and hotter. Just let this moment end, *please*.

She pulled her fist back again so he could do nothing but stare at her, knees wobbling, eyes somehow dry. He couldn't see Fionne anymore—the alley door had swung shut behind her. Everyone else could run from this.

"Stregoni," he hissed. The fire flipping and rushing around her only grew stronger. She shook her head, hard, but it wouldn't go out. Gristle heard a car door slam out there, and footsteps clacking toward them. This was it. It was over.

Hawthorne whipped her head to face the alley entrance with a huff of sparks bleeding from between her teeth, the fire snarling defensively. Gristle couldn't watch the world be ruined twice. He shut his eyes, slid to the cold, real ground, and waited for the purity of an apocalypse.

It didn't come. Part of him was disappointed.

From behind his closed eyes he felt the smothering heat dampened. His vision switched from diffused-gray to black. He touched gingerly at the raw wetness at his stomach and his chest. The burns ached dully, but the pain was distant.

"Easy, love," he heard ahead of him, a voice tight but familiar. "Breathe, Hawthorne. Just come down now. Focus on your breathing. I'm here."

Gristle's eyes opened. The world focused in, piecing the shadows into something coherent. The alley was dark again. Fionne was indeed long gone, the Dogfoot door closed snug. Faintly, in the silence after the roaring flames, he heard quiet music from above.

Ahead of him, Hawthorne stood extinguished with a thick iron-laced coat pulled around her, the embroidered capelet stiff over her still-trembling shoulders, smothered into the chest of a tall, lean-framed figure in a wide-brimmed hat and a duster.

Gristle's stomach lurched. *Daddy?* a squeaky, juvenile part of his mind still asked. But Gristle Senan Maxim Junior knew, with logical certainty, that his father was ash.

And so, it was Shona Maxim who held Hawthorne against her chest, solid and sure.

"Easy," she said again, slow, with her hand on Hawthorne's back. Hawthorne was shaking, knees weak. "It's over. You're alright. Just breathe." Only when Hawthorne managed two shuddering breaths, and then another, more even one, did Gristle's aunt look around. Gristle couldn't see her face under the shadow from her hat, and yet he caught the moment that she nearly missed him crumpled against the dumpster before her eyes settled on his. He knew it from silhouette alone, and the exhaustion in her voice.

"Ace," she breathed. He swallowed, prepared for what would come. "What the hell happened here?"

University of Stoutshire

"The Fey Condition"
Effects of Iron on Fey Persons

by Doctor Sonder Secondchild, MD

"THE FEY CONDITION" has long perplexed and astounded mortal persons, giving way to countryside whisperings and superstition. However, as we move forward, we are able to unravel some of the mysteries of the fey. We have discredited claims that Faerie Disorder can be caused by environmental factors such as elevated sugar in small children (Bahai et al., 204-6) or through mental or bodily trauma (Tien, 24). Contained studies have proven that fey are not "swapped in" for stolen children as once thought, but that latent Faerie Disorder can be detected in infants, and possibly even in pre-born fetuses (Flanagan, 308-13). More and more we are coming to understand the genetic causes of Faerie Disorder, and so too its ties to class, region, and criminality.

The Secondchild study of 51SC uses a series of trials consisting of 200 randomly selected fey children between the ages of 3 and 13 cycles old, and confirms that fey are not "burned" by iron, as the old speculation and limited scientific data would suggest. Rather, pure metals (such as iron and silver) are distressing to the sensitive olfactory and cutaneous senses of fey. Small amounts raise distress signals, and so may heighten minor fey traits to process this adrenal change. However, large amounts administered via discs sewn into jackets are able to "smother" the nervous system and fey power center, slowing oxygen levels and cooling the body to prevent symptomatic surges that can encourage and enable "madness." This may even point toward possible medicinal uses of pure metals, which could act as an ongoing suppressant.

In this study, also containing a test group of mortal children, children were asked to play with an alloy or pure iron toy. While the mortal group played equally with both, none of the fey children were able to touch the iron toys without distress, with 30 percent experiencing minor symptoms and one particular child experiencing a heavy flare that nearly resulted in the complete transfiguration of the subject's body from flesh to stone. This has proved

HAWTHORNE STREGONI IN
"THE LONG RIDE"

I wake up with my head feeling like cotton, and my iron jacket over my shoulders. It smells like frozen blood and weighs me down, keeps my heart from racing off again. I swallow and it feels different, sharp. Shit. Musta grown some teeth in there when I wasn't paying attention. Funny how I can only change when I'm not trying to.

I know what I just did. And the worst part is that I meant to do it *then*, even if I know *now* that it was wrong. I can feel the symptoms stalking under my skin still, the impulsive high burning brighter since I fed it. One slipup, and I've promised myself that it'll only get worse from here on in, after everything I've done to be better.

The world's bumping, dipping—I hear tires on pavement, smell leather and something smoky sweet like charred fat. Light flashes by, but it's not so bright as at the Dog. I try to wrestle my vision straight. I *need* to get it together.

Things crash into place. I'm in the back of my aunt's long car with the top pulled up, lying across the leather seats. We're driving fast, whipping past streetlamps.

"I told you to check on her," my aunt says, voice tight and almost teary. The shifter clunks. We lurch faster. From how I'm laying, I can get a good look at her face when she turns to him, her eyebrows twitching. "And I find her lit up like a pyre at the most radical fey spot in this entire city. We're ruined if someone saw her there *without* the flames. And with what went down at the docks—we're lucky if all they do is test her."

What happened at the docks? I try to make words but my throat's too tired, all docile like something drugged. Like those mad fey in the institutions.

I'm eighteen now: if someone saw me, they could be building a case for a stress-test. I knew that, or should have, and I did this anyway.

In the middle of all the racing, I can hear someone breathing a little loudly. Not crying or anything, not breathing fast, just slow and deep, like he's trying his hardest not to puke.

"I know," Gristle says from the passenger side of the front bench seat, so calm and even. I want to punch him all over again for just taking it, for being so damn rational while I can't manage that. I want him to just hate me out loud and give me the fight I deserve. And like he heard me, the tiniest nerve pumps into his voice. "I checked in on her, like you said."

"And now?" she asks, *snaps*.

"It's not my fault she doesn't listen—"

"You and I both know she's not always rational," my aunt says. "I don't need to hear excuses about it, Senan."

A flash of memory rips through my head, of my stepdaddy haloed in smoke and folding pamphlets about dirty cities and the people they crush. But when the memory dies in a mad blast, after Senan gets himself burned up where his sibling wasn't there to save him, there's just the semi-silence of wheels on road.

I hear Gristle lick his lips and open his mouth. He exhales the name "Gristle" to correct her, without much commitment. Part of me wants him to break down screaming and crying. Just be imperfect too, lug. I'm tired of taking the fall.

My aunt tries to breathe. "Gristle," she mutters, in the same way you might say an apology. But neither of them seems to have the heart to pick the conversation up again. Neither of them wants to fight or scream or hurt each other like I do.

And so I just lay there with my eyes wet as a blistering burn, feeling the whole world come crumbling down. I wish I was better. I thought I was, but dreams ain't reality. I'm closer to an institution than I've ever been to moving out properly.

And Fionne saw that. It's a fresh panic, fighting against the heaviness of my coat. Where is she now? Does she hate me? It's a selfish, stupid question.

My aunt carves us off to the side of the road. Through the window, the boutique across from our apartment looms into view. Home safe, or almost. She crawls to the streetside and stops the engine. I wonder who's gonna break the silence first: my tough old aunt, or Gristle, who doesn't ever talk unless he has to. If I wasn't here, would either of them ever say anything? Or would they just stare out the windshield, waiting.

Finally, my aunt sighs from so deep in her stomach I think she'll bust up into tears or just collapse into a puddle. "*Gristle*," she says again. Her hand paws sideways, landing solid on his shoulder. "I don't have any right to talk to you like that. It just took me by surprise." She looks out the driver-side window. "I know what it's like, to have a sibling you gotta keep an eye on. I didn't keep a close enough watch on your daddy, and next thing you know..."

Next thing you know.

"I just know what it's like, being responsible for someone," she finishes.

He nods. From behind, their silhouettes look exactly the same, down to the solar system embossing on the high collars of their dusters, and the starry ribbons around their hats. Twins.

"I messed up," he says from low in his stomach. "I know that. She's been . . ." I hold my breath. I don't want him to say it, but I know I deserve it. "She's been sneaking out for a while, with Fionne Eze."

"Victory and Táyò's Second," she says quietly.

"They're not like that anymore," he says, probably meaning that Fionne's family ain't shouting for revolution like in Mum's day.

"She's a fashion girl, right?" my aunt asks. "*Dolly Day* fan?"

She's too smart: she knows the Dog was Fionne's idea, that I'd never be that bold on my own.

He doesn't have to answer. "They never went far. She always came back when I asked," he tries to explain. She opens her mouth, but he knows what she'll say. "I should have known it would escalate."

Her hand falls off his shoulder so she can pull a half-smoked cigar from her pocket. The spiced clouds smell like her and Senan both, a mirror set up on the line between dead and here. The type of twin who knows how to make a life from the scraps given, and the type of twin who dies from dreaming too big in a city you can't turn your back to.

Which one am I?

"Eze seems like a nice girl," she says in all the smoke. My throat hurts so bad I can't even swallow. "But I don't think she understands the gravity of what Hawthorne's going through. Same as her parents: they thought Hàzell was being metaphorical, talking about destruction. I know they regretted it after and they're good folk now, but . . ." Another plume. "That doesn't bring anyone back."

He nods.

Fionne asked to see the sparkles, and the Dog, where everyone was dancing to the song of their own bad blood. I doubt I'm the only one who had a mad trip after that. How many other fey bust up there and crawl home exhausted and scared to be caught?

The two of them stare right ahead while she puffs slowly. From this angle, I can see the cold line of her pale cheek, the buckshot freckles blasted everywhere, the tip of her button-small nose. It's Senan all over. Gristle's got his mom's rusty skin and her dark eyebrows and whatever else, but when you look at them together, anyone can see he's got Maxim in his blood.

My hand's in front of my face, each finger a greeny-gold. A strong Verdossi fey, Mum would have said. In the curve of my nose and tan of my skin and glossy curls so thick they could break a brush. Where we've got stories of how the fey could listen to the tall pine trees and the tan-brown mountains to tell the mortals where to farm and build and dance. It's Old World, too damn idealistic.

I need to take this seriously. I wanted to think Fionne could too, but it's asking so much of her.

"Alright," my aunt says, loud and snappy, like she's gotten out everything she needed to. "Are you sure you don't want me to look—"

"They're not that deep. We have a medical kit," he says, and he opens the car door. "I'll send the pictures in."

"Tough old jack," she says, voice lighter like a forced smile. "See you tomorrow night, Ace."

"Rain-right." And then he's out, and gone, and fine. Because everyone else can just tough it up while I feel like I'm breaking apart.

My aunt smokes the cigar right down, fogging everything up, and drops the butt out onto the road. And then she just sits, like she's waiting for something.

I reach out my hand, put it on the back of the cool seat, and poke one finger into her shoulder. She doesn't flinch, but takes a slow breath.

"Did you hear all that?" she asks.

I don't say anything, 'cause I know I'm a bad liar. She turns and looks at me in the yellow-white streetlight coming through the windshield. It cuts under the brim of her hat, showing her green eyes.

I need her to tell me why tonight is so bad, besides the obvious part.

"What happened on the docks?" I ask, as if I even deserve the truth.

But I'm not Gristle, who can deal with the hard shit. So she leans back and puts her warm hand on my cheek. "You sparked up a bit, but we're home now, and no one saw. I'll call Doc Secondchild and tell him what happened. I'll make sure this stays quiet."

Of course she will. "Gristle," I say. My throat's all burning, aching, and exhausted. "I really socked him."

Her thumb sweeps slow. "He'll be alright," she says. "He knows you didn't mean it."

It's convenient, to say I couldn't control myself. "What if I did mean it?" I ask her—it cracks and squeaks like breaking glass. "Auntie, what if I wanted to hurt him? What if I'm going mad like Mu—"

She doesn't even let me get it out. Already she's twisted right around and pulled me up, even with the seat between us, hugging me against her so I can throw my iron-heavy arms over her shoulders and hide my face there, shaking, and letting all the exhausted tears come out.

Her voice is fierce, same as it always is when I force her to remember Mum. "You're *not* like your mother," she says. I can barely remember Mum—just these burned-through flashes, feelings more than memories. "We're getting you help, and she never had that. I know you're going to be alright."

"Senan thought Mum was alright," I breathe. He strolls through my head like a ghost. Dancing with my mum to that old radio that was always getting hit by the door in our too-small dockside apartment. Arms around Fionne's parents, the same as they were around mobsters like the Gattanos and murderers like Mum. Too damn trusting. "What if I tricked you?"

"I don't know how much you remember," she starts. I hear the words trying to form in her chest. "But Sen—" Her voice breaks. We both breathe. "He was in and out of detention houses since we were small, never learned how to trust the right people. I'm not like that, neither is your brother. We learned what happens when we don't protect each other."

Is that enough? Three of us against the world? "Auntie," I say, quiet like a kid, "what happens if you don't get elected?"

She holds me tighter. "You let your brother and me worry about politics," she says. She lets go, sitting me back so she can push my tear-soaked curls away from my eyes. "You just focus on getting better, alright?"

And if that means listening to Gristle even when he makes me feel like a dumb kid, and no more parties, no more gin and swing, maybe even no more Fionne? Could I even stand that world?

But the way she looks at me, and how sturdy her hands are, I know I have to try to be better. For all of us, so we can finally stop hiding and hurting and just be normal for once.

"Alright," I say. "I'll be good."

16-CYCLE-OLD DOCKYARD DELINQUENT AND TWIN LOCATE SENATOR'S MISSING CHILD

"MAXIM & MAXIM" TWINS SOLVE MURDER OF TROLLEY WORKER

"The police weren't even looking!" says Maxim Secondchild.

IN SHADOW OF POLICE UNION LIBEL SUIT, MAXIM & MAXIM JOIN PPPD INVESTIGATION

"A chance to mend fences," says Maxim Firstchild.

THREE CHEERS FOR MAXIM & MAXIM!

Wonder twins locate missing jewels alongside PPPD.

WHERE ARE THE MAXIMS?

Amidst rising crime, the recently named dockyard duo has shut up shop.

THE DOCKYARD TRIO?

Senan Maxim presents bastard child, says he "will not be ashamed."

MAXIM & MAXIM ARE BACK!—33 ARRESTED IN GANGLAND BRAWL!

MAXIM & MAXIM: THE PEOPLE'S HEROES

Duo provides "shocking" evidence against factory management—awarded "Citizen of Distinction" by Ironworkers' Guild.

"TROUBLEMAKERS WITH A COMPLEX"

PPPD takes stance against Maxim & Maxim after Senan Maxim defends fey thief.

MAXIM SPOTTED WITH "FEY RADICAL" KNOWN FOR INCENDIARY PAMPHLETS

Could a new love affair be the cause of the duo's recent "pro-fey sentiments"?

"I STAND WITH MY FAMILY"

Shona Maxim defends brother following his "wild and disorderly" public marriage to fey radical.

SENAN MAXIM CHARGED WITH MISDEMEANOR AT ILLEGAL PROTEST

"The police are mad dogs without a leash!" he says.

"WE HAVE A DUTY TO PROTECT OUR CITY!"

Police contemplate arrest of Senan Maxim and wife for "threats of violence" related to "pro-fey organizing."

GRISTLE SENAN MAXIM JUNIOR IS "THE MAN IN THE MOVIE"

Gristle Senan Maxim Junior sat in his room, which wasn't so much a bedroom as a mothball-smelling broom closet in the office. When he and Hawthorne moved into the Maxim & Maxim office with their aunt, Hawthorne got the single bedroom down the hall, and this was at least better than the office couch his aunt was sleeping on: he got his own bed, and could crack the door open to talk to her until he fell asleep.

In the shared grief of those first strange moons, when Hawthorne was wilder than a windstorm with no savior in sight, his aunt had told him everything. About how the city had been darker before the iron boom. How his grandparents had abandoned both Maxim children early. About how the two had slept on wooden pallets near the docks just to stay out of the mud, back when every shadow had monsters in it, when every alley was a mouth. The cold winters, the blazing summers, the people who ignored them, and the other kids who went missing. How Senan Maxim, then Maxim Secondchild, had always been running into trouble, a good-hearted kid too prone to trusting.

These days, his aunt made enough money to also rent a small apartment closer to her 6th Street campaign office, which left Gristle alone that night in the concussion-black dark, mindlessly winding film into cylinders. He had dabbed a wet cloth over his burns, which didn't hurt as long as he kept his mind moving. He could picture his daddy, young and reckless, ripping through the revolving door of detention houses for another petty crime, another hurled insult or rock despite his sister's pleas, and screaming with bloody teeth as he was hauled off of an officer at a bread riot and thrown straight into a jail cell with one final warning. Gristle could feel the creak of broken ribs under jailers' boots better than his own burns. In the dark, he could see his adolescent aunt standing outside the penitentiary after six moons, with a train ticket in her hand for the quieter countryside where he might be better off. But then her twin, with a face so much like hers, came tottering out to collapse into her arms, and she knew she couldn't abandon him. There had to be a better story for them in this filthy city.

Gristle wound the cylinders, prepared them for the chemical vat that sat, sealed, at the end of his bed. His aunt had told him to send in the pictures, and she had always been the brains. She was the one who'd known how to smooth that criminal legacy. Took some pix to find a lost cat, some roundels to track down a stolen locket, even more to catch the culprit in a string of working-class burglaries, leading up to the moment they found a senator's missing kid, and suddenly her brother was a heartwarming story of carceral reform.

And yet, still, whenever she turned her back . . .

"He would have believed the devil was his friend, and he'd be gone before you could tell him better," she'd said once, when Gristle was barely older than the day of the fayre and just begging for answers. Hawthorne had been attending her very first clinical study at the university, so his aunt had taken him to a nice east side park, bought him an ice cream, and sat him on a bench to watch the duck pond. "That was his curse, Maxim: he believed too much in folks, optimistic to a fault, and everyone could smell it on him. He told me to trust him, but . . ."

Now Gristle shifted closer to the end of his bed. He knew there were details that didn't make the news. Sometimes they spat up through his head like silhouettes in front of the projector. Sixteen cycles old with dead rats on their doorstep and shadows around every corner after his daddy mouthed off to the police the first time. His sister stalking grim-faced to the precinct to offer any apology necessary. And it had worked, until his daddy abandoned everything to run off with his tutor, and she died, and he crawled back with a toddler he could hardly care for. Another cover-up. Another reframing. More lies to hide the truth:

That the younger twin was an accident waiting to happen, and the unseen older woke up every day ready to patch the sky before it fell in on them.

Gristle knew the feeling.

And, finally, Senan Maxim fell one last time, siren-sung along into Hàzell's spiraling madness. It was the last straw that even Shona Maxim couldn't stop. Gristle had heard too many people speculate that his daddy knew Hàzell was planning to self-destruct, or that he didn't, or that it was an accident, or that he was a victim in a devastating plot. None of it was pretty enough for a picture show.

Like an eighteen-cycle-old boy sitting alone on his bed with two fist-shaped burns in him and a sister he couldn't save.

Gristle nearly crushed the celluloid cylinder, too small in his grown, shaking hands. He opened the chemical vat, let the smell swim as he dropped the film in. Things had been *fine* before that night, and he needed to put everything back on the track that had served his family since his aunt had learned how to make a good story from a bad one.

Gristle clunked the lid closed and told his mind to do the same. "No more," he whispered to himself. His aunt had a plan, and she'd taught it to him. In another few moons, they'd win the election, and more funding, and the tragedy would be resolved. Hawthorne could be saved.

This time, despite it all, the Maxims would win.

Puck's Port Herald

51SC, Summer Solstice

TRAGEDY AT THE SUMMER FAYRE
300 KILLED BY "MAD FEY"

Devastating tragedy struck today when, at approximately twelve bells, on what should have been a day of celebration to welcome in the summer moons, known fey anarchist Hàzell Stregoni, 38, self-destructed as a result of growing madness. The fayre grounds were completely leveled, with tents, booths, and rides reduced to rubble and matchsticks. Stregoni's body was incinerated, along with that of her husband, Senan Maxim, 30, the controversial younger member of the infamous firm Maxim & Maxim, Private Detectives.

The only survivors within the radius of the blast are Maxim Child and Stregoni Child, both 11 cycles, who suffered only minor trauma. At the time of the implosion, both were on the carousel nearby.

"I was going for the prize ring," Stregoni told reporters from their hospital bed. Maxim Child was unavailable for questioning, having suffered a head wound. Due to the fey nature of the blast, Maxim is currently experiencing a total inability to perceive color. It is unclear if this is temporary.

As for Hàzell Stregoni, her motive is uncertain. Stregoni has been given a posthumous diagnosis of "madness," a classification that marks a fey as dangerous to themself or others. When left untreated, "mad" fey are driven to engage in increasingly erratic behaviors, which ultimately result in self-implosion if there is no intervention. Until today, the deadliest self-implosion killed only three, including the fey themself. However, investigators are unable to determine if Stregoni's implosion was an act of mad desperation or a pre-planned attack.

"Stregoni was a radical, considering some of the materials she'd been handing around, but that was covered by freedom of speech laws," Police Chief Dermott Ashley III told reporters. "Now at least 144 children are dead, including a Second, Third, Fourth, and Fifth from the same family. Our laws need changing to stop this from happening again." Ashley plans to donate a substantial sum to this family, the Tanners, and urges other citizens to do the same.

Investigators are still determining

Senan Maxim's involvement in this event. The younger Maxim twin's well-known criminal past has long inspired speculation, with some suggesting that Maxim & Maxim began to cover up his history of public disturbance and juvenile arrest after assaulting a police officer. While the twins have stated that Senan Maxim came to respect law and order, an anonymous tip reports that he was increasingly erratic and paranoid before the event, perhaps in anticipation of the massacre.

Shona Maxim was unavailable for comment, but family friend Táyò Táyò, the printer responsible for Stregoni's incendiary autobiographical pamphlets, has stated that "Senan and Howell were phenomenal parents and friends who wouldn't hurt anyone, let alone risk their own children." Táyò is currently being investigated for possible involvement, alongside a few others who have come forward to defend Maxim and Stregoni. This group includes an individual known to be connected to the Verdossi mob, as well as journalist Victory Eze, who only recently published another article alleging excessive violence from the Puck's Port P.D., which included a statement from Senan Maxim.

Staff at the University of Stoutshire's Department of Fey Studies urge the public to remember that Stregoni does not represent all fey, and that "madness and self-implosions can be prevented by access to treatment." They urge the public to make donations to the department to fund research into treatment methods.

Maxim Child and Stregoni Child are expected to be released from the hospital soon into the care of Shona Maxim. Those still attempting to locate a loved one in the aftermath of the Summer Fayre Massacre are urged to call 777.

PART TWO

HAWTHORNE STREGONI IS "SOME KIND OF FEY"

I know there's something going on, worse than me toasting up last night. And I know someone who might just give me the scoop . . . as long as she ain't holding seven iron bars when I get there. It's terrifying, and it does involve sneaking out my window again, but I oughta talk to Fionne even while my skin still itches from last night's high. I'm not the monster she saw last night. I won't show off anymore. Quiet hands, quiet mind. And it helps that I'm sober now too.

Before Gristle wakes up, I sneak into the washroom to splash some cold water on my face and try to smooth my curls out, put on my daffy little school uniform (high socks, shorts, a round little collar like a toddler's), and slip out the window while the moon haunts me from behind the flat, corniced roofs and quiet places filled with quiet people. From there, I turn east.

Midtown shifts slowly until the pavement switches to cobbles and the buildings ease from boxy businesses and apartments into east side, days-gone-by "charm," all swirling, tight-packed streets barely big enough for a one-way lane. Some buildings still have thatched roofs, or are plastered white with chunks fallen off so you can see the stone underneath. The iron lampposts are running electric now. It's the only thing that makes this place not look like a piddly middle-country village.

I twist down the streets quick as a cat. When I step into the ocean of fog piling up in the old city circle, I try not to look at the platform in the middle—I know that's where the pyre would have been. We don't do that anymore, which means things are getting better even if they feel like they ain't.

But I still have to pass Oakpost Road, where I can't stop myself from staring toward the quaint houses with wooden shutters and tiny little gardens. One still has black crepe in the windows nearly a septennial later, because you don't lose your four youngest kids in one day and just forget it. I remember standing up on that top step, a moon after the massacre, half-hiding behind my aunt with Maxim stoic at her side. The Tanners were alright enough to accept her condolences through their tears, and I remember Maxim shaking their hands like my aunt did. I didn't try to shake, because I could tell by the way they were watching my mismatched eyes and sharp nails, and how their Firstchild was glaring at me, that they didn't want to shake the hand of some fey. Especially not the one born from the one who killed their kids.

We all lost people. I was crying too, but most of that was guilt.

I rush forward into the next street, a bit faster. Birds start chirping the sun awake—they speckle the high roofs and telephone wires striping against the lightening sky. I want to count them. More mist rises from the mud between the cobbles to itch against my bare knees and soak into my socks. Closer now, a thundering *chug-chug-chug* booms a heartbeat down the lanes. A mis-shaved spot on my jaw itches deep in the pores. It's all singing.

I squeeze my fists tight. I shouldn't have fed this last night. I should have just let it go hungry in my chest until it shriveled instead of letting it carve even stronger paths back to the surface.

A boxy van rounds the corner and goes wobbling past me, the canvas sides flapping and the back bed empty, aside from a few folks who stare at me walking all stiff. Their eyes feel like slashing knives.

It just keeps cycling through my head, digging deeper and deeper.

Just one flame, just one tiny release, just *something* to make it all *stop*.

"I won't," I say, out loud, so it's true. I cross the street, running my feverish fingers across a wall of cold stone and wet ivy. It's a good feeling, almost enough to get my head on straight as I duck sideways through the gate toward the *Puck's Port Herald*'s printing factory.

Across the courtyard, the printing house sits wide and tall, three levels with lots of chimneys and shingled roofs, ivy all over, and the windows glowing warm in the early morning. Through one, I see some jack with a wrench and ink all up their arms, shoulders flexing under their roughed-up shirt as they tune up the presses for the morning edition.

I could do that—get in only a few bells past midnight, spiff the machines up, carry the heavy toolboxes and make sure the city wakes up to the news they need. I will, when I'm better. Just gotta make it through, like my aunt knows I can.

I take a solid breath and walk up the ramp and through the heavy door. The front area's cramped and dusty, just big enough for stairs that lead to up-top and stairs that lead to down-low, and doors that go off to the narrow halls of distribution offices. I start to head down.

I always joke that Fionne's baba must have some fey in him, considering how sharp his hearing is. "Is that the birthday lady?" I hear him call from up-top, in his low Ileian accent.

I straighten my cap and make my posture good, even though I know it probably doesn't matter considering how long he's known me. But it's one thing to know someone when you're a snot-nosed little tyke splitting egg creams with their kids in the back of Cat's, and another when you're courting their Second.

And after your mum pretty literally burned down the whole friend group and threw everyone's good names into question.

I can't let my blood hurt this family twice.

I step onto the sturdy wooden stairs so I can look up to see him leaning over the carved banister, the first bit of dawn light coming through the rooms behind to light up the dust glittering around him. He's wearing his little glasses that are like Fionne's reading ones, and a wide-necked Ileian shirt with the bright colors and patterns smeared with opening shift ink.

"One sun late, Mister Táyò," I shout up over the sound of the presses.

"She's still in her office," he says right away, 'cause while I do love him fierce and have been sneaking out here pretty regular since I was fourteen, he knows I'm never here for him.

I frown. "Ain't she done yet?"

He opens his mouth as Fionne's oldest sibling comes out from behind with his plait beads clicking under his hair kerchief and three whole cases of lettered stories stacked in his arms. Psh, I could do that.

"Hey, Ify," I call.

Ify looks down at me with gunmetal black eyes but doesn't say anything. My skin shrivels. He shifts his smooth jaw in a gesture I don't quite get, and then jerks his chin at his dad in a "I've gotta take these" type of way. He disappears down the hall.

A tiny chill carves down my spine. I think to tap my toes, but I don't want to amp myself up. Deep breath. "You . . . you seen the stories yet, sir?" I ask Mister Táyò, careful now.

Even from down here, I can see his eyes glaze for a second, like he doesn't wanna say. But then he just snubs at his wide nose. "You get to call me Baba Ify," he says, wagging his finger at me. "Now go tell that girl to hurry up before the bell goes. I don't want the paper-kids throwing rocks."

"Sure . . ." I say, but I can't find a way to talk to him like we're family, so I just fumble my hand into something that ends up looking like a real corny military salute, beat myself with a crowbar in my head, and then turn tail before the embarrassment makes my body ache worse.

I escape down the narrow stairs into the brick-walled lower hall tight as a tomb with sconces glowing into the dim. I speed past offices where folks are setting ads. But none of those people feel "safe" to me; they all feel like they're watching, even if they're not. I want to believe that the last office on the left will wrap me up warm, but Ify's eyes still cut.

Did Fionne tell him? Does he hate me now? Does she?

I stop just short of the open door and close my eyes for a second to get myself together. It's been one thing for Fionne to know I'm fey, or even to know my mum, but it's another altogether for her to know how much power I've got in me waiting to shoot through the cracks.

I think about what my aunt said. Yeah, Fionne didn't know. If she did, would we have been more careful? Or would she have run to report the dangerous fey, like Senan should have?

I step up to the arch-shaped doorway and look into Fionne's office, at her thick wooden desk and her nice cabinets with all her different kinds of type that she coos over. The iron composite for the morning edition front page is already finished on her desk, all the little letters slotted into their place, but she hasn't put it into the dumbwaiter to send it up to the presses.

Instead, Fionne sits on a crate in the corner, staring the composite down like a hard math problem. Her glasses are hung off the apron pinned over her puffy, checkered work dress and her hair's wrapped up smooth with a nice little brooch on the front. She looks like a girl in a *Dolly Day* magazine, smoking slowly with her chin on the heel of her hand and her elbow in her other palm, the cigarette hanging from her brown fingers and the smoke coiling up to the spidery lights. I wish I could just stand here looking at her forever.

I knock my knuckles against the doorframe. She looks over and I wait for her to dive for some ash wood or iron. She doesn't, just stares at me, like we both want to keep this moment lasting longer.

I don't know what I'm supposed to say. I don't try to walk in. "I thought your boss told you not to smoke down here," I try.

She stubs her cigarette out on the crate. "Don't tell the boss, then," she says. "Or Ify. He's been on me all morning."

Did she tell him what I did? Dread creeps up my legs. I wait for the cold shoulder (bad) or for her to just smile like nothing happened (worse). Instead, she stands up and holds her hands out, and, really, who am I to say no to that? I try not to run right over like I want to, and instead I walk through the dust and the smoke. Her arms fall over my shoulders, her forehead tipping down into mine.

"Feenee," I say. I almost tell her I didn't mean to go all mad on Gristle, but that's not true, so I just say, "I'd never hurt you."

Did Mum say the same to Senan? Can any of us really promise that?

"If Gristle's good, so am I," she tells me, so fast it's like she ain't even thought about what I've said. "End of story."

I frown a bit. "You don't wanna talk about—?"

"Nope," she almost snaps. Her eyes look frantic for only half a second, until she shuts them soft. "If you want, H. But it feels rotten to make you sorry for something you can't help."

But I *can* help it, can't I? Isn't it my fault that my brain's so fried? It's nice she wants to be all sympathetic, but at what point is that just rotten for her instead?

"Last . . . last night was a wake-up call," I tell her. I can't look at her eyes, so I stare somewhere past. Am I looking for a way out? Drop her before I crush her in my hand like a covetous fey? "I'm not ready for what we said," I tell her. "Parties every night. Living just us. I've gotta focus on school, and it could take a bit, and I don't want you resenting me any while . . . " I have to take a breath so it all comes out smooth and not creaky or rambling. "I won't be mad if you want a break or something."

Her thin eyebrows buckle in. I want to take it all back, every word I've ever said, until I fold into myself and disappear. "Do *you* want a break, Hawthorne?" she asks. Her arms stiffen over my shoulders. "'Cause you're sounding awfully serious about this."

No! My thoughts are getting all rushed and annoyed, and I know bad things happen if I can't cork that fast enough. I close my eyes and keep beating myself with that crowbar in my head. "You're allowed to be upset at me," I tell her, so quiet I'm not sure she can hear even right ahead of me. "Everyone treats me like glass, or like I'm . . . like I'm this animal they gotta feed themselves to no matter how much it hurts."

I hear her open her mouth, maybe to argue.

"I can't have you doing it too," I say, opening my eyes to look real hard at her. "I'm not gonna hurt you, but that means I need to know you'll tell me when to stop if I do."

Her lips close. The silence sits. I want to take it all back, but I won't. I'm too old to be hoping—I need to work for the things I want.

"I . . ." She can't get the thought out. Her arms slide until her hands are light on my shoulders. "You scared me last night, H, you really did. And I hate thinking I was rushing you—"

"I should have said something too."

She swallows. "I still trust you, but now, with the stuff in the paper today..."

My knees stiffen.

Her eyes are glassy. "I'm guessing Gristle didn't tell you."

"You gotta," I tell her, almost like I'm begging. "Please, Fionne. Just keep being honest with me." We're not kids anymore. We have to be serious, and honest, and realistic, and everything that isn't fun. "I can't help if I don't know how."

She nods. Her hands slip down to tangle with mine, cautious but still strong.

"I know it wasn't you," she says first, "but a fey killed someone on the docks, and I don't trust folks to be reasonable about it."

Puck's Port Herald

57SC, 3 Winter Moons, and 4 Suns

"EVIL RUNS IN THE BLOOD," MAD FEY AT LARGE

At approximately two bells past midnight last night, police received an anonymous tip concerning suspicious activity at Dock #2 of Puck's Port's coal yard, in front of the Feu Family iron smithy. A patrol was sent to investigate what was suspected to be a routine misdemeanor by a local "hobo," a rail-riding individual come to the city on the coal train looking for work.

However, they found the body of an unidentified person, burned beyond recognition. While initial hypotheses included an intoxicated individual and the smithy's stove, crime-scene photographer Gristle Senan Maxim Junior (of the once infamous Maxim & Maxim, Private Detectives) arrived on scene.

"I'll be honest, we didn't expect much of the kid. He was there for photos," Sergeant O'Riley reported. "But he caught the shadow on the wall. The bricks were all scorched like a kiln, except for where the victim had been standing when they were hit."

"It's clear we're dealing with a mad fey," said Police Chief Laura Bazik. "While mad fey are indeed escalating offenders, their heightened state makes them erratic and easy to track. The majority of cases are solved within forty-eight bells. Until then, we advise citizens to report any suspicious activities."

President Dermott Ashley III offered his own comment in an early-morning radio broadcast, saying that he believes an increase in fey-related crime is inevitable as long as "certain fringe groups" encourage "hand-holding" rather than strict laws.

"We learned our lesson less than a septennial ago: there is no dialogue that works with a criminal, only action," he told listeners. "Evil runs in the blood. It's here in Puck's Port. We ought not to let the same sort of corruption try to convince us otherwise."

This story is ongoing. Details will be posted as they become available.

Gristle Senan Maxim Junior hadn't slept. Mostly he'd just let his consciousness sink into the chemical smell, until he heard a knock on the office door sometime just before dawn, at which point he handed the photos over to the delivery kid. He thought to add a roundel, too—bribery to get them to say that Senan Maxim's son was cooperative—but he knew what his aunt would think about that.

Things would have to be "by the book" for a while, respectful and all. Frankly, that was Gristle's wheelhouse. Stick to the law, the cops would get this sewn up soon, and the Maxim campaign would just have to ride the wave.

Gristle changed his bandages, changed into his usual oversized sack suit from the office armoire, grabbed his camera bag and hat, and went out for the morning. When he stepped onto the front stoop of the apartment building, the dawn-drowned air was misty and cold, split only by a few kids on bikes racing past and tossing newspapers onto doorsteps. Three landed at his feet, swallowed by his broad shadow. Gristle cautiously leaned sideways to let light from the doorway's sconce leak onto the front page, so stark against the concrete.

> "EVIL RUNS IN THE BLOOD,"
> MAD FEY AT LARGE

He didn't have to be a genius to know who *that* comment was from. And he didn't have to read it to assume Ashley would be throwing a bad light on both Gristle and his aunt for Senan Maxim's mistakes. But it was frankly laughable, borderline cartoonish. Hell, maybe this would even do the Maxim campaign a service. Gristle might be able to head to his aunt's office to plan a good response for the evening paper. His daddy sure hadn't gotten out from under the hunt of whatever wrongness swam in his head, but Gristle hadn't inherited it, he swore.

That was progress: knowing people could be fixed if you pushed them hard enough.

Gristle Senan Maxim Junior had roughly one bell of free time before he needed to walk Hawthorne to school, and so in sharp contrast to the wild wanderings of his daddy, he had perfectly honed his morning routine like an oak tree coaxed into a fist-sized pot. He was the first person into the morning-bright diner on the bottom level of their building where he startled Miss Kîsisam, who apparently never heard him come in despite the bell on the door. He knew he didn't have to say his breakfast order but he did anyway: Askiyn fry bread, two eggs cooked all the way through, venison bacon, and a cup of coffee. He ate at his usual table off in the back corner. He wasn't big on smiling, but he always faked a flat one for Kîsisam when she refilled his cup (twice), a habit learned during his schooling cycles. He finished quick, left a twenty-pix tip on the table, and hurried out the jingling door.

He could have ordered take-out lunch from Kîsisam, but the deli at the other side of the block stocked desserts from a Jahagee bakery a few streets over, rose sugar donuts and saffron cakes and the like. He knew very little of his mother beyond that she'd been his father's tutor, that she'd despised Shona Maxim for warning her brother against having a child so young, that she'd died and left his father stranded on his sister's doorstep with their bastard baby. And that she'd been from a Jahagee family.

And so, in an act of strange and desperate longing for something he'd never known, Gristle entered to find his usual paper bag on the counter, and opened it on the usual chicken sandwich (cut horizontally), a gray-toned soda that he reread the label on a few times to make sure it was the usual lime, and the chef's pick of dessert: three cardamom biscuits leaning against each other. It was one tiny, unplanned surprise each morning, and yet it always made him feel strangely guilty, like a schoolchild sneaking sweets.

Never mind. He left cash on the counter, stopped at the grocer for his weekly bags already packed plus an additional bottle of whiskey, and headed back toward home right on schedule. By then the sky had lightened to white, autos puttering awake and commuters wandering to the trolley stop. Gristle strode back for the thin stoop of his building, honed in like a marksman. He fit his toe under the last remaining newspaper and popped it up seamlessly into one of his bags before shouldering his way into the dozy light of the wooden stairwell. Gristle trotted up the polished steps, looking forward to the mundanity of taking Hawthorne to school, coming back to the office, and purchasing new flashbulbs.

He stepped to the switchback landing, where segmented light shone through a stained-glass window, turned toward the stairs up to the sanctuary of the second floor, and realized, with sudden, sinking dread, that the day would be no more ordinary than the previous night.

Up the well-lit steps, into the dark shadows of their hallway, a *huge*, roving shape paused to sit itself between the carved banisters. Gristle nearly thought it something demonic until he managed to discern its shape in the gloom: a lean black dog, with deer-thin legs and a snout so sharp it seemed pincerlike. Gristle had seen medium-sized dogs, and large dogs, and even dogs big enough to make most folk nervous, but this one seemed larger than any four-legged mammal ought to reasonably be allowed to grow. It could have put its paws on his shoulders with ease; each was the size of his deli container.

Gristle jolted back into the warm window with braced knees, but the dog didn't move. Inanely, Gristle looked up to the third-floor stairs, as if he might see the upstairs neighbors wandering down to collect their common pet.

But there was no way on this mortal plane that a dog of that size and intensity belonged to the painfully ordinary families that lived in midtown. Gristle's already sunk stomach sloshed down toward his heavy feet. The dog's eyes gleamed as intensely as Gristle's. Not just any dog, he felt certain.

That right there was someone's familiar, which meant there was a fey somewhere in the building. Gristle blinked. The dog did not.

A door creaked somewhere past the stairs, off in the direction of the office and bedroom. Every hair on Gristle's body itched rigid. A stranger was up there, and so was his sleeping sister, and so was a business he was meant to mind.

"Easy now," he breathed, as if a dog could possibly understand him. He crept up with one hand reached out before him, skating his eyes to the hallway now coming clear around the stairwell bend. "Good poochie."

The dog stared at him even more intently, as if it despised the notion that it was a "poochie," let alone a good one. When Gristle was nearly all the way up the steps, the dog growing no smaller as he approached, it resignedly pointed its sharp snout off to the right. Gristle, finally, was able to see past the bend.

Down their tidy hallway, Hawthorne's door was still shut, as was the small bathroom across. However, closer, one wedge of early-morning light leaked out onto the gray-floral wallpaper, unobstructed by any frosted glass. In the whole closed-in hallway, the office door was stuck ajar. Even the air was wrong up here—something sharp needled through Gristle's sinuses. Perfume. Not the kind rich folk dabbed on their wrists at election parties. This was cheaper but no less fine, like velvet barrooms and smoke-laced furs.

The south side had followed him home, like a ghost. Gristle hated everything about this, and yet knew what he had to do. The dog had gone back to staring down the stairs, and so Gristle slid carefully past, set his groceries against the baseboard, and pressed his back to the wall alongside the doorframe.

This was his office. He was in control here. With his breath held, he poked his head sideways only enough to see who was creeping about the famed Maxim & Maxim office so early in the morning.

Sun burned through the blinds, until the slender-limbed smudge in the middle of the room became a person. A girl, or rather a woman, he supposed, older than him but not by much, with smooth Hannochian features. She was dressed far too lavishly for the daytime: a silver-fox scarf tossed around her neck, a small clutch purse held in both hands, and a drop-waisted dress that faded from patterned silk into drapes of jewels glinting across her legs like light on a pond. Her dark hair was rolled and permed to a perfect black cloud of sculpted waves reaching no lower than her chin—she touched at it and turned her face to inspect the armoire he'd left open.

There was something cautious about her, and yet her voice rang with the clarity of an actress. "I was told you were in the business of helping people," she said over her shoulder, without even looking at him. "Now I find out you're in the business of sneaking around like a schoolchild." She gave the armoire a very obvious scan. "And wearing horribly out-of-date suits."

Despite the unexpected intrusion (and the terrifying dog, and being called unfashionable for the second time in twenty-four bells), Gristle was settled by her statement: she was looking for a detective. They didn't have any of those here anymore, but she wasn't the first to wander in thinking she'd find one. Saints, they oughta fix the door—his father's name still stared from the frosted glass, incredulous.

Small talk was easy. "You can't ever be too careful, miss," he said, striding in and tapping his hat brim. The office was wide and warm in the morning light, all the filing cabinets gleaming, the wallpaper smartly simple, the desk moderately tidy. It was a fine day, Gristle reminded himself. "Though I will say, I'm not used to there being anyone here so early in the morning."

"Well," she said. From a distance, he'd thought she was closer to his own towering height. But stepping up to her now, she had to tilt her chin up to face him properly. "I'm sure you could change that."

Gristle felt like it was almost innuendo but wasn't sure, and wasn't given much of a chance to parse it; the woman smiled shyly and extended her delicate hand. He took her fingers on well-practiced impulse, face flat and intentional.

"You have a very . . ."—she paused. Her eyes moved like lightning bugs, zipping electric across every stitch and freckle—"*severe* look about you, Detective Maxim."

He'd never perfected eye contact. He attempted to keep his voice welcoming. "That's *Mister* Maxim," he said, with the same flat affect that never did learn to bend. He let her fingers fall from his and stepped back behind his desk, motioning to the extra chair ahead of it before tidying the election posters aside. "Detective Maxim was my—"

The empty whiskey bottle tipped. The woman stopped it with one long finger. "Father," she finished, pushing it forward with a glass-on-wood screech. He'd meant to say "aunt," but that was all the same. Her eyes still searched him, tremulous as she clutched her purse closer. "Spirits . . . aren't you a detective as well?"

Laughable. He removed his camera bag, setting it on the desktop. "I specialize in evidence collection." He sat, thinking she would too. But she was still standing over the desk, looking back over her shoulder and touching one diamond-drop earring. "My aunt offers professional opinion. Apologies, miss—I assumed you'd know that we haven't been in the nose-to-the-ground detective business in quite a while."

Her chin dimpled so dramatically that she looked like a pouting portrait in a magazine. She pulled a Maxim & Maxim business card from her clutch in a frantic flash. "I was told you were the man to speak to about getting problems solved," she said, holding the card out between two fingers. He had only a moment to see his new name scrawled in pen before she tucked it away. Word traveled fast . . . but it traveled wrong. "Unless that wasn't you in the paper this morning?"

Last night wasn't a solve, just an observation. Nevertheless, she was clearly frightened, and he did feel for her. He still didn't know how to make his voice sound sincere the way others did. "I'd do you no service by sticking my neck where it's not needed," he said, nodding slightly. Her chin dipped too, more a mirror of him than a look of understanding. "The best I can do is forward you to the real detectives at the triple-P D."

"Oh . . . the police," she said, in a way that made Gristle's spine ripple like a cracked whip. Was she more powerful than he thought, scared of inviting a stress-test on herself? Or was she just mindful that a dog that large wouldn't sit easy around cops? And even with feyness aside, Hannochian southside businesses tended to step light around the police, for a gaggle of reasons.

"I can call in a favor," he tried to say. "My aunt knows some of the softer folks there. I assure you that this is best."

Her mouth wrinkled further. From other angles, the woman's face had seemed sharper. It must have been a trick of her hair—now her cheeks were cherubic. She looked innocent, kind, impossibly young, like an eleven-cycle-old child thrown from a carousel without anyone to catch them. He didn't know why he was thinking that, but—

"P-perhaps I have some alternatives," Gristle said, like a gasp. He picked up his legal pad and a pen, forcing his hand not to shake, "if you can tell me what the gripe seems to be?"

Her face opened. She smiled, small and tight. "Very well, Mister Maxim," she said at last, finally easy enough to sit down in front of him. Her nerves were fading, but he couldn't be sure what emotion had replaced them. "My 'gripe' is that there are some strange things happening at my place of work. Things that go bump in the night, you know."

Not uncommon. "I can connect you with some local tradesfolk to upgrade your locks," he offered, and he began hashing out details. "What's your business, miss?"

No response.

He looked up. She was staring right at him, as intense as her familiar, her face like the center of a storm. For a moment, he was certain her eyes had flashed yellow against the tan-brown of her face. But then everything was gray again.

"My business?" she asked.

A creeping dread twisted up into him like climbing vines. They wriggled into his organs, tightened toward his throat. He understood that she wouldn't just tell him where she worked, but exactly why she had come *here*.

"The Dogfoot Club, on Aziza Street."

Suspicious activities at the Dogfoot. Her smile started in her eyes, and dripped to her dark lips.

This dame knew something. Gristle needed to get *far* away from this, away from the place where his sister had lit up, but also away from the sorts of fey too much like his wild stepmum. Was all the fear just an act to sedate him into her claws? Had he really felt sorry for her, or had she messed with his mind to inject that in? And now the silence was too long and he needed to come up with something.

"You . . . seem quite young. To own a club like the Dogfoot."

She raised an eyebrow at him, still with that entertained smile. "It was my uncle's establishment until earlier this cycle, when I returned from my schooling. But he grew tired of Puck's Port, and my eldest sister thought it might give me some . . ."—her mouth moved strangely, as though someone had wound the tape just a second behind the picture—"*direction*. I've fixed it from his liking to my own."

Regardless of who she was, there was a process for this. "Most suspicious activities fade off once the perpetrators know you're serious. I can recommend some security contacts," he said quickly. He debated if it was worth pulling out the big guns, those connections that his aunt had done well to lock away when she'd ascended past the docks. But Gristle needed to fight a threat with a threat. His aunt had never messed with anyone close to the Verdo mob (besides Rory Gattano, a declawed kitten compared to their eviscerating brothers), but her twin had. Gristle could remember them all playing cards at the dockyard apartment, and how one or another of them would slip a few pix or licorice drops to Hawthorne and him to spy on someone's hand—it should have been a sign that they weren't good folk. Still, Gristle knew the names of a dozen minor members who could flash their mob tattoos just long enough to scare anything away.

He wrote them down. This would end. Gristle ripped the page out of the pad.

"This is all I can offer," he said simply. She was washed in the strangled light coming through the blinds, and he was a grim shadow that could not be moved. Over. Shut. Done. "Cheers, miss."

A momentary strike of emotion speared across her face like a gunshot, a widening of her eyes, a softness to her parting lips. He'd hurt her. Gristle's throat caught. He thought she'd grab the paper and rush off, maybe in tears. Well, that was the job, wasn't it? People got hurt.

And some people, Gristle knew, didn't take well to hurt.

"Gristle, Senan, Maxim, Junior," she said, which made him stop. He retracted the paper slightly, shocked that a stranger would think to name him in full. She was standing now (when did she stand?), staring down at him with the gems on her necklace shining yellow and purple and—"Something is amiss at my club, and if you knew better, you would know the Dog has no lack of strong-arm connections from folks much more fit than whatever rascals you *think* you control." Every word rumbled, like the battering gusts of tornados swirling up in the countryside. Gristle felt as if he'd shrunk in his chair, back to the size of that eleven-cycle-old with no one to catch him. "What we *do* lack is a detective, and you would do well to fill the role. My office is against the back wall of the club, Mister Maxim, and I often have a late-night *smoke*."

Gristle's entire body contracted. Every word out of this fey's mouth twanged strange through his body, seemed to come from everywhere, like a voiceover track closing in on him.

She toyed with the whiskey bottle, tilting it to one precarious angle. "So imagine my surprise when, last night, I looked outside to see a certain beloved fey go wild and put two holes in her lovely brother."

Clack went the bottle, back to level.

"That sounds awful surprising," Gristle said with a flat, dead tone.

She rapped a decided finger on the cap. Again her features fuzzed, almost hurt, and yet livid, and yet completely calm. "Fortunately, I don't much care about your political games. I care about *my* problems," she said, laying overdramatic fingers across her bare collar. Gristle could get no read on her. "So you will investigate my club without squealing to the pigs—"

Did he have it in him to call the police? Hope Hawthorne and the Maxims had enough favor to evade the accusation? Maybe his aunt could—

"*Or* your aunt," she went on to say, teeth sharper now. "You will find the source of my suspicions, or I will tell the police what I saw. And really, I think now may not be the time to announce that your sister can't control her own body, yes?"

Gristle pressed his hands against the desk and rose quickly to his feet. He had to tilt his chin up to meet her eye; she was taller now, in an instant he'd missed. Gristle knew he was dealing with a horrifically powerful fey, cruel enough to be mad. But Shona Maxim's nephew would not be tricked nor bullied.

"Miss," he said, his voice dropping low, which was the closest he would get to any sort of snarl, "understand who you're dealing with."

"Oh!" she said, her mouth a perfect oval. She reached into her purse, pulled out a ten-roundel bill and slapped it on the desk, leaning forward to meet him. "I know *exactly* who I'm dealing with,

Mister Maxim. Here's payment, and I'll see you tonight at 216 Aziza, twenty bells sharp." Her eyes kept drifting around his face, dipped below for some length, and then slipped back up. "And do buy yourself a better suit. I hear there's a sale at Goodfellows'. We can't have you there looking like a copper." She lifted her hand up as though she'd touch his face. He could do nothing but tilt his head so a bit of light showed his pinched glare. Her smile twisted worse. "We all know you're too soft for that, doll."

The words lashed out unplanned. "If I'm so soft, then why hire me?"

She curled her fingers back to her clutch, watching him. "Well, I simply have nowhere else to turn." She sighed, sweeping one finger under her incredibly dry eyes. Gristle was used to acting: this was mockery.

She gave him one last awful grin before trotting out at a very easy sway, pulling the door to swing lightly shut behind her. Through the frosted glass, her image was warped. He didn't even hear her go.

Gristle stared, feeling the sky coming down on his head in glacier-sized shards, and the film reel of his life melting through.

He was glad he'd bought that whiskey.

The Diary of Hàzell Stregoni, "Radical Fey"

44SC, 3 Summer Moons, 19 Suns

In all our shantytown struggles, I have found one person who has reminded me of the reason for it: Senan Maxim, a young man with a handsome child the same age as Stregoni, to the fated day. In fact, we only came to meet when Stregoni insisted upon it, tugging my hand to draw me toward Senan's child hiding behind their father's legs at the trolley stop. While Maxim Child seemed nervous of Stregoni's avid babbling, I found Senan Maxim to be as bright and open as a Solstice daisy. He is currently living with his sister in midtown, where he works (unhappily) as a "private dick." I understand this to be something akin to a police officer. I do not yet know what to make of this.

But there is something about Senan Maxim that drew me in from the start. When I later learned he spent his childhood in the very same slum-yard neighborhood I've found myself in, moving through cell doors and court stands, I understood:

Both of us, I in my "disorder" and he in his "delinquency," understand what it is like to be discounted. We are further tied by our children's fast friendship. They do not seem to wholly understand the other, Stregoni with their raucous screaming and elaborate stories, and Maxim more intent to listen silently while lining up orderly tinfolk across the worn floor of our apartment. But when the two sit bare-chested and innocent as soft flowers, they seem content not to know the other fully. In those moments, Stregoni's feyism seems like a cannon blast etched into their pale eye.

Senan and I talk on this difference routinely, him fumbling along and admitting that he knows very little of the fey, beyond that Maxim's late mother believed her father to perhaps be fey in "shameful" secret. I tell him how we rarely find fair work, which he well observes, given my rotating positions as a washer, or lighting fires in the smithy, or tending the looms of the shirt factories. He nods along and does his best to keep pace. Where he fails, he asks. And in return, he has shown me the sunnier sides of these dockyard streets he used to roam: the fine Verdessi community at a local cantina, the union houses where Stregoni can be cared for during the days I must work. When my rattling hands mark me fey, Senan's generous spirit calms the room. He is, it seems, a man who trusts in the goodness of every soul.

When he learned of my reason for coming to Dale, he was keen to introduce me to — j—————but he has known since a student protest of his wild youth, a Dale-born Ileian woman called Victory Eze who has taken an interest in both me and my struggles. She has offered that, if I'm willing, she may edit some of my writings into a series of autobiographical pamphlets. We would do our best to hide the identities of those involved, and her sweetheart has access to a press through his work. If fey might read of my rage or mortals of my struggles, perhaps they too could join the cry for justice. A moon ago, I would have said this would be of no use.

I have been convinced not by Senan, or Victory, but by Stregoni and Maxim as I write this entry. I'm sat at our terribly small table in our terribly small apartment as Senan attempts to untangle Maxim's hand from Stregoni's without waking them on the hearth rug. They know they're different from the other but haven't yet been taught to fear this. I should hope we can wake them into a world where they never have to know.

I understand what we risk by boldly demanding change. I understand why Senan has not told his sister of our friendship. We could well be walking into our own doom. But for our children, who refuse to break their hold on the other, I know we would give most anything.

Let tomorrow be kinder, and let us play some part in it.

HAWTHORNE STREGONI IN "THE BIG PICTURE"

I walk home with Fionne after her morning shift, which is the most we see each other in the daytime even if the sun is barely up. But today, while our shadows fold over the crosswalks and shiny mailboxes, my head hums. I can feel blood pulsing through my brain, filtering out the impulsive sparks and whatever else. I'm trying to be happy that Fionne's still keeping pace beside me, still linking her hand through my arm and unsubtly pointing at the better-dressed pedestrians to say what she thinks of their hats and skirts and fabrics, and yet there's a whispering in there that doesn't buy it, knows it should, wonders if it's worse to question.

She says she knows what I really am, but does she?

We step up toward the apartment building and the alley. I take a long, smooth breath. Maybe last night was a slipup, but there ain't gonna be a second time, no matter how much more fragile I feel today.

"School," I say, all sure of it. "Get some sleep before you head in for the evening edition."

"Hmm," she says, which is Fionnese for "not likely." She's got a notebook poking from the pocket of her baby-doll pink wool coat, pen in the spiral binding, with a city full of possibilities. It ain't right to be jealous. She squeezes my hands in hers, like her own way of trying to say she's here. "You just go on to school and get it all sorted. We're not stopping the party because of one bad night."

It's a metaphor, right? She knows there won't be any more parties? I watch her face in the morning light, trying to find some clue that says she understands me better after all this. That I can trust her to back out if I'm hurting her.

All I can do is watch her go, all long legs and easy step as she struts off fast toward a higher-end boutique flipping its sign open. I could probably stand here for a bell wondering what she'll get up to all day without me (and maybe worrying some about her, because it ain't me who killed that dockworker but, shoot, *someone* did), but I need to see my doctor and get this all sorted. If anyone's gonna know how to get me past the first twenty-four bells when my head is still hopped up, it's him. And then we can just chug ahead.

I run up the dew-dropped fire escape that rings under me, pop the window, and duck in like always. Except instead of getting a chance to fold my bed so Gristle hears it and thinks I just woke up, it's already been tucked up against the wall.

I smell whiskey.

In the middle of my tiny room, with the daylight washing in over every scrap of paper pasted over every hidden burn mark, Gristle's standing ahead of my wide-open door.

I feel a whip of fire race up my spine. I swallow it, but it doesn't help my rage. He never comes in here! He's not even looking at me sneak back in, just staring at all the yellowing pages on the walls—newspapers and magazines and pamphlets and journals and obits for people I never knew. The morning sun throws a sharp line of light right across a series tacked up near my bed. They're a bit faded now, dry on the edges, but the words are damn clear.

"You still have it up," Gristle mutters.

"The police said it's mine," I tell him. I really do sound like a covetous fey. It's covering up a bad smear of ash from when I was twelve and wild, but I can't pretend any of these are random papers. "They only needed the copies, now that the case is closed."

His mouth wrinkles up just a bit. He skims his eyes over Mum's old diary entries, rambling journals of Dale's disrespect. The edited-down pamphlets are around here too, but they're too secretive about the finer details, not personal enough. And still none of it clears up whether Mum planned to blow up the fayre. Maybe it was spur-of-the-moment madness, or maybe Mum was trying to take us all out of this dirty world together—a murder-suicide thinking it would martyr us and start a revolution—but us lucky tykes slipped the net.

I don't feel lucky.

Gristle's eyes are stuck on a line, and then they scan quickly and stick again. I wait for him to be angry I'm still poking and prodding around the worst thing to happen to us, but he doesn't say anything about it.

"You seen the paper?" he asks.

No sense lying, not that I'm any good at it.

"Yeah," I say. It still stings that he didn't tell me and made me go out to figure it out myself, but I keep that feeling down where it can't hurt me. "Some fey went berserk. It wasn't me."

"I know that."

"Fionne says she'll vouch. Secret's safe."

"Not quite." He looks to the corner, maybe because that's where his old trundle bed was when he was crammed in here with his daddy and Auntie before I came around to drag him west again, and maybe because an article about Senan in his erratic, accusatory, not-so-glorious end days is pasted up there. Maybe I *am* a freak.

"Hawthorne," he says. His hand twitches to the paper, but stops and grabs the side of his slacks. "We're in a bit of a ring."

My skin prickles. Gristle's always pinched about something (usually me, so he'd pinch less if he got off my case), but this seems different.

"I *saw* the paper," I say, forcing my voice to stay all even. "Nothing about me. I didn't appreciate you leaving me out of your little chat with Auntie Shona last night, but it'll blow over. The doc will get me sorted out."

He turns his face to me. In half a flash, a bit of light catches his eyes to turn them a pea-soup-y hazel, like oak leaves in autumn, before the shadows close in over him again. "Someone saw you go mad last night. They've threatened to go to the police."

All the air snaps from my stomach. Gristle just stands there like nothing could knock him down, but my whole body's a kiln building pressure. The world's twitching at every edge, sounds and smells and feelings trying to swarm in. Is it some folk with a vendetta—do I gotta be worried about going up on some makeshift pyre? I at least gotta be worried about getting stress-shocked to hell and landing in an institution, never seeing Fionne or my aunt again, going right out of the frying pan of school to the fire of being locked up for life and knowing I ruined *everything*. Spirits and saints, how the hell—heat crackles in my pocketed hands, begging to be let out through my palms, so much louder than yesterday. I lock my spine like rebar. Keep it together!

"Well, why haven't they?" I almost shout, catching the flame in my throat.

Gristle's voice is so level I wanna scream worse. "She says she needs someone to investigate something at her club. It's blackmail."

I try to shove my feet into the ground as hard as I can, willing everything to sink. "Which club?"

"The Dogfoot."

Of course. I went to a place filled up with fey who don't respect rules or manners, and now that's coming back to bite me. Can I even blame him for it? Well, if he hadn't shown up, it would have been fine, right? Do I really believe that, though? *I* was the one who nudged the cap off my power, and now I'm braided up with people who get their kicks from doing that, who don't realize the kind of shit they're feeding. I've read about the owner, and they're *not* good people.

"You called Auntie Shona?" I spit.

He doesn't even move. *Just do something, you asshole!* "The owner said not to."

'Cause our aunt wouldn't take shit like he is. She woulda called the cops in, bolder than my stupid brother who couldn't even punch me back.

I clench my jaw tight, even if I can feel heat reaching for the first row of teeth. I fight to breathe and wash cold air into my stomach. Slowly, I take my hands out of my pockets and press them tight together until my wrists ache.

My voice sounds too low, like I'm gonna be sick. "So what are you gonna do, Gristle?"

"What am *I* going to do?" he asks. He tenses, like he'll step to me—something vindicated purrs in my skull when his voice turns sharper, even if his feet stay rooted. "I'm not the one who lights herself on fire whenever she feels like it."

"It's not on purpose!" I tell him, stepping forward.

"You could have stopped it," he snaps. His teeth flash in the light. *Good. Fight me, coward.* "Isn't that what school's about? To make you not so damn . . . damn *selfish*."

If he knew how hard I'm trying not to lose it on him right now, I think he'd be grateful for school. And I think, staring at me, staring at him, he sees how hard I'm trying not to be some covetous little sprite who burns him to ash just to get him off my case, because he gives a frustrated huff and turns one foot away from me.

"It's not a hard job," he says, more to himself. "The owner just sounded scared of something. Comb the place, get some security pamphlets, and it's golden."

Hearing that he's got a plan lets me give him a little more credit, so I can just keep breathing like I was taught and not have to go anywhere near that club. "Then hop along, Maxim," I say. "I need to get to school so I don't light on fire again and *inconvenience* you."

"Oh no," he says, pointing like I really am a child. "I'm not letting you out of my sight tonight. You're going to school, and then you're coming with me."

What?! "I'm no detective, asshole."

"Real mature," he says. I wince out a smile. "I'm not either. But considering whatever"—he waves his hand around so wildly that it looks like that mad fey rattle—"this crime-scene-hoarding *freakshow* is, you can scribe me some notes."

I cross my arms, digging my nails in. "It's to cover the burns," I tell him. "Evidence hiding, huh?"

"Then why are they all about . . ." I can tell he's trying to figure out how to phrase it, maybe so I won't get mad or so he won't burst into tears. "About *that*?"

"I've got a moral deficiency." I couldn't grin if I wanted to. The fire's cooled now, and I don't know if he's ever gonna notice how close I was to torching him. That could have been the final straw before self-destruction. Sometimes that feels peaceful.

"Maybe I need someone with their brain all on wrong," he says, fixing at his hat that hasn't even gone crooked. "This dame's got the condition too. The faster we get her off us, the safer we all are . . . including Auntie's campaign."

And me, and the school. Sometimes I wonder if he forgets that we really are all tied up with each other: oak, thorn, ash. We either guide, or hide, or burn.

I close my eyes tight and throw up my hands. "Fine, Gristle." I can't remember the last time we did anything together besides walk to school. In my gut, though, I know it was the fayre. And look how that turned out. "I'll deal with your ugly mug until this is closed."

"Good," he says. But I don't know if it really is. And then, because I think he resents me still—might forever—he adds, "You gonna burn me again, Hawthorne?"

I open my eyes, wanting them to be fiery, but I just feel all immure and sort of scared. And he looks like it too in the warm light of his childhood room ruined, all because he met me. "Don't touch me with your mortal hands when I don't ask for it," I say. "And I won't touch you neither."

He nods. I don't think either of us much trusts the other. It doesn't matter. If we can keep our aunt's campaign all clear, then I'm on my way to getting better. And when I do, he won't have to be my warden no more. And I won't be the person who can hurt him.

"Deal," he says.

We're in this ring together, so we'd better start dancing.

ON THE 33RD SUN OF THE 4TH WINTER MOON...

VOTE MAXIM

FOR A SAFER, BRIGHTER, EQUAL TOMORROW

GRISTLE SENAN MAXIM JUNIOR IN "SOUTH SIDE SHUFFLE"

Gristle Senan Maxim Junior's day progressed in achingly normal fashion, as though the usual scripts and patterns were mocking him now while everything else was burning up. He walked Hawthorne to the trolley in silence and they took it uptown. Her schoolhouse had been built a century ago, as a little farm-style sanitorium a decent walk from the village, before everything started changing and it was engulfed by the creep of progress. Now, it seemed a whitewashed "historic" eyesore amidst all the rearing stone and wrought iron, or the newest high-rises of sharp steel and glass. Gristle waited until she'd trotted up the porch and through the doors, waited an extra beat to be sure she wouldn't creep out, and then wanted nothing but to return to the trolley stop and head home.

But he had a case to work, and that case entailed heading toward the tailor. He hated everything about that; turning toward Goodfellows' felt like ripping off a limb. Still, he forced his usual purposeful posture and strode north. It took him past the Presidential Building, tall and columned and made of flat gray stone with quite a few long steps up to the wide wooden doors. Gristle allowed himself to dwell on the senators streaming in and out, or haunting around the benches in the front courtyard to smoke and gossip. Among them flitted their interns, all eager eyes and slightly scuttling walks. If his aunt won, Gristle would be one of them, he was certain. He wasn't sure if he wanted that so much as he understood it to be true, a fitting sequel. He'd be off the campaign trail—no more late-night bar conversations discussing strategy, no more chaperoning Hawthorne, who would be getting twenty-four-bell support.

And if they didn't win? If the whole campaign spiraled out into chaos?

Clunk!

A cab door swung out into the middle of the sidewalk. Gristle stumbled to a halt.

"Sorry, old boy," the passenger rushed to say, stepping out to meet him. "I didn't even see you there." But then they drew up to their full height, both got a good look at each other, and kept their mouths buttoned.

Gristle knew how much was on the line if he bungled this case, and here was the cosmic warning.

President Dermott Ashley III shut the car door and waved the cab off. He was a broad-shouldered, bull-faced sort of man, with the pale skin and slicked hair of someone who had grown up in the numbered streets of the north side and been hammered into form by his time as the chief of police. And now with a presidential sash tied from shoulder to hip beneath his fine suit jacket.

"*Mister* Maxim, eighteen at last. Allow me to congratulate you twice," Ashley said, with shockingly transparent insincerity. Gristle didn't even bother trying to smile or show his eyes—there were no senators or cameras to be civil for, not even his aunt who encouraged him to "play nice." "Honoring your name with a dockyard solve. Quite the detective, I hear."

"Evidence collector," Gristle clarified.

Ashley stared at him for another second, as if waiting for more, then cleared his throat in an attempt to bust past that stony silence. "Well, if my police are any good at what they do . . ." he mused, touching at his tie. Gristle steeled himself against what would surely be bait. "They'll have that mad fey locked up in no time."

Watch it. "If your police were any good at what they do . . ." Gristle said, with his droning voice and flat face and ticker-reel of dockside curses running through his mind. He knew he ought to be law-minding, but couldn't stop. "Then they would have stopped all the crime cycles ago and hung up their hats."

Ashley took a beat as if to consider whether this was an attack or a joke, but then just clicked his tongue, like Gristle was still a child. "You sound just like your father."

He hadn't been trying to. His burns had gone quiet, but began again to prickle with pain that made his throat tighten. The last thing he needed now was to become his impulsive father.

"I'd hoped you'd learned his lesson for him," Ashley said. He leaned in, almost conspiratorially, like they were two good friends. "I think we all found out just what happens when criminals go unchecked, didn't we? At least the Tanners did."

Gristle knew Ashley didn't give a damn about the Tanner family on any personal level, but four dead children were even more tragic than Shona Maxim's two surviving wards. Ashley wouldn't have gotten into office without it. Still, Gristle didn't know what to say. His daddy *was* a criminal, and Hàzell *was* mad, and those stains didn't wash out.

The city hummed around them. Gristle wanted to disappear.

"Well," Ashley finally said, leaning back yet extending his hand. His eyes were a sharp, lethal gray over his smile. "I suppose the winner will decide just what to make of this country. Give my regards to your aunt—at least *she's* willing to compromise."

Gristle wanted the moment to end, so he clapped his hand into Ashley's, waited for Ashley to let go, and then watched him march through the courtyard without another word, whistling to himself. The pitch was painful as bells.

Home, Gristle thought with blunt certainty. *Get me back to my office and then everything can be normal for just a few bells.*

He dodged someone who almost walked right into him and carried on down to 8th and 2nd to slip into the dark-wood tailor's and order a "whatever's on-fashion right now" suit. After submitting himself to the humiliation of many mirrors and many prodding hands with many measuring tapes and bolts of fabric that all looked the same to him, he returned to his office, marched up the steps, and at long last collapsed into the worn leather of his chair.

Finally.

Gristle breathed out all the tension in his chest, watching the dust sparkle and scatter in the light coming through the blinds. He then proceeded to sink into the comforts of his ordinary routine: ordering flashbulbs, giving his police statement, checking in on some unions that were still loyal. It lulled him into an easy rhythm of the winding phone dial, of his pen scratching, of the steady hum of the radiator under the window. He ate his lunch, hardly felt his burns, had a drink, ignored the clock for more than gauging glances.

If he didn't think about it, then things would be alright. Sure, the Dogfoot owner was a powerful fey, and sure, she'd hinted she had mob connections. The Hannochian Court was an easy guess, but whose territory did the Dog actually fall under? Gristle didn't know the underground crime scene, not like his daddy had before caring for dangerous people got him killed. Hadn't Gristle learned from that, as Ashley had said? He'd be smarter, as his aunt had taught him to be. She trusted him.

She trusted him to ask her for help. Gristle's stomach churned. He looked to the phone, shining in the light through the blinds like the dark shell of a carnivorous beetle. He imagined picking it up, calling her, telling her exactly what was happening. Would that make her proud? Or would it be better to solve the case, wrap it tight, show her how well he'd done? Was it better to be a diligent child, or a capable adult? And which was which?

Gristle's vision felt sharp at the edges, like a picture focused too close. His burns sank a toxic pain into his blood, tightening every organ. No one had prepared him for decisions like this. He knew how to take photos and ride the trolley and had thought he knew how to protect his sister, but this? The dust seemed to scream at him, flashing by in winks. In it was the memory of Senan Maxim, the delinquent child grown into a reckless radical, who either didn't see the end he was bringing by scorning honest folk and befriending dishonest monsters, or had welcomed it.

Gristle could feel his cells dividing. The world was turning upside-down and shaking everything good and proper into shattered chaos. Gristle was so damn aware of it.

A knock on the door jolted him from that thought, nearly sending him to his feet in time to see a shadow rush in. He braced like a man with a gun.

Instead of anything terrifying, it was only his aunt's fussy and bespectacled little VP. Somehow, that was worse than flying bullets, but at least it was typical.

"Afternoon," they said, more customary than kind. They were a Jahagee-Daleish folk with gray skin a few shades paler than Gristle's and twice as many freckles, thick hair chopped to a storm of bright peaks on top, dressed in a plaid-and-floral suit more midtown than north side. They beelined for the stack of posters on his desk with their briefcase already pried open between two leather-gloved hands. "I'll be taking these." In went the posters with one sweep.

And then the evidence-collecting nephew offered, "Fine by me," despite understanding that "Egghead" (whose name had been lost somewhere and thus replaced by his aunt's charming moniker) would sweep through like a hurricane either way.

"I'll also need any notes you're keeping on iron production." They turned for the filing cabinet on the wall and raked a drawer open with one polished shoe. The globe balanced on top wobbled slightly. Gristle's veins twitched. "Your aunt wants to discuss the logistics of an iron fine at Cat's tonight."

Gristle's eyebrows furrowed slightly. "Cat's . . ." he muttered, and then it clicked. He was supposed to get drinks with his aunt that night! *Saints.*

"I really need us to put our heads together on that one because I promise you this is not as simple as outlawing iron when everyone west of Chestnut makes their money on smithing. Cat's was built by that union," Egghead was saying, while Gristle could only stare with dread building in his stomach and the world still too sharp. Egghead wrenched a handful of files out and stacked them into the briefcase with their mouth still going. "I believe in fey rights as much as any decent jack but we *cannot* afford to alienate the only people who would respect a president without a degree."

Egghead was, frankly, correct. They were correct about most things, really . . . painfully obvious things. Gristle wondered if they actually believed in the platform at all or if they just knew how slim political options were for Jahagee-Daleish folks born below 14th Street. Gristle (who was himself a Jahagee-Daleish born below 14th Street) figured he ought to feel a bit of kinship in that, but he couldn't stand the reminders that he knew *nothing* about politics, and now the reminder that he was going to miss drinks. How many balls had he dropped without realizing? How many more would he drop while trying to fix the world?

Egghead had the briefcase held open and balanced on one hand, the other pulling files, one shoe toeing open another drawer, like a circus act that *never stopped talking*. "Ashley is already blowing this dockyard death far out of proportion." *Snap* went the drawer as it closed. Gristle's ears rumbled. "And now all he has to do is say the words 'Maxim doesn't care about the industrial workers' and we've lost the majority of our voter base—he really only knows one trick and it's 'monopolize on fear and tragedy until you can trick people into worshipping you'—are you listening to me?"

They whipped their head over to him, the lenses of their glasses catching the light in two blinding circles like car headlights.

Gristle wanted to be struck head-on. If death ended this, then so be it.

Egghead's posture relaxed. Every intent feature softened, from their dark eyebrows to the fierce purse of their lips. "Saints, kid," they said, despite looking less than two septennials older. Gristle would have scowled if he remembered how. "Are you alright?"

His aunt was going to find out, she was going to find out, and he'd be as big a disappointment as his daddy, and he knew *nothing* about politics beyond what he was told and—"No," Gristle wheezed. His eyes watered. Was he about to cry? Like a pathetic child? Egghead gently clasped the briefcase and stepped toward him. Gristle forced himself to find a reasonable lie. "I think I'm coming down with something."

Egghead looked to the new whiskey bottle on the desk corner. "Uh-huh," they said dryly. They clicked their tongue, the second time that day that Gristle had been treated like a child. The first time had made him livid, but now he just felt hollow. "Aren't you a bit young to be day-drinking?"

Gristle's shoulders tightened. "I'm eighteen," he said.

They shook their head. "Yes, you really are." It didn't seem to be about Gristle, though he couldn't place the tone further than that. They inspected the remaining cardamom biscuits in his open lunch container, gave them a small nod of approval, and slid the box closer to him. "Sugar and carbs to soak all that up. Don't come tonight."

Any other day, Gristle would have been horrifically insulted that *Egghead* was telling him what to do. Instead, he was forced to grit his teeth. "Tell her I'm sorry to miss."

Their voice was just as sharp. "I will, but I'm not." They pushed his lime soda toward him too and then sped out. Gristle wasn't sure he was meant to hear them muttering "This is what we get when people treat politics like a passion project. Such a joke," but then they were gone.

Maybe being a bit bitter was a good thing; they were so caught up in the yammering that they probably bought Gristle's half-baked lie.

Gristle collapsed back into his chair and let all the kept air out from his lungs.

His aunt called within the bell to say she hoped he felt better soon, even if she was a little short and he could tell she was irked to have to spend the night alone with Egghead. Still, "better to keep an eye on Hawthorne," she said. And at least Egghead knew something about keeping a platform afloat. Gristle was wondering if there was anything he was actually good at. He wanted to tell her what was happening, but couldn't worry her again. Not after the previous night, or the fayre. She'd already had a lifetime of worry.

He put the phone down, ate a biscuit and drank his soda, and groaned softly to himself with his head on his desk.

Adulthood was awful, and his burns were aching fierce.

No more incident for the rest of the afternoon (besides missing three trolleys before the fourth stopped for him), including when he picked up his suit from the tailor. He changed in the shop without caring to inspect how he looked, shoved his usual sack suit into a briefcase he'd brought along, pulled his duster and hat and camera case back on, and marched right out to pick Hawthorne up from school. By then, the sky was solid, slate-gray overcast; most pedestrians had umbrellas at the ready as they slashed through steam fuming through the grates.

He popped up the embossed collar of his duster and followed his usual path while crunching down two vervain tablets. He needed to quell the pain fizzing up in his charred skin. By the time he made it to the schoolhouse, wandering up the path and squinting to make out Hawthorne reading a comic in one of the rocking chairs outside, his body still felt like a live wire.

He stepped up to the side of the porch. His voice sounded wrong. "You ready?"

Hawthorne dropped her comic book into her lap with a start so violent that Gristle expected to see flames. He didn't. It was only a small consolation.

"Saints," Hawthorne hissed. She scraped the book onto a side table. "We oughta get you a bell."

He narrowed his eyes, even if she probably couldn't see it under his hat. He was already on edge, and now he was going to bring along a very literal fire-starter. He'd thought it was better than leaving her alone, but could he be sure of that, or anything?

"I picked up my suit," he said through the porch rails.

She gave him a look down and raised a bushy eyebrow. "Want a medal for it?" she asked, but did take a minute to inspect him even while he cringed. "You almost look like a real person."

Something about the sarcasm split through him. He turned back toward the street, letting her shout, "I'm off, Doc!" through the doors as always before racing down the wooden steps to catch up. He heard a muffled call of agreement from inside and promised himself that the doctors wouldn't let her leave if she was an active hazard. Or at least that they wouldn't do it two days in a row.

"*I'm* going to fit in," he said, clomping toward the street. "You're still dressed for school."

She walked steady, not even kicking the wayward pebbles or leaves in her path. "Fionne's bringing me a change after she sets the evening pages."

Gristle's brain sharpened.

Hawthorne squinted up at the clouds. "It's gonna rain," she observed, as if she hadn't just confessed to ruining the case before it started.

Gristle stopped dead in the path, right before the sidewalk. "You told Fionne?" he asked. His voice was sharp—he felt it. "Why the hell would you do that?"

"Hang it up," she said, snapping her fingers at him. It was a very Hàzell-like gesture, Gristle thought quickly—*no no, back in the memory vault where you belong.* "I just said you and me were going to the Dog tonight, and she said she'd come too."

Okay, okay, okay. "So Fionne doesn't know this is detective work?"

She opened her mouth. Closed it. Sucked her teeth. "I didn't tell Fionne this was detective work," she said with precision.

That only meant that Fionne was clever enough to figure it out herself. What other reason would Gristle have to start going out, and to a place like *that*?

He was obvious, and clumsy, and was going to ruin everything. Cars rushed by and his whole body ached. He opened his mouth.

"I had a good day today," Hawthorne suddenly told him. Her eyebrows were still tight, annoyed, but he could see her nose wrinkling and un-wrinkling like she was fighting it. Better than him, he realized, only then feeling the pressure across his tight jaw. "I know this shit is important, and I know I caused some of it—"

"All of it," he muttered.

She huffed, but no sparks leaked out. "*You* let yourself get blackmailed," she told him, and yet was somehow mature enough to drop it as she stomped past him toward the trolley stop. "I'm not letting Fionne see me like that again. Maybe it's a good thing she's coming."

Gristle didn't want to ask why he alone wasn't enough incentive for her to behave herself. He felt ridiculous arguing, and ridiculous for the staticky panic flitting through his veins. Since when was *she* so solid as she stepped up alone to the trolley stop post? Since when was *he* so frantic?

"Fine," Gristle said, raising his hand as trolley bells rang nearby. "But we're there on professional business."

She gave a grunt of agreement.

The trolley passed them.

◆

The south side was new, and so ever-changing, which Gristle didn't care much for. Once the Confederacy had brought laws and education and industry, and the iron trade grew, Puck's Port had started booming out. It put money in people's pockets even below the government districts past 14th Street: the toilers on the west docks, the white collars of midtown, and the growing scholars in the east all had cash to burn. So they leaked their bawdy houses and pubs and theaters down into the countryside of the south, swallowing what was once nothing but racetracks or gambling houses for the rich. The entertainment district grew as a place for everyone. It was, on a surface level, a mighty fine thing that proved their country was moving along.

Practically, it was far more disorienting than the clear-cut districts where Gristle knew what to expect. Even his aunt's stories were of little use: the district that she knew in her detective days was nothing like the one pouring out beyond the trolley's last stop. As Gristle stepped off into a thin mist of drizzling rain that made Hawthorne grimace, he understood that the south side was already different than it had been the night before. It was warping as he stared at it, melting like icing. Unknowable, unpredictable, and so, terrifying.

Gristle didn't say a word as the two of them walked toward what could very well be the beginning of the Maxims' final feature. There was no one else out on the streets.

They were a bell early when they approached the still-dark Dog, silent as a grave, with the unlit marquee hanging out over the sidewalk like a tombstone. A glint of light burned across Gristle's eyes: Fionne, waiting for them ahead, tilted her compact to check that her patterned hair wrap was still twisted up tight. Her white coat glowed in the mist.

When Gristle and Hawthorne slipped under the overhang, Fionne snapped her compact shut with a definitive *click*. Her grin was so wicked it was nearly fey. "So the lug's got some dancing shoes after all." She appraised his suit. Gristle wanted to shrivel away. "It's hot, G."

"Don't call me that."

The corner of her mouth twitched. "And you got paid to get it? If I didn't know any better, I'd say someone's prettying you up."

Hawthorne snorted. Gristle refused to dedicate even a single millisecond of brain activity to the idea. He set the briefcase containing his old suit down by the doors and looked through the glass, trying to stare past his reflection.

Fionne kicked at the suitcase beside her. "There's a diner open just down the way for H to change into hers, and we should get a bite to eat." He could hear her grin. "You'll need your smarts tonight, right?"

Gristle looked back over his shoulder, voice low and rough. "How much did you get out of her, Eze?"

She hummed placidly and turned off down the street with her hand tangled in Hawthorne's, toward the glow of the single lit window on the strip. Hawthorne trotted alongside her; Gristle knew how reckless she could get when she was peacocking for her girlfriend, and didn't much trust them to be as mature as Hawthorne promised.

Gristle's reflection stared after them. He closed his eyes, forcing a deep breath through the prickling building in his chest where his heart beat quick and weak. He couldn't spend the whole night waiting for the world to self-destruct—he'd get no work done that way, and then it really would. Hawthorne had said she was serious about this; he had to hold up his end of the family before he let the whole platform collapse.

Puff up, Ace. No use crying. There was too much on the line for him to be a coward now.

And so, with forced fearlessness, Gristle locked eyes with his reflection. He took a long enough breath and tapped each toe into the soles of his shoes, enough to feel himself sink into his body and calm his haywire heart. His new suit was all sleek mohair with high lapels, pale gray (he assumed) with gaudy pinstripes. When he shifted, some two-toned image bled through the light, of leaves or eyes maybe hidden in the pattern. It *was* "hot," but what was more, it actually fit instead of swallowing him into a shapeless shadow. The jacket fell evenly across his wide shoulders, no strain about the middle where nearly everything pinched, and the slacks were smooth at his legs in a way that wouldn't chafe like most things did, hemmed to sit nice against the tops of his wingtip shoes always kept perfectly polished.

He looked good, *tough* with his father's gunpowder-blowback freckles, his mother's dark brow and wide cheekbones encasing his eyes in shadows under his hat.

That's Shona Maxim's nephew in there. The thought came clearer than most. He became very aware of the monologue in his head rolling along over the soft rattle of rain and some distant siren. *That's her crack-along right-hand who keeps the gears turning, who was taught damn well, and he's not afraid. He's a bit nauseous, and the vervain doesn't feel like it's working, and he's tired, and yes, his whole life's been a tragedy since he was born a bastard and his mum jumped and his daddy spiraled and his sister punched him charred, but his aunt has made him too damn tough to fail her. And even if everything feels strange, he's real.*

The rain misted down. Gristle swallowed and dared himself to try one step further.

I'm real, he practiced. His skin ticked once, but stilled. He held eye contact with his reflection. *I'm real, and I'm not naive like my dad, and I can fix this all tonight.*

The south side lay quiet as a crypt. Gristle knew what he had to do.

The body of Kitt Atwal, age 20, was found today on Puck's Port Beach. Atwal is thought to have jumped from the nearby dockyard close to her residence after an ongoing battle with melancholy, according to those closest to her. Raised by two schoolteachers and a librarian, Atwal was an assistant teacher at Bridger Elementary and an active advocate for free and fair education. May the spirits guide her home. Om Sadgati.

HAWTHORNE STREGONI IN "THE OLD WORLD"

I know these ain't my clothes; Fionne must have taken Eze Fourthchild's, which is fine by me if I ignore the fact that the tyke's getting big enough for us to share. Corduroy trousers with a silk runner of a forest-creature pattern up the sides, suspenders that match, a flax shirt (and a cotton undershirt so it won't rub), and flower-stamped boots which are actually almost too small, so Fourthchild ain't so grown yet. Known that kid way too long for them to get big on me now.

Anyway, that's not so important. Maybe I'm just nervous and getting ramble-y. I lean into the wall of the washroom stall, prop my foot opposite me, and carefully pull the laces into a bow.

The whole time, I breathe in through my nose and out through my mouth just like Doc Secondchild told me to in the alley at lunch. The younger kids were still in classes, doing trade practice in the laundry press room. I could see them down through the little basement window behind the bench. When another student hauled a soaking sheet from the bucket, I could damn near feel it all cold and slimy against my arms, hear the rattle of the drying presses as they turned and the splash of bleach-reeking water hitting the cement floor.

One of the kids closest to us gave a full-body shudder—spears of frost crackled out from under their feet, clouding up the window. The kid snapped their hands together, offering a window-muffled apology to the nearby doctor. They were little, had time to sort it out before they could be stress-tested, but the power was already so strong. And the more they fed it, the worse it would be.

"Easy," Doc Secondchild said next to me. I realized my fingers were flicking. No sparks . . . yet. "Breathe."

I huffed, but tried to focus on the roughness of the bench under me as I breathed back in slow and out slower. There might have been one spark that leaked out like a firefly, but I kept the rest locked tight in my stomach. "I should be in there," I told him. I wanted to shuffle my legs up, but dug my heels into the gravel to keep everything loose. "Getting the practice, you know?"

He sat next to me, cigarette burning bright orange in the autumn-y alley gloom and eyes all clear blue through his wire-rimmed glasses. "Last I checked, you were fine with laundry shifts," he said.

A shudder ripped up through me, same as that kid, but I bit it back. "I don't like them much," I told him.

"And I don't like getting out of bed when it's still dark out," he offered. He blew a smoke ring. That made me smile a bit. He's somewhere near my aunt's age, and I've known him since I was twelve when I was part of some toy study way before the school was even an idea, so he's something like an uncle. More like Auntie Shona was before she had to get serious. He'd left his lab coat inside, and so sat with me in his shirtsleeves, all casual with his tacky-bright suspenders and tidy beard and always-there smile. "It's not about how you feel about it—it's about if you can tough it up and get it done right without hurting yourself. Last night was a minor setback, right?"

Ask my brother how minor it feels. I just stared into the bricks and pipes across from us. I wondered what would happen if I said, "Doc, someone saw me last night and they're trying to string me along"? Would he toss his hands up and let them take me away, pretend he didn't know I was actually bad enough to be stress-tested? Try to save his hide, and the school, too?

He wouldn't, I'm so sure of it, but you never can know what someone's capable of when the chips are down.

He just nodded and said, "You're still farther along than anyone could have guessed when we met you. Don't lose hope on yourself, alright, Stregoni?"

"Expectations were pretty damn low," I muttered, even if I knew that wasn't much fair to myself.

I didn't know if he was going to say something about it, because footsteps came crunching down the alley, and we both turned to see my aunt come striding toward us with her deli container, tailed duster streaming behind her and hat on a slant just like a movie hero. Doc Secondchild stumbled up to standing, more like an unstrung puppet in a bad sideshow.

"Miss Maxim," he said, with that stupid grin. I corked my laugh. He put his hands in the pockets of his baggy slacks. "How goes the long haul?"

"Rain-right," she said. She gave him a real professional brim tap and sat down next to me. Doc slumped but took his leave, disappearing inside. I'm pretty sure he's got some cute little crush, but she's way too busy for friends, let alone something serious.

"How's it heading?" Auntie Shona asked me, close and low.

There was a newspaper under her arm. I stared at it, and then at her.

My aunt set her hat beside her, and put both hands on her deli container like she was trying to put the thoughts together. "Hawthorne," she started.

"You could have told me last night," I said to her. The smell from her lunch was a lot on top of everything else, but I let it all filter away. "I could have handled it."

She closed her eyes and swallowed. For a second, she looked real old. "I still remember when I met you—you were so small we could have carried you in a flower basket, just this little thing," she said, nodding slow like it was all jumbled in her head. "Max—Se—*Gristle*, he was quiet since he was born. I'd give him a bottle or a box of toys and he'd be set for the day. But you were all over the place whenever I had to look after you, when . . ." When Senan and Mum were at rallies, or meeting at Cat's, or wherever. I shuffled my leg into hers. "You just always had so much to say and always needed me to listen, you know? And now you're named, and I thought things were going to be alright."

My stomach sank low. "Me too," I said quietly. I looked over my shoulder, enough to see that the frost kid wasn't down there anymore. Probably had to go cool off, try again the next day, keep trying.

"Hawthorne," she said again, getting my attention back. She put her hand on the top of my head, smooshing my cap into my hair that crinkled like kindling. But her eyes were so deep and soft and *trusting* that I couldn't mind it. "I'm sorry last night happened, and that I didn't tell you what you ought to be told. I'm not perfect."

None of us are. "Me neither."

She opened her mouth. I wondered if she was going to tell me that I couldn't be at fault, which would have only made me feel worse. "You're never going to be alone in this," she said instead. My throat choked a bit. "Once we win, and I can get Doc Secondchild some proper funding, he says there's a dozen more methods we can try to be certain that you'll be alright."

I have to keep that in my head. "Then I could work, maybe at *Dolly Day*?" I asked.

She blinked at me. Her eyes seemed to line my face. I wondered if she was remembering when Senan started out on his own. "Yes," she said. "Some day."

I got one of those big rushes of feelings, not hot really but warm. That's all I want, being out in the world, and knowing she's proud and still has my back. I leaned into her shoulder and she kissed the side of my head, and we ate lunch, and I knew, *know*, she believes I can do this. And I can make her proud.

I finish off my shoes, throw on my cap, push everything else into the suitcase, and haul out of the stall while I sling my suspenders up over my shoulders. Maybe solving this is the price I oughta pay to know I can be that perfect girl buried under the flames. I'll let her out before my mother's bad blood burns her alive.

I'm not sure I know who she is, but I know folks can't wait to meet her.

"*Scusami, bello*," someone says.

I turn, all calm.

Another person's standing beside the sink: a man probably close to eighty cycles by now, all hunched down with wrinkles and pudgy bags under his eyes, and a crooked hand balancing on a cane. He says something else, again in Verdossi. Suddenly I recognize the proud swoop of his nose, and thick curls, and the embroidered flowers on the hems of his shirt and sash. He must recognize the same on me, even if I'm not wearing a stitch of tradition.

He smiles a toothless grin. "*Parla Verdossi?*" he asks in his crackling voice.

Saints . . . it's been a while since I heard a voice like that. I ain't even talked to Rory Gattano in cycles. "Uhh . . . no, *zio*," I try to say, which is really the most I can do. "Came when I was small."

He squints at me. A tiny itch digs into my brain, pricking out. *That's a shame*, I suddenly hear, resounding from somewhere in my skull. My eyes widen. It's almost words, and yet more a meaning than a sound. *You're one of those tots from the fayre, e?*

He looks totally normal, not a scale or pointed ear, with his eyes too milky to tell if they shine like mine does. But this is some serious mental trickery. I know I oughta be wary, but . . . "Guilty," I tell him. I really mean it.

Lucky baby, he says, shaking his knobbly finger at me. Small sparkles trail from it. No, not just sparkles, but a dark mist like a star-swarmed night sky. I lean back. *Big blast, but you're still alive. Lucky lucky.*

Ask my brother how lucky he feels. I slowly inch one foot away, ready to scramble back. "*Grazie*," I say. I don't all the way mean it, but the word fits nice in my mouth.

My hand's on the sink, and he puts his over it, warm. But then, from that contact, his face slackens into gaunt shadows under the soft light coming from behind him.

Powerful child, he says, all round, low sounds. He doesn't sound scared but almost . . . reverent. *I feel it sing in your blood.*

His pulse beats down into mine, dissonant for a moment before they slip together like harmony. A taste of something sprints through my sinuses, pine and mountain air and the beginnings of smoke from the growing city centers as Dale's industry leaks out even to our wild homeland. It goes straight to my stomach where it starts to spark. My throat tightens and heats.

I snatch my hand back to clutch it into my chest. My other fist tightens on the suitcase to block out all the humming. "Sorry," I spit out.

Ah, bello, he says, almost sadly. My nose crinkles. *It's very fast in your head. And angry, like a fire.*

I can hear all the lights humming, and the water in the walls. *Stop that.* "I'm not the one who killed that person on the docks," I say. The boots feel awful tight now.

He shakes his head. *Pah. That's obvious.* Sparkles dash off of him—a few hit the wallpaper and leave dark burns, like mine did last night. No, not burns. A different, darker smell: mold.

Despite the milkiness of his eyes, there's something that says I'm caught in his sights. The bathroom feels like it's shrinking. *We are living in dangerous times. Our body is an altar, child, and it breaks under pressure.*

"I . . ." I start.

Around his feet, creeping tendrils squirm across the tiles. Those spots on the wall grow, spread. Uh-uh. No way. This sounds too much like Mum, saying how chaos is beautiful, destroying her head with it. I won't turn out like that.

I step back, but he steps forward, blooming another puddle of mold out from under his shoe. His teeth flash, each of them black at the end like a snake's. *They can't have their pyres so they hide them inside us like lightning-trees—from the inside-out, we burn. We are dangerous times.*

The wallpaper curls and disintegrates. Madness, I know it—a swarming impulse running amok in his head and building the power stronger and fiercer and worse. Who is he, under that? Does it matter?

"I g-gotta get going now." My heart is slamming. If something starts to happen, do I sock him mortal-style? Or does this have to be fey on fey, fire against rot? I'm so fragile without the flames, skinless and toothless. "A pretty girl promised she'd take me dancing."

The old man stares me down. His snarl calms. "Handsome girl," he says, in an accent so heavy I nearly think it's Verdossi too. It's confusing, and painful. The mold still stains the bottom of the mirror, but I know that in it we look more similar than my aunt and I sitting shoulder to shoulder in the school alley. "*Vai a ballare.*"

I know that one: You go dance. I will, and I'll be better than what we left behind, even when it tries to trick me. Verdosso is ancient, will be swallowed soon enough, and it does no good to dream for something already dead.

"*Grazie, zio,*" I say once more, just to be polite. I ease backward, and then I'm tearing away from him, standing in the half-shadows with his pale eyes and stoic face. I rush out toward Fionne waiting for someone sane enough to survive this filthy city.

I'm newer than myth and legend. I'm nearly better, and tonight I'll prove it.

School's in Session

U OF S'S NEW SCHOOL WELCOMES FIRST STUDENT, CHILD OF NOTORIOUS MAD FEY

4TH WINTER MOON, 52SC

For the past two cycles, Puck's Port has watched the only survivors of the 51SC Summer Fayre Massacre grow before their very eyes. And for the past cycle, they've seen the children's guardian (Shona Maxim, of the once highly praised Maxim & Maxim, Private Detectives) work with the University of Stoutshire's head of Fey Research, Doctor Sonder Secondchild, to build a science-based school for fey children. Today, the school opened its doors to one lucky student, Stregoni Child, aged 13, one of the two fayre survivors.

After their first day at school, Stregoni sits politely in their tidy shirt and shorts, fidgeting as fey do. Doctor Secondchild waits nearby, in case of any mishaps.

Dolly Day Reporter: You look sharp, Stregoni. Did you dress up?

Stregoni Child: This is what I have to wear for school. It's itchy.

DD: Sorry about that, jack. How was your first day here?

S: Alright, I think. We did a lot of math, 'cause I'm not good at it so I've got to catch up. Then I had trade practice—today was kitchen work and tomorrow's gonna be laundry. There's some comic books here that are funny.

DD: People are dying to know, Stregoni—what's the difference between this and regular school?

S: I guess that my friends aren't here ... but also I learn some tricks so I don't get all worked up into an episode. We do exposure therapy to get me ready for the mortal world. And I practice sitting still. [They notice they're moving around as they say this.] I'm still learning. [They sit on their hands.] It's hard.

DD: And this helps your symptoms?

S: I guess so! Sometimes I go too fast and make fey things happen. So I'm practicing not doing that, even if I want to. Getting my life skills, keeping quiet hands, not fiddling. [They look very intent.] Paying real close attention, like this. I have a responsibility not to indulge my moral deficiency.

DD: That makes sense. I have another question, but it's a tough one. Can you swing with it?

S: Oh yeah, I can swing. Whatcha got?

DD: Do you wish your mother could have had this opportunity?

S: ... Well ... I miss her a lot, and Senan. I think it would have been good for Mum to get help, so a doctor or someone could have noticed she was heading down a mad path and helped her slow down, like I am. Put a pause on it. But I don't really know what she would have been like if she was slower—that was just who she was, you know? I'm not really sure. Can we do a different question?

DD: Sure, jack. The floor's yours. Anything else you'd like to say?

S: My auntie's making a petition for more school funding, and everyone should sign it. She says she can help more kids come here for help instead of being all alone and scared. That'd be great.

Gristle Senan Maxim Junior paced outside the Dogfoot's shining doors, waiting on Hawthorne and Fionne. Every thought was precise, like a scalpel. It was still only half-past nineteen bells, and the painted signs on the glass said the club didn't even open until twenty-one. He scanned the street, where there wasn't a single flashing light or burning marquee, just dust-soft rain whispering down to the pavement. Gristle was alone, and wasn't a damn lick scared of mad fey or anything else that bumped in the night.

Tonk! Tonk! Tonk!

Gristle snapped his hand onto his camera like it was a pistol holstered at his side, whipping around to face the glass doors.

A Dogfoot worker in a tidy vest and slacks was standing back there, a few lights turned on to half-illuminate the wide lobby. She looked rather surprised to see him, or maybe just dubious about his pacing.

Gristle smoothed his features and lifted his hand. She unlocked the door beside the revolving carousel.

Showtime.

"Saints, miss," he said as she swung it open for him. He swiped his briefcase up after him and strode through onto the plush entry rug. "Almost gave me a heart attack."

"Well, if you do keel," the woman said, "I've got some staff who can mess with your adrenaline." *No thanks.* She seemed mortal so far, but he wouldn't underestimate anyone. "Let me take your gear."

Gristle handed her his damp coat and the briefcase, but motioned that he'd keep the hat and camera. With that, she slipped off into the coatroom nestled behind a carved marble desk.

It gave Gristle a moment to scan. The electric sconces crackled low for now, but he didn't need perfect vision to see that the lobby was large, made of white marble with carved pillars on the walls and some long lengths of dark drapery bordering a few expensive paintings. Above, the elaborately molded plaster ceiling swirled toward an unlit crystal chandelier. He had to squint and tilt his head back and forth to discern a spiral of stairs up to a second-floor balcony on the back wall, above what he assumed to be the dance hall and barroom.

Layout gauged, he ought to cut to the chase. "Is the owner about?"

"Should be," the woman said as she wandered back, hands hooked in her pockets. She was just shorter than him, perhaps a septennial-and-a-bit older, with dark-gray hair slicked straight back, gray skin, and pale-gray eyes. She gave him a slow size-up, one foot farther back than the other so she was just barely turned from him. But finally . . . "Fifthchild O'Taglio," she said, sticking her hand out. "Head barkeep."

Gristle understood the "traditionalists" who kept the same name they'd had as children, but it was strange to meet someone who'd seemingly swapped their place name and family name around. Then again, *Gristle* was named after the first noun to pop into his head in an unexplainable panic, so he supposed he shouldn't judge. There was surely some story there, though he doubted it much pertained to the night's mission.

"Gristle Senan Maxim Junior," he said, clapping his palm sturdily into hers, looking her right in the eye like he was always told to.

She stared right back, matched his intensity. "Maxim," she said, almost carefully. She held fast, scanning his face slowly. He felt suddenly stupid to have given his real name. "What brings you down here? I didn't think this was your side of town."

He ought to save this—he shouldn't announce the investigation of "suspicious activities" and rile everyone up. "Appointment with the owner," he said. "For insight on how my aunt's platform can support fey businesses." He realized too late that his "Vote Maxim" button was on his duster, not his suit lapel. He felt strange without it.

Finally, she loosened her grip. He took his hand back. "I thought you'd be talking to tidy little bakers or that, not sorts like Hien."

Hien. Gristle hadn't gotten the owner's name before. "What do you mean?"

She just shrugged. Gristle could almost feel a little disdain, something about the wrinkles near her eyes. "You lot seem by-the-book, and this place ain't that. It's all just fidgety kids dropping bottles and broken mirrors every other night when someone pops off the handle."

Did she mean madness, or just a bit too rowdy? Gristle wondered how illegal things could get around here.

O'Taglio buzzed her lips. "Hien revels in that, won't hear anything about toning it down. Says it's"—she splayed her fingers in something close to jazz hands—"*repressive*, which pretty much shuts down any argument I could give."

She was definitely mortal, and the Dogfoot was exactly as his aunt had said: fey building pressure, racing toward oblivion, unwilling to cap it. At the center of this, the owner, Hien, reigned as wild as Gristle had thought. And there were those mob ties...

"Why work here, then?" he asked.

She shrugged again. "I've been here since the old owner. Got too much love for the old place. Hien's going to get bored eventually when something shinier comes along. Then maybe I'll get my Dogfoot back how it was."

Understandable, really. Gristle nodded, drawing himself up. "Well, maybe we'll have a swell conversation about the education center plans, and things will get a bit more up to code," he offered. She gave a snort to say she didn't believe that, but it didn't matter. "Where should I be heading?"

O'Taglio jerked her chin up to the balcony. "First door up there."

"Thank you," he said, and twitched out half a smile. "My sister and her girlfriend should be around soon. Let them in, will you?"

The corner of O'Taglio's mouth twitched too, sending a strange glimmer through her eyes. "The whole family's here," she said, seeming to taste the idea. "Ain't that sweet." She slapped his back and strolled through the batwing doors into the barroom, whistling.

The lights blinked overhead again. He heard O'Taglio tell someone to knock it off and stow it up, which he appreciated. He couldn't imagine working in a place like this, but also understood how some perfect past could get its claws in you.

Gristle took a solid look around the lobby, saw nothing of merit, and strode up the thin spiral staircase at the back. The sconce lights melted as he climbed, pressing him up into the black-gray shadows. In the gloom, again, he was met by a roving shape that stopped to sit between the banisters.

The impossibly large dog stared at him. No panting, no sniffing.

This time, Gristle wasn't afraid. "Evening, poochie," he said easily. He hurried up the last few stairs and sidestepped past it. The dog didn't growl, or lunge, just stared. He wasn't certain if that was a good thing.

Up there, away from the lights, Gristle had a hell of a time discerning anything. There was one door immediately to his left, and then what he thought were several more ahead along the balcony—at least, he assumed as much from the way the banister shadow dipped against the gray.

He was doing mighty alright so far, and was actually proud of himself. He tilted his chin, rolled his shoulders back, stepped to the first door on the row, and knocked.

At practically the exact moment his knuckles collided with the wood, there came a startlingly clear "One moment," an equally startling lack of footsteps, and then the door opened much too quickly in a blinding sweep of light and a rush of that perfume that clogged in Gristle's throat.

He didn't dare cough it away, because he thought it'd be rather rude to cough on the shirtless young man in the doorway, dressed in only a skirt wrapped around his wide hips. Gristle froze and calculated.

"You're early," the man said, leaning into the doorframe. He was almost as tall as Gristle, with broad shoulders in stark contrast to a slightly boyish face under fashionably tousled hair.

Buck up, Ace. "I'm looking for the owner," Gristle said. "On business."

The man grinned. "If you're looking for the owner's *office*, it'd be *that* door." The man waved a lazy finger to the door beside the stairs, and then wagged it back the other way to keep pointing down the row. "*These* are all bedrooms. A different kind of business, unless it suits your pleasure."

Gristle opened his mouth. Nothing came out aside from a blush attempting to creep up from his neck. Behind the man, he could see a small but decidedly decadent bedroom, with chaises longues and bookshelves and the glow of a fire on one wall shining light toward a four-poster bed. Behind the sheer curtains there sat the shadow of a long-limbed woman.

The owner, Hien, he had to think. Different kind of business.

Gristle breathed out slow through his nose. He would not be derailed by one slipup, despite the aching rot of embarrassment carving out a gap in his chest.

"You've got a stare to make every spirit fall in line," the man mused, seemingly charmed by batting Gristle around like a mouse. "I see you got your new suit. They do work fast, those Goodfellows."

Gristle's jaw tightened. "I—"

"But your shoes are brown," the man noted, again with that pointing finger and unbothered smile. That smile that didn't move even when he spoke. It was not just that he smiled through his words, but that his lips stayed tight and grinning, like a ventriloquist puppet-ing something else. And yet still, words clear as bells rang between Gristle's ears. "And your hat's black. Doesn't match," said those unmoving lips.

Wait. Gristle forced himself to see a bit clearer, even if it just made the rotten embarrassment ache tenfold. The lights were flickering again and sending strange shadows onto the wall and against the man's black eyes. Yes, they were black, but Gristle had this peculiar and terrible feeling that they had been yellow at some point. Somehow the man was all at once mundane black-and-white, and yet in color, too? The awareness of color and yet not the image, like knowing names in a dream.

The man leaned farther into the doorframe and grinned with his tongue on his bottom lip. As though he had felt Gristle's hunch, or tasted it.

Chest a mess, burns on fire, and yet willing to dance with

anything the night threw, Gristle still felt certain of the impossible. "I never noticed my hat and shoes were different," he said. "I'm color-blind."

A rush of something speared up through Gristle, fizzing in the spaces between his teeth. He knew that wasn't coming from his own mind—someone had put that rush in him. The man kept his satisfied grin and turned his face over his shoulder without looking away from Gristle. There was some unspoken interaction, a heavy silence. The woman on the bed slipped out of the curtains, wearing the slate-gray uniform of a cleaner. She was an Askiyn dame with a long black braid and wide dark eyes, certainly not who Gristle had thought she was based on the vague silhouette. She slipped her shoes on and bustled out past them without a word, giving the dog a familiar pat as she passed. Through the back of her dress, two feathery wings were neatly folded between her shoulder blades.

"Alright, Mister Maxim," the man said. Gristle began to notice that he bore some small resemblance to the owner. "Now what kind of color-blind are we talking. Red-green?" Suddenly the spot where he was standing blurred; he came back in yellows and blues, wearing an evening dress and long limbs and diamond jewelry. The person standing in front of him now looked exactly as she had in the office that morning.

"Or yellow-blue?" she asked, but now Gristle could hear the echo more clearly. The more he thought about the voice, the more distorted it sounded, as if his brain was pulling it apart. The owner had sounded the same way in the office, just slightly *off*. Again, the figure blurred, Gristle's throat turned to sandpaper, and there stood the man, skirt red and skin more green than bronze.

Which one? the strange figure asked, except didn't ask it at all. Gristle heard the words, but the figure's mouth hadn't moved.

It had *never* moved, he realized. He had assumed it had because he knew it should; his mind had filled in the gaps that he hadn't paid attention to. He'd never met a fey this powerful, this seemingly controlled—not since Hàzell. His aunt was right: mad sorts of fey held court here. He'd been using logic on a person who operated only in chaos.

Now he was wising up. "Black and white," Gristle said.

The figure didn't repeat it, but Gristle felt something in his head that seemed to taste like grayscale and the faint visual chatter that freckled his vision. The figure in front of him blurred again. In the split second where the illusion changed, there was still a hazy cutout left behind, something too tall and impossible to decipher. Gristle strained to piece it together—his eyes stressed as if under pressure.

But then the trickery snapped back into Gristle's mind's eye, and there was another clear-as day person, willing as he didn't observe too closely. Hannōchian, with lean limbs but broad shoulders, black hair tied back, a gauzy shirt tucked in from the front with billowing tails fanning down to the person's knees from under their waistcoat. All was a proper, regular, mundane black-and-white. Gristle had righted the world.

He'd thought perhaps this person would be his aunt's age, but their smooth face and bright eyes seemed barely older than his own. Then again, he was still sure this wasn't the real form of the Dogfoot's owner. Tricks on tricks on tricks.

Every moment felt like a test, but Gristle was used to that.

The person held out their hand with elegant down-turned fingers and faint glitter in their nails. *Phong Hien*, they "said," just words pressed into Gristle's mind like a gramophone reel. Hien's mouth stayed in that same puckish grin, their chest puffed and their stance professional. *Welcome to the Dogfoot Club, Mister Maxim. I had my doubts about your skill, but I'd say you're off to a very good start.*

Gone to the Dogs

AZIZA STREET'S DOGFOOT CLUB GAINS NOTORIETY AS FEY HOT SPOT AFTER OWNERSHIP HANDOFF

5TH SUMMER MOON, 57SC

When the Dogfoot Club first opened its doors on the south side of town, it was a hot spot country club for wealthy elites, boasting a shimmering gold lobby and delicate chandeliers fit for election parties and bashes of the like. But with fortune raining down on Puck's Port, it's not just the rich who can have a ball. Now, working-class folks are getting their money for cars and gin and swing. And with Shona Maxim climbing the polls for the upcoming election season, putting "fey" on everyone's lips, it seemed high time the old Dog changed its tricks. And so, a change of ownership was arranged, shuffling the Dog into exciting new hands.

Phong Hien, barely twenty with a smile to put anyone in a ring, sits with one foot rested on their other knee. Their colossal black dog, known simply as "Quen" (the Hannochian word for a "familiar," a fey's companion animal), sits proudly nearby. Hien is in fact fey, and can influence the perception of others, as much as their energy will allow. They use this to feign an ever-changing appearance, or to defer to a simple blur to conserve strength. This same mental trick lets them put their voice in someone's head.

"I was never one for talking out loud," they explain. "I knew what everyone was saying, had my opinions, but had to find my own way of voicing them. But folks tend to find this a tad *invasive*. Frankly, I think it's equally rude to expect me to talk like them."

With the University of Stoutshire gaining notoriety for its Senan Maxim School for Fey re-education center, which hosts a program of trade skills and cognitive training, the current dialogue suggests that fey should refrain from encouraging their symptoms, as this degrades impulse control and leads to increasingly erratic and impulsive behavior, which in turn exacerbates symptoms to dangerous levels. When asked what they think of such statements, Hien's eyes flicker red.

"And what would you have me do instead? Keep my mouth shut?

I've got a pad and paper here, for short-and-pleasant answers. But I figure there wouldn't be an interview if my answers were all 'yes' and 'no' and 'lovely weather we're having.' I'd make for a great employee in a factory, though, wouldn't I?"

Instead, Hien has encouraged fey staff at the Dogfoot to embrace their symptoms, despite the clear danger. They say they've learned from experience that suppressing symptoms only worsens them. As the youngest of thirteen, Hien tells the tale of accidentally decompressing their sister's lungs as a child for about thirty seconds, a common story for dysregulated fey children. However, rather than hide their child in shame until the legal age for stress-testing, Hien's mothers sent them from the family estate in the Daleish countryside back to their home country of Hannoch.

"The culture is better there," Hien boasts. Indeed, Hannoch has reported only three fey-related deaths in the past half-century, though some Daleish experts argue that Hannoch intentionally underreports to undermine Dale's ordinances. "I spent a few cycles at a specialized school, was set up with a local mentor when I returned, and a job, and Quen." According to Hien, they could "win a match with one of those repressed Senan Maxim School brats any day," though they refused to elaborate on what sort of "match" this would be.

According to Dr. Sonder Secondchild, the institute's head researcher, "freewheeling" attitudes may seem liberating at first, but will only escalate. Young fey may not realize the damage they're doing to their minds until it's too late. "Discomfort is a fact of life that we all need to adjust to, including and especially fey. Adapting to new coping mechanisms is difficult, but necessary," he explains. He has suggested that loose regulations contributed to the 51SC Summer Fayre Massacre that began with the violent self-implosion of mad fey Hazell Stregoni. Stregoni had earlier immigrated from Verdosso, where mass poverty in outlying villages leads to a lack of fey regulation and education. Friends, family, and personal documents have explained how Stregoni grew up letting her symptoms flare liberally, ultimately resulting in increasingly criminal behavior and symptoms strong enough to destroy three-hundred fayre-goers in a single second.

Hien says they have no worries about so-called "mad fey." "Why is the Fayre Massacre any more unsettling than the number of fey who die in madhouses every year? What gives you lot the right to call police on us whenever you choose? You don't listen when we talk, you call us mad when we argue. Statistically, I ought to be more afraid of an anti-fey mortal planting a bomb under my club than someone having a bad night." Hien neglected to give any further comment.

The Dogfoot Club continues to be a swinging spot, with live jazz, dancers, and always-flowing taps. Even if you're mortal, the Dog seems to be the place to get down.

"My [mortal] kids are there every other night," says Rita O'Mallory, an iron factory employee. "I'm worried this is becoming a trend."

Ileian-born Dogfoot singer Cab Kazah Junior laughs when told this. "Classic," he says as he prepares for his next set. He does not disclose if he's fey. "The new world ain't just for the mortal Daleish folks above 14th Street—we deserve our piece of the pie as well."

The lights on the marquees are starting to come up as me and Fionne dash through the rain, in and out of the dry patches of overhangs and then finally under the Dog's. The damp's digging into me, pulling all the heat out, but I'm weirdly alright with it. I can be, if I try hard enough.

"They just gonna let us in?" Fionne asks, staring through the dark glass, craning her neck. Her hand hovers near the opening of her coat—I see that little spiral notebook waiting in her inside pocket. "You said Phong Hien hired him, right? You think we'll get to meet them? I've read every damn article and there aren't ever any pictures."

"Maybe," I say, stiff. Can't say I ain't curious myself, but I've read "every damn article" too and I know that's a fey we shouldn't mess with. Especially if they're the one blackmailing us. "Let's just be careful, alright? This ain't a party."

She smiles, all secret-like, but already she's pulled her notebook free.

I can't get the same smile. "This could actually be dangerous, Fionne." My voice comes out so low and steady that I swear I see it sink into her skin. Her thumb pauses on the cap of the pen. "We don't know these people, and they play wilder games than I do."

She purses her lips and turns back to look inside. "D'you know what we're looking for when we get in there?" she asks, more careful now. I appreciate that, but hate it a bit, too, that I made her be nervous about a place she'd been so excited about yesterday.

I pick up the suitcase and keep steady. "Anything suspicious, play like we're just chatting," I tell her, just as I see movement in the shadows.

Some kid, maybe only thirteen, trots out from the coatroom toward the batwings. I bang the glass with the side of my fist and they jump almost right out of their little vest and slacks before they come swinging over to haul the door open.

"S'cuse you, dollface. Please don't smudge up my glass," they spit. They have a little snaggletooth, and straight black hair pulled into a sharp ponytail to show off two stubby goat horns. A fey kid. "I work real hard to keep it nice and shined."

"Aw, shoot." Fionne laughs. "Aren't you a peach?"

They almost blush when they look at her (me too, kid) but just lean into the door twiddling their hands into their pockets. "Are you the Mad Blast girl? She said you'd come," they tell me, giving me a quick sweep. "O'Taglio, I mean—you look the part."

Guess there's no getting away from what Mum did, especially when my reflection in the doors looks so much like her. "Howdee, kid," I say. I walk in before they can really let me, so all they can do is step aside. "You got me. Name's Hawthorne. This is Fionne."

"Charmed, I'm sure," she says in her dolled-up, night-on-the-town voice. She shrugs out of her big white coat. "Be a good sport, jack?" She's wearing a satin dress underneath, no pockets, so she just wedges the notebook under her arm and sticks the pen up into her hair wrap.

"Yes, miss. I can take your coat, and your case," the kid says, swiping the suitcase from me. "My name's Robin—I do work here most nights." Pause. "My mothers own the tailor but I'm not . . . so good at that as I'm so good at this."

They've got one of those vocal patterns I'm always hearing about, a real specific way to put the words together. I wonder how much it hurts not to. Maybe they oughta start breaking the pattern, getting used to it.

"That a family name?" Fionne asks. "Robin?"

They shake their head. "I'm try'n' it out for when I pick, that's all."

The Dogfoot seems a lot bigger when there's no one here yet, and a lot simpler when there isn't music playing from the barroom, and when I'm not a bottle of gin deep already. "Hey, Robin," I call just as they come kicking their way back from the coatroom. "Has some big lug talked to you yet?"

"No, Miss. I haven't talked to an'one yet," they say, shaking their head. No sparks or nothing comes off. "O'Taglio says the lug is a dick."

Fionne has to slap her hands over her mouth and turn around, wheezing out a laugh.

Well, looks like he ain't subtle about why we're here. I put my hands on my hips and smile with every tooth. "He's a dick alright," I say, and make sure to go on with, "That means a detective." I should stop talking, but my runaway mouth won't let me. "Also means something else, but—"

I know what a dick is—I'm not some kid, I hear in my head, and I look at Robin grinning like the devil. *I'm a Sixthchild. My big siblings, they talk.*

My stomach drops. The kid looks innocent enough, but I'm not worried *by* them. I know better than anyone that it's harder to stop something that's already started, and this is some powerful stuff.

Robin sticks their little nose up. "But between you and me and her, most folks . . . here won't talk nice with cops. A dick's the same."

Course. Mum and Senan were like that too, and then look what happened. My teeth start to grit, but suddenly Fionne's hand's on my arm, with the pen uncapped between her fingers.

"Oh, course," she says. "We're not here *with* him. I'm writing an article." Robin's eyes narrow. A flash of color ripples through them. Fionne flips her notebook open. "You ever heard of *Dolly Day*?"

She's a star-favored genius.

Robin grins so wide I swear they must have twice as many teeth. "Boy, howdee—I love *Dolly Day*. Thanks, miss!" Robin says. They take a skipping sidestep toward the barroom, shaking out their excited hands. "You want a tour? I can do that real fast."

Fionne shoots me a slightly apologetic look, but I ain't regretting the fib one bit. And hey, maybe she'll get something for her portfolio.

I nod a few times. "Take the lead," I say as they back up through the batwings into the barroom. "What's it like to work here?"

Robin taps the heels of their hands against each other. A crackle moves through the air every time their hands collide. It prickles up my arms.

"Real nice. I like my family lots, but they . . . ain't fey as far as I can truly tell," Robin says. There are a few keeps behind the horseshoe bar. That same singer from last night is pacing between the tables, running scales that clash with the band tuning on stage. I squint a bit. "Was it nice to have a fey mum, before?"

I really hoped we were gonna brush past being Hàzell Stregoni's one-and-only child. My spine tightens. Fionne eases up beside me, darting her eyes from me to Robin like she don't know what to say or do here.

"I'm not here about that," I snap.

"We want to hear about you," Fionne says, which sounds a lot less mean. "You sure are grown-up, being here all night. Does anything strange ever happen?"

Robin doesn't take her bait, just tilts their head at me. The trumpeter on stage blasts out a sour note. A ripple of weird goes up through me. Robin flinches too—their shadow lashes strange across the hardwood like something dying. I press my shoes into the ground to keep it corked. "I wish I could have met her," Robin says. Of course they say that. Eyes all glassy, shadow all strange, too odd to just answer the questions without getting distracted by the thing they want. "She sounds swell."

The memories come slashing back through me, of her hands under mine, of pulling sparks to the surface, flames for the fireplace, laughing until everything was orange and wild and my brain was burning.

"Well, she's dead, so that's a damn good warning for you," I tell Robin. Fionne touches my arm but it just presses everything in worse. A barkeep looks up at us. "So you oughta cool the tricks 'fore you end up collapsing in on yourself just the same."

"Hawthorne," Fionne says, like a warning. She side-eyes me, the whites all wide, then gives Robin a big-sister smile. "Say, Robin, it might be good for us to talk to more folks too. Can you see if anyone in the kitchen wants to chat?"

"I won't end up the same," Robin says, stepping forward instead of back. The horns grow a few inches. A waiter slams a chair off the table onto the ground. "I'm well practiced."

My skull whispers. "And so was my mum," I snap, ripping from Fionne. My breath's coming out hot but I can keep it together. *I'm well practiced.* "But she got too big for her body. You know what I mean by that?" Robin's lips crease up but I'm not stopping now. Not when they're actually listening to me. I wish this was me. I wish someone noticed and saved me before *my* mind got ruined. I'm so close I can crouch nearly eye-to-eye with them. "Being fey killed her. So every time you make your happy little horns or twist up your shadow, you remember that. She'd *still be here* if she wasn't fey."

Robin blinks hard at me. "I have a mentor who keeps me in check," they say. Their voice is coming out a half-squeak now.

A burn sprints up from my stomach, like TNT going off in a tunnel. "You want some 'mentorship'?" I ask, low and quiet and so close to them I can see myself in their eyes, and the fire building behind my pupils. A few sparks come trickling from my mouth without my permission. "Cool the tricks before you just get yourself hurt. That's what my mum taught me."

Robin's face twists up. The antlers shrink a few inches. They open their mouth like they might say something, but just turn quickly on their heel and rush toward the kitchen door, mopping an arm over their eyes. A barkeep with half their face made of bark gives me some serious evil eyes before they zip over to follow them. But I ain't sorry. The truth hurts.

I breathe out the rest of the air in my lungs. Puffs of smoke trickle from my nostrils but I pack the rest in. It goes down easier and easier.

"Damn kids," I start to say, trying to smear a smile back on as I turn to Fionne. "Maybe we start with the band folks and then do the kitchen."

Fionne stares at me. Her lips are parted a bit, notebook and pen held close. I don't get the look on her face in the low light, where the shadows are all pulling out strange and thick. "Saints, Hawthorne," she breathes. A wave of goosebumps moves up my arms. I step toward her and she leans back. She didn't even do that this morning! She caps the pen and tucks it into the spiral binding, movements all rough. "You didn't have to be so damn mean about it."

"Someone needed to say it," I tell her, like I can possibly explain it to a mortal girl with a mortal family who just reads about fey in magazines—I know that ain't fair to think, but it bubbles in my stomach. "We're gonna get out of here by the end of the night and never have to think about it again, alright?"

She bites at her lip. For a second, her eyes dart around. Does she want to come back here still? Chase the fashion trend?

From the stage, the singer whistles. "You were here last night, miss!" he calls. It echoes out through the barroom, still prickling with me and Robin bristling at each other. "What's your favorite? Give me a warm-up."

Fionne turns to him. "Something to dance to," she says. It's stiffer than she usually is. "From an Ileian singer."

He laughs and whistles to get the band crashing together. I get why she likes it here, in a place where there's no expectations, where it feels like anything's possible. Where we can all get what we want. But that's how Mum made us all feel. That sort of optimism is always fixing to blow.

I wait for Fionne to slip off to the dance floor without another word. She saw the horrible thing inside me, worse than flames, and I understand why that's terrifying.

But she stays with me. "No yelling at kids," she tells me, trying to be serious about it. I can see how her eyebrows twitch. I need her to keep it up. "I don't care if you're right—you don't have to be cruel."

And if I can't cap it? "Alright," I say. I'm going to keep it together. I keep saying that, but it has to be true eventually, right? "Thanks, Fionne."

"We can find a better club after this," she says. "I'll go to every single one for you."

I shouldn't go to clubs at all. I say nothing, so she just smiles and takes off to dance.

Why does it feel like we're growing in two separate directions? And if we are, which one of us is gonna call it off first? All I can do is stare after her and try to breathe until the anger's gone. But I still have so much shit to be angry about.

I wish Mum could be here to dance with me, all fancy free and fine. Instead, we're cursed in this tragic city, so all I can do is fight what I am.

The Diary of Hàzell Stregoni, "Radical Fey"

45 SC, Winter Solstice

The newspaper has announced our relationship to the world, and so there's no longer any reason to hide. Today, on the Winter Solstice, with the sentimental fancy that it will hurry the sun along faster in the lightening moons, Senan and I have chosen to braid our paths through marriage.

Given the spontaneity, we have forgone the church or courthouse. Instead, Senan and I spent the morning calling on every soul we know. By the time the sun began to set, we were able to invite nearly one hundred people to fill Chestnut Street, from the Gattana garage down to Cat's, even as snow fell. Tippi officiated the ceremony in a jumbled mix of Daleish, Verdossi, and Ileian tradition. We were not picky about this, just as we were not picky about the reason. Many marry for love, I am told, or perhaps money or title. I do not understand these things. Perhaps it is my fey blood that distorts mortal reason and emotion. Instead, I knew only this:

Senan Maxim and his child are dear to me, and I to them. We see the world through different eyes, and yet are challenged and emboldened. He has been called a crazed idealist by even those closest to him, and I a mad fanatic, all for imagining a future where folks—mortal, fey, immigrant, young, old, poor, working, harmed, and tired—are as free as those with money to throw away. Our struggle is the same. And so, the dancing congregation of our celebration looked not unlike a riot crowd as fireworks broke apart in the sky to mark midnight. I don't know who baked our wedding cake, or whose pen I am using to scrawl this upon a notebook from my apron pocket while Stregoni and Maxim dance with Victory and Tãyé's children and others I cannot name.

As the suns progress longer, we cannot sit in silence. I am aware of those who fear us, who question our methods or foretell our downfall with glee, but I do not fear them. Because I know that those who only love a heeling dog know not what to do when it breaks its leash. Perhaps that is what I hope Sey can teach mortals: that there is beauty in the uncontrollable. We do not need to accept leadership, or order, or law.

Senan's sister has been, unsurprisingly, bitter about the whole affair. Tomorrow we will tell her of his plans to move both himself and Maxim back from midtown to the dockyards. I'm unsure what will come of this, but Senan is a grown man, and I do not intend to let my husband be kept from me.

GRISTLE SENAN MAXIM JUNIOR IN
"SWING AT ME"

Gristle Senan Maxim Junior was certainly unnerved by his new "boss" but refused to be fazed. He was waved toward the door to the left of the spiral staircase, not any of the bedrooms that sprawled out overtop the barroom. Hien said nothing as they strode in, the dog after them, and then Gristle. He found himself at one end of a long, tidy office. Past the sitting area and ornate fireplace just ahead, past a grand desk in the middle, and up into a backsplit study of imposing bookshelves, Gristle saw billowing curtains framing bifold doors, open just enough to let in a slight breeze and the sound of rain. In the minimal lighting of just one banker's lamp on the desk, he could only guess that there might be a balcony out there, presumably where Hien had stood to see Hawthorne go up like a mad pyre. It was a painful warning of exactly what was at stake here.

There came an echoing whistle, high then low. Gristle let his gaze drift down to see that Hien had seated themself at their desk, and was motioning to the wood-and-leather chair across from them. The dog sat just beside them, staring.

"Not much for talking," Gristle observed as he walked over and sat down, carefully unbuttoning his jacket and hiking the legs of his slacks.

Hien pushed another thought into Gristle's head, something between an image and a feeling that *seemed* like *no*.

He'd hoped the theatrics would stop now that he had proven himself a clever enough detective to notice he was being deceived by mental trickery, if that was what this was about. But he was getting the sense that the show was always on with Phong Hien. Whatever image of them he was looking at wasn't even real, just chemicals in his head. Well, truly, wasn't everything just chemicals in your head?

He needed to stop thinking about that before he gave himself a headache.

"I'm sorry about earlier . . . in the bedroom . . . with that woman," he said, even if his face began to burn again and his words kept congealing. Gristle had never had many friends, had certainly never had anything more serious than that, so wasn't exactly personally familiar with . . . *intimate activities* was the only way he could think of it without burning up as bright as Hawthorne. "If I interrupted anything . . . personal."

Hien gave him a slow look, and then quirked that puckish grin again. Gristle felt a spark of anticipation needle through his brain, as if they had nearly decided to say something, but thought better of themself. Hien instead shook their head. As the rain smell swept in warm, they made a large show of breathing in, raising both hands on the inhale, and lowering them on the exhale.

Gristle stared at their strange image a bit closer, trying to ignore the suddenly deeper neckline of their shirt. "You were helping her with her breathing?"

Hien nodded, leaning back in their chair with both arms lying lazily on the rests. *The human body is a natural element.*

Some fey can make plants grow. Hàzell, and the foxgloves. Gristle shut the memory out. *And some of us can force your body to pry its lungs open.*

Gristle didn't like the sound of that. "Sounds like you're a doctor," he offered.

Hien smirked. Their eyes seemed to look through Gristle's, rather than into them. *Unlicensed*, they said. *I trust you won't tell anyone. I figure some may think I'm getting a little too wild. I have no desire to waste a day on a stress-test.*

Gristle had to admit that Hien seemed fairly sane, more helpful than harmful with their symptoms. But, then again, so had Hàzell. He stared into Hien's unfocused eyes and wondered if he might somehow see a dangerous plan in there, or else the pin-trigger impulse switch to stop every heart in the building if they weren't getting their way.

They swept their eyes over his suit, as if entertained. *I can smell your neurons firing.* Gristle's heart stuttered. Hien's smile grew worse. *But I can't tell much more than that. I'm no mind reader, so you ought to say why I've made you feel so guilty all of a sudden.*

Guilt? Not guilt, but fear. What did he have to feel guilty about while sitting across from someone who could destroy him? But they couldn't, because they needed him. Maybe Hien *thought* they were in control, with their strange senses and overbearing confidence, but they needed his services.

Gristle had to stop letting himself be dragged around. "We ought to get to business. I'll need a clearer portrait of what's going on here, Mx Hien," he said, adjusting the slouch of his hat and sitting firmer. "You said you've been seeing suspicious activity?"

So professional. Hien didn't look away from him. Their smile didn't change. *It might be faster to show you, Mister Maxim. If you're up for it.*

Had something grisly happened already? He wasn't afraid of pictures or evidence, not when he'd heard every story of dead-rat threats on doorsteps and murder investigations. He'd seen a burned body just the night before—nothing could shake him.

"Alright, then," Gristle said. "Show me."

The light from the banker's lamp shone into the pits of Hien's strange eyes. Each tooth gleamed, just a bit too sharp. *Very well.* They didn't reach for their desk drawer, they just raised one hand up near their face, knuckles out and fingers loosely curled so Gristle could see smoke swirling in three strange rings.

Gristle's lungs suddenly locked. They refused to inhale. *Wait!*

It's always a pleasure to put on a show for such fine company, Hien said. *Survive this and maybe you'll see more.*

Gristle couldn't tell if that was innuendo. Hien suddenly jerked their wrist so their palm flipped toward him. Gristle fell back in the chair with his head a rip-roaring blur.

◆

Gristle felt like he was face-down in a river, with everything rushing past. And then (less like falling into it, more like focusing his eyes to find he'd been there the entire time), Gristle was sitting on the other side of Hien's desk. There was an empty chair ahead of him.

Something was wrong.

The banker's lamp scrawled emerald-green shadows over the paperwork he was sorting through. He was taller, *much* taller. His limbs felt odd. But more than that, the world was painfully vibrant around him. Not the colors (he found those rather annoying, actually), but a sort of sharp clarity on the edge, a weight to it more than a flat picture show. The smallest sounds of the radiator humming pressed into him, the tiniest sensations of the velvet chair beneath him, and the steady rhythm of Quen breathing evenly from its wide wicker bed beside the fireplace.

This was a memory. Hien's memory. By instinct, Gristle knew it was from just past closing two nights previous, the morning approaching Gristle and Hawthorne's naming ceremony and then Hawthorne's mad fit. The rest of the staff had gone home and locked up, but it was a known secret that Hien rarely left the sanctuary of the Dog.

The radio was tuned to a jazz station, letting the croon of a slow trumpet wind through the air like lazy smoke while the fireplace crackled. It smeared Quen's shadow up the wall. Gristle saw those already large ears twitch once before honing toward the door. The dog woke to raise its head off its clodhopper paws.

Through the office door's frosted glass, a nervous sliver of shadow had leaned in. Oh . . . so perhaps not all the staff had left. It wasn't unusual for one to come knocking, especially if they were looking for assistance. Gristle felt a tad tired but gathered his weary energy.

The sharpness on the edges of everything kicked up a notch, pouring humming and rustling down into Gristle's chest, where it harmonized with every cell. A steady pressure came whispering out, calm as countryside wind. It flowed for the door and the figure behind it. There was indeed the vague suggestion of a person back there, though he couldn't pinpoint their identity.

Who is it? Gristle felt himself ask, but the internal voice echoed. The words hadn't sunk into anyone. He wrapped the power around the sound of a heartbeat and brain waves and frenetic energy. *Who is it?* he asked again.

The same echo. He tensed, unsure now.

The shadow swayed as if it would open the door, to *his* office. Gristle snapped to his feet, forced the radio's hum into his pores, let it sing his rivulets of calm into forceful intent. Every hair and scale (*scales*, Gristle was sure, but couldn't look down to see them in this fixed memory) pricked up. A sweeping tension locked down the entire length of his spine. How could the person avoid his voice? He'd never had that happen before. *Who's there?* A warning rattle shook about the room, like a snake before it strikes from the high grass. *Don't play games with me.*

A shriek of metal as the doorknob began to turn. The room pulsed with colliding sounds and smells and sights and feelings and tastes. Gristle forced himself to ignore the cacophony while he yanked open a drawer, flipped open an ornate Hannochian-made box, and pulled out a snub-nosed pistol with a jade handle. Sweat carved hot lines around his horns and down into every eye.

The door cracked open—a sudden reek of iron shocked through Gristle's sinuses and straight through his body like he was drowning, every nerve and pore frozen. He stumbled away from his desk with the back of his silk sleeve to his nose. He couldn't remember how to spin the gun's barrel.

And yet there was Quen, thank the spirits for Quen, who galloped over and reared on its back legs. Its huge paws bashed the door shut with a rush of wood on wood. Quen kept scrabbling and barking and snapping with all of its huge teeth, spit and foam flying from the corners of its jaws. The iron smell lingered. Through the glass and his watery eyes, Gristle could see the shadow had retreated quickly.

A molten-hot rush tore through him. All anger. *No*, they didn't just get to peer in on him and walk away. He'd figure out why the hell his voice couldn't touch them and then he'd turn their every pore into an eye so they could watch a million versions of him bear down on them like Armageddon. They'd wish for death, and he might just do it.

Heel, Quen, he thought, then he crossed the office in a few quick strides. The movement made his face burn, as if he had countless cuts slit open to the air. Quen dropped back onto all fours, stoic, while Gristle wrenched the door open and aimed the gun down the walkway.

The iron smell was sunk into the carpet. But there was no one there. Below, dawn light burned through the lobby doors and windows, throwing muntin shadows against the empty floor as well. He whirled around and looked up to the ceiling as if the culprit might be perched there like a spider. They weren't.

The world was screaming for his attention. It speared at him from every angle. Someone had gotten into his club, had gotten near his *office*, a place where he shouldn't have to worry about peering eyes. Suppose the person had a camera and caught a snap before he could catch them? Beautiful creatures were given interviews and fame and tragic admiration, and monsters were given nothing.

Gristle felt as if his whole body was being filled by hurricane-force winds, the sort that flatten homes and snap apple trees. It was too much, pressing out against his bones, singing to be let out fast and rough and desperate. Tear it all down around him. Quen reared up to put heavy front paws on his shoulders. It forced his feet into the floor.

This power could kill him, he knew, rip him up along the fault lines of his skin until he was a dazzling mist. The thought actually brought him calm. This power *could* kill him, but he was trained not to let it. He wrapped his arms tight around Quen and—

♦

A whistle, high then low.

Gristle blinked his eyes open with a feeling like a hangover from hell. Everything was still a little blurry. But at least the blur was regular old black-and-white. It would have been one thing to get in anyone else's head, but the body he'd been in was too large and strange to be his own, as if he'd been vaporized to fit the space. And in that vapor rushed all the singing of every sensation in the world, and of growing madness heading toward a self-implosion that he'd felt stalking on the horizon.

Gristle didn't like the feeling of being fey, not one bit.

Something cold nudged into his hand. His fingers fumbled to take the crystal glass.

The chill was grounding; the blur focused. Hien had swung his chair away from the desk, and stood ahead of him. Over the course of showing him their memory of the "suspicious activity," they'd also changed their image to include short hair so heavily greased that it caught the light like a star-speckled night sky. A gauzy scarf seemed to hold the same constellations in its stitches.

The thought of adding alcohol to this already unsettling job made Gristle even more nauseous. "I don't drink," he lied, tipping his chin to the pale liquid.

Hien waved to the glass anyway. Gristle raised it up under his nose. A faint burn, but not alcohol. Seltzer. Alright, that would do.

He sipped. Hien seemed content to take a step back. The dog was sitting by their side, eyeing Gristle just as warily as Hien.

"I'm guessing you don't take people for that sort of ride very often?" Gristle muttered. He felt violated, if he was honest, but at least the seltzer was easing his stomach.

Hien smirked again. *Ask nicely and let me buy you dinner*, they said. And yet Gristle could feel a nervous edge floating under the innuendo. The dog had sat itself on Hien's shoes for some deep pressure. Gristle understood their concern now, why a fey as strange as this would be livid about intruders, considering how thrown Gristle had been just that morning by Hien waltzing into his own safe haven. A jack ought to have one place where they didn't have to put on airs.

Just because he sympathized didn't mean he trusted. He'd learned that at his father's deathbed.

"And there's no chance they got out through the Dog's main doors before you could catch them?" Gristle asked, standing up and setting the glass on the desk. He remembered how high his eyeline had been in the memory. Now, Hien was presenting as quite a few inches shorter than him.

They shook their head. *Back to the game at hand, I see*, they said. They sounded disappointed that they wouldn't be bantering more, but gave him a vague mental understanding that all the club doors were still locked when they checked.

"Locked to exit, though?" Gristle probed. "Did you check everywhere?"

A faint pressure in his head said he'd struck a nerve. *I understand my club, Mister Maxim. No doors were opened. I prefer you not waste my time on useless questions.*

Alright, alright. He didn't wholly believe them, but knew better than to push. "If I find out how this person got in and fled the scene, are we done?" he asked, motioning stiffly between the two of them.

Hien stared at him, face so unmoving it was like a stone bust. *I'm far more interested in who they are*, they said. Gristle felt his pores prickle, as if preparing to change. *Me and mine will handle the consequences.*

He'd heard just what Hien planned to do with intruders. He was supposed to be past the dirty days working with dangerous people.

Unless you want to leave, Hien said, raising an arrow-shaped eyebrow. Gristle was given a faint flicker of memory, of standing on the balcony and watching with entertained curiosity as Hawthorne roared up in flames and punched some sad sack named Gristle Senan Maxim Junior. *In your absence, I may have time to call the police you seem so fond of.*

Gristle gritted his teeth, but refused to respond. Instead, he took a slow, roving look at the long room.

Start with the evidence.

He pulled his camera from its bag and took a cautious step forward. His legs and head were still holding him upright. The room was semi-dark, but with a *pop!* and a sudden flash, the details all screamed and ran into view like startled mice. The crown molding, and the ceiling medallion, and the dramatic rear window and doors. Despite some more modern furnishings, the smooth, nearly-unsettling beauty was certainly older than the past few septennials.

The broken pattern was interesting. "You mentioned you inherited this from your uncle," Gristle said. "Was it built for him?"

He said he won it in a game of cards, Hien said, cleaning a set of glasses now, without much attention.

"Do you know what it was before that?"

Hien huffed, an easy way to say they didn't care. But Gristle knew that the south side roar was recent. Before that, this was just countryside, and none of the architecture here was recent enough to be post-Confederacy. If he had to take a guess (and there weren't really any guesses when you were being logical, he figured), this had been a country home, a mansion to some rich folk wanting to escape the noise.

"I may be wrong," Gristle said, tapping his toes slowly in his shoes. He shocked himself from the friction and so stepped forward to press his fingers to the wallpaper. It was a deep-toned shade of gray (or rather, plum, he remembered) embossed with shimmering scallop patterns. Up close, he leaned and turned to look along the length of the wall. The pattern blurred, but despite focusing so close he feared he'd grow nauseous again, Gristle noted something uneven. "But are we above the kitchen by any chance?"

Another huff.

"And the wallpaper is new," he said, to a slightly entertained hum suggesting they were glad he'd noticed something fashion-adjacent, considering the sorry state they'd found him in.

Gristle didn't appreciate the condescension . . . and so he felt no shame in stepping back to swipe a penknife off the side of Hien's desk and striding to cut a nick in the wallpaper big enough to hook his fingers in. He wrenched it off the wall like hauling skin from tissue.

A searing pang like a scream tore through his chest before he heard the dog jump to put its paws on Hien's shoulders. Gristle's heart raced back to life as he whirled to face Hien.

"I'm helping!" he snapped back, which didn't feel very "professional." He almost didn't care, because as the dog dropped back to its four huge paws, Hien's onyx-black eyes widened from beneath a heavy cloud of kohl. Gristle turned too, already certain of his hunch.

They were just above the kitchen, and the building was old, and so it followed the expected blueprints.

The wallpaper sloughed to the floor like a shed scab. Behind it, built into the faded wooden wall now mottled with old paste, was a small door. Gristle nudged it with his shoe. The hinges gave a rusty, unsure *creeeeeak*, but did in fact swing to reveal the cobwebby blackness of the unseen servants' hall.

Gristle nearly grinned. It was a foreign impulse. But it didn't matter, because there'd be paths all around the Dogfoot. Gristle bet that some of them weren't fully papered over, at least not anymore.

You can hide something away all you like, but it's still in there when you look.

"There's your answer, Mx Hien," Gristle said, a low mutter. The iron smell swam through Gristle's memory, more sinister than suspicious. He didn't think the culprit was just trying to snap a picture or spy. This felt much bigger. "I think you have someone sneaking through your servants' halls."

Notes on Dogfoot Staff

"Robin" Goodfellow Sixthchild, Waiter.

Fey. Gets "mentored", probably by Hien. Youngest employee.

Cab Kazah, Junior, Singer.

Hired by Hien. Loves working here. Says the stage is "off-beat." Can't elaborate.

Chet Arthur, Musician.

Mortal. Been on for a few cycles—prefers Hien who pays overtime. Says dozens of folks left with~~ ~~ is a jilted ex-employee?

Thomas Proud, Head Chef.

Fey. Hired as sous chef a few cycles ago and promoted under Hien. Says all employees who left were given good severance.

Rastova Firstchild, Barkeep.

Fey. Related to a day staff member. Hired by Hien specifically for mentorship opportunity. Says the cellar stairs creak.

Derry Wahua, Barkeep.

Fey. Not a big talker. Says everything creaks and Rastova is whiny.

Echo Finch, Barkeep.

Fey. Wouldn't talk after scuffle with Robin.

HAWTHORNE STREGONI IN "THIEVING SPIRITS"

I'm not gonna bust up at anyone else, so I let Fionne take charge of the interviewing. She's nicer about talking with them, makes it more like a conversation than an interrogation. I'm not sure how it all patterns out, neither is Fionne, but even just getting it is a good look. Hopefully Gristle's doing something more impressive.

The Dog unlocks its doors right at twenty-one bells, letting in a rush of people with pointed ears and scales and eyes that change color. Cab welcomes everyone in and introduces the band and the little menagerie of dancers real quick, and then the party starts up. We pull a few folks aside to ask if they saw anything strange last they were in. Besides some folks saying the lights blipped last night around the time I had my bust-up (I'm glad there's no windows in the dance hall), they got nothing. They love the Dog, and the staff, and they're gonna swing till the sun comes up.

"Only place I don't worry," some dame says, looking right mortal if not for suggesting she's fey. I wonder what she's capable of. "Let the magic flow like the taps, right on?"

I button my lips, let her go on her way, and look to Fionne. "Let's wait it out," I tell her over the wailing trumpet and Cab singing so damn pretty. "We can tell Gristle what we got and go from there."

"Alright," she decides. There's still ink on her fingers, and a little bit on the corner of her mouth from chewing her pen. She'd had her glasses hidden in her stocking, but hasn't taken them off since she started writing. "You good?"

Besides being worried, and maybe even a bit frustrated, yeah. I'm good. "Rain-right. You?"

She frowns at me, but then nods. "Yeah," she says. The corner of her mouth twitches, but it ain't as bright and beaming as usual. "Interviewing folks is good *Dolly Day* practice. My mama would be proud, I figure."

Is it weird to want mine to be proud too? At least the part of her that wasn't bad?

We find two stools right at the front of the bar to watch Cab wave on those same dancers from last night. I lean my elbows back and Fionne has her legs crossed, all dolled up like she does while she parses her notes. I look out over the swarming mob of folks at the tables or farther out dancing. I keep my hands in quiet fists.

"Evening, ladies," one of the barkeeps says while they sidle on over in the low light. It's that scrawny kid, Rastova. Family name—they're still a cycle out of getting their real one. They got themselves some pointed ears and snake-pupils that stare over our heads. Something tells me they changed it all that way on purpose. "I know you probably shouldn't drink on the job, but I can bring you waters if—"

"What did I tell you about convincing people *out* of paying?" Another barkeep—that taller, older mortal lady with a handsomely rough face—pops her rag at them. We never did get around to interviewing her. She slides a drink over to another person waiting and turns back to us while she slings the rag over her shoulder. "I met your brother, if I'm not mistaken."

This is O'Taglio, then. "So *you* met the lug," I say with a smile, swinging around. "Robin said you figured out he was here on detecting, so I guess he ain't been holding his cards too close."

Fionne jams her elbow into my side. "We don't care what he's doing," she says, tapping her pen into the notebook. "We're here to interview, for my *Dolly Day* portfolio."

O'Taglio shrugs. "Doesn't matter to me what you're doing. I'm above board," she says, dodging another barkeep slipping past, taking the rye out of their hand and tossing it to the other folk that's calling for it. She moves like she's done this for a good long while. "Drinks? I'll give it a light pour if you really are worried about your wits."

Fionne purses her lips at me. I shouldn't. And, for the first time maybe, Fionne seems to remember that. "Two waters," she says with no missed beats. O'Taglio shrugs and plucks up a cup to click it into the tap.

Saints, maybe this job ain't all bad if it's getting us on the same page.

A crystalline crash sounds from the other side of the bar. Next to me, a fey jumps up to their feet so fast that their legs shift into something goat-like. Down the line, two folks start laughing louder than howling dogs.

"Are you kidding me?" O'Taglio mutters. We all turn to look, and there's Rastova with a bottle shattered between their shoes and a blank sort of look on their face. "It's coming out of your pay."

Their eyes narrow. "It was an accident." Blue-green smoke trickles from Rastova's nostrils. The color glows and shines off of them. I tense, but O'Taglio ain't afraid.

"Get another bottle from the cellar then take it up with Hien," she says. The smoke rushes more, like Rastova's just building pressure in there. "*Now.*"

They huff, jump over the bar exit in a smear of smoke, and push at the wall . . . a section of it swings sideways so they can walk into a little downward stairwell. Rastova shuts it behind them so loud the bottles jump. Those two folks are still howling laughing.

"What a plum," Fionne says dryly.

O'Taglio drops a water in front of her. "Howdee," she agrees, and gets to pouring mine too. "That doesn't scare you two, does it?" She looks at Fionne when she asks it. I want to open my mouth, to say I'm not that sort of fey, but that folk with the bark-face—Finch, I think—is staring at me just the same as when I barked at Robin.

Fionne chews at her cheek and skates her eyes to me, like she ain't sure what to say. "If you're not scared, I'm not scared," she decides. I'm not sure if she's saying it to me or O'Taglio, but her voice is too light and pretty for anyone to argue with much. Still, she leans a bit closer to me, like she knows the answer should've been "Yes." O'Taglio and Finch both nod a bit for their own reasons, going on their ways.

That same trumpet player from last night is blaring loud, and Cab's keeping up, and people are laughing and dancing and the kitchen doors are swinging open. I see Robin zipping through the crowd with a rag to clean a now-empty table—their shadow pulls out wrong behind them, like it's melting or dancing or flailing like a dying thing.

"And water number two," O'Taglio says, putting mine down. She wipes her hands and checks her watch. "I need to sign off for the delivery," she says to Finch, then heads for the exit of the horseshoe bar.

We haven't interviewed her yet! And I want her to know that she doesn't have to be scared of me. "Want me to help?" I ask her as she slips toward the back exit.

She pauses for a second, looks me over, but flinches when

someone in the crowd shouts out a cloud of rainbow light. "Give it ten minutes, and if Rastova ain't back, go get them," she says, softer than the roughness from before. "That'll help plenty."

Alright. She heads off, and I feel like I'm still trying to prove myself to everyone. I'll be perfect soon, I know.

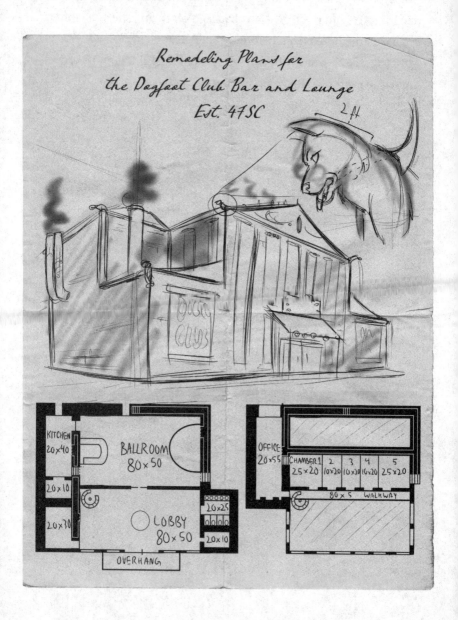

GRISTLE SENAN MAXIM JUNIOR IN
"SOMETHING IN THE WALLS"

Gristle Senan Maxim Junior hadn't been sure how the night was going to go, but he certainly didn't expect a sinister shadow living in the walls. This was getting out of hand, and fast.

"Alright," he began to say, but Hien wasn't listening. Harsh ripples of frustration swirled about the room—a distinct breeze that hadn't been there before tugged at Gristle's pant cuffs. Hien pocketed a flip-lighter off their desk, skimmed the bookshelf, and produced a folded sheet of paper. They tossed it like a playing card cutting through the air. Gristle scrambled to catch it. When he unfolded the dry paper, he saw a very old blueprint that clearly hadn't been looked at in some time. It included all the servant halls.

Hien wanted them to investigate.

"I don't think—" Gristle started again, but he was cut off by further creaking of the hinges. Over the top of the blueprint, he saw Hien stride through the servants' door with the dog at their heels and a pistol suddenly glinting in their hand.

"Saints," Gristle hissed, following after them. He stepped away from the glow of the banker's light behind him, ducking his head to slip into the narrow wooden hallway. A spear of path dove off beside them, out behind the chambers of bedrooms, but Gristle could hardly see three steps down it. To his other side, a bit more dust-dimmed light bled up from the floor, sparkling between hastily-hammered boards that didn't match the rest. The blueprint showed that there had once been a stairwell there, further confirmed by some poorly patched studs in the walls.

That only made Gristle even more unsure: this map was clearly out of date. Who knew what was waiting for them in here?

"This is more serious than we thought," Gristle tried to explain. "You and I both seem to agree that whoever was trying to get in your office isn't a friend—we have no promise that they've ever left these hallways."

Wind still whispered to blow dust into Gristle's eyes. *And they have no promise that I won't tell their brain to shut them into a permanent nightmare of every regret they've ever experienced.* The distant banker's lamp shone across one side of Hien's body; the rest was eaten by the impenetrable shadows. *I won't be told how to run my own due process by someone who still thinks law and order can save him.*

Was it worse to die, or to be wrapped up into Hien's horrors? He'd signed up to investigate, to do his job, not to be an accomplice.

Gristle hadn't even said anything out loud, but he didn't need to when Hien was *still* in his head. They snorted and stepped to him, smiling like a snarl. *Glower all you like, but you were only hired to investigate, not to be judge or jury.* In the light, they were again the woman from the office, with her dimpled chin and frightened eyes that *still* made Gristle's heart jolt. *I'm awfully frightened, Mister Maxim. Won't you help a girl?*

He despised the stutter in his chest, the ache in his hands to help. "You're the devil," he muttered.

The devil is in awe of me, Hien said simply, more businesslike than threatening. And yet the wind was rising enough to make Gristle's tie tug and fight against its pin, and the dog was nudging at Hien's hand. They were getting worked up. Gristle knew what that could become. The gun glinted, barrel wagging in his direction. *I won't be undermined in my own club, not by you or any rodent in the walls.*

For a moment, Gristle swore Hien looked exactly like Senan and Shona Maxim. One dead because he was a foolish child, one still struggling to clean that up. Gristle knew what he was supposed to do.

Whatever worry it caused, he'd rather give that to his aunt than a nephew arrested for accompanying a mad fey murderer . . . or a casket.

Gristle's voice was quiet. "You have everything you need from me," he said beneath the sneering wind. He turned for the door. "I should be getting along."

A warning rattle rumbled through the tiny room, kicking up an acrid smell. Hien side-stepped ahead of him, blocking the exit. *What was that?* Hien asked. There was something distinctly snakelike about their voice. The dog whined, bouncing its colossal front paws off the wood in preparation to rear. *Speak up, dickie.*

The wind blustered against his pants and his jacket and up under his hat. The weak office light burned around Hien in an unholy nimbus. "My work is done here," Gristle said, louder now but still middle-line, reasonable, something his aunt would say too. He tapped his hat brim, mostly to set the shadows firmer over his eyes. "Good evening, Mx Hien."

The second you have a chance to actually *help a fey instead of just peddling politics, you turn tail?* Hien snarled. The smell was getting louder, a prickly burn, like being strangled by that old dress Maxim had worn so long ago that never lost the smell of three hundred charred bodies until he threw it away. Was Hien forcing his worst memories to the front? *You really are a coward.*

Gristle couldn't catch the thought before it speared out between his teeth, so sharp he swore Hien's eyes lit up white in response. "Screw you."

There it is, Hien said. Their voice was both snarl and grin. Wind buffeted into Gristle's face, slashing away the heat racing into his cheeks and the rage trying to build. *So he can say more than scripted niceties.*

Gristle's burns were still aching beneath their bandages. The smell was so thick he nearly gagged.

You can leave right now, Hien said, stepping closer. They were his height now, with shoulders to match his own, in some flowing robe-dress that struck Gristle as deeply "Old World" if not for the modern addition of skin-close trousers beneath. Gristle held his ground, simmering. *But the consequences still stand, so you'd better be sure you're paying your own penance instead of someone else's.*

The only reason he was even *there* was to cover up Hawthorne's faults, because his aunt wanted him to, because they needed money Ashley wouldn't give, because Hàzell blew up the fayre, because his daddy encouraged her. Everything in Gristle's life was planned as a patch-up to someone else's failure! And now he was here, with the burning smell so fierce he feared insanity, knowing he oughta run. He *should* run. He'd been taught not to tangle with sorts like this, that they were only dangerous, that his daddy was a fool and so there was no room for him to be one too.

Gristle opened his mouth, unsure what he would even say.

Instead, another scream sheared through the fey wind

blustering in the tiny room. Gristle flinched. The dog barked under its breath. Even Hien startled out a stronger rush that nearly swept Gristle's hat off.

"What—" Gristle began, but a voice followed from somewhere close.

"Help! Somebody help!" More shouting, hurried talking, quick consolations. The dog leapt up to put its paws on Hien's shoulders, cutting the wind to sudden silence. The burning smell still lay thick as ash.

Gristle turned, back toward the spears of solar-flare-like light rearing through those hasty boards. The voice echoed from down beneath. "SPIRITS—SOMEONE HELP!"

Despite everything, Gristle moved without thinking, a gut instinct. He leapt sideways and slammed his foot down into the boards, raising a puff of dust. They creaked. He was sweating already, soaking through his brand-new suit, creasing his perfectly-polished shoes.

He snapped his foot down. Someone needed help, and he wanted to help, and that was his own impulse, right? Had his daddy thought the same when Hàzell tricked him? Did she intend to? How could anyone know what they actually wanted?

With one final slam into the creaking boards, they all splintered at once. Gristle dropped through in a descent neither heroic nor graceful; he smacked down into the landing of a flight of stairs, almost managed to stop himself there, but instead went sliding down with the debris in a blundering of bruises and aches into queasy half-light that smelled like wine casks and straw and malt, but mostly like charred bodies.

Gristle collided with the packed-dirt ground of a wine cellar lit by one hanging bulb. The air rang. His whole body hummed, not pain so much as shock. When he opened his barely-focused eyes, he was almost face-to-face with the grinning teeth of a charred, lipless corpse. One eye was melted into white-gray sludge, the other glassy with a snake-thin pupil.

Gristle gasped out a curse and scrambled back, his camera bag flailing beside him and wrenched, aching limbs quickly ignored. The body was seared right at the chest, burned with a force so hard the ribs had snapped in on a black-crisped lump he was sure had once been a heart and the collapsed tubes of the corpse's airway and throat.

"M-M-Mister Maxim?"

Only then did Gristle look up and see some barely-named barkeep over the body, his eyes wide and skin drenched with cold sweat. His nameplate said Wahua. Gristle's eyes snapped about the room for more evidence: a bottle smashed on the floor beside a half-fallen, burnt shelf; tipped wine casks, from a struggle; the brick wall the victim had been scorched against, stained with a negative image.

And there was another person, pressed back into the corner with hands over mouth.

Hawthorne locked mismatched eyes with her brother, her entire body frozen as still as a picture, nails glowing with barely fought pressure.

No. Saints *no*.

"They were just sent to get a bottle," Wahua breathed, eyes flickering through fey colors fast enough to make Gristle feel even more ill. "They were taking their time—O'Taglio had to sign off on a delivery and Finch went to check the kitchen and it was just me up there and your sister said she'd check—" Gristle's heart threatened to tear out of his body. Tears were flooding down Wahua's face, catching the hazy light. "I couldn't have watched the cellar door if anyone came in or out—"

Hawthorne whispered something behind her hands. A spark let loose between her fingers before she dared to speak louder. "W-we came down together," she squeaked.

An alibi. Thank the saints and the spirits and anything else. But that didn't explain the dead body ahead of them.

Gristle heard footsteps up the stairs—not Hien's, but the clomping of a crowd coming in to investigate the screaming.

That dockyard's mad fey was in the building, this claustrophobically small cellar was a crime scene, and again the Maxims were at the center of it all.

```
                              777 Call
                          Case #:____
                           Time:__:__
                    Attendant: M. O. Gui
```

777 Call Transcript

Caller: Hello?

Operator: Hello. You've reached emergency services. Are you in need of assistance?

C: Yes, alright, I'm calling from the front desk of the Dogfoot Club at 216 Aziza.

O: Please slow down.

C: Someone's hurt, a kid I work with. There was a crowd. I couldn't get close. My name is Fifthchild O'Taglio.

O: Are you in need of medical assistance?

C: Send everything!

O: Please tell everyone to be cooperative and to keep their hands in view. Ensure that no one leaves the scene.

Additional voice: Wait, wait—the owner says that they don't consent to police on the premises. Just send medical!

C: Are you kidding me, Hien?!

Caller line goes dead

HAWTHORNE STREGONI IN "THE FEY BLUES"

I don't know what to do! We called for help and now everything's all moving too quick—even Gristle is looking shaky, staring through the lobby at the half-drunk crowd trying to get to the doors. O'Taglio's got them locked, because I know she thinks just listening to the cops is best, and I want to think it too, but do I?

Everyone's swirled out of the barroom into the lobby. We're all shouting and shoving, the crowd moving in waves. Gristle brought some other person that I can't even see through a headache whenever I try. They've ducked back behind the main desk with their huge familiar who keeps jumping up onto them. We're just in front of it, on the edge of the crowd.

"Folks!" Gristle shouts, hands over his mouth like that'll do shit. His dandy new suit is scuffed from his fall, his hat crooked and camera bag strap all twisted even if he don't act hurt. The smell of Rastova crisped up is still swimming in the air. "Folks, I need—"

We're shoved backward into the desk by everyone whirling. Fionne pushes back next to me, gray and panicked. She barely manages to hold onto her pen and notebook, and can't seem to figure out what to do with them when her dress doesn't have pockets. "H—" she starts to say. Someone stumbles into me and almost takes both of us down so I crack my fist against their arm, no flames but just enough to get them away. I can feel the pyre in my stomach burning louder but I'M IN CONTROL!

"Hawthorne," Gristle chokes out, staring up and over the crowd still pushing for the doors. They seem forever away across the mess. "When the police come, you're running."

What?! Since when is he so keen to lie? "Gristle, you know I didn't—"

"I *know*," he says. More screaming. O'Taglio shouts for everyone to stay calm and take a seat but that's no use, jack. A thousand auras and panics rip through the room. Fionne clutches onto my arm. "But if either of us gets caught near this..."

They'll tell Auntie Shona. The shame is its own sound and feeling.

"Sh-she didn't do it," Fionne says for me, but her voice is shaking. She points the notebook at him: it's pastel purple with flowers on it. So out of place here. "That barkeep can vouch."

I bare my teeth, just to make a scene, to snarl and growl like a fey. "Gristle, you know—"

"You could have," he says back, just as angry, his eyes too hard. His hat's been pushed back in the mess. I never see this much of his face, or this much emotion from him. Now here's all the rage I'm due. "Notes from your girlfriend won't mean jack besides getting her corroborated, just like last time."

Fionne's hand stiffens on my arm. Just like her mama and baba, getting all tied up with mine, barely clawing back their good names. I can only think of how Ify looked at me just this morning, like he knew what I could be.

"This is the kind of shit that grants stress-test orders for anyone who looks at the cops sideways," Gristle goes on. "You and I both know you'll light that room up after the first shock. We need a *plan*."

He's right. It doesn't matter what I've done, it only matters what I could do. I can't answer him while terrified flames leap up my throat. There's another shove at the doors. Are folks trying to get out 'cause they want away from the murderer, or because they wanna be gone before the cops come in?

"Hawthorne," Fionne squeaks beside me, and nothing else to say if she agrees with Gristle, if she wants to escape with me, if she wants me to just put my hands out. I put my palm on hers over my arm, but what else is there to say? "I don't want any trouble."

I should have let her go when I had the chance.

"If we could all please—" Robin calls. Through the ocean of horns and heads and shouting, I see them jump sideways on top of the coat-check desk when someone with vines of hair growing longer leaps to get cover behind. "If we could all please listen, that'd—"

Then come the sirens. Over the top of the crowd, the windows into the street flash with red. There's a collective inhale, a rumble of aura waves rippling out, of growing scales and horns and tails, of tiny flashes of flowers in hands or frost from breath to desperately cool the system enough to survive.

Is that feeding fey madness, or just good sense? I wish I could make a tiny flame without feeling guilty for how I'm ruining myself.

"Get behind the desk, Fionne," I whisper. Her claw-stiff hands fall off my arm.

The front doors bust open with the smell of iron ripping through the crowd like the plague, sending waves through it when the people in front of the door collapse back into the fray. In the split second where every fey in the joint cringes with their head tipsy, Gristle grits his teeth and tries to shoulder forward.

"Officers, I'm here with Maxim & Maxim—"

Above the crowd, a gun barrel goes up.

One silver shot rips into the ceiling, sending the chandelier swinging to glint diamonds across everyone.

"All fey against the wall NOW!" some officer booms.

The room roars up, folks screaming and trying to run, auras and voices and thoughts tangling together, Gristle stumbling back toward me. Everyone's running back the other way, trying to get into the barroom, even up the stairs, just to get away from the cops tearing through the crowd and forcing people into the walls. They're dressed like old knights, wearing iron armor. I throw my arms out ahead of the desk blocking Fionne, even if I'm shaking like a dog and covered in sweat from holding every muscle as tight as it will go. I *won't* light up. I can keep it together. The lobby is clearing fast, everyone running or pulled away.

And that's when I lock eyes with Robin across the room while everyone's zipping like rats. I see their little hands shaking a mile a minute trying to calm down, their freckles blinking and rearranging into constellations, their shadow smearing across the wall and jolting strange.

"No cuffs, off'cer," Robin tries to say from the top of the coat-check desk. The cops have cleared a way up to them, everyone else shoved into the corners and told to stay real calm while the fey clutch their rattling hands and go dead-eyed. Why do they look so much like Gristle? "I do not like the sm—"

"Hands out, kid," one of the cops says. Robin's eyes flash different colors. The lobby's nearly empty now besides held-aside suspects, and us too scared to flee. "Just make it easy for us and we'll hand you to your parents."

"No cuffs, off'cer—"

"Come on, kid, give us a hand—"

"No c—"

"I need backup for this damn *sprite!*"

Robin's eyes strobe white, just their pupils in the middle. All I can do is stare across the open floor while I know what's coming. That kid already burns so bright, already has a mind all fey, and now they've been pushed to the edge like a stress-test without the padded room.

"Fionne," I breathe over my shoulder, without looking away from them. I hope she understands. The least I can do is get her out of here. "Keep your head down, baby."

The cop's hand catches their little wrist; Robin's arm turns jet-black. Not dark-skinned, or burned, but like someone's cut away the world in the shape of their arm, and then their entire body is just a shadow, except for two glowing red eyes.

The voice is a vibration: *Foolish.*

The word rumbles up through the walls in bubbling lines of smoke, cracks plaster from the ceiling. The lights on the chandelier spark down on the last cluster of people, who cover their heads and sprint for the barroom, plunging us into shadows burned red from siren lights through the windows. I wait for the shock of energy like an overbright star. Just like last time, when Mum ended everything before it could begin.

The end doesn't come so quick as before. Instead, Robin's grinning mouth opens on a flurry of teeth that go all the way down their throat, and blasts out a shockwave of sound.

"DON'T TOUCH ME!"

It storms out like a rock-solid wall. The police skid back on their heavy boots. Gristle and I slam into the desk. I grit my teeth and look up in time to see Robin's head twist and reel on a too-long neck like a snake. Their shadow jigs across the marble walls while the officer with the cuffs explodes in a cloud of scarlet butterflies. They flap up only four beats before they turn to blood and shower down.

One dead. How many more?

It's one burst of power after the next, another impulse and another impulse and another entertained. The other officers run for Robin with their batons ready. Robin's hair turns to snakes then twigs then hands then back to hair but it's bright yellow now. Their legs shift into goat legs that tear out from their slacks. Robin's small, cat-clawed hand reaches up and squeezes—the semicircle of rushing officers drop to their knees clutching their chests. The batons fall harmlessly to the ground, where moss grows to cover them.

"The kid's mad!" an officer shouts. The fey already know; the ones on the balcony have herded each other into the rooms up there, and the ones that were corralled into the corners are clawing for the front door while the cops just let them go. "Everyone out!"

We're too far away from the bar entrance or the stairs or the front door. Gristle gives a stunned moan because we know there's no way to outrun this, like last time. We can only watch it get worse.

Robin twists, grows three times their size, and then shrinks down to nothing I can see, like a star.

The fayre massacre was so fast. I remember my hand on the carousel's brass ring, and then?

Click.

Bang.

Here it is: the end of the world.

Robin's replaced by a seed of fire. It busts open like the beginning of everything. Against that, Gristle leaps in front of me. I see only his black silhouette against a blast of green-blue fire scorching out from where that kid went total bust-up like my mum. But this feels worse than that simple trigger. This is wild. This is fey madness. This is the old world myth that leads travelers to their death.

This is what happens to that selfish fey rattle when you feed it. Some part screams to make them pay.

And then you do.

And then you're the bad guy.

Puck's Port Herald

51SC, 1 Winter Moon, 7 Suns

"WE WILL NOT LIVE IN FEAR"
CHIEF ASHLEY PROMISES AN END TO "THE FEY PROBLEM"

Since the self-implosion of Hàzell Stregoni that killed over 300 Summer Fayre attendees, including Senan Maxim (of Maxim & Maxim, Private Detectives) and 4 children from the Tanner family, the city has been held in anxious suspense to see what will be done about the "Fey Problem." While Puck's Port has experienced "mad" fey before, and even similar escalations of power resulting in self-implosion, there has never been one of this physical magnitude, or resulting in deaths on this scale. The University of Stoutshire claims that without proper infrastructure to understand the Fey Condition and supports for an "increasingly desperate people who cannot keep up with a growing country," there will very likely be more of these large-scale attacks.

Chief of Police Dermott Ashley III claims he will stop this fey problem in its tracks. "We don't need another one of these radicals to show us who the danger is," he said at a press conference held yesterday on the steps of the 1st Precinct. "300 are dead, parents are without children, and this is all because of one careless fey who thought herself too proud for our Daleish laws."

Stregoni was known to be a fey, but since mandatory stress-testing was banned at the ports and borders in 41SC, she was able to immigrate from Verdosso without unveiling the full extent of her symptoms. Those closest to her have suggested that her condition worsened over time, leading to increasingly erratic and inflammatory behavior as well as paranoia. Ashley suggests that stronger border protocols, increased police funding, and tighter fines for public use of feyism will weed out these "mad" fey before they can endanger themselves and others.

Ashley, a presidential candidate, has seen his popularity in the polls rise by almost 40 percent since speaking out in response to the Fayre Massacre. "Maybe this is the only way to solve this problem head-on," he said to his 3,000 spectators. "If elected, I will ensure the police budget is increased to adequately train and equip officers to deal with the fey threat, and I will increase funding for prisons, testing facilities, and madhouses. Will we wait for another fey to slip the net? To callously let their own feelings destroy us? For more threats to invade our way of life? Enough is enough. We will not live in fear."

However, family friends have stepped forward to ask for further investigation into the actions of Hàzell Stregoni. "It's easy to call her mad, and to call Senan Maxim a criminal. What's harder is to listen," reads a collective statement brought to the *Herald* offices by printer Táyò Táyò, one of seven radical activists now being investigated for possible involvement. This includes Táyò's wife, journalist Victory Eze; a switchboarder with alleged ties to the Verdossi mob; and others. "Both of them were shaking this city up. It's awfully convenient to discredit all of their work." Indeed, Stregoni and Maxim made a stir in the western dockyard, organizing for fey liberation, immigration, education, workers' rights, and more.

"Fey are often incredibly charismatic, and not always in a bad way," says Doctor Sonder Secondchild of the University of Stoutshire's Department of Fey Studies. "They're quick to act, and bring great passion or great logic. But as we've seen over the past several suns, this can easily be corrupted by their own imbalances. Still, there's a reasonable person trapped in there by all those negative thoughts. With the help of psychology and medical intervention, we can bring that person out and teach them how to build a life in Dale." **(More from Ashley on page 7.)**

Gristle Senan Maxim Junior had known things were wrong since he'd met Hien that morning. Seeing some kid going full implosion was the horrific shining star on top of it all. It shouldn't have happened. There was no rhyme or reason or logical pathway. Because sometimes (most times), horrible things happened despite your planning. Because sometimes (*most times*), life wasn't a movie full of daring heroics and step-by-step patterns.

He'd tried to live a perfect life, and now this punishment, all the same.

The fayre had been ruined in a single second, like the click of a lighter. But that wasn't what happened here tonight at the Dog. That little fey kid was death delayed and extended so you could get right up close and see how rotten everything was. Gristle had watched the kid twist and fight against themself, sending plaster spattering from the ceiling and cracks up the walls that sprouted flowers and ivy. Then the kid had crushed down to a grain of salt.

Something bad is going to happen, a voice in Gristle's head said.

It was so clear he thought it might be Hien's again, but it came in his own timbre, or something like it. A younger, smaller, more sure part of him knew what to do, as it had known that day on the carousel. Was Hien pulling memories out of him? *Cover them.*

While the last patrons scrambled out, and the cops tried to turn tail in slow motion, Gristle saw every hard edge and dust mote and bit of reality with blazing, sickening clarity. And yet still he leapt forward in front of his sister with arms extended, out of loyalty, or love. He didn't know the difference.

Wasn't that sad?

BOOM!

The kid self-destructed. Gray flames sprouted like a flower from where they'd been. Gristle didn't move. If the world was upside-down, maybe he had to be, too.

A rush of static ripped through the air, with a *crack* like lightning. A circle of squiggling white carved itself in a great faerie ring around Gristle and Hawthorne and the desk. Static blared over their heads—Gristle looked up to see white energy knitting itself together only a few feet above him. His jaw dropped; his knees loosed like bad hinges. What the hell was this? He stared as the threads of it crackled into a dome around them, achingly slowly. But past it, the fire was inching forward even slower. Time was frozen for a second. He was frozen too, able only to watch as the police officers were swept into the gray flames. He heard their screams echoing, smelled the iron growing red-hot against their skin to boil them. Three hundred dead before from just a simple self-implosion. How many would this kill? The whole city? The world, like a wolf swallowing it down?

This was the life he lived, horrible and terrifying and painful. They could pretend things were dandy in their flashy city, but outside the windows, the band doesn't play. And then the energy dome closed around the desk, protecting him and his sister, and behind them Fionne and Hien.

Hien. They had to be the one doing this. Feyism was keeping him safe.

Gristle saw the police drowning in flames, felt every scream and saw every thrash. His own burns ached like cavities. No matter how he tried to set his hat, his whole body hurt from that tumble down to the cellar. The flames crawled forward and Gristle felt them. Felt his feet on the ground. Felt his thoughts coming together like a gramophone reel spinning.

This city is broken, his daddy always said, wreathed in garlands of cigar smoke, or the mist under the raised tracks or clawing in off the ocean. *The fearful people wade into the filth of Puck's Port and make themselves broken too and hope to win someone else's game. Few do. Mostly, they hurt. But oh, oh, don't cry, Maxim. The most wonderful people, the most brilliant, are the ones hurting. Because they're changing, and adapting, and one day when the world ain't ready for them yet, it'll be them who's ready first. And then this rotten city will flip right over onto its back so the underbelly can breathe. Because every bough breaks, jack. Every story has its end.*

"First, it's gonna hurt," his delinquent daddy used to say, while folding pamphlets at the dinner table, face gray and nervous, always looking over his shoulder. But then he'd smile and ruffle Maxim's hair. "Then we're gonna win, Maxim. Remember that."

The pain before the victory, or the pain in the victory. Gristle felt it singing through him, horrible history wailing behind and ahead. And yet there was something exquisite about living in a body alight. Every impulse was brighter, every sensation fresh and frighteningly fierce. He wished he could run or jump or scream or cry because it would feel better than it ever had in this strange moment beyond the usual pale.

Gristle Senan Maxim Junior watched the fire hit the side of the veil-thin, fey-made dome that had closed them in, then crash back like beautiful seafoam. Beyond it, the world was in ruins. But inside, he felt so damn free. Someone had kicked over the picture show projector. Someone had torn the script.

Gristle let the fantastic hurt consume him for one last moment, let himself *be* for a few more seconds, and then collapsed to the lobby floor.

OBITUARIES (Cont.)

Tanner "Owen" Secondchild, 13. May the spirits guide them home.

Tanner "Leo" Fourthchild, 10. May the spirits guide them home.

Tanner "Tag" Thirdchild, 10. May the spirits guide them home.

Tanner Fifthchild, 5. May the spirits guide them home.

HAWTHORNE STREGONI IS "HOME FREE"

I don't know what the hell that was. One second Gristle's in front of me, and then there's this dome around us, all silvery and lightning-y and *fey-made*. I feel like I recognize it, something from a dream. But then Gristle collapses into a pile with his face against the carpet and his hat spilled off. Robin's fire fades out. The dome snaps away in a crack of thunder. The lobby smells like boiled iron.

Everything's dark aside from the slow strobe of red siren light leaking through. The silence rings. I don't wanna know how many people are dead. I can't be in the eye of the storm again.

But still, I slowly look out from behind my arms, blinking in the dust. The windows are shattered, busted out so hard the wall around them is in cracks, with vines and flowers growing from them. The floor's covered in glittering crystals catching the strobe, all of them placed in precise whorls like the veins of leaves or frosty fractals of ice. They twist around the feet of the folks who didn't make it out: the cops are all still here, stuck standing gray and cold. They've been turned to statues. Three Dogfoot patrons blink and fumble their hands over themselves, checking they still got all their limbs and no extras.

There's no harm done. Even the stone police, I see them shaking like baby birds out of eggs. Rock puffs off and falls to the ground as one busts a boiled-red arm out.

Alive.

So it's just that puddle of blood-turned-to-rubies near the coat check, where the officer tried to grab Robin. The desk is cracked straight down the middle and bowed inward. Atop it, only a thicket of branches left to say a life was ever there. It throws a horrifically still shadow against the wall.

The desk looks like an altar. Robin's dead. Self-destructed. Mad. And gone.

My throat lurches, the first bit of feeling coming back. *The power got away from you, kid. This place was breaking down your control bit by bit with every rush of chemicals that made you feel too damn high on being alive. Made you think anything was possible.*

It is.

That's the terrifying part.

Something's tugging at my ankle. I look down to see that big black dog's caught hold of my pant leg with careful teeth. It turns its head back, to where the blurry person's moved aside one of the long, ornamental curtains draping down the marble wall; behind, there's a little servants' door. Did that blurry person make the protection dome? I hear a big chunk of rock hit the ground as the police start busting their way out. Through the shattered windows and the torn-out doors, more cops are crowding in the street and getting ready to come in with riot shields.

Fionne pokes her head up over the desk with her face stiff and eyes wet. She takes one look through the shattered windows at the riot cops gathering and darts for the servants' door. I lean after her, but Gristle's still collapsed behind me, passed out. The blurry person strides toward us.

All I can force out is a strangled "*What?*" but they don't stop. The dog's already stepped over to Gristle. It lays its head and front paws on his chest as the blurry person kneels down. They hurt to look at too long.

One hand rises over Gristle's head. Cloudy shadows drip off their fingers in slow, wispy strands. They fall to cradle Gristle's temples and sink in there.

My stomach churns. I want to shove them so they stop touching my lug brother with their messed-up magic after we've been shown just what happens when you try that. But then Gristle's eyes snap open. He's alright.

Behind me, I hear Fionne's breath coming in whistles. For the first time in a while, I'm torn between her and my brother.

It hurts some to leave Gristle as I turn back for Fionne, to rush for the servants' door so fast I nearly trip and have to shove both hands into the jamb on either side. My dark shadow cuts through the red light coming in behind me, folding over her collapsed against the wooden wall opposite, blinking off at nothing with her breath shuddering in and out, the notebook and pen shaking against her chest. Her eyes are so damn wide behind her crooked glasses, with wet tracks down both cheeks.

I don't think I've ever seen Fionne cry. It's another barb through my skull.

"Feenee," I breathe. I step through the doorway. Her head snaps up to me, hands flexing around the notebook like a pretty little shield. I stop where I am. "That kid—Robin—they . . ." They what? Does it matter that I'm not like that when we both watched *a kid die and take another person down with them*?

What do I even say to make that better? Is there anything?

Fionne's voice comes out stilted, like a scratched-up record. "I came here to dance," she mutters. "Didn't think we'd get a party like that." It's words I expect from her, but the tone is all wrong, while her voice splutters and squeaks. "H, I . . . Saints, I never . . . how the hell did we *get here*?"

I warned her, didn't I? But how can you warn anyone about this?

"We're gonna get home," I say.

"We're still surrounded," she breathes. She presses one hand to the dusty floor, enough to push herself up the wall and stand. "If you . . . if they *see* you, won't they try . . . ?"

Hello stress-test, goodbye campaign, goodbye school, goodbye getting better and helping other folks do it too. Robin could have been one of them. How many people could I be letting down tonight?

I *won't*. No more.

"We're getting out of here," I tell her, as serious as I can. "On my name, I wish you didn't have to get tied up in this."

"I know that," she says. Her lips stutter. She closes her eyes, trying to breathe. "I never thought," she says. End of sentence.

Shadows bleed into the tiny hallway. Gristle steps in, and that blurry person. Fionne's eyes dart to them.

I step back toward her, turning to face the doorway and keep a barrier between her and them. Gristle trudges in with his hat back on at its jaunty angle. He's blinking hard like he just got kicked in the head, wincing as he walks with the dog leaning into his legs. The blurry person closes the servants' door and packs us all in like little canned fish.

The pitch-black gives me a few seconds. Slow. No panic. "What's the plan?" I ask in the dark.

Gristle's voice is low as always, but there's something that shivers on the edges, threatening to twist it higher like a tuning peg. "I think those suspicious activities and our mad fey murderer might be connected," he says. "It all comes full circle, Mx Hien."

I clue in. I have enough magazine articles slapped on my walls.

"That's why you ain't letting us look at you proper," I say. One bell ago, I think Fionne would have been squealing about this, but I feel her shift further behind me. "Because you can't mess with all our minds at the same time."

I could, but you're hardly worth the strain. No free peep show, Phong Hien says in my head. I can *feel* the wink, and that rush of too-precise power. Slick and mobile. I want far away from it, and soon. *Your girlfriend's adrenaline levels are off. I can help her with that.*

"No way," I snarl, but I can feel them look to Fionne, and some question slithering past me in the dark.

"I'm alright, thank you," she says from behind, real polite even if it's stiff.

There's a heavy silence, a metallic shuffle, and a sudden *click*. A lighter burns to life in Hien's blurry hand, bright enough to make me flinch. It's just enough to see Gristle wincing.

"M-Mx Hien wants me to say that the child who went mad was triggered by the crowd and the iron," Gristle forces out. In the lighter glow, his face is a mess of pinched, flickering shadows. He doesn't look good, or much like himself. "They also say that . . ." He pauses, coughs, and presses a knuckle into his temple. "That an officer of the law consents to violence, but a child does not. Mx Hien would like us to consider this when deciding our sympathies."

"What the hell," I mutter. I'm seeing that moral deficiency on full display. Fionne shifts closer to me. "I know you were 'mentoring' them. *You* got their brain all hopped up!"

A warning sound shifts around the tiny room, something between a snake rattle and a growl. Gristle snaps his arm out ahead of Hien, as if that would do anything. The dog sits on their feet like an attack hound at the ready.

"H-Hien says..." Gristle spits out, with the lighter glow splitting around him, "that they can't expect us to understand proper fey training."

"Can we save the pissing contest for once we're out of here?" Fionne mutters.

"Seriously—" I start to say, but an image gets shoved into my head, of long pavilion hallways and soaring ceilings, big lecture halls like at the University of Stoutshire and quiet study rooms. A fey teacher with antler horns and black-pearl eyes, looking so old you think they should have been dead seven septennials ago. Fey children throwing orbs of molten metal between them, sprouting horns, screaming colors into the overcast sky.

Those images ain't the important part, really. It's the feeling of Hien clicking their tongue at me, and assuring me this was no grueling laundry shift or learning to steel your skin. *What did "science" ever know about fey? The new world has built itself without us. You cannot tear it down playing by their rules.*

Mum used to say the same shit.

My temper wants to flare, and I won't let it. I want to survive *here*. Doesn't matter how many fey have been killed by mortals—Mum leveled that scale and more, didn't she? And now there's some mad fey in the building, so we're not exactly looking good in the public eye.

"If you hate science so much, then go back to the old world," I say. "I came here for something better, and I'll get it."

Will you now? their voice croons.

Watch me.

Outside the servants' door, there's a clunk and shuffle as the cops go past, probably kicking the rubble over. The iron stench weasels in. "I can't get caught hiding like I'm guilty," Fionne squeaks. "It took cycles for my parents to get their good name back after..."

After Mum turned everyone around her into suspects. "I'm *not* risking my future on this."

"Someone must have seen you with us," Gristle says, voice thin, but still so damn logical. "Even if we got you out of here, they'd be at your door sooner or later asking what you know about Rastova... and us."

Her hands fall off my arm. She steps for the door, like she might actually throw it open. "I'm a *typesetter*. I want to work at a silly fashion rag that no one over the age of eighteen actually takes seriously, not be a suspect in a *murder investigation*," she says, snapping the toe of her shoe into the floor. Hien hums, like a warning to quiet down. "Can we *please* think of a way to get out of this without looking like the bad guys?"

That's all I've wanted. And, maybe, I've got a chance to prove it now.

"What if we get evidence about the mad fey," I say, less a question and more a command. Fionne's posture relaxes ever so slightly. "Whoever cooked Rastova can't have gotten out, right? If we're surrounded?"

"They could have slipped out before," Gristle says, but he tilts his head like he's really thinking it over. His copper-brown eyes shine with the lighter. I always thought they were a bit more green, but I'm not convinced enough to say anything. "Could still be some evidence worth finding. We just need enough to get the heat pointed somewhere else."

Exactly.

"Great," Fionne says, like a gasp.

Hien's silent. Good.

Gristle swallows and pulls a sheet of paper from his pocket, spreading it between us to show that it's a map. "This is what we can work with," he says, tracing his still-shaking finger down the lines. "There used to be a second staircase off the cellar, up to the second floor. I smashed the floor out, so if we can get up through it, we can get most anywhere in the club: upstairs, downstairs, behind the stage."

The stage. Why do I feel like I've been thinking about it?

"Th-this man we talked to, Cab," Fionne offers, flipping the notebook open past all sorts of sketches and pasted-in bits until she finds our Dogfoot notes. "He said something about the stage, that it was 'off-beat', but he couldn't explain it. It seemed odd."

Gristle nods. "Odd's good. Let's start there," he says. "Do you know about anything happening with the stage, Hien?"

A pause. Hien's blurry shadow shifts, like someone popping an arrogant hip. Gristle narrows his eyes.

"Asshole," he mutters, which is the most pointed I've ever heard him. "Stay here if you want. Fionne too."

She takes a second, but the clattering from the lobby makes her tense. "I'm on board this sinking showboat," she says, with lighter light flickering over her smeared makeup. Hien turns as Gristle does, so I guess they're coming too.

Hien and Gristle head off down the hallway first with the dog clomping behind, Fionne and I following, but we don't get far before our way is blocked by a wall of wooden boards that stream glistening, dusty light through the gaps. Gristle sidles over, I come up beside him, and we peer through.

Ahead, it's a straight shot down into the dark cellar. It seems like the cops have already taken all the photos they need to, but to the right, the service door's wide open on the dance hall crawling with officers still questioning the Dogfoot's fey workers. How the hell do we get past that?

I don't like Gristle's answer. "Hien," he whispers. He looks up above the stairs, toward the bashed-out gap leading to the dark second story. There's sweat crawling down from his hair. "Any chance you could make us invisible while we climb in?"

I let a slow grumble rustle through my throat. A bit of wind slides past me, some sentence I can't hear.

"I can't 'do it myself,'" Gristle says, snapping his head back with the light falling across his face in stripes. His voice really is sharper. "That wasn't exactly in the job description."

"This fey's getting to you, huh?" I whisper. Gristle tightens his jaw. "We get out of here and I don't wanna hear another word about the Dog."

Gristle hums. Might be the first thing we agree on.

"Stow the argument," Fionne says, in something close to her big-sister voice. She tucks her pen into her stocking. "Make it happen."

Hien leans against the wall, allegedly keeping us covered while we pull the boards away as quiet as we can. Apparently, we're not going to be so much invisible as the police just won't notice. Eyes will see, brains won't compute. Gristle's all tense while he explains.

We get through and step out from the hall into the little stairwell. The map says there were up-ways stairs too, twisting back from this landing, but now there's just that toothy gap with a distant bit of light tracing the jagged edge we'll have to boost up to.

As soon as we know the coast's clear, Fionne rushes forward first, tosses her notebook up ahead of her, then steps off the banister to catch the ceiling edge and haul her tall self up. I hold my breath until she's safely perched. Then she reaches back to help me. I boost up and hold her hand as soft as I can, like she can feel that I'm alright and in control.

"It's okay," I say. Behind me, there's a clattering as the dog's hoisted up too. I don't even wanna think about how strong or tall someone would have to be to lift that thing over their head. "Fionne, I'm gonna get you out to send that portfolio to *Dolly Day*, alright?"

"You better," she says. "I'm serious."

I can't read the tone. When Hien and the dog slip past us, Fionne touches my side just fast, and then turns after them. Hien kicks the office door closed as they go to shut the lamp-glow out, and then turns right around a corner. The lighter fades to leave us in the dark. Jerk. Fionne follows close.

In the last bit of visibility, I turn back to see Gristle awkwardly waddling his elbows forward, trying to crunch one knee up.

"How you faring, dickie?" I ask him. In the dark, I step forward and grab a fistful of his jacket at each shoulder to start pulling. I'm not sure if I'm actually helping, especially when I feel him wince. "The boss didn't want to help you up?"

His arm finds its way over my shoulder, like a strange side-hug. It's better when I can't see him. He's warm, not weirdly warm or anything, but person-warm in a way I somehow thought he wouldn't be.

"They've been pretty... pretty *moody* since I told them I wanted to quit," he grumbles. "I think they're making a point."

"Hate to think what that might be," I say.

He tugs on me less when his leg gets up proper. I let go of him as soon as he's able to start standing. Ain't anything more to say on that. I step off first after Hien and Fionne, with one hand on the right-side wall to feel for the corner, and my heels digging in just enough for him to know how to follow.

We turn into the long hall. Far down, I see a brown stain of light cutting Fionne's outline. I think to run up to her, but I know we're overtop the barroom and I don't want to clomp too heavy in my boots. So I bite the feeling of wanting to leave my brother and just walk a few steps ahead of him, like always.

He breaks the silence first, with the last thing I ever expected to hear from him.

"I'm sorry about last night," he says. I could almost ignore it, pretend I didn't hear or I don't need any thanks, but he swallows and keeps going. "I shouldn't've been such a jerk about you coming home. I thought I was doing the right thing, but I'm not so sure now."

Getting me home from the club full of implosion-hazards seems like a pretty right thing. I furrow my eyebrows. The light pauses at the end of the hallway, waiting for us. This feels like a mile-long gauntlet. "It's fine, Gristle," I say. "You were just doing what Auntie asked you to."

I hope that's the end of it. I'm not doing this, not now.

"My dad was just doing what he was asked. That's what everyone says," he mutters. I let my eyes un-focus like I've closed them—anything to get out of whatever this is turning into. "He just went along with things he didn't understand, and that's how he ended up in all those awful jams. And now I feel like I'm doing the same."

It ain't all true. Sure, I remember Senan sitting across the table from my mum with both their mouths flying as fast as the other's, grinning as wide. I remember him playing cards at Cat's with bigger thugs than spineless Rory, or the days when we'd come home to see trench-coated folks loitering around the apartment entrance, and he'd send Gristle and me on some useless errand before disappearing for a bit. But more than that, I remember Auntie Shona practically begging him to stop, to live with her in midtown and bring us too, to at least tell her what he was doing so she could prepare for the fallout. He didn't, and then?

"Auntie Shona ain't exactly a mad fey radical," I say. Not like Mum, who braided my hair and kissed my cheeks, and could have killed me. Still could with how she hurt my head. The light ahead slips sideways down a staircase I can barely see. "She said not to tangle with this sort of thing, and now look where we are. Even if we get out of here alive, there's gonna be hell to clean."

"Always is."

Fair enough.

We get to the top of the stairs, where the light just touches the edges of the banister. I turn back to Gristle, for just a second. "I'm going to be better," I tell him. "I've decided that. This shit's a mental problem, and so I've mentally decided that I'm not going to hurt you ever again. Not you, not Auntie, not Fionne or her family, *no one*."

No matter what it takes.

He squints at me, opens his mouth, closes it, and then tries again while he looks past me instead of at. "And then when everything turns up a notch?" he asks. His voice is small, like that eleven-cycle-old crybaby I used to love. "Things are always changing, Hawthorne. It feels like it's just getting farther and farther out of control. How are we supposed to protect ourselves from that?"

I don't even know what to say to him. Below, Fionne's finally realized we might not get that paradise future she was planning. I knew that already, but I at least thought there would be *something* better than we got now.

What if our aunt isn't some radio-play hero who knows everything, and winning this election can't fix this awful city?

Gristle's head snaps up like someone's called him. "Alright, alright," he mutters. He gives me one shy glance from under his hat but then shimmies past me down the stairs. I can only follow.

At the bottom, both Hien and Fionne are waiting. The hallway here is wider, with no cobwebs, at least in the part we can see before it leads off into gloom. This is a well-worn path. The shadows are all squirming out there, like anything could come running for us.

"You smell that?" Gristle asks.

The dog's nose starts twitching like a rattle. It takes a second before I smell it too. I can't figure out what it is: almost sweet, but thick and sharp.

"Diesel," Fionne says, eyebrows together and focused. She's kept her glasses on. "It's what the delivery trucks run on."

Why would there be auto fuel in here?

We set off. Between Fionne and Hien and Gristle trying to get to the front, I see some sort of light sparkling around the edges of all of them. Real small, yellowish like a cheap lantern. I notice the dog is hugging close to Hien's blurry side. The light gets stronger and stronger.

Finally, we walk up to a little open doorway on the left, one that leads under the six-foot tall stage.

"Bingo," Fionne mutters, hollowly. Under where the dancers swing and the big band plays, there's a little maintenance room, or what used to be one when all of these hallways were used and they hadn't boarded up everything 'sides the cellar. It ain't a maintenance room no more, even with the hoses and pipes still on the walls, and crates stacked up. There's a shanty trundle bed on the right, a few crates of canned food in bulk boxes like the kitchen would get, and a whole mess of machinery on one wall that I don't much understand.

"Someone's been squatting in here," Gristle says.

There's no one else here, at least right now. "If that someone's a mad fey," I mutter, as we walk one after the other into the greasy glow, "then it ain't the hiding out part I'm worried about."

The dog's whining worse than a bad-tuned fiddle. The burnt reek clouds all around, mixing with the smell of old food from a crate of empty tin cans, and of iron, too, which doesn't make much sense for a mad fey. I know it'd give me a headache if I stayed in here too long. I can feel Hien cringing and holding their breath.

I step toward the smell by the left-side wall, even if I have to stand a little stiffer to stop the pressure from building. There's four tanks of diesel lined up, just like Fionne guessed, but the real reek is coming from a mess of straps and plates jammed in the oily dark. I might not have recognized it if not for tonight.

Gristle pulls his camera out to take a picture, lighting it all up brighter. "Iron armor," he says. Like what the police wear. "That might explain why you couldn't get in the person's head, Mx Hien."

My skin prickles. "Could a fey even wear that?" I ask.

Gristle narrows his eyes. He opens his mouth, pauses for a moment, and says, "Hien says some fey are less sensitive than others, so it wouldn't be impossible."

Alright... there's something else there next to it, some contraption thing made of a rucksack and hoses that I don't understand. "What the hell is that?"

Gristle looks from it to the tanks on the wall. *Pop*, flash. "Mx Hien, do you have something I could write on?"

Hien produces a paper and pen from somewhere in the blur and hands it over fast, maybe just so the dog can rear up and put its paws on their shoulders. While Gristle tries to pattern it out, I turn to see Fionne picking up a box from the bedside, made of iron too, from the smell. Why would a fey have so much iron? Maybe this ain't the fey after all? Someone else? That don't make sense.

She sits back on the very edge of the moth-chewed blankets. Even with the smell (Robin, I get why you flared up to avoid those cuffs, I really do), I step over and crane my head to see her unclasp the lid of the box and pull out a stack of envelopes.

"All from the same address," she says, showing me one as I crouch ahead of her. It's a simple white envelope, with a return address for a random post office on Chestnut Street. As she rifles through the open envelopes, I see her lips begin to part. She tilts the box down and holds an envelope open so I can see what's inside.

"Saints," I whisper. Each one is packed with 20R bills. That iron-and-diesel smell is getting worse, swarming up my head. I swear I can hear the cops outside the stage. We were dancing right outside of this room, with probably 1000R just over here in fat white envelopes.

She gets to the last one. There's only one bill, but a letter, too. We read it quickly—I have to wipe my hand over my mouth so I don't gasp or nothing. I thought this place was gonna tie our loose ends into fancy little bows, but it's just making this more complicated.

If being mad makes you impulsive and volatile, how could you be calculating enough to set this up, too?

"Okay," Gristle says. He steps toward us, sinking to a crouch beside me. "I've got a suspicion about all that. What did you lot find?"

My mouth is kindling-dry. "Money, and a letter," I tell him. The dog leaps up onto the bed behind Fionne, who accepts its heavy head on her shoulder. Hien keeps their distance. "Say, Gristle, I don't think we're hunting a mad fey."

He taps the pen into the notebook with his eyebrows pressed tight together. The light above and behind makes him look sick. "Who's doing the paying?"

"It doesn't say, but that's the thing." I'm staying calm. I'm alright. I can handle whatever comes at me. "This can't just be someone who's out of control. If it *is* a fey, then they know exactly what they're doing—they've just been making it look like random madness."

"Well, fey or mortal, I've had about enough of this," Fionne says from behind me. She snaps the box shut. The dog whines. "This is enough to hand off and get us out of here. I say we go before they come back. Gristle can explain his doodles on the way."

I agree. We start to stand.

But before we can hightail out, I hear a voice. And it's not Hien's.

"What good observations, dickies," someone says from behind my back, in the direction of the door. "You know, I really underestimated you brats, but I'm still leagues ahead."

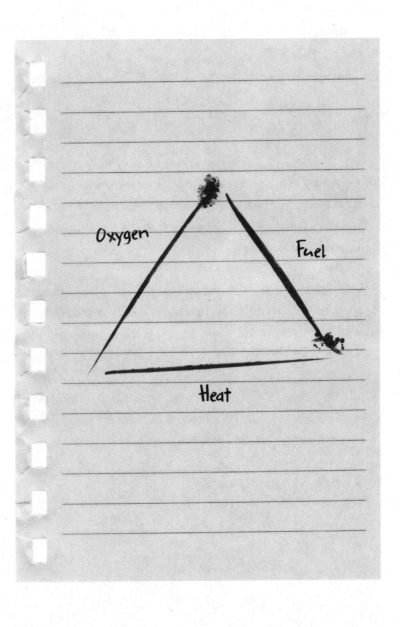

Tanner Firstchild
444 Oakpost Road
Puck's Port, Dale
57SC Summer Solstice

Tanner,

I understand today is a day of mourning for you and many, so I will be as brief as I can. I've seen the black crepe on your family home for the past six cycles. I've seen your parents cry for justice while the city shuts its ears. I sympathize, and I'd like to offer a chance to amend everything that's gone wrong.

I have a proposition that I think may interest you. If the job doesn't, then perhaps money will. Know that there's more put aside if the job is finished as requested. There are ample opportunities for you to take your own liberties.

Details will follow. Please contact Rory Gattano at the switchboard office to be directed to me. We can make this country remember who the real victims are, and who can save them.

I look forward to collaborating.

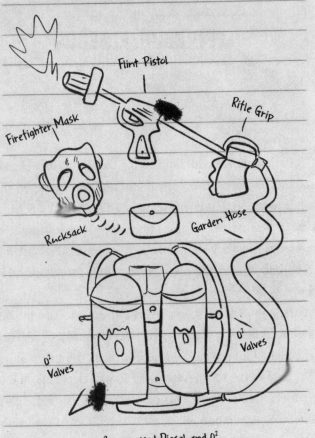

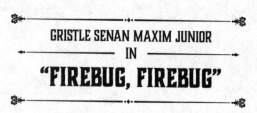

GRISTLE SENAN MAXIM JUNIOR
IN
"FIREBUG, FIREBUG"

Gristle Senan Maxim Junior hadn't felt right since Hien dragged him awake on the lobby floor. The world was too sharp, the sounds too loud. His burns seared and his muscles ached and his stomach was nauseous and his head was now a mess with the knowledge that they hadn't just been caught, they'd fallen for it.

His daddy said the hurt came before the victory. He didn't believe victory was even possible.

Gristle spun around on one bruised knee to face the door with his whole skeleton screaming, shoulder to shoulder with Hawthorne on his right, Fionne, shocked, behind them, the blurry haze of Hien at the back of the room refusing to show a clear face, and one new person in the doorway. This person was missing their scrapyard flamethrower, abandoned in the corner, but instead they held a pistol, aimed not at Hien but at the diesel canisters.

"No sudden movements, Hien," Tanner Firstchild said as she stepped in. Except she'd picked her name at eighteen, and so now they all knew her better as Fifthchild O'Taglio. "And don't think about trying to sic your dog on me again—I'll send us all into the stars." Her teeth tightened under the cold, blank mask of her face. Gristle recognized that sort of detachment. "I've got folks prepared to say you made me do it. You freaks go down for this either way. I'm just glad I could get Hàzell Stregoni's kids in on it too."

This was the old Fayre Massacre debts coming back.

The "mad fey" was never a fey at all, but terrified mortals cared more about order than truth.

A warning rattle rumbled in the room like a hidden snake, but O'Taglio's features were all hard set, though there was a slight sheen across her skin. Was she bluffing?

"You, miss." O'Taglio jerked her chin to Fionne, who tensed. "You don't have a hand in this. You take the mutt on out of here. Not too far, though."

Fionne didn't respond. Gristle hated the silence and the stillness, terrified it might never end.

"Feenee," Hawthorne said, impossibly level somehow despite her rumpled clothes and frizzing curls. "Just take the dog out."

The light flickered overhead. It was the dog who hopped down first, with a clatter of claws. "A-alright," Fionne finally breathed. A rattle as she set the iron box back upon the bed. Her heels touched (*clack . . . clack*) onto the ground. "Come on, Quen."

Quen? They started for the door, Fionne with one hand on the dog's rough back so it would act as a barrier between her and O'Taglio. Quen . . . yes, that was the dog's name. How did she know that, when Gristle could barely remember? Well, surely the dog's name was in some article somewhere? But as they slipped through the doorway and into the unseen hall, he swore he saw the dog's silver eyes dart to Hien for just a moment.

Gristle's breathing wheezed sour. Hien had a plan, had told Fionne and possibly directed Quen with whatever strange fey-familiar link they shared. Gristle waited to see the metal-and-jade pistol, for one quick shot to save them, to bring the law in like blood from a wound.

The light above flickered again, fiercer. Hien, powerful as the devil, stood still.

"Saints, this is better than I thought," O'Taglio said with tight teeth. Her hand tightened at the trigger, eyes boring into Hawthorne's, while the gun was still aimed at the canisters to ruin them all. "You're a much better face for this, aren't you?"

"Face?" Hawthorne muttered.

Gristle knew. It was so simple. "She wants to frame you—for the dock death, and Rastova." The room was full of evidence in their favor, but . . . "She'll hand you over to the cops and get rid of this behind her. Blame you, or Hien, maybe both."

O'Taglio's eyes narrowed. "Bravo, dickie," she said, but the solve had come far too late.

The light burned brighter, glowing into the shadows and turning every dust mote into a burning star. "Y-you can just keep the money," Hawthorne said.

"It was never about the money," O'Taglio snapped, so violently that Gristle flinched and waited for the bullet to shatter them apart. "Taking all you freaks down'll help three hundred people sleep better in the soil. I would have settled for Hien, but fate's on my side tonight. Get up."

Hawthorne stayed rooted. Should Gristle call for the police? Could he be certain they weren't in on this, or that they wouldn't take the envelope bribery? That they wouldn't break him apart? Could he be sure of *anything*?

What would his aunt ask of him here?

O'Taglio's face twitched once. Hien didn't move. O'Taglio snapped the safety off her pistol and took a step closer. "*Now!*"

And yet, a sound came from somewhere deep in the back of Gristle's brain: a whistle, echoing as though in a long hallway. High. Low. Out of the corner of his eye, with just the slightest tilt of his chin to see them, the blur of Hien didn't change.

Would you like me to present an alternative solution, Detective? Gristle's every cell rippled. A ticker reel of horrors screamed through his skull. *Or would you like to continue solving this in your lawful fashion?*

He'd been certain before that Hien couldn't hear his thoughts exactly, but he was becoming increasingly worried that they'd been underselling the act. All his life, he'd believed just what he was told. His mistake, maybe. *Hien,* Gristle thought, a desperate attempt to be heard even in his own head. *Just get the weapon away from her.*

No response.

Hawthorne didn't stand. Every muscle was locked, eyes vacant, and yet voice so level. "We can make this go away. My aunt—"

Could bend rules too, but only so far as this city allowed.

O'Taglio's jaw tightened. Gristle could practically see her cool exterior fracturing. "Your aunt thinks you can be fixed," she snarled. The hand not holding the gun tightened into a fist. Sweat beaded down her clammy face. "But if you really understood how dangerous you are, you'd get behind bars to prove it."

"I'm getting better!" Hawthorne said, voice pitching. Sparks twisted through her hair like burning steel wool, in a room so ready to go up. "I'm not gonna feel . . . feel *guilty* for something I haven't done."

The choice is yours, Mister Maxim. It had come from somewhere above, slithering through the low rafters, and yet he couldn't drag his eyes from O'Taglio. Hien could snap their fingers and end this now, and it would be awful. *Will you still think I'm the devil after I've saved your hide?*

"This should have been over after the fayre," O'Taglio spat. Her face looked three septennials older in the gnarled light. "That should have taught everyone that you freaks can't be saved from yourself—you'll get us all *killed*." She cracked the hammer back with her thumb. Her eyes were fierce and flat. "If you won't walk with me, then I guess we stick with Plan A. I love this place, but we all gotta make sacrifices."

They'd all burn, like his daddy and stepmum, and who would ever believe that a mortal had done it?

Time's running out, Hien said from somewhere in Gristle's synapses. The blur hadn't moved, and yet a shimmer of light flickered, too fast to catch. The dust swam through the air in irregular currents under the light buzzing furiously as a hornet's nest. *Imagine, killing yourself to abide by laws that never served you in the first place.*

The laws of the same city that had arrested his daddy for a bread riot, locked Hazell from proper work, burned fey at pyres so recently that their platforms were still visible.

"I'm not like my mum—look at me!" Hawthorne said, nearly a screech. Heat rolled off her like summer pavement. Gristle tensed and screamed in his own head. The searing light above them was turning everything stark as an ink drawing. "*You've* killed more people than I have."

O'Taglio's mouth twitched at the corner. "You're about to be guilty for every death here tonight," she muttered. Her bloodless finger tightened on the trigger. "Same as your mum and daddy were when they decided to be heroes."

"What does that mean?" Hawthorne started to ask. But Gristle didn't know. He hadn't known anything his entire life, only that nothing was going right. And now the trigger action tightened, ached to release, to strike a spark deep in the chamber that would smell like a dying star as it sent lead burning into diesel. Heat to fuel to all that oxygen alongside it. They couldn't have survived it all just to come up short again. Just to be ruined again. Just to hurt and never win.

The patterns had never worked, and never would. Everything needed to change.

Snap! The bulb went out. Gristle grabbed Hawthorne's shoulder and yanked her into him in time for—*BANG!*

A shot went off. There was a *crack* as it hit something wooden. Gristle and his sister collapsed to the cement floor in a tangle of limbs.

"She knows something—about Mum and Senan," Hawthorne wheezed. The smallest bit of light glowed from between her sharp teeth, just a monstrous mouth in the dark. "We have to—"

"Hien!" O'Taglio shouted. Her voice speared through the dark, screeching hot as sparks off train tracks. "You and I both know you can scramble off from this! Leave it between the three of us."

They were all answered only by another purring laugh. They said fey were covetous, selfish. Gristle knew Hien would not walk out on this insult. Wind raked up around the room, violent as a twister. Gristle's hat flew somewhere unseen. His thick hair was thrown into unruly peaks. Crates creaked over. The canisters chuckled and fell with ringing clangs.

Gristle could feel burning heat from Hawthorne now, tiny sparks zipping down her hair, from her teeth.

"Hien, don't you dare," she whispered. Was she hearing them too? "We need her witness statement!"

Statements. What good had statements ever gotten them? Gristle himself had been prepared to lie to the police that very same night, and still would. He would *not* let some washed-up, low-level, brainwashed thug be the death of the Maxims.

From behind, a clawed hand closed on his shoulder, just as the light burned on again so bright that every shadow cringed back behind the destruction of broken crates, papers gone flying, and O'Taglio standing stark in the middle of the room with her pistol aimed again for the lopsided canisters.

The blur of Hien was gone. O'Taglio looked to Gristle first, then her eyes rose up behind. That claw grew tighter on his shoulder.

O'Taglio's features widened past natural fear. Gristle felt a rush of vindication that nearly made him grin. He became certain that, whatever Hien was back there, it looked nothing like the nearly mortal person he'd been seeing tonight. Was that another trick? Or was this perhaps the real Phong Hien, without the illusions? Gristle was part of that fear, this power.

"Do it," Gristle whispered.

The hand clutched hard enough for Hien's claws to ache through Gristle's suit. *Pleasure doing business with you, Detective.*

Hawthorne's sharp teeth gritted as she turned to look over her shoulder. "Don't you—"

The claw let go, some quick arrow of light and wind shot over Gristle and Hawthorne's heads, and the show began.

O'Taglio shrieked as her hand evaporated in a rush of mist, leaving her sleeve to droop with not a drop of blood spilled. The pistol fell to the ground. Gristle refused to look away.

"Wait—stop!" Hawthorne screamed. She leapt to her feet. Light bled from her mouth, but her hands stayed in fists at her sides.

It was too late. O'Taglio's remaining hand jumped to her throat, blotchy color blossoming over her face as her lungs refused to expand. "You're monsters," she croaked. Dark veins like vines tangled across her exposed skin. Hien kept up the tricks, twisting this mortal body into something monstrous too: O'Taglio's eyes shifted into snake pupils, and her tongue forked when she gasped for breath. Yes, a snake, like damn Rory Gattano, and like whoever this led back to. This was so much bigger and worse than whatever happened in this room. Did that justify Hien's brutal puppetry?

A heavy pause. And in it, the pronounced *click* of someone snapping their fingers.

The wind stopped. O'Taglio drew in a long, rattling breath. Gristle's hair prickled, like grass swaying to a song. Behind her, an image of Phong Hien stood, crystal-clear and waiting, dressed in a corseted vest and looking mortal if not for everchanging tattoos up both bare arms.

As the world seemed to slow down around them, they tilted their head toward O'Taglio and looked to Hawthorne.

Hawthorne swallowed. "No," she whispered. "You're just proving her right, Hien. Can we please just talk—"

Civilities would only shove back the lines they'd drawn. Hien gave a showman's two-fingered salute, none too serious.

"NO!" Hawthorne shouted, but it wasn't enough. Hien's hand snapped into a fist.

Whatever O'Taglio knew, it was going six feet under.

O'Taglio's face washed suddenly blank. Her eyes, her tongue, her hand had all returned to mortal. There was only enough time for her to clap one palm to her chest before her legs went wiry.

She collapsed on top of the gun.

Her eyes stayed open, staring right at Gristle. He watched the last tears drain out of the last Tanner child.

Dead, just like that.

The chapter was closed. Was this victory?

Hien hooked their hands into their pockets, so calm that Gristle couldn't consider them mad, just brilliant, to hold so much power and wield it so well. He wanted to lunge for them, to ask for any sort of clarification, some balance between this rip-roar making everything a carnival of chaotic little lights and sounds and feelings, and the order that he knew was swallowing him.

But then Hawthorne screamed, not scared but *angry* as she leapt to her feet. Gristle didn't even think, he just stumbled up to grab her arm and clung to it like they'd skipped back so many cycles.

"Hawthorne—"

"SHE KNEW ABOUT MY MUM!" Her voice rang out so loud that the cops would hear. He didn't want them back here. O'Taglio's dead eyes stared at their shoes—she was right to think the cops would believe her over any fey. He wanted to settle this behind closed doors like his daddy used to, because he didn't trust the law to keep him or his sister safe. "SHE COULD HAVE TOLD US WHO HIRED HER!"

Hien stared at Hawthorne. Gristle knew they'd said something to her, felt it rush past him and sink in with arrogance dancing on the edges.

"You're a monster," Hawthorne snarled. She ripped her arm from Gristle, throwing her hands around as she spoke and snapped her fingers like Hàzell used to. Sparks came glittering off her. The stress was hitting mad levels. "She should have put you on her pyre—I'm *nothing* like you."

Hien sent a lash of wind out like a challenge. Two landforms were about to meet. It was exhilarating in a delirious, dangerous way. Anything could happen next. The whole world could burst into glittering sparkles, and would that be better than this?

Prove it, Stregoni Child, Hien said for both of them to hear. *Prove that you have any control at all.*

They started to raise their hand, but Hawthorne was quicker. She snapped her arm up, palm out. Hien didn't even flinch, unperturbed. Gristle knew exactly what his sister was capable of. His whole body was racing with adrenaline.

Without a word, a torrent of flame blasted from Hawthorne's hand, so bright that Gristle swore he saw the color of it in

Hawthorne's pale eye, so bright that every shadow lit up. Hien's eyes were indeed yellow in all the gray. A snarl of wind rushed from between their teeth, out to meet the flames.

Gristle watched the fire tear right through, neither diverting nor diminishing. Hien's eyes widened. The tattoos on their arms paused as if startled.

The rocket of flame struck Hien directly in the chest. It burned at skin, at fat, at muscle, at bone. Gristle heard the cells dying one by one.

There was no rejoinder.

Hien was sent crackling and burning straight out the open doorway.

They landed sprawled, chest burned into just a carcass of ribs, eyes flashed open.

The air smelled like three hundred dead.

The light bulb flickered, unsure.

Gristle waited for the punch line, laughter already poised in the bottom of his throat.

And yet, everything was horribly quiet and horribly still. In those moments, the illusion faded out: Hien lay in the hallway, a rather ordinary Hannochian folk wearing just a pair of simple trousers and an organ-deep, shattering burn. They'd have looked mortal if not for an iridescent shine to their bones that matched the scales across their flat nose. Gristle waited for the trick to finish, for Hawthorne to be struck next by a sudden attack from the shadows. But there was no final word. There was nothing.

There was only Hien in the hallway.

Dead.

Hawthorne's hand slowly dropped to her side. Gristle's mouth fumbled open. The two of them stared.

"I thought," Hawthorne breathed. Her hand twitched for Gristle's, but then she snapped both to her stomach, each hand cuffed around the other wrist. Her voice came out stuttering and sick. "I didn't think it would . . . I thought they'd fight back . . . I thought someone might actually . . . finally . . ."

He'd thought that too.

Gristle couldn't say anything. The adrenal rush through his synapses dried quickly, filtering from his blood like a mad fey high. In its absence, the sensations in his body began to dull, and the sharpness of the world began to soften. Had Hien been putting that in him? Making his thoughts so sharp and strange, singing him to this chaos? In its place, he was left with only a sinking, irrefutable heaviness that could have pulled his bones down into the soil far below the Dog.

"Hawthorne," Gristle breathed, but he could find nothing else.

Gristle heard the dog bark, the sound splitting into a howl that rocked through his entire body. It shook the electricity from him. The horror was doubling. Two dead bodies ahead of them. Cops outside the door. The impossible future bearing down like a train. And, now, he was aware of it. Hien had only begun to cut him off the track, hadn't finished the job.

It was one thing to exist in a game you couldn't win, and another to know it.

"*Maxim*." Hawthorne's voice came out as a creaking squeal, nearly a sob, and too damn young. "We have to tell Auntie Shona."

I don't know if she can fix the mess we're all in, Gristle thought. *I don't think anyone can save us from this city.*

Puck's Port Herald

57SC, 3 Winter Moons, 5 Suns

THE DOGFOOT DEATHS
"MAD FEY" CAUGHT IN NIGHT OF CHAOS

Five are dead at Aziza Street's Dogfoot Club in a strange conclusion to the city's recent "Mad Fey Murders." Just before 22 bells, Rastova Firstchild, 17, was found burned to death in the club's liquor cellar.

"At first, we thought it was a mad fey, possibly the same one who killed that person on the dock," said Gristle Senan Maxim Junior, 18, who was called to the Dogfoot earlier to investigate the seemingly unrelated claim of a possible intruder. "We turned out to be right, but not in the way we expected."

Investigation by Maxim and his sister (known fey Hawthorne Stregoni, 18) led to the discovery of the home of an apparent squatter underneath the Dogfoot's stage.

"It was clear that someone was living there," said Maxim, who is the spitting image of his aunt, presidential candidate Shona Maxim. "We really thought it was that mad fey, but we found some papers that pointed to motive, and I identified the weapon."

This weapon has been classified as a makeshift flamethrower, used to replicate fey attacks. It was built and owned by one Fifthchild O'Taglio (formerly Tanner Firstchild, the only surviving Tanner child following the Summer Fayre Massacre), head barkeep of the Dogfoot Club. The weapon has been tied to the deaths of both Rastova and the unknown victim on the docks. However, the death did not end there. In the chaos of capture, O'Taglio attacked and

"THEY WERE ONLY 13": MOTHERS PLEAD "NOT GUILTY" FOR THEIR MAD CHILD

Amid the chaos at the Dogfoot Club, with the "Mad Fey killer" caught and a deeper conspiracy brought to light, O'Bron These and Tania Goodfellow (of Goodfellows' Tailor) were not told what became of their child for several bells.

"A staff member had to tell us," These said, still in tears. "The police gave us no answers. And then we heard that Sixthchild was dead [from implosion]."

"Of course we knew they were fey," said Goodfellow to curious reporters. "We were told this job would be good for them, give them an outlet with others like them." According to Dogfoot workers, Goodfellow Sixthchild (aka Robin) and many other employees were receiving killed Dogfoot owner Phong Hien, 20, who Maxim claims had most likely been a target since the start. O'Taglio then died of heart failure, possibly due to the stress of the events and related to a congenital defect found by coroners.

However, Maxim suggests that this conspiracy extends beyond the Dogfoot. Investigators led to the squatter's small room beneath the stage found a series of envelopes containing bills amounting to 1260R, and a letter instructing O'Taglio to cooperate with an unnamed party through a person known to be connected with the Verdossi mob. Investigators plan to follow these leads. Details will be made available as they are known.

Maxim gathered reporters to take a very bold statement. "I'm sure these attacks were made to fuel hatred against the fey. They were made to make people like my sister look like uncontrollable monsters and their supporters like fools. It's a result of over six cycles of mishandling my stepmother's case. While it was tragic, and the death there will never be changed, the way people have responded—with more iron justice, and less funding for institutions such as U of S's Fey Studies Department—only lights pyres that should have died centuries ago.

"Something has to change," he went on to say. "We need to stand by the idea that this will end, that Faerie Disorder will be understood through science, that fey can have a life like mortals can, and we can all build a new and better future without suffering. The episode in the lobby may go unheard tonight amidst everything else, but we've got to remember that tragedy too."

The reported self-implosion (more on page 9) of mad fey Goodfellow Sixthchild, 13, claimed the life of officer Daniel Blake and injured 12 other officers, though the Puck's Port Police Department was able to secure the area to prevent further injury. It is yet unclear if the Blake family unlicensed "fey lessons" from now-deceased Dogfoot owner Phong Hien.

"If we had just been there," These said. "The staff said the police were interrupting them, and had iron. The whole brigade coming at them is not what they needed. They needed their mothers, some understanding, and some compassion."

UNIVERSITY OF STOUTSHIRE REBUKES GOODFELLOW CLAIM

While O'Bron These and Tania Goodfellow suggest that their child's mad implosion was brought on by external factors, experts in the fey condition urge caution.

"Yes, these factors can exacerbate symptoms," Doctor Sonder Secondchild said. "However, saying that these are the root cause is dangerous—with proper training, a fey can withstand even the most uncomfortable situations without a single symptom. Goodfellow's death is a warning to us all: without funding licensed education centers, we'll only see more tragedy."

Doctor Secondchild

will press posthumous charges against Goodfellow. Shona Maxim was on the scene and elected not to speak, but her running mate, Calligan Firstchild, was happy to comment. "O'Taglio's hatred isn't just about the fey," they said to gathered press. "That's two working folk dead, and I don't believe Ashley will serve justice for them. We will. These deaths will mean something to the greater good. I've got to believe."

says that, amidst high tensions, citizens must remember that his department is on the forefront of research and medical innovation to control symptoms of Faerie Disorder.

"Goodfellow is a victim of ignorance," he went on to say. "How many more children will we allow to be stolen by this disorder?"

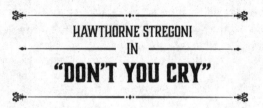

HAWTHORNE STREGONI IN
"DON'T YOU CRY"

I killed someone.
 I killed Hien.
I killed them and they're dead. I killed them and I saw them hit the ground with their chest all burnt. I killed them and it smelled like the fayre. I killed them and Gristle didn't even scream. He didn't do *anything*. Mum killed him once, I think, and I keep him dead.

Prove it, Hien had said. Prove that I can control myself, or that I can protect myself, or that I can be left in charge of anything.

Why did you let me win, Hien? If I'd known I'd make myself a monster anyway, I would have gotten O'Taglio to talk. Now I have nothing.

Gristle led me out, told the police he was there with Maxim & Maxim, told them to call our aunt and get three cops with him to investigate. Fionne wasn't there. She must have heard O'Taglio drop, and ran. While some medical jack took me aside, Gristle was all tall and strong and marching off like a detective, and I was given over like a kid. I could feel the fire tingling under my skin, but not even trying to flare. Just trying to make me know it was still alive, was always gonna be, like a taunt.

You killed someone. *You killed someone.* You let the flash impulse leap out, and now you can't take it back, and now you know you really are mad. You always have been. So many people have been lying for you. Why are you so special? Why should the world bend in your favor but no one else's? Mum's dead, Robin's dead, Hien's dead, and you?

Why do you get to walk free, Hawthorne Stregoni?

I got led out to the front of the Dog, where ambulances and police cars were clogging up the road. Cops were trying to hold back peering crowds half-drunk from the other places. All the marquees burned down over us. The air still smelled like Robin, bloody but green with flowers and trees. There were people sobbing.

Press cameras *pop!*-flashed, swarming like gnats. "Officer! Can you comment on the state of the club! Can you tell us—"

I felt too far away for all the noise to bother me, like I'd been tossed right out of my self. Tires screeched—I looked over to see my aunt's car weaseled right up to the edge of the crowd. She whirled over the door to run to me, her duster flashing behind her, eyes wild. She looked like that sixteen-cycle detective dragged into the job because her kid sibling was causing problems, and all you got is family, so you do what you have to if it means protecting them. Even lying.

She crashed into me like an iron bullet, wrenched me into her arms and away from the medic and said she had it, screw off. Egghead was fast behind her, still clutching a briefcase to their chest with papers out the corners. They sniffed and fixed at their glasses, then squinted up at the Dog with leaves and flowers coming out the cracks like smoke.

"A comment, Miss Maxim," some reporter was saying.

Pop! Auntie Shona turned me from it and told Egghead to say something good for the reporters, she didn't care. They got all snivelly and "I really think it would be best if you—"

"Leave off," she snarled. She held me tight tight tight, 'cause she's never had to worry about breaking the world in her hands. "Do I look like I give a shit about my campaign right now?"

They sulked off, gnashing their teeth while their glasses went white with the *pop!*-flash of the cameras.

"Saints, Hawthorne," my auntie was whispering in my hair while I clutched her like a kid. Her voice rambled. "Saints, I'm glad you're alright. You shouldn't have been here. All this awfulness—why were you here?"

I wanted to cry but I had the peppery feeling all over and was scared that crying would make it burn. "Auntie," I whispered, while Egghead led the press away so we could just stand by the bricks. "I did it. I did *it*," and I knew she'd know. Maybe not the details, but that I'd busted up bad like everyone knew I would. That I was as much a wreck and a kid as everyone thought.

She held me tighter. "No more," she said. I could feel her look up and around at the swarming cops. "When we get home, alright? Tell me then. I'm sure you didn't mean it."

Why do the rules go out the window for me? I wanted to tell her Hien hadn't even threatened me, just annoyed me, and the fire blasted up like packed dynamite. I'd been trying to hold it in too long and it lashed out louder. But she'll just say I'm not a monster, that she knows I'm good. What the hell does *good* even mean now?

"Tell me your brother's here, Hawthorne. Tell me he didn't leave you."

He's handling it all, just like you taught him.

But over her shoulder, easing along the edge of the crowd, I could see someone in a sparkly dress, hair wrapped, holding her coat and her notebook in her hands but looking too gray to know what to do with either. Fionne. She was staring at me, all blurry from behind my tears. A little moan crackled up from my throat.

My auntie must have turned to look where I was 'cause she said, "Get along, Eze. I'm sorry, but she needs space after tonight," and then, "Officer, can you see this girl gets home alright?" and I knew it was the end of it, and that I couldn't look up and see Fionne tell them that she was fine, that she'd called her brother and oughta be meeting him. Ify was right to be wary of me. I knew it, and yet?

"I'll call Doc Secondchild," my auntie was saying, sounding a bit far-off too, like she was realizing how badly everything was going. "We're going to handle this."

"I want to fix it," I told her. No, that wasn't true. "I need *you* to fix it," I spluttered out. "Auntie, just do anything."

She raked me closer, holding me while the tears came out hot but the fire couldn't light. "We will," she said. I didn't know how, but I trusted her to do it. If I could just stay out of my own way, just sit down and let myself be saved by people who know better. "We'll make you safe."

PART THREE

𝔓uck's 𝔓ort 𝔥erald

57SC, 5 Winter Moons, 1 Sun

"A STEP IN THE RIGHT DIRECTION"
SHONA MAXIM WINS PRESIDENTIAL ELECTION AFTER LONG-HAUL SEASON

After the disaster at Aziza Street's Dogfoot Club, the country has watched anxiously while so-called "anti-faeist" Dermott Ashley III and newcomer Shona Maxim warred over votes. In a nail-biting finish, Maxim has secured the presidency with 43 seats on the senate floor. Ashley, leading the official opposition, claims 40, with Marlowe taking 12 and Holmes 5.

Maxim is Dale's first president who was not born in the north end (above 14th Street), and who has not received a university degree. "I have to admit, I'm not sure how we made it here," said a visibly stunned Shona Maxim in her victory address, her wards on either side of her, and VP Calligan Firstchild present as well. "I was ready to step away from this after [the Dogfoot Murders]. It was you, all of you and your fierce support, and these children here with me today, who reminded me why I couldn't do that."

GATTANO & BROS. MECHANICS

CARE YOU CAN TRUST
366 Chestnut Street

Present at the front of the crowd were a dozen students from the Senan Maxim School for Fey, a fey re-education center that has been promised nearly 10,000R of federal education grants, on top of the large charitable donations sent since the so-called "Dogfoot Murders." They plan to expand their school to include more students, hire additional staff, and fund new research and groundbreaking treatments.

"I'm grateful to Gristle Senan Maxim Junior for apprehending Fifthchild O'Taglio," said Calligan Firstchild during their speech. Just like Maxim, they have had a surprising political career, being the first Daleish senator with a community college degree, the youngest person to run for VP in Daleish history, and now the first person with Jahagee ancestry to earn the role. "Had O'Taglio been able to frame the fey as she'd have liked, we surely would have lost to public panic. But now we can forge new futures for the underdogs of Dale. Today, we fund fey education. Tomorrow, I hope to lift up my alma mater and other underserved establishments below 14th Street who haven't seen new funding in septennials."

"I think [the Dogfoot] was a wake-up call," said Gristle Senan Maxim Junior in his own address. "Very few people hate fey enough to pin murder on them, but many don't support enough to take their iron handles off."

Since the murders two moons ago, the University of Stoutshire reports that 60 percent of citizens believe in supporting fey, and only 20 percent still support "iron justice," a term popularized by Senator Dermott Ashley III. This control method believes in strict criminalization of feyism, the same kind that caused the death of 13-cycle-old Goodfellow Sixthchild at the Dogfoot Club, whose funeral was attended by hundreds of fey sympathizers and parents.

"We're behind Maxim, because no one else was behind [Goodfellow]," says O'Bron These, mother of the deceased.

"This is more than we could have ever dreamed for, and I include my late brother in that," said President Maxim. She raised her glass to the crowd, as did Stregoni and Maxim. "To family: mine and yours."

GRISTLE SENAN MAXIM JUNIOR IN
"LOVE AND LOYALTY"

Gristle Senan Maxim Junior dusted off his hat in the soaring marble entryway. The wreathed lights hanging from the ceiling flickered once, throwing yew and holly shadows across the tiled floor and up the pillars along the walls. The smell was thick, uncomfortable in his sinuses. Gristle was glad to see that the Presidential Building lobby was otherwise empty.

He let the snow fall off him and then strode forward with his chin as high as he could handle, unaware if it was convincing when his sack suit fell limp past too much lost weight and yet still rubbed wrong. The elevators stood open with no attendants, so he trotted up the wide staircase at the back. The stained-glass window had a pyre in the middle of it, a "historic artifact" that couldn't be swapped. Things never change too much, he thought, and wriggled the uncomfortable prickle from his spine.

Gristle wove his way up the stairs and through the long, dark halls with their fine wainscoting and festive garlands on each light fixture. Most of the offices he passed were empty, but not the office of *Senator*

Ashley, whose door stood wide to spill a wash of light into the hallway. Gristle tensed as he approached. Thanks to some minuscule gram of luck, he could hear Ashley occupied by a phone call.

Gristle hazarded a peek inside as he passed. Ashley sat with the phone jammed up into the side of his face, his other hand splaying pale fingers across his forehead while he stared down at his desk, a sharp profile against the stained-glass windows of the back wall. His posture was all pinched under his fine suit.

There was something vindicating about seeing a previously confident man become so twitchy. "I don't care," Ashley spat. He wedged the phone into his shoulder to scribble something into a notebook. The pen squealed. "I asked for a report suns ago and I'll damn well get it. Do you know who you're speaking to?"

Gristle knew better than to prod and trap himself in a useless back-and-forth volley of insincerity, but he told himself to take pleasure in Ashley slamming the phone into the cradle and flipping violently through his filing cabinet.

The victory was still hollow. Most things had felt that way, since . . .

Watch it, he warned himself. Gristle steeled himself, went up a short flight of stairs, and was released into one of the grander hallways. The floor was buffed to a mirror-like shine, showing his own face swirling in the marble-grain. He drifted past Egg—*Calligan's* office. Though the door was closed, he could hear the typewriter going. He approached the next door and knocked. Each rap boomed like a cannon. He didn't wait for an answer, was merely announcing his arrival, and tried to enter with the sturdy confidence of a political son.

The office was large, not too boastful but still sure of its status: dark wooden walls, a cozy waiting area surrounding him with a few leather chairs and a table topped with magazines, and his aunt's study past the backsplit. Gristle went up the three stairs to where the fireplace glowed from behind his aunt's proud desk. She was just a black silhouette with gray flickering at the edges.

"You give this to your mother," she was saying to one of her volunteers, handing them a parcel and fixing their collar with her other hand. The volunteers were practically wards at this point, seven fey adolescents she'd brought on as a new initiative. "There are shoes for Tenthchild and some banknotes if she needs them. And some bells, for the holiday spirit."

"You're too kind, miss," the kid said, perhaps only fifteen. They swept their eyes over to Gristle just fast enough to see him, and then snapped back to look at President Shona Maxim. "You know she won't take it. Says she don't need no mortal help." Their flat tone made it hard to catch the joke.

But his aunt smiled anyway, the light warm across her cheeks. "Then you give them to your sibling anyway and put the banknotes toward something," she said. She shook their hand. "Happy Solstice, Barrah."

"And you, miss," the kid said, then bustled off with the package under one arm, their shoulders tight to their pointed ears. They gave Gristle a very obvious eye-contact-and-nod. He gave back a very obvious eye-contact-and-nod. His neck ached.

"Happy Solstice, Barrah," he echoed.

"And you, sir."

That stung for no reason at all. Gristle felt very old, or perhaps just very intimidating.

Barrah slipped out into the hallway, sealing the door tight behind them.

On with it, even if he already knew how it would end.

Gristle gathered his breath and stepped forward toward the desk, drawn up to his proper posture. "Hello," he said, which felt like a very weak start. He blinked the dryness out of his eyes.

His aunt turned back to her desk, both hands on it as she looked at her nephew. The firelight glowed against the evergreen on the mantle and a framed picture of her and his daddy, taken from a *Dolly Day* article, a reprinted photo from the day they solved their first case. Identical, with their straight mouths and slightly narrowed eyebrows, mirrors of the other aside from the faint hunch that curved his body around his broken ribs, and the exhaustion obvious under her eyes. Gristle knew the article had been about Maxim & Maxim celebrating two septennials on the job, and so it was both his young daddy looking at him and yet still one much closer to his death.

His aunt had gray in her hair now, as her brother had when he died.

"Gristle," she said. Her eyes were as exhausted as they'd been at sixteen, like nothing had gotten better. "What brings you?"

Say it, he told himself. *I know what she'll say, but say it anyway.*

"I thought we'd have Solstice supper," he offered, not even trying to sit, and so standing awkwardly with his hands clenched around the strap of his camera bag. "I figured you could be looking for some company, since Hawthorne—" Her name choked in his throat. He hadn't seen her in over a moon and was supposed to be happy for her. Push on. "Hawthorne is staying at school tonight. And if you're busy, then I can help with some of the work. Calligan could find me something to—"

"You let the egghead crunch their numbers," she said, easing back in her leather chair and never looking away from him, like one second might let him slip off. "If they want to bitch and complain about balancing budgets, then they can do the honors."

"I just meant . . ." he started, forcing himself to hold her eye properly, aiming for not too intense or weak but just right. "I just meant, we could have dinner while we work, take a bit off their plate. We could order in," he tried to say, looking through her forehead. "Maybe from Cat's?"

"They're closed on Solstice—I don't have time." Her voice snapped, firmer now. He knew he'd done it. "Ashley's been stabbing at our platform all moon to find a fault line, Secondchild says they'll need another round of funding for their next treatment model, and public interest is going down. The sympathy vote only lasts so long—we got what we wanted, but now we have to keep it."

Why had he even tried? "That's why I could help—"

Her shoulders tightened. Her teeth were white and frantic in the fire glow. "Because you were such a help the last time?"

Gristle's breath caught crooked in his chest. He could see her lip twitch and knew she hadn't meant to be that cruel, but still the pain ebbed through him like a tide. Since the Dogfoot, Gristle had forgotten how to make the hurt roll off himself.

Her voice was quieter now, threatening to be lost under the crackling of the fireplace, but it was no softer. "Ace, what she did was textbook madness, plain and simple. Do you know how close we were to losing her?" She looked down at the desk, like she couldn't stand seeing him in front of her. His throat choked. "I had to pull every string we had to cover that up, with folks I said I'd never go back to once I got us out. You had me in rings with dangerous people again, all because you wanted to go on and act like your father—is that it? Be some hero to the people and leave her on a chopping block?"

Gristle sniffed and said nothing. He knew all the gray in her hair was from the Dogfoot, or the aftermath, when she was out every night trying to find whoever had paid O'Taglio. The Verdo mob closed ranks around Rory before they could say "rat," the spineless police had barely pretended to investigate, and Rory had disappeared so completely that Gristle worried their brothers had let the rest of the mob dump them off the docks. Interviewing O'Taglio's parents and neighbors led nowhere. The case went cold in her hands, and Gristle was forbidden to so much as think about it.

That was fine. More and more often these days, he felt as if he couldn't say or do anything right. His routine was shot to shit, leaving him completely unmoored in his guilt and shame.

But the school was fully funded, more would open, new treatments were being piloted, and Hawthorne had twenty-four-bell care. This was supposed to be victory.

He'd stopped believing in a finish line, or progress, or himself, or anything really. He barely believed he was real.

"I'm sorry," he said, for what felt like the millionth time. His voice had a shiver on the edge, petulant.

His aunt sighed. Her eyes were glassy, her nose wrinkled. He felt suddenly sickened to think she might cry before he did. "You're so much like him," she muttered. That felt like an insult. "I know I'm hard on you, Ace. But it's only because I don't know what to do. Sneaking around with radicals behind my back, putting us all in danger, ignoring the rules and the laws and everything I've taught you..." Her eyes skated to a picture on her desk. Gristle refused to look at what he knew was himself and Hawthorne as children. "I'm still waiting for the other shoe to drop on the rest of that Dogfoot business, and when it does, we're stomped, one right after the other—your sister, then me, then you."

He lifted his chin, barely. This wasn't the world of windstorms from nowhere, of evaporating hands, shimmering veils, something strange and unpredictable and so fantastically horrifying that even death and destruction had an addicting sort of grace. That night might as well have been its own picture show.

Hien was dead. The moment was over. The world was the same, even if Gristle wasn't.

"I'll call you a cab," she said. She reached forward and flipped the picture frame down. Maybe she couldn't stand him either. "Go home, Gristle."

He couldn't deny her.

Turn around, he told himself. *Don't puke on the rug. It'll just hurt worse. Just turn.*

Even if it took every remaining shred of energy to send the signal down, his toes lifted, heel ground into the carpet, and he faced back toward the door.

She allowed him to take one step. "I loved your daddy every damn second, even when he knew how much he was hurting us," she said to his back. Gristle would have begged for a story about Senan Maxim that wasn't a tragic warning. He stared ahead, where a clutch of carved marble angels glared back from above the door. "I feel the same for you, Ace. I just can't trust you yet."

He closed his eyes for one split second of rest. "I love you too," he said. He'd keep trying, because he knew he should.

And then he was floating off toward the doors that were already opening so another kid could come trotting in. They had a scaly tail out the back of their trousers. He felt so jealous he thought he'd combust.

Maybe she'd forgive him then.

♦

Gristle sat outside the Presidential Building, at the edge of the courtyard near the road, where an ice-cold bench pulled every bit of heat out of him. The full moon stared from behind the tall buildings boxing him in. Full moon on Solstice—that was supposed to be good luck. But Gristle found no cheer; it meant that, even if the air smelled sweet and spiced and there were wreaths on all the posts and columns, this was the darkest night of the cycle.

He agreed. Gristle dragged his eyes up to the clock on the bank across the road: it had been nearly half a bell since he'd sat down, and still no cab.

She forgot about me, he told himself. He tried to swallow the lump lurching up into his throat, but it wouldn't ease. He shuffled a tin from his jacket pocket and shook two vervain tablets into his palm. When they split between his teeth, he could remember Hàzell burning vervain when he had scarlet fever, dabbing cold wine on his forehead, parting his hair while his daddy hummed something old and faintly haunting. It dulled the pain but couldn't kill it. His mind wouldn't go back to sleep again.

There was a hush of wheels through slush. Gristle looked up, eyelids sagging under cold exhaustion, to see a cab sat just ahead of him with its headlights boring into the falling snow. The cabbie stepped out and onto the sidewalk. He hadn't been forgotten! Gristle felt grinning warmth whisper its way through him and began to stand.

But then Ashley came streaming down the cement path, overcoat flowing behind, face so severe and pale against the darkness that it seemed to glow. He went straight past Gristle without acknowledgment.

"Senator Ashley," the cabbie said, opening the back door to spill light onto the icy sidewalk. "Where will it be?"

"A personal call." Ashley slid into the back seat and settled in with the ease of a man who never drove himself anywhere. Gristle wondered if he wanted that sort of wealth. More than that, he wanted that sort of security. He wanted to be able to stop caring. "Swing me by Number 8, 1st Street, and then to Cat's Cantina on Chestnut."

Why the hell was Ashley going to a dive bar like Cat's? It just felt like another mockery. The cab peeled off and away. Maybe he ought to meet Ashley at Cat's, be like his reckless daddy and throw stupid punches, tear the world apart with his teeth. Maybe this was *his* moment to break down.

The streetlamp ahead flashed angrily. Gristle's knees tensed to stand.

"Gristle?" he heard, and jumped. Calligan had come up the walk beside him, straightening the fur collar of their plaid coat. There was a streetlamp on Gristle's other side, painting their glasses blinding white in the cold gray gloom. "Shouldn't you be home?"

Gristle wiped at his eyes—they were damp. "C-cab," he managed to shiver out. The street was comically empty.

Calligan seemed to weigh that. "Mind if I sit?"

Gristle didn't have time to hear their bitching and whining and snively complaining, but also didn't have the energy to say so.

Calligan settled in beside him, rubbing their gloved hands together. "It's damn cold," they said, that small talk Gristle never knew what to do with. "My husband's bringing me dinner but I wish he'd hurry."

Gristle swallowed. "I didn't know you're married," he grumbled.

"'Course not," Calligan said. Their breath fogged up in the air, catching the light. Gristle couldn't begin to read their tone, besides to hear something distinctly dockside creeping in on the edges. "Why would you? Not sure how much I know about you, neither, outside work."

Gristle said nothing. Calligan said nothing. Gristle really had no idea how to talk to people, especially lately, when every stumble in his words or possibly sour glance made him feel like gum on their soles.

There came a set of crunching footsteps and a faint jingle of bells. Gristle and Calligan turned to where a man was walking down the way with his collar flipped up near his grizzled chin, holding a paper deli bag tucked under one arm and the hand of a toddler flouncing along in a bell-studded Solstice dress.

"Daidí!" the kid howled. They tried to run—their tiny shoes slipped on the ice but their father kept them up by one wrenched hand until Calligan raced to sweep them onto their hip. They took the bag and kissed the man's cheek.

Cute. Adorable, even. It was more awkward to sit there than to leave, yes? Gristle stood, despite his aching knees and the rough shuffling of his clothes on his skin. The cab wasn't coming. Press on.

"Oh, Gristle," Calligan called, and then lowered their voice some. "This is Gristle Maxim. You know, her nephew." Gristle wanted to scuttle off, but he turned anyway and tried to fix his posture. "Gristle, this is Calligan Child," Calligan said, while getting their glasses pulled off by grabby fingers, "and my husband, Davis Weekusk."

"Pleasure," Davis said, holding out his wide hand. Gristle clasped it and shook, very mechanically. "I heard you cracked that rotten business at the Dog."

Would he ever be free of it? "Tried to, anyhow," Gristle droned for the thousandth time. At least Davis wasn't another senator or journalist or benefactor at a gala, but there was almost something worse about having to lay the story out for some ordinary man who looked more like the burly dockyard workers of his youth than the rich cats he circled now. "But the case went cold. O'Taglio was good at covering her tracks at home and . . ." As for work, the Dogfoot staff had all disappeared like smoke the second the police cleared them. Gristle suspected those "connections" Hien had mentioned had played a hand, but Hien wasn't exactly around to ask who or how or why. "And we've just heard that the Dogfoot's been sold for land to build some sort of community center, so all's well."

Calligan nodded. "Well . . ." they said quietly. Davis touched their arm. Gristle wasn't sure why. Calligan just sighed and shook their head. "Let's just say we have a lot of work to do from here on in," they decided on, which seemed to be a much gentler version of what they were actually thinking. Davis took the cue and plucked Calligan Child away to point at the wreaths and stars and moon reflected in Calligan's glasses still held in their tiny fist.

Calligan looked at Gristle a little longer, eyes so very deep and clear without their always-shining lenses, and then did the last thing Gristle expected: they lifted their hand and laid it on his shoulder, grip warm and well. Gristle tried to look at Calligan properly, with that intense stare to make every devil fall in line. He couldn't remember how to pull it off. He feared he looked as young as he felt.

"Your aunt won't tell me all of it, but I know something rotten went on at the Dog, and I still know that Ashley would have won if you hadn't broken that case," they told him. Calligan Child shrieked with glee as Davis flew them through the air like a shooting star, ringing all the happy bells. Gristle's mouth creased into a wrinkled line. "You've been helpful, Gristle, but you're also good-hearted. Don't let anything stamp that out of you, alright?"

Gristle couldn't hear this. "Thanks," he said, even if he knew his voice never sounded as sincere as he felt. He tapped his brim, sloughing Calligan's hand away. "Happy Solstice."

"Oh . . . yes," Calligan said hurriedly. Their eyebrows pressed together. "You know, Davis and Calligan Child are going to the Solstice bonfire at the Jahagee Cent—" But Gristle was already turning swiftly on his heel.

"Happy Solstice to you too, jack," Davis added, and whispered something before . . .

"Happy Solstice!" Calligan Child cheered.

Gristle raised his hand to return the gesture, and maybe so it wouldn't look quite so obvious that he was wiping his eyes clear.

He wanted to get home, if you could call it that, and shut the world out until his aunt called on him. At the very least, he had whiskey there, and more vervain. Being good-hearted hurt, and dulling the pain was a temporary fix. *Fine.*

Gristle took off for the trolley stop, fast enough to fear his feet sliding out from under him with no one to hold his wrist up. The windows of the fine shops sent square light over the icy pavement and blustering whirls of snow. A trolley bell rang from the distance. Gristle squinted and sped to the stop just ahead, raising his hand into the light. He could have sworn he saw the driver look right at him, and yet the damn thing kept on chugging past, throwing dirty slush over his shoes and soaking into his socks.

"Saints," he hissed, fumbling back and shaking out his feet. The chill still sank in deep, right to the bones that weighed lead-heavy inside him. Couldn't anything go *right*? It was all spinning so far from his grasp, whirling into madness. What if his aunt never got a handle on the O'Taglio case? What if they never found out who paid her, and so Gristle was never forgiven?

He would just live with this guilt forever, wouldn't he? Alone and terrified of the future he could see coming, unable to shut his mind to the oncoming pain.

Something hot stabbed into the back of his leg.

Gristle gave an undignified yelp, jumping around so quickly that his feet skidded. He stumbled back into the hard trolley stop post, hands flailing to get a grip on it.

One small light above a closed bookshop door caught the falling snow and radiated out around the dark, impossibly large shape that stood ahead of Gristle. Its eyes, glowing under bat-like ears, did not blink.

The shape gave only one little huff of breath. Gristle's breath came out in a similar puff.

"Quen?" he breathed.

The dog's tail gave one considerate swing. Had he ever asked where it went after the Dog? Had it slipped out and been running wild since then? Its fur was still sleek, eyes still bright. Had someone in the neighborhood taken it in? Those were the most logical answers.

"Good poochie," Gristle started to say. Quen cocked its head, swung its nose from him, and suddenly took off at a southbound gallop.

"Damn it," Gristle muttered. Not at Quen, but at his feet that had already gone slamming after it. His body was moving without thinking, like there was a tether straight through his ribs and into the soft insides. Quen sped down the block, a black comet caught in the temporary telescope's eye of the decorated streetlamps. Gristle's lungs ached but he didn't stop, even when he passed a phone booth to call another cab, even when Quen turned west across the quiet intersection, heading off the trolley route and deeper into the snowy city.

What the hell am I doing? What the hell do I think is happening?

Gristle slid around the corner just in time to see Quen's tail disappear between two buildings. He rushed up, almost sliding into the barely pried-open gate between a soaring apartment complex and an office tower. Beyond, the alley was blocked and black.

He shouldered in even as the rusty squeal echoed down into his marrow. In the impenetrable gloom so far below the stars, Quen's paws rattled through the alley's gravel and snow.

And then they stopped. Gristle did too, with the taste of blood and bile heaving out to billow against his sweaty face.

"Quen," he said again.

The dog let out a faint whine, just enough to say it was there in the dark. A dull scraping sound rustled ahead of him, claws on metal. They'd hit the end of the alley, where there must have been a door. The morgue, Gristle suddenly feared. The familiar was trying to get back to its dead master. Gristle's throat tightened. No, surely Hien had already been buried... were they near a cemetery instead?

Somewhere just steps ahead, hinges squealed. A thick smell washed out in smoky, herb-green billows that smothered into Gristle's pores. He recognized it almost immediately, at the same time a spear of cast-off shock needled into his brain.

Vervain, for pain.

Ahead of him, seemingly with no one touching it, a light buzzed alive from past the opened door. It showed an apartment complex basement, filled with furnace room pipes and a boiler. And it bled out around the blurry edges of something impossible to describe standing backlit in the doorway, a smear of horns and feathers and eyes and teeth and scales.

Gristle's cells sang out. In an instant he missed, he was suddenly staring at the warbling shape of a Hannochian folk wearing a silk robe over a simple singlet and trousers, a cigarette of pain-killing vervain hanging from their thin lips. Though their expression was placid, Gristle could feel spatters of panic burning into him like sparks off a grindstone, feel exhaustion swarming out to pull at his bones.

Quen slunk forward almost guiltily, to sit heavy upon the slippers of the one and only Phong Hien, who'd left Gristle behind.

"You're alive," Gristle breathed. Then came the first thought that rose unprompted into his head, the first un-patterned moment after moons of cruel logic. His skin burned, and he said it. "I oughta kill you for dying."

Hawthorne Stregoni
Number 3113, 8th Street
Puck's Port, Dale
57SC1W20

H,

Firstly, Fifthchild wants to know what it's like to live way up on 8th. They saw the pictures from that grand opening gala and got all giddy about it. Last week they made Iffy drive them and Fourth past the school just to get a good look. They told me they wanted to see you but I said you were studying hard. They understood.

Now that you're settled, I think we should talk.

With love,
Feenee

Hawthorne Stregoni
Number 3113, 8th Street
Puck's Port, Dale
57SC16W42

H.,

Did you get my last letter? I'm hoping it's some postal jam, so we'll call it evens. How are things? Fourth and Fifth keep stealing the paper looking for you. We caught that interview a moon ago—you look real happy in the picture. Well-rested I guess. It's funny... I never noticed you looked so tired until I saw that you didn't.

Dolly Day just wrote to tell me that I've got the intern spot. I start in the new cycle. I have to go apartment hunting soon. I feel like a real grown-up. It's not as scary as I thought it'd be, or at least it's good scary.

I want to talk to you, about that, and everything. I'm not sure what we are now that you're there and I'm out here, and we haven't talked at all. I guess I knew things could change, but I never saw a world where we weren't at least friends when it did.

Write me back if you're getting these.

With love,
Feenee

Hawthorne Stregoni
Number 3113, 8th Street
Puck's Port, Dale
57SC16 W123

Hawthorne Stregoni,

I called your brother and asked how you are, and he says you're not seeing anyone, but that you're alright. So I guess you're alright. He's sounding rough. I think the Dogfoot did him something awful. I want to say I'm too good for that, but I don't think I am. I'm more scared than I used to be, like I got the sense kicked in. It's sort of sad, but sort of good.

I'm at Wolly soon. Everyone from school's got roommates and no vacancies, so I just signed for this tiny basement apartment uptown. It's not worth what I'm paying for it, but it's mine starting in the new cycle.

Happy Solstice, Hawthorne. Phone me up when you're able. I guess we can see what page we're on then, if it's the same enough. I can't say I won't have any hurt feelings if we call it quits, but I can say I'll survive it. You taught me that I'm tough enough to get through hard things.

Fionne

HAWTHORNE STREGONI IN
"SAFE HAVEN"

I'm giving up on thinking I'll get better. Now I just have to figure out how to make good with what I've got.

Between donations and grants, the school could afford ten more doctors, and to move us out of that tiny sanitorium to a nearly mansion-looking place up on 8th off toward the antique east side. It's all clean, brown brick and sharp roofs and spires on the outside. Inside, the dark wood halls echo, and the classrooms have tall windows to shine warm light onto the chalkboards. They brought in two dozen new students. I'm still the oldest, the uniform is the same kiddy clothes, and classes aren't much different.

That's fine, 'cause I stay here every day, all day, so I don't care what we do or don't do. The patterns are easy.

Tonight, for Solstice, we're eating dinner in the big meal room with its checkered floor and usually bland walls strung up with green streamers we made. The doctors are at the head table near the kitchen window, wearing their white coats and chattering while some kid with scales stands up there and lists all the trees they know in alphabetical order. They hold their hands behind their back, fingers around their wrists, and don't even sway when they say them. I wonder if listing makes the symptoms burn under their skin, asking to be released, screaming for one more beautiful disaster. My pores feel like match heads.

"My mum says she'll come after dinner," the kid across from me says, pulling me back. They're one of my roommates, just a cycle younger than me, but their name is always leaking out of my head. They line their carrots up beside each other, some not-thinking motion while they talk. "The docs say she can stay until one bell past the Solstice, so we can celebrate it together."

The other kids hum and chew.

My roommate glances up to me. Damn. They weren't big on talking when they came in, but the doctors coaxed out a slow, precise voice. "How about you, Hawthorne?" they ask.

I hold my fork tighter. "My aunt's gonna call."

"She's not coming?" a littler kid down the table asks. "What about your brother?"

I click my teeth against each other. "They're busy," I say, just low enough that the kid looks away. It's not a lie, but it ain't exactly the reason I haven't seen either of them face-to-face since I ended up here. And it's not for my aunt's lack of trying on each nightly call.

I blink hard to stop the rumbling off every breath.

"My poppa ain't showing up," that same little kid says, elbow on the table, cheek shoved into their hand. They flick at a piece of their dry turkey. "I think it's 'cause my Third is still scared."

"What'd you do?" someone asks.

I can feel the heat twining through my curls, burning in my palm. I remember how it lashed out. It's still in me, I know it is, that same fire waiting for my guard to go down.

"Turned my fingers into spider legs by accident," the kid says. I guess they had enough control to change them back, but there are still spiny black hairs up each finger, like a reminder. They huff. "I was *trying* to make my whole body into a spider."

A few kids laugh.

Spider-kid blushes. "Well, if I practiced more, then I could do it," they say. The hairs twitch. My skin tightens. "I hear folk in Jahag can."

"Folk in Jahag are Old World," I say into my plate. Every word feels carefully put together. "Spiders don't get to drive cars."

They go more glum than angry. "Spiders don't have poppas who tell them to get lost," they mutter. Their eyes are glassy—blinking hard doesn't clear it. "Spiders get to leave the house if they want."

"Spiders don't hurt themselves if they get too rattled," my roommate offers. That puts a nice blanket of heavy calm over the table.

We all know we're just accidents waiting to happen, with pin-trigger impulses.

Some kid another table over drops their glass. It shatters into a million shards, each of 'em ringing and catching the light. A shock sweeps through the room—the pyre in my stomach roars, lashing into my blood. Orange heat flushes across my cheeks and nose. It gets louder every day.

I drop my fork and put my hands under my legs, tighten my shoulders, and stop breathing. My roommate accidentally grows three porcupine quills out each cheekbone before they take the same position. Everyone else at the table matches it, backs straight and eyes unfocused dead ahead. We look like soda bottles all down the line, ready to *pop-pop-pop*.

Keep calm, I think. It's the same shit as always. Bigger school, but we don't have anything new yet. It's still the same old tricks that don't work for the people already ruined. *Keep calm. Keep calm.*

We do. But there's a snarl from behind us that says someone else didn't keep their cap on well enough. I turn to see a kid a bit younger than me twisting and writhing at the table behind. A pulse of pressure spears off them. Dust puffs from the ceiling—our plates hop. The kid falls off their chair, tumbling into the aisle under the light hanging from the middle of the room, pitching and moaning as one of the bigger teachers races over with an iron jacket. When he tries to reach for the kid, their thrashing head sends another burst of air pressure to slice raw-red across the teacher's hand. He swears but clamps the coat down over the kid, smothering their nervous system, while three other teachers come rushing over to soothe and pat.

We all turn back to our plates when the snarling turns to tears, and the teachers try to bundle the kid out for the medical office. The iron-coat smell fogs up the room. Chew. Swallow. Drink some water from the glass cups. If they were wooden, they wouldn't break, but that won't much prepare us for "the real world." As if we'll ever get there.

"Poor jack," my roommate says, staring off toward the door. Spider-kid is crying, silent. I can't think about it all. I just pick my fork up again and try to get a potato on it and get that fork to my mouth and chew and swallow.

Doc Secondchild stands up and tucks his chair with a horrible little squealing sound that I don't let bother me, and then he's walking over. I look to my roommate; they push their carrots out of a perfect line, even though it makes them wince. One by one, the quills evaporate from their skin.

Secondchild smiles, striding past me with his clipboard under his arm and his shoes striking the tiled floor. "Come on, Stregoni. Let's get that phone call started." When he walks past, I see everyone straighten and keep their hands in tight fists. One kid flicks their eyes back to round-pupiled blue before he can notice.

I swallow, but carefully stand and lift my chair up to tuck it in. I put my feet down cautiously to speed out after him, through the wooden doors wrapped with annoying little Solstice bells and into the hallway.

When the door seals shut, it's like we're the only two people in the world, apart from the echo of someone's radio somewhere playing Solstice carols. They twist toward us like a ghost.

Secondchild jerks his chin off down the arch-shaped hall and I step up next to him, hands held behind my back 'cause I know it ain't proper to put them in my pockets. I just stare ahead of me, let it all melt to a caramel-colored blur.

"How was dinner?" Secondchild asks.

I nod a bit. "Fine. Yours?"

"Fine," he says, but a bit slower than me, almost a question. "How are classes? How's math? What about shop? You like shop."

He knows how my classes are. I flunked my last test, and I haven't finished my shop project because I won't be putting my steel-and-flint hands anywhere near timber. I don't want to say it, and I don't want to hear him say it either, so I just shrug.

He stops trying to talk to me. We climb up a wide set of stairs toward the third floor. Out the towering window on the landing, the front courtyard spills into the antique east end of 8th Street, with the sky mostly clear to show the bright, round moon. Supposed to be good luck when Winter Solstice is on a full moon. My throat is tight again. If I'm lucky, I'll get through this phone call without bursting into tears. I can already feel them prickling in my nose. But it's just a phone call. I can fake some merriment for that long.

We turn off down a smaller, darker hall where us students don't go often. The doc steps to his office door between two electric sconces, unlocks it.

He doesn't step in, just freezes in the doorway—I almost run into him. Around him, I can see the phone sitting on his desk and backlit by a dramatic arch window all full of jewely stained glass, but he doesn't move for it.

I cuff my fingers around my wrists, so I won't think to shove him. "Come on, Doc," I say. My eyes start prickling worse. "Phone call, right?"

He breathes in slowly through his nose, turning to rake his eyes around my face in a way I don't love.

"Hawthorne, your aunt's called me four times today asking why you won't see her," he says. My stomach swims. "It's Solstice—"

"That doesn't change anything," I say, a bit too fast. He doesn't flinch, even when my teeth are tight and I can feel my eyes watering. I hunch my shoulders up, cool my voice. "I'm not taking chances," I tell him, quieter.

"It's commendable," he says, pushing his glasses back up his nose. "But you can't avoid her forever."

"I'm not ready for it," I say. Even when I *thought* I was in control, I killed Hien. Something isn't working. And how different am I now? Besides a bigger school, what's actually changed? My voice cracks. "There's still all this *bad* in me, and if it gets on her then—"

"Alright," he says, soft. He reaches out and I step into his side, pressing my forehead into his shoulder hard enough to keep the tears back. His other arm lands heavy around my back, giving me two good pats. It's all clinical, stiff, 'cause he ain't family and he knows that. He's just a doctor, with his expectations managed.

I don't want to be around people who think I'm gonna be alright. I can't let them down again.

"I know things are tough," he says. That makes the tears burn up to soak into the stiff, starched white of his coat.

"I thought I had it handled," I cry. "But the Dogfoot—no matter how hard I work, I ain't gonna be able to change my blood and cap this—and being here, maybe I don't have . . ." *Freedom*. And yet, there's the smell of Hien cooking. The look on Gristle's face. Shredding Fionne's letters in the envelopes so I won't be tempted to bring her anywhere near me. The pyre bashes at me. I want so badly to let it win so this can all just end. It's all coming apart, but at least I'm away from the folks I'd disappoint. "I'm *not* getting better. I-I'm not ever going to—"

"You don't know that, Stregoni."

"'Cause you're such an expert in what I'm feeling," I snap. His arm tightens, like I've hurt him as bad as that other kid slicing the air apart. My skull screams to keep doing just that, cut him down inch by inch until he understands. That's madness. It all is. *I* am.

He doesn't respond. Instead, I feel him take a slow, even breath. He lets it out above my head. "I might have something that could help," he says quietly. It floats around all the empty space, off the polished walls. "It's something new we've been working on. It's cleared for trial now—we figured we'd start after the Solstice, get consent forms signed when parents come in tonight. But you're eighteen, so if you want . . ."

My skin's still prickling, but I step back from him. He's still a bit blurry. Even wiping my eyes doesn't make him clear. "Something new . . ." I say. Is it some alternative meditation technique? A stricter exposure therapy regimen? Is he gonna hand me another journal so I can "write out my feelings" for two weeks and then forget about it, or say my daily newspaper is "too stimulating" and replace it with kids' books? There's this cringing in my chest. I can't much tell what it wants. "I'm not a lab rat, Doc," I tell him.

"Obviously not," he says. A bit of his usual smile comes back, but he's still real serious. "Otherwise, I've been writing your species in wrong this whole while."

I roll my eyes, but the joking at least makes me feel a bit better.

"I'd really like you to get to see your aunt. I mean that," he tells me, solid like he's always been. "This new treatment isn't a permanent fix, but it might help things slow down for a bell or so." His eyes are all bright behind his wire-rimmed glasses. "A Solstice miracle, if you will."

That actually makes me laugh, just a buzz through my lips. "You're sounding real superstitious, Doc," I say, grabbing my own wrists tight as cuffs. "What happened to science and logic?"

"Well, I can bore you with that, if you'd like," he says. Finally, he's willing to turn in to the office. "We can try this out, and see how you feel. If we're still not sure, then a phone call is better than nothing."

I ain't making any promises. Optimism is for chaotic kids, but I can't stand the idea of letting one more person down.

"It's nothing invasive," he says from the middle of the room, looking back at me still frozen out here. The rug he stands on is soft maroon and gold, cheery garlands hang from the bookshelves and fireplace mantle, and snow falls gently behind the window that frames him with his kind smile and tacky Solstice necktie. It could be the beginning of something nice. "Try it? For your aunt?"

I wish I could give her the niece she deserves. I wish I believed that person was still in me somewhere waiting.

"Alright," I say, stepping into the office. There's nothing to lose, really, not in a school that's safe as a madhouse. "Hit me with it."

PUCK'S PORT POLICE DEPARTMENT

Form A-316 (Coroner's Div.)   Autopsy Case # 22

Victim's Name (Last, First, Middle)

Hien, Phong

Status	Age	Race	Wgt.	Ht.
Fey	20	Han	150 lbs	5'2"

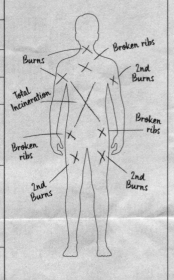

DESCRIPTION OF BODY
Severe burns to the abdominal and chest area

EXTERNAL INJURIES
Third degree burns from the navel to the clavicle, radiating into second degree down the arms, pelvis, and jaw

INTERNAL INJURIES
Incineration of all internal organs, and burning to the spine. Ribs 1-3 and 10-11 suffered splintering, the rest burned to ash

MEDICAL DIAGNOSIS
Cause of death: trauma to the internal organs. Victim appears to have died nearly instantly due to shock

NOTES
No signs of struggle or additional injury. Brain chemistry indicates high fey capability, though does not suggest fey symptoms within the last bell of life

INVEST. OFFICER	RECORDING OFFICER	DATE	DELIVERY
Chief Bazik	Deputy Ma	57SC/3W/6	H. Abebe

CORONER P.H. Sống

GRISTLE SENAN MAXIM JUNIOR
IN
"ELECTRIC IMPULSES"

Gristle Senan Maxim Junior was supposed to be leaving everything alone. But ahead of him in the alley's-end doorway, Hien stood smoking, and not in an incinerated sort of way.

"You faked your death." Gristle choked up. His throat felt vise-tight, like all the muscles might splinter against each other. "You made me think my sister *killed you*, Hien. She *still* thinks that!"

Was that the plan? Had Hien known the killer was in the building, known they could hire some daffy little half-baked detective to pretend to solve it just to make it someone else's problem? Known Shona Maxim would clean it all up?

Hien just stared in their robe and singlet and trousers, no makeup or trickery or pageantry, like they couldn't even be bothered to pretend they respected him.

A surge of anger ripped up through Gristle. He slammed his hand into the doorframe, palm screaming with fizzing pain from the blow. "Say something!" he snapped, boring his eyes into the black pits of theirs. The rest of their body twisted and churned like smoke or shadows, flashes of indescribable visions that cleared only when he tried to catch them. Hien existed only in front of an audience, and came apart everywhere else. "You goaded me into watching you kill someone, and now you're the coward?"

Hien rippled with a spluttering pulse of wind. It vibrated into Gristle's skull like a dull drill, forcing him back a step. He should leave, he thought, listen to his aunt. He just needed to get out of there and accept that this was all over. The thought itself tugged at his muscles, as if it would peel them back from bone. Did Gristle himself want to leave, or did Hien want him to? Were they whispering pain and cowardice into his marrow so he'd finally forget them, now that the job was done? Gristle's whole body twisted in on itself. He almost doubled over.

Quen nosed at Hien's hanging hand. It was just enough to convince Hien to turn away. For a moment, Gristle saw a shock of bright hair falling down their back, but then it was again dark and close-cut. They stepped inside and reached to shut the door on him.

Gristle's voice came out on its own, spilling from some back corner so long forgotten that it sounded timid and young. "I did everything you asked me to," Gristle said, while every smell of ice and gravel and metal clawed through his sinuses. "Were you just using me?" Why would anyone want to hire him, really? Had he thought he might still succeed? Might still become something? Might help that scared dame in the office? "I can't believe I ever felt sorry for you," he said.

A plume of exhaled smoke rose from Hien's turned-away face.

The door shut suddenly, boxing Gristle back to blackness. He tensed his leg, ready to kick the door until his bones snapped. It would do nothing to help him, but neither would every other choice.

Gristle drew his foot back.

Hien's impossible voice wound up in his head the same as it had before. *I can speak to you, or show myself, but it's a strain to maintain both*. Gristle could have sunk to the ground right there. *I'm not as I was*.

The world had stayed constant, but in it, they were different. Gristle's rage refused to dim. "Me neither," he breathed in the dark. The vervain smell still clung to the air. Whatever Hien had planned for that night, Gristle doubted they'd anticipated an injury. Maybe they deserved that. "She hit you, then. You weren't just pretending."

The doorknob creaked, but no light came out. *Not quite so serious as I had to feign, but yes.* A flash of memory. Heat speared up through Gristle's chest, blocked by something heavy like armor and yet still stinging. The pain wasn't a burn, but panic that killed any confidence. Gristle was used to taking shots, but Hien? *Your sister is quite powerful*, they decided to say. *I've won a number of duels, but I hadn't anticipated how much she'd pack behind her punch.*

Gristle could have told them as much. Somehow, that made the corner of his mouth twitch despite the churning frustration still coursing through him. Snow fell against his hat, an infuriating series of tiny nudges like death by ant bite. "She's at school now, twenty-four-bells," he decided to say. "They'll help her so that won't happen again."

He heard how rehearsed it was. Who was this person who just droned on with Gristle's mouth and voice? He closed his eyes against the pulsing under his skin.

A small breeze slipped through Gristle's synapses, as if Hien had prepared to speak and then stopped.

"You left," Gristle muttered. The hinges shivered open ahead by the tiniest fracture. He wondered if he might see Hien, see them for real, if he just dared to open his eyes. But somehow it was easier to say this to nothing but the black behind his eyelids. "You broke everything I thought was true, you had me on your side, and then you just dropped me. And now nothing feels normal—it all feels *fake*."

The door opened a bit more. There came no arrogant hum. No chuckle. Hien's voice was quiet, even in his head, like faintly reverberated words barely beyond a whisper. *I shouldn't have toyed with you as I did, and yet you must have expected this from the start, Mister Maxim.*

Gristle scoffed. He *had* known Hien would hurt him, so what was he hoping to get from a dead jack who abandoned him to the cops and press and politicians of this damn city?

A reset, he knew. If there was no way to fix anything, then he'd at least like to go back to the days before he knew that. He wanted to fall for it.

The door opened the rest of the way, so he kept his eyes squeezed shut, terrified that he'd jinx this one chance. A sudden, heavy warmth settled in the center of Gristle's chest, crinkling his shirt into that old burn scar. Gristle felt every digit of Hien's fingers there, every crease of their palm against his rough clothes that never fit so fine as that Goodfellows' suit.

His heart thumped loudly, as if Hien had shot it up with something. When Gristle opened his eyes, Hien was again some strange blur ahead of him, the suggestion of diamond earrings and a Hannochian snow leopard coat and slicked hair, tricks on tricks. And yet their face was soft, eyes tired but shining in the back glow that pulsed through their unreal figure.

"Nothing feels right since the Dog," Gristle whispered, unsure what he was even asking. "I don't know what you did to me back there, but I want it reversed."

I didn't do anything to you. Nothing permanent, anyhow, Hien said, image flickering with strain. Their palm warmed against Gristle's chest, yet he could feel tiny pinpricks like frustrated claws. *Do you really think so little of me that you believe I'd alter you without permission?*

Well, why not? No one else liked him as he was, and here was someone who could actually change his mind into exactly what they wanted. Was it so hard to believe they would?

Right here, right now, if Hien could snap their fingers and make Gristle into a perfect nephew, he'd take the chance. That's what this was, he understood.

"Then here's your permission," Gristle said with gritted teeth. He lifted his own hand and set it on Hien's wrist to keep the contact steady. It was like grabbing water. "Fix me. You asked me what I want. I want that. Fix whatever the hell is wrong with me."

Hien paused, mouth twitching. Gristle didn't care what they thought about him. Finally, Hien's palm turned, creasing hard into Gristle's shirt.

Gristle waited for the world to seep back to blurs and smoothed senses, to a life of sleeping awake. Or maybe just to wake up in his broom closet room ready to accept every pleasant mundanity without feeling destroyed by the weight of this uncaring city. The light thrummed louder from inside the building's basement. The icicles dripped. Quen breathed hot huffs of nervous air as it nosed Hien's legs, fur shearing against unseen fabric. The cigarette still in Hien's mouth was burnt down nearly to their lips. There were a million stars in the sky. It was the opposite of what he'd asked. Gristle wanted it to stop, and yet felt a gasp wrench its way from his lips.

I, Hien struggled to say. Their image pulsed. Gristle saw a glimpse of something he couldn't describe, but wanted to. Hien's hand shook and Gristle kept his grip. Bright flashes of color and tastes and sounds and smells strobed through Gristle's mind in rhythms, in patterns. *I l-learned my lesson about meddling in matters beyond my purview, but I don't regret . . . telling you to grow a spine.*

What the hell did that mean? The light back there burned up so bright he thought it might explode. It bled through the swarming vision of Hien ahead of him, which was waning like a candle. They were so strange, against everything mundane and awful that he was tired of. And they were here with him when no one else was. They'd opened the door when no one else did.

What do you want, Mister Maxim? Hien asked. *You. Just you.*

He'd just said! And yet in the pulsing and screaming of his body, against Hien so bright ahead, he still wondered. Was that his own hesitancy? Was Hien injecting it into him? Did that matter? They were still a rush of something impossible, and yet the swirling maelstrom took the cigarette away to grin with a mouth of eel-sharp teeth.

"I want everything to change," Gristle breathed amidst his screaming senses.

He understood that he could have that, could have anything, if he only dared to grab it.

And then Gristle was pulling Hien into him by instinct and smashing his lips into theirs, clumsy and ill-practiced and yet insistent enough to believe he could. There was a shattering of glass from ahead that said the light bulb really had popped. In the dark, Gristle's tie was in Hien's fist for some sort of leverage to pull him even closer, then his hands were on Hien's hips. It was all a half-spun dream. Was it really happening? He didn't know. He couldn't be sure.

He didn't really care. For one moment in his sorry life, he didn't feel broken or invisible.

Hien thought a sound between a snarl and a purr, and Gristle could have looped it on a gramophone just to hear something besides his own far-removed narration. His lips crashed into theirs so hard he thought their teeth would scrape. He wondered if Hien's were actually sharp, and was answered by a sudden spark of pain across his bottom lip and the faintest tang of copper on his tongue.

Gristle's back crashed into the doorjamb. Hien's ice-cold fingers hiked his shirt loose and pressed against the soft skin of his waist.

Gristle hissed, tried to catch his breath but couldn't. He pulled back from Hien—the alleyway darkness pulsed ahead of him, fraying around the faint shape of something out there.

"You terrify me," Gristle wheezed. His lips were both numb and red-hot. He wasn't sure his legs would support him if he pulled his feet back under him properly.

Likewise, Hien said. Funny how they were only honest when he couldn't see them. There was something still tentative about them, their words bold but their aura moving carefully as their hands fell back from him. *Why are you still here, Mister Maxim? Don't you have some fancy political gala to be at?*

The truth poured from Gristle's lips like liquor. "My aunt won't even look at me since the O'Taglio case died. Whoever hired her is still out there."

Hien shifted. *That does put my skin in the game*, they said ahead of him, even if it wasn't true. They'd disappeared as completely as mist in the morning sun, and could do it again. *Nothing came of Rory Gattano, I imagine.*

"Could be dead," Gristle muttered. Weak link gets the chop, was that it? "Quit work at the switchboard center, hasn't been seen in moons—"

They offered another truth: *I could always ask my sister for some assistance from the Hannochian Court.* There it was, the confirmation that Hien knew mobsters in high places. Here the Maxims were again, tangling with faces from the underbelly. Gristle refused to feel guilty for it—the old way wasn't working. *Surely someone at that grease-sodden diner overheard something with enough promise. We could give some prods.*

Diner? Gristle paused. Stars were shooting through his neurons, nearly making connections.

A flame pricked on, just enough to illuminate the end of another vervain cigarette floating in the dark. *Come now, Mister Maxim,* Hien mused. *You might not know enough about the underground, but surely you know something about the city layout.*

An image warbled through Gristle's mind, just out of grasp: the faintest shape of a smudgy black tattoo, and the feeling of iron in calloused hands. Gristle squinted and tried to reach for the thought.

The neurons clicked together. They sang out in every color behind his eyes. Gristle's lips parted. His stomach dropped out.

Cat's was just down the road from the Gattano garage. And he knew someone who was on their way there, with a lot to gain by framing fey as unchecked monsters—after all, he'd used it to win once before. He must have been clever to keep Shona Maxim off his trail, but he hadn't expected Gristle to overhear him from that bench.

"Phone," Gristle fumbled out. His heart was still slamming. Should he tell his aunt? No. There might not be time, or she might tell him to leave this, and he *couldn't*. She already distrusted him—there was nothing to lose by diving in deeper, but everything to gain if he resurfaced as a hero. "I've got a call to make."

He began to sway back toward the street, to spill from the alley and find a phone booth.

For the record, Hien said, from where the faint glow of their cigarette almost touched a thousand planes and glints of imperceptible things, *I may not be as powerful as I was, and I ought to be reserved, but I'm still prepared to accompany you, despite your disappointing backslide in fashion.* Gristle narrowed his eyes, but the next part seemed more sincere. *Consider this payment on my debts, Mister Maxim.*

If tonight was going how he thought it would, he wanted all the support he could get. And if Hien was stowing the show-off, it would be mighty fine support indeed.

"Please do," Gristle said. He was waking up to a world of possibility, even the chance that Senan Maxim's son might finally win. "Thank you, Hien. Sincerely."

University of Stoutshire Institution for Fey Re-Education

Student Name: _Stregoni, H_   Date: _57 SC/6W/WS_

Doctor: _Sonder Secondchild_   Session Number: _236_

Disciplinary Meeting: y / (n) (if y, please fill out Form J)

Reason for session: _Experimental treatment to control fey symptoms and delicate fey sensitivities in order for smoother integration into mortal life._

Observations: _____

Attentive	Inattentive	Session lasted < 5 min	If a student has exhibited any symptoms, please describe in Form J
Verbal	Semi-verbal or selectively verbal	Non-verbal	
No power flare	Small power flare	Large power flare	

Form A: Page 1

HAWTHORNE STREGONI IN "THE DRINK RUNS DRY"

I walk into the doc's office where the lights glow warm like pancake syrup, better than the cold wood of the Maxim & Maxim office. It's cozy, but I'm gonna stay realistic here. Maybe this works, maybe it doesn't, but at least I can say I tried. I ease over to the chair in front of the doc's huge carved desk and sit.

Doc Secondchild leaves his lab coat on the coatrack, all casual in his vest and sleeve garters as he swipes up a clipboard and a printed form.

"You look like someone's butler," I mutter, hoping the joke can make us all forget how raw my eyes still are.

"Manners," he says as he sits, but he's still smiling, so I know he ain't serious. "We're excited about this treatment, Stregoni. It's more than just cognitive mitigation—we're getting to the baseline."

"Big words," I say.

Two more flourishes before he tosses the pen and form aside and rolls his chair back to the bookcase behind him, popping open a tiny cabinet there. "This won't be a permanent solution just yet, but hopefully the start of one."

He pulls a smooth, silver bottle from the cabinet, and a crystal glass. Okay, so it's just a medicine, like cough syrup or something to help you sleep. That's not bad. And compared to years of meditation training and slogging through trade classes, drinking something feels pretty easy. "Now you look like a bartender," I try to joke. It comes out a bit steadier than before.

He laughs and pours. The liquid shines like melted silver, all glimmery and opal-ish. "We'll give you the standard dose and monitor from there."

I tilt my chin up a bit, tracing my tongue over my teeth. "What's in it?"

"It's a silver-based solution, with stimulants."

"I thought I was over-stimulated."

"You're *under*-stimulated," the doc says, tipping the bottle toward me. "That's why symptoms emerge, to fill that gap. With some chemical consistency, you won't be compelled to do that."

I know I can't control my impulses, but if I never have them at all? I sit forward. "And the silver?"

"A suppressant for an overactive nervous system. See?" He slides the cup toward me. His glasses gleam in the light, just like the medicine. "Science and logic. A lot more predictable than superstition."

It's true. The medicine swims around in the crystal, reeking like tarnished silverware and churning and mixing in gray and purple and blue. Like magic, but it ain't magic. We're too far along to believe in that.

I know there's no ultimate fix to save the world from me, nothing to erase what I've done or Mum did or anything else. But this little step is something, right? My skin prickles and my skull mutters.

"Best do it quick," the doc says, dragging his clipboard over again. He nods to the cup, but doesn't take his eyes off mine. His smile is sympathetic. "It's a bit of a doozy."

I've been through too damn much to be scared of one drink. And when this is done, I can call my aunt.

I lift the cup and tip back all of the thick liquid. It slides smooth past my tongue, then burns in the back of my throat, sears the whole way down, bubbling thicker until all that freezing heat fills my stomach.

"You were right," I croak, and cough a bit. "That's awful."

The doc laughs. "Good medicine tastes awful," he says, scribbling some notes. "Let me know what you're feeling, if you can."

If I can? "I'm all good," I say. I smile . . . it comes out a little wonky.

The fizzing zips out from my stomach. Shooting through me, galvanizing my veins. It's all cold, not in a nice autumn-y way, more like the chill off gunmetal. I think I groan.

"Easy now," the doc says. He sways ahead of me. Why's he swaying? My thoughts start sliding into each other.

"Feels w-weird," I mutter. I hold the chair arms and keep my feet planted. Breathe. "It's cold. Heavy." I can't feel my skin anymore.

"Good, Stregoni," he says. He's farther away, everything swimming on the edge like I'm looking at him through a backward telescope. "It's always worst the first go-round. Give your body a minute to process."

Does that make my body stronger, to know how to power through something wrong? Doc, give me something else. Where's my aunt to sweep me up in my jacket and hold me tighter than truth?

Where's my mummy? Why am I thinking about her? My breath tightens in my chest. Foxglove sweetness twists through my blood. The world around me is stiffening and turning fake. Like I'm watching a picture show, not like I'm living it. It shouldn't be doing that. I know that. I shouldn't be letting this happen!

"Just keep calm, alright?" the doc says. Everything around his face is spinning up silver. "What are you feeling now?"

It's like something could shock me and it wouldn't mean jack.

It wouldn't get to me in here, the girl in the bomb. My body's just a shell.

"I don't feel anything," I say.

Doc Secondchild nods, and checks something on the page.

◆

Hawthorne Stregoni felt her pupils widening, felt her brain melting inside her skull, and felt herself drifting back from the movie screen as every sense of control fell from her grasp. She expected her body to roar up with unbridled flames, but there weren't any. That was almost *more* terrifying.

"We really think this is it, Stregoni. It's working faster than we thought, too," she heard Doctor Secondchild say. He was grinning almost deliriously, pen whipping through lines. "A daily dose of this, maybe twice a day . . ." His pen paused. He looked off like he was thinking. "I wonder if we should monitor your response levels. Would you be up for a stress-test?"

She'd be shocked until she lashed out with a vengeance, or collapsed exhausted.

"I feel sick," she whispered. Not in a way where she'd throw her guts up, but like she didn't have any to throw. *This don't feel right*, she wanted to say—her lips could only move so much.

"Let me see if the stress techs are still here," Doctor Secondchild said, standing. "If they're ready for you, I can tell your aunt to come see you after. That'd be nice, right? Something to give her for Solstice?"

She didn't know what to say, or if she was even speaking. She swallowed and tried again. "Can I call her first?"

Maybe it was the silver, but his face seemed more shadowed. "Now I'm not sure about that, Stregoni," he said, laying one hand on the phone like a warning. "You're not quite stabilized just yet. Best to wait so we don't frighten her, right?"

Wrong. Her energy spiked up. She told herself not to let it make a flame, but became perilously worried that it *couldn't*. And then it suddenly didn't matter if her brain worked too fast, or if she was too angry to control herself, or if she wanted to learn how to be as smooth and controlled as Hien, so horrible in that secret room beneath the stairs, or in the moment they knelt on the lobby floor to coax her lug brother awake with a power she couldn't call cruel.

When she tried to look inward, to see the pyre burning in her mind, there was nothing but a black gap. The party had been cleared out, and now there was nothing wonderful or strange or miraculous. There was nothing to fight back with.

Perhaps, after so many cycles of madness, sanity was supposed to feel like you'd been skinned alive. Hawthorne Stregoni, who'd wanted to be mistaken for mortal, had become one. The thought was terrifying, but she knew this was best for everyone, and so she tried to trust.

Dockyard Drama

AFTER TWO SEPTENNIALS ON THE JOB AND RECENT "PRO-FEY" SCANDAL, WHAT'S NEXT FOR MAXIM & MAXIM?

6TH SUMMER MOON, 51SC

Amidst the industrial growth of 37SC, Puck's Port P.D. were searching high and low for Senator Spade Rosewood's six-cycle-old child. After three moons, they were starting to lose hope... that is, until two red-haired twins from the coal-cloaked dockyard streets arrived on the scene.

"We didn't know what the hell to make of them," says Police Chief Dermott Ashley III, who was then only a sergeant leading the case. "Suddenly you've got these two kids the same age as our newest privates, one of them with a criminal record, and they're asking for access to our evidence."

When the police refused, the twins took to the streets themselves, gathering witness statements from locals and calling in favors from friends.

"A strong web is important," says Shona Maxim, now thirty, with her brother at her side in their Ashwood Road office. "Knowing people, and knowing how they operate and what to do to make the gears spin, that's the fastest way to get a case wrapped up."

Within three weeks, Rosewood Thirdchild was located in the company of their estranged mother (who had not been seen publicly in several moons), and returned to Senator Rosewood by officers on the scene. The twins went on to solve a mix of cases: from robberies and murders, to exposing workplace or tenancy violations, or exonerating victims of unlawful arrest or wrongful conviction. These cases have split the public over the Maxim twins, with some considering them working-class heroes, and others calling them troublemakers. Ashley has publicly stated his distaste for the twins, saying they "enable the worst sorts of people." There have indeed been allegations of collaboration with organized crime members, felons, or undocumented people, but (in the words of the twins' lawyer) "It's not illegal to have friends."

"We'd like it to be known that we respect the law as written, and the people who write and enforce it," Shona

Maxim reiterates. "Rules are there for a reason. We know what a lawless world looks like: we grew up in the belly of it, with no one to watch our backs. I won't let that happen again."

Senan Maxim nods his assent, but declines to comment further. However, he and Shona agree on one thing firmly. "This is about protecting our family," Senan says, and he happily shows a picture of his child (whose birth promoted a two-cycle-long hiatus for the twins), his fey stepchild, and his fey wife Hàzell Stregoni. Stregoni has caused yet another stir for the duo. While the Maxims claim to defend the law, Stregoni has been known to disseminate incendiary pamphlets calling for dissent against the police and government in the name of a city that accepts all people, fey and mortal alike.

According to Shona Maxim, Stregoni's calls are metaphorical and in no way suggest unlawful activity. Still, Senan's marriage has put the twins back in the spotlight, opening age-old debates. Some sources are again suggesting that the twins began their practice only to hide Senan Maxim's criminal delinquency.

"I've never been shy about that," Senan Maxim tells us, with the same tooth-bared conviction he displays on the witness stand. "As long as politicians claim that criminality is a blood curse or some sickness, I have more in common with the fey."

"We're doing the best we can to help this city, for everyone," Shona Maxim clarifies.

In order to better serve the country, the twins plan to take on a more expansive caseload, including jobs from outside Puck's Port. Recently, the town of Hinterland has reported a large-scale robbery of 2400R from their local bank. Shona Maxim has expressed her interest in working alongside Hinterland's precinct to locate the missing sum, in order to build trust with non-local law enforcement as a first step to mending relations at home. "We're committed to weeding the troubles out of this country," she says. "It's a delicate dance, but we'll get there, as long as we all play our part."

GRISTLE SENAN MAXIM JUNIOR
IN
"BANG ZIP POW"

Gristle Senan Maxim Junior strode from the alley with a racing pulse and yet a mind stunningly clear. Ahead at the curb, a gray car had pulled over with its top up; the driver slid over into the passenger seat to look out the open window. She wasn't wearing white fur, but instead a very sensible wool overcoat and bell-shaped cap.

"This better be as important as you said it was, Maxim," Fionne said. She didn't smile, which seemed grim, her whole face rippling with frustration. "I have a Solstice dinner to be back for, so you'd better explain why you were calling for the car like the sky was falling."

Quen came plodding up to Gristle's side, followed by the click of Hien's heels as they stepped onto the sidewalk. Fionne's eyes sank into wide shadows.

"Saints," she breathed. Already she was pushing the door open while the car idled, and already Gristle was rushing to her. She grabbed hold of his arm, yanking him into a barely private huddle. "Gristle, what the hell is going on?"

"I think I have a lead on who hired O'Taglio," he said. "I'll pay double for gas if you let me drive to the dockyards right now."

Up close, he could see that the shadows under her eyes weren't just from the lights. She looked cycles older.

"And Phong Hien isn't dead," she hissed, darting her eyes behind him. "Are you gonna explain that one to me?"

The idling car only made his heart slam faster. "Please let me explain while we drive," Gristle said. Her face creased harder and he desperately swept his hand up, pushing his hat back so his face wasn't all shadows. The open air dug at his skin, but it was a good reminder that he was really doing this.

Her eyes skated over his face, to every freckle and crease. "*Triple* for gas, and only because I'm out first-and-last rent," she said, stabbing her finger into his chest. Her voice trembled a bit, formed each word with careful precision. "A-and you better promise me that what happened last time . . ." She looked to Hien again, or at least the blur of them as they popped the back door open for Quen to hop in first. Her hand curled back slightly. "I work tomorrow. I don't want a party tonight."

This was not the Fionne Eze his aunt knew of, who didn't understand the weight of this city. The patterns were changing.

"Hien's hurt. They can't do as much as they could, and they know they have to rein it in," Gristle told her, quieter. "But you and I both know they're still the most in-hand fey we've ever met. This isn't like that kid, or Hawthorne, and we'll have Quen if they get carried away. I need the backup to catch Ashley."

Her shoulders tightened. "Ashley hired O'Taglio?" He didn't get a chance to answer. There was a faint glimmer behind her glasses, somewhere between the girl who loved swing and gin, and her parents in their wild cycles before it all burned down. "Damn it . . . alright. Explain the rest while we drive. I'm not going in without a plan, but hell if I let you stake that scumbag alone."

Gristle could only nod and put a heavy hand on her shoulder as some form of thanks, and then he was sliding into the driver's seat.

"And I want an exclusive with you," Fionne said to the back seat. "I don't care if I have to pretend it's from three moons ago. You're telling me everything about designing that club."

Hien must have said something good enough, because she pursed her lips, touched at her glasses, and finally swung into the front seat with her arms crossed and her chin up.

"Drive, Maxim," she said, as if to a chauffeur. He didn't need to be told twice. He dropped the car into gear, swung out into the road so fast Quen growled under its breath, and the car raced off toward Chestnut Street.

"No scratches," Fionne hissed, while Gristle waved a barely apologetic hand out the window at the lonesome car they cut off in the intersection. "Explanations. Now."

"I saw Ashley getting in a cab," Gristle said, punching the car faster to avoid the traffic stop. There was hardly anyone out on the roads; with twenty-three bells just crawled past, most folks were at home, preparing for midnight. They carved southwest off the numbered streets toward the western edge of town and the industrial smoke. "He was going to Cat's Cantina."

Her voice slowed. "That doesn't seem right . . ."

"That's what I thought, too." Ahead, the traffic guard was letting a few cars from the other lane go. Gristle stopped and took the time to fumble into his pocket without taking his eyes off the guard, raring to race. "But Hien's reminded me that it's right next to the Gattano garage."

"But I thought the police cleared Rory?" Fionne asked.

"They did, but that doesn't mean jack." Gristle pulled out his notebook, with a pen threaded through the binding, and handed it over his shoulder. He felt Hien take it, the faintest brush of their fingers. "Someone had to pay good to get them off a hook that big and cover up all their mistakes. I thought it was just their brothers, but..."

"Someone like an ex-police chief could move those strings pretty easy," Fionne muttered. "He really only got elected because of the fayre, right? Maybe he thought he could fake another tragedy."

Gristle's thoughts exactly.

She seemed to hesitate on the next part, but then plowed ahead. "We need some sort of evidence of that, don't we?"

Gristle's camera bag still weighed heavy at his side, wedged between his thigh and the car door. Was he just going in for some photos? Snap some shots of clear collaboration? Bring them where? To the police, who would just be bought off again?

"I'll get some photos and talk with my aunt about it," he said. And, this time, he wouldn't let her say he should leave it alone. He'd dig his heels in and prove he was grown. Together, maybe even with Hien to prove the Dogfoot business wasn't just a mistake, they could get a path forward. "She'll know what to do."

Fionne nodded. Hien was silent. The traffic guard held up both gloved hands to the other lane, spun, and waved Gristle forward.

It was time for Ashley to be finished once and for all. Gristle had no time for games, and very little room for mercy.

◆

They turned onto the high end of Chestnut Street, a long industrial road filled with silent warehouses and garages and dirty windows glinting in the moonlight. Despite the burn in his temples that wanted to lead-foot through the gentle snow, Gristle shut off the lights and drove slowly through the long shadows of the brick-and-steel buildings.

He stopped the car at the curb, and looked past Fionne through the passenger window.

The Cat's Cantina stared back at him, its faded sign nearly impossible to read. Without any lights pouring from within, he couldn't even see through the painted windows, just the reflection of Mr. Táyò's fine car. All the better, he figured . . . last time he'd been here, it had been with his daddy.

"Closed," Fionne confirmed, sounding just as wary of the memories. "So where's—"

The street shifted. It took Gristle a moment to determine what had caused it. But when he looked out the front window, a new light had flicked on ahead: at the end of the block opposite them, a second-story window glowed awake. From this angle, Gristle could just make out the sign above the rusty main-level door:

GATTANO AND BROS. MECHANICS

The entire street was quiet, aside from that glowing window.

"I'm heading over there," Gristle said. Before anyone could respond, he popped the door open and swung out into the middle of the street, camera bag ready and hat set back. "Hien," he said, looking to the blurry figure in the back seat, reclined with one leg over the other and an old *Dolly Day* in hand. "Come along, please?"

They sighed, dropped the magazine into Fionne's bag, reached into a hazy image of a coat, and pulled out their metal-and-jade pistol. They held it up to Fionne in the front seat.

"Hien, she doesn't want a—"

Fionne lifted up the corner of her dress and pulled a snub-nose from her garter. Gristle nearly had to collect his bottom jaw out of the slush. She spun the barrel daintily, then caught the look on his face. "Oh, so the lug and the louse get to go snooping around but the dame stays in the car with nothing to protect herself?" she asked, wagging the barrel in his direction.

"Don't wave it!" he whispered. "Where did you even get that?"

"Last time we had a fun party, Hien died," she said. Hien chuckled. She didn't. "I'm not gonna be playing patty-cake while someone else builds a damn *flamethrower*."

He wanted to be frustrated, but he understood.

She cut her eyes to Hien as they stepped out after him. "If you die again, I'll trash your name. You hear me?"

Hien's blurry hand swiped an X over their heart, a slightly sarcastic promise, but Gristle figured it was the best they'd get. Fionne rolled her eyes and settled back into the seat to watch the road.

Hien held their own pistol out to Gristle, swinging by the trigger guard. Gristle was well aware that he was going into the business place of folks who swung lead pipes first and asked questions later. Plus, he was cornering himself with a man he suspected of hiring a patsy to toast up fey just to prove they needed harsher laws. Now was not the time to go with his camera as his only protection.

He sighed and took the pistol, pocketing it for now, and strode off with Hien and Quen silent behind. The garage was only two stories of dull brick; greasy warehouse windows peered in on the lower-level shop, with a door crammed between. Gristle gave it a quick scan, just enough to see that the snow on the three cement steps was unsettled. But in the alley, dark prints led toward the back.

Gristle kept his eye on the lit windows above, all of the curtains pulled. He knew there was an apartment up there, and his aunt had surely staked the place for any sign of Rory, who must have been clever about staying hidden. Ashley didn't have mob-family subtlety.

"Upper access is through the back," Gristle whispered. The two of them carved down the narrow passage toward a back lot jammed with half-junked cars covered in snow. As suspected, there was a small landing. Two heavy footprints were sunk ahead of it, with no sign of nervous pacing. Gristle became more and more certain of his hunch.

The door's iron handle was so cold it nearly burned, but the knob spun open. Even with the door barely cracked, just enough to send one stripe of light down into the dark back lot, Gristle could hear voices.

"With no damn respect, I've got bigger fish to fry than the leftover giblets of that job," said a voice with a fading Verdossi accent. Rory Gattano. Gristle held his breath for . . .

"You made your choice moons ago," another, lower voice said. Ashley. The hunch had panned out. Gristle readied a hand on his camera and motioned for Hien to move toward the darker corners of the back lot. "These aren't matters you can simply step back from when you choose to, or send your brothers to bully me back."

"Then I leave Dale," Rory said. Their voice was fierce, and yet still quivering. Gristle's insides cringed to hear them like that. Wasn't this still an old friend of Gristle's daddy? Of Hàzell too, despite it all? "Verdosso's got its own troubles, but it don't have you, now do it?"

Gristle bit back the sympathy and unclasped his camera bag. He just needed evidence. He wouldn't let his feelings bungle this, but hadn't it been proved that perhaps those weren't so bad after all?

Ashley's voice snarled low. "Do you really think the fey radicals there would have you if they knew what you did?"

What you did. This was still a folk who'd tried to torch Gristle's life alight. What did he care for the fear in their voice?

From above, a glass shattered. Rory gasped.

Gristle, too damn good-hearted, moved without thinking,

slipping through the door and up the narrow stairs, where the damp cold of the building smelled like wet plaster and burnt Solstice pine. Before he'd recognized it, the gun was in his hands instead of his camera, almost too light to feel lethal.

"Don't you dare step to me," Rory sneered, but in a voice bubbling with weak-link panic. Gristle rushed for the apartment's flimsy door. "I-I'll call my brothers down on you."

And there was Rory in the middle of their humble one-room apartment, Ashley bearing down on them, forcing them back against the rotting plaster of the wall. A glass of almond liqueur lay shattered on the ground—the saccharine smell turned Gristle's thoughts to a syrupy haze. Still, he slipped through the door unnoticed, clinging to the black shadows next to some old crates.

"Gattano," Ashley breathed, with Rory crinkling under him in only trousers and an undershirt. The Gattano cat tattoo was faded on one gangly, aging arm. "You and I both know Maxim is a piss-poor president. She'll send this whole country up in smoke to keep herself warm."

Gristle's stomach turned. What did he care about Ashley's opinion of his aunt, a woman he knew to be benevolent and kind and fiercely loving—perhaps frighteningly so, but wasn't that all to keep them safe? To keep the bad things back, including people who made him doubt the plan she'd laid?

Focus, Ace.

"I know good fey," Rory snapped, despite being cornered. Gristle's chest heaved to hear it: they may have been a low-rent mobster who'd let themself be roped in thus far, but at least they were barking back at the end of it, breaking the pattern, to do better. "Hàzell Stregoni was practically kin, and Senan Maxim was a good man. I stand by them, and by their tykes. I ain't gonna be . . . be *strong-armed*."

"You think Maxim cares about you?" Ashley nearly shouted.

Gristle's heart lurched through the smell of the liquor swimming in his head and the damp of the apartment. The world was beginning to thrum on the edges, pouring every sensation into him.

"She's been a puppet master since she crawled off the dock. Tell her 'no' and see how fast she cuts your strings, same as she did with her nephew."

He thought of Calligan on the sidewalk, eyes warm, even Calligan in the office telling him to cut the whiskey and rest. But they were just a jabbering egghead know-it-all, right? Hien was a monster, Fionne naive, his daddy a fool, and Hàzell a mad mastermind.

"And yet here I stand, free and right," Rory said. "The only one who lost was you, *Senator*."

Too far. "Maliano Rory Gattano," Ashley said, pronouncing the entire name like a threat. He reached into his coat. "I don't care what sort of gang war this starts: I won't have Maxim thinking she can win."

Gristle saw the shine of a metal barrel, sleeker than a camera. Hien's gun weighed nothing in his hand.

BANG!

The room froze for an eon, where Gristle stood with the gun up and the shot gone off, and Ashley stood over Rory with his own weapon ready. Gristle watched the world through the smoke drifting from the barrel.

Would his aunt have done the same? Would his father?

Beneath that, what did *he* feel?

Ashley's pistol dropped to the floor. He tore sideways with a snarl and a flash of black, very-real blood, collapsing into Rory's drying laundry. The blood splattered onto the worn wood. Rory screamed and turned to the door. For a moment, they looked more confused than frightened, and then they jumped as their eyes settled into Gristle.

"Maxim Child?" they said, squinting into the shadows. "What the hell are you doing here?"

He'd caught Ashley. He'd caught the Mad Fey Murderer. He'd done it . . . *he'd done it!*

"No matter," Gristle said in a determined daze, rushing forward and kicking Ashley's gun off into the shadows cast by a worn-down couch.

Ashley stared from the ground, blood pooling out from a shot just below his ribs. "Senan Maxim Junior, so intense," he hissed, with his bull-like face and his too-proud stature while he gulped in air. Gristle was sure his lung had collapsed. *Good.* "You look like the Reaper."

"It's Gristle," he said in his usual flat voice.

He still needed answers—confessions, ideally—but at least Rory was alive to squeal. He slipped the gun back into his coat. Behind, Hien's shadow leaked up the stairwell, twisting and writhing with something unreal.

"You may bleed out, Senator. I have an associate who could stop that from happening, as long as you confess right here."

Blood foamed between Ashley's teeth. "I want none of your . . . fey . . . *abnormality.*"

Gristle turned to where Hien had stepped into the room, smoking vervain and radiating waves of drowsy pain. Their note was ready and written:

I do not care if he dies or lives, Mr. Maxim.

"He hired O'Taglio," Gristle explained, jaw beginning to ache under his deadpan expression. "If he dies, we never get justice."

What is justice anyway? To you?

Ashley let out a gurgling laugh while the pen scribbled again.

Rory was staring from the floor where they had sunk, with their skin paler, mouth trying to fumble an answer.

Gristle couldn't do this right now. The man who had hired a mercenary was bleeding out and choking on it, and he was supposed to sink himself in some ethical conundrum?

"I need a minute to think—keep him breathing," Gristle said. Hien's hazy blur shifted haughtily. Commands wouldn't suffice. "*Please*, Hien. A favor."

Reciprocity did the trick: Hien sighed and strutted past. A rumble of wind pushed through the room, Ashley let out a moan so tortured that Gristle felt certain Hien was proving a point, but Ashley fell quickly unconscious for Hien to crouch beside him. They kept one hand on Quen's back as it lay next to them, and the other poised to pour cloudy oxygen through the wound like a bullet in reverse.

Gristle needed answers. *Now.*

He turned to Rory on the ground. They were just managing to pull themself to their feet. Gristle grabbed the liqueur bottle off the crooked table and poured some into a new water-spotted glass. He caught his reflection in the bottle; he looked so like his father.

"Thank you, son," Rory said, nervously tipping it to Gristle and then taking a sip through dry lips. It seemed to stand them up a little more solidly, or as solidly as they could look with their rake-thin frame and one hand braced against the exhaust pipe of their sleeping woodstove. "You were always good to me, like your daddy. He was a good man, Maxim. I'm right sorry he ended how he did—I know we all are . . ." They shook their head and took another gulp. Gristle's pulse was climbing. He could smell the liquor rotting into their teeth. "The least I can do is stand by his sister—I do. I swear I do. It falls into place in the end, Maxim. You're kind, like him."

Gristle really didn't have time for the ramblings of a shaken folk three seconds from thinking they'd die.

"I'm asking you to be good to me now, Mx Gattano," he said, forcing his voice to stay quiet and calm. This crook had tried to kill him, and yet perhaps they'd been forced. There were a thousand explanations other than them being a monster. Gristle dropped both broad hands onto Rory's rickety shoulders. "I need you to tell the police about Ashley hiring O'Taglio, so we can put it to bed, alright? We'll get him behind bars."

Rory looked confused. "It would be easy to frame him now, with the gun," they admitted, swiping at their grizzled cheek. "I oughta ask my brothers, though."

Frame? "What the hell are you on about?!" Gristle said, so loud the light in the hall flickered. "It was Ashley who hired O'Taglio. He said so!"

Well, he hadn't, had he? Never admitted to letters, had only come to tell Rory off for the whole ordeal. He was pyre lighting and bringing hell down on the Maxims and their cause as he'd always done. But if he hadn't hired O'Taglio, then who had? Gristle thought he had put clues together, but he had *NOTHING*!

"Maxim Child," Rory breathed, with the same gentleness as Calligan on that street corner, one that felt too unfamiliar to be comfortable. The blood smell and the sound of Ashley's lead-plugged lung and the sound of a cat yowling three blocks over, the sound of Gristle's cells multiplying. The sound of sounds. "She told me you were in on it. I woulda never done it otherwise."

Why did everyone think he knew everything? Why did the world treat him all at once like a heroic adult *and* a stupid kid?

Gristle felt something in his head snap.

No matter how hard he tried, how much he thought he'd changed, he wasn't enough.

"Tell me what's happening!" he screamed. Something jolted in the center of his chest, like two live wires tapped on each other. It sent a spark that sank into the wooden floor and spiraled out in searing fractals, zapped up through his arms and into Rory Gattano, who had known him since his youth, who thought his father was a good man and Gristle was too. Gristle heard their heart flick off and back. A spark of light glowed in the pits of their chestnut-dark eyes.

They dropped limp to the burned ground at his feet.

Every hair on Gristle's body stood on static end. Quen nosed its way over to him, heavy head pushed into his leg. Gristle's hands were still held up. He couldn't feel his body enough to lower them to his sides.

Madness, Gristle thought. That was exactly the word for whatever unknown power had ripped up through him . . . at least when a fey did it.

Senan Maxim's son was mortal. He'd been told that all his life. Been told so many things that he hardly knew what he wanted, or what he was. He thought he'd learned in that alley with Hien's mouth on his, but already the memory was distant, as if it was being overwritten.

Gristle Senan Maxim Junior stumbled back into the table away from Quen, hands balled against his chest, whispering for spirits and saints. Rory was still breathing inside the target of all those fault lines. Gristle kept staring at them, hoping they weren't real. Perhaps if he thought it hard enough, this too would end.

Mister Maxim—

"Hien!" Gristle shouted, turning to them. Ashley was passed out but breathing evenly, Hien leering over them. Their blurry image heaved with labored breath: limbs and hands and eyes and teeth. Gristle snapped his eyes to the ground between his feet. "Hien, what the hell is this? What did you do to me?!"

I've already told you that I haven't done anything.

Ashley choked once, spluttered in his sleep. He couldn't die! Gristle needed someone to take the fall here; it had to be Ashley! Saints, even if it wasn't Ashley who did it, did he have the guts to pin him anyway? Their platform would run easier, Hawthorne would be fine, and his aunt would trust him again . . .

Was that what he wanted?

Quen whined. *I'm tired of this, Maxim*, Hien said, almost a growl as they stepped up to him. Waves of emotions ripped through Gristle's sinews, like being battered in a bad current. *You're waking up, but you're still stuck partway.*

"I don't know what the hell you mean," Gristle wheezed. Everything had been fraying for some time, but there were certain truths that Gristle understood irrevocably. That his daddy was dead because he'd been a stupid punk, that his aunt was all he had left, that his sister was fey and he was the mortal who had to protect her properly, because she was both his daddy and her mum: too innocent to know better, and yet renegade enough to murder them all. And Gristle was beloved so long as he obeyed.

He knew what was wrong, he'd seen it in Calligan's eyes and Ashley's teeth and the dockyard duo up on that mantle staring back at him, but the answers would destroy *everything*. He tried to pack them back.

"Hien," he said, begging for something he didn't know.

I can give you some clarity, untangle your brain waves, Hien said ahead of him. Their voice was still fierce but lower, rumbling like tectonic plates. *But I can't make choices for you.*

The choice to let go fully and completely. To sever the last grip on order, on sanity maybe. To rewrite the world from his own eyes, not anything he'd been told or scripted. To get control of himself, something he feared he'd never truly had.

You told me off, even when you knew I could have killed you, Hien said quietly, as if they didn't want to admit it. The blur flickered uneasily. Hien put something hand-like to Gristle's chest again, creasing in good pressure. A strike of shivering exhaustion trembled through Gristle's body. *You're not a coward, Mister Maxim, but you've been very alone.*

Their hand pressed harder. They didn't have to complete the thought. They understood, in a way Gristle felt certain that no one had. Perhaps that was why Hien terrified him.

Perhaps that was why he was told to stay away from the folks at the Dog, who might give him one final piece.

The indignation was enough.

"Stick by me," Gristle whispered. He didn't need Hien's response.

Gristle slammed his palm into Hien's wrist. It was like touching another live wire. A flood of acid-hot adrenaline rushed from Hien's touch and into his every bone. His entire body roared up as Hien winced in time with his own snarl of pain. Memories sped past like kids on roller coasters: his daddy screaming at the police, his stepmum laughing to the stars, Hawthorne on fire, his aunt's tears and sturdy hand and cycles of political planning. The feeling hit Gristle's skull, wrenched the wiring. With it came snaps and twangs of everything coming down like a collapsing suspension bridge.

And yet, within the carnage inside his head, Gristle could feel something else bleeding through.

I'm waking up, Gristle thought in the haze. *I'm waking up, and it's going to hurt, but at least it'll be real.*

Fey Under Fire

JAZZ CLUB OWNER PHONG HIEN STRIKES OUT AGAINST SCIENCE

1st Winter Moon, 57SC

Above Aziza Street's Dogfoot Club, its notorious owner, Phong Hien, sits in the plush armchair of their office with a cigarette balanced between fingers and their loyal familiar nearby. Hien wears a long, crystal-studded dress draped over broad shoulders, with the faintest dusting of sparkling fey freckles, at least they appear to. As they smile a particularly puckish grin, the image of them wanes and blurs.

Dolly Day Reporter: I'm guessing that's not how you actually look, is it?

Phong Hien: [Laughs] It's a mental trick—an image of me in your head. I think I might frighten folks if I walked around looking like I really do. I had a bad flare-up as a child, accidentally shifted myself.

DD: Could you change back? I know some fey have good control over that.

PH: I don't care much. I get along fine like I do.

DD: Is there anyone who's ever seen the real you? Maybe someone special?

PH: How salacious. Besides my immediate family, no. It might be dangerous for me. Some folks have a very limited idea of what "human" looks like.

DD: But if it's so dangerous, why not learn to change?

PH: Would a mouse want to turn into a cat?

DD: Probably depends on how close it is to getting eaten.

PH: Exactly. Ask me these same questions when fey aren't being forced to hide, then we'll talk. Until then, the question's fixed from the start.

DD: That's a fair point. You're very wise.

PH: If I didn't talk so fine and look so pretty and participate in this funny little economy, Dale would find a way to call me a monster, and you wouldn't be interviewing me.

DD: What do you think happens to those fey, the ones who don't talk so fine?

PH: They're in breadlines or sleeping under bridges until they snap, and then they're in madhouses or prisons. And if they're not there yet, they're clamoring for someone to tell them how not to get that way. They'll do anything to stop it, even kill themselves for it.

DD: I suppose you're talking about Shona Maxim's fey re-education schools. Is it wise to speak ill of the one pro-fey candidate?

PH: Maybe I'm not as wise as you said I was. Would you still love me then, or am I getting too fey for you? Putting someone on a pedestal is the same as putting them in a cage—I don't aspire to be an example.

DD: Any advice for us mortals?

PH: Stop destroying everything that doesn't bend to you. And stop crying when we snap back.

HAWTHORNE STREGONI IN "A CALL HOME"

Hawthorne Stregoni was still in the chair across the desk, feeling the silver solution fade to a dull murmur in the back of her skull. Like a child hiding from a monster movie, both rationally terrified and sickly curious, she tried to peer into herself to find that fey wild pyre. It was superstitious, old-world outdated, nothing more than a chemical image, and yet she dared to look.

She found nothing. No building energy to keep an eye on, no shakes or fidgets or wayward emotions or guilt or anger or *anything*. There was simply nothing.

There was only Doctor Secondchild with the phone jammed between his shoulder and ear, waiting to see if the stress-test room was available. When its current lit her body up, there would be nothing she could do to make it stop. She'd be forced to accept syncope. Logically, she understood that it was the fancy way of saying "being fried until you pass out," but she could feel no fear.

She would be mortal. Harmless. Harmed.

"Rain-right," Secondchild said. His smile smeared in Hawthorne's vision, like a film run wrong to leave ghosts of movement and little pinpricks of grain and noise. When he stood, the screech of the chair legs ground through Hawthorne's silver veins, but went nowhere. "Let me tell the others—I'm sure they'll want to see it."

"Doc," she heard herself say. What was she just thinking? She might be losing time. "I'd like to call my aunt, please, before I go in."

"How do you feel?"

"I feel . . ." Silver coated every conductor in her body, tingling cold under her nails. "Mortal," she said.

He smiled, the same kind smile it had always been. "Well, that's the idea." He picked up the entire phone and clunked it in front of her. "Here you are, Stregoni. We'll be done that test within the bell—she's more than welcome to come after that, no matter which way this turns out. We couldn't have gotten here without her funding."

Hawthorne wanted to scream at him, even if her brain couldn't quite remember why. He headed toward the door, patting her shoulder as he left with no fear that it would burn him. She was safe now, the weapon pried from her hands. She could do anything next, yes? She could work at *Dolly Day* and mind the presses . . . she couldn't remember why *Dolly Day* had mattered that much to her. There was that pretty dame who had loved her ever since they were small and pressing wildflowers in their schoolbooks or throwing bread to the pigeons gathered in the *Herald* lot, but even that felt more like a name than a person. A memory of someone who was already gone. Maybe it was just the irrational, wild parts that had loved Fionne Eze.

Was "Hawthorne" some new, realer person now if she wasn't a fey? A squirmy little baby stepping out of the bomb and ready to face the world anew?

Hawthorne's heavy hand swung forward to drag the phone up. She stood, or was standing, unsure how the moments connected.

Afterimages swam between her eyelashes. Her finger fumbled into the cold iron that didn't burn.

Click. Whirrrr.

The phone should have echoed, too loud, but it was just a phone. Everything was just everything. Her stomach was an empty engine. Alright, she thought, it's okay. The emptiness would ebb. The stress-test would be quick, and then just a dull memory.

Click. Click click whirrrr.

Hawthorne swallowed, dry with the taste of metal still swimming in her mouth. The operator picked up.

What was her aunt's number again? She couldn't recall. "Shona Maxim, the president," Hawthorne requested. Her voice sounded wrong. "It's her niece."

"Putting you through, sweetie," the cheerful person on the other end said.

Hawthorne nodded as if they could see her. The line tolled, tolled. She wasn't sure what she was going to say. Was she relieved?

"Hawthorne?" her aunt said. "I expected you to call half a bell ago—what took so long?"

"Auntie Shona," she whispered. She could hear Doctor Secondchild outside the door, and excited murmuring between new voices. "I'm . . . I want to see you. Now."

Her aunt's voice lightened. "That's wonderful!" There was the decisive smack of a ledger closing. "Oh, it's been so long since we had a nice family Solstice."

It had been. Everything before had felt stilted, but now? "Can you . . . can you bring Gristle?" Hawthorne asked.

The slow creak of a chair rolling back from a desk. "He's been a bit off lately. I'm not sure how merry that would be," her aunt said. "I can be there in time for midnight. Maybe we can invite the doc for a drink too."

His ecstatic voice rang from the hall. Hawthorne cringed, unsure why.

"I thought . . ." Hawthorne started. Shouldn't a family Solstice have Gristle too? Was he too frightened of her? Still? "Why 'off'?" she asked. Her voice sparked just slightly, the last reserves. "Is he alright? I haven't really heard from him."

A guttural unease edged into her aunt's voice. "You haven't asked about Gristle in moons," she started. "Come to think on it, you haven't even wanted to see *me*."

Things were different now? Better?

"You sound a bit odd, Hawthorne," her aunt said. "Are you feeling alright?"

Yes? "New medicine." She felt something caged throwing itself against silver-plated walls. She tapped her fingers, snapped them, and waved her hand so her wrist felt loose, but there was no fire. The baby inside the bomb was pink and skinless and hurt. "I'm all slow. It's just putting some stuff in perspective, I guess." Her throat ached suddenly. "I want to see you, and Gristle. Right now. I'm . . ." What was this feeling? How could she name it in her new body? She made a low moaning sound, the preamble to tears that wouldn't come. "I'm sort of scared right now—I really want to see you both."

The answer was quicker than angels. Of course it was. Anything for Stregoni Child. "I'm on my way," her aunt said. "I'll get Egghead to handle things here. Where are you?"

And would she bring Gristle? Why wasn't she bringing Gristle too?

"Secondchild's office. They want to bring me for a stress-test."

"Tell him that you won't be doing that without your legal guardian present."

Hawthorne was eighteen. She was supposed to be her own person. Could she deny the test herself? She couldn't even ask for her own brother. What was his number? Was he at the office? Where was Senan Maxim's son? Where was Senan Maxim?

Where was her own mother on family Solstice, and why did she have to feel so damn guilty for wanting the one person who might understand the weight of losing everything? Wasn't this exactly what her mother had warned of?

Hadn't her mother been wrong, though? Wasn't Hawthorne better, safer, *cured*?

"I'm sure the doctor knows what he's doing," her aunt said. It was true. His degrees shone on the wall, the glass glinting like scalpels. "I'll be there for you soon."

"Alright," Hawthorne said. And that was that.

She set the phone down and turned for the door. Her brain waves were settling with sounds like the carousel groaning and flipping sideways. Sounds like the sporadic laughter of people racing past on roller coasters. The smell of popcorn, or of the dockyard apartment, or the ocean waves on the journey to this filthy city. Everything was churning slowly into darkness, fizzing quieter and quieter the longer she let it. Perhaps Secondchild *had* been right: despite the strange coldness of her body, her thoughts were aligning through the static.

"Your body is an altar, Stregoni," she heard her mother say, a memory that frayed and pulsed on the edges. The diary pages cutting across the walls of her room. The nights she heard typing until the dawn. Senan with his shadowed face slipping papers into passing baskets. Her mother writing another and then shaking out her hands all stained with ink. Petals that fell around her, and antlers curling out. "Don't let anyone tell you what you ought to do with it."

And then? *Boom*. What did her mother know?

Hawthorne stepped forward but her head swam with a wave of vertigo. She fell onto her bare knees. In her haze, she imagined falling into her mother's strong arms smelling like herbs and smoke and *home*, and hated herself for it. Her aunt had sounded so much like Senan, and yet Hawthorne still wanted to find comfort in the fey who killed him and three hundred others. Who had ruined this family. Her quieting mind found the memory reel and fit it into the projector.

Click, click, click, click. Alright. Roll the tape. *Evening, folks, are you ready for a show?*

She needed to remember why she deserved clipped wings, and limited choices, and why this numbing was a gift.

The Diary of Hàzell Stregoni, "Radical Fey"

51SC, 6 Summer Moons, 32 Suns

There are forces working against us. There always are, but all have been defeated by our bonds: the police who know better than to tussle with Senan, the politicians who cower against Rory's grin and looming family, Victory's easy words for the fearful mortals, and Tàyè's fearless art. The lot of us, our web of reaching hands and braided arms, is stronger than their ignorance.

And yet, I knew that there are variables we cannot control. That there will always be a higher price, a bigger threat, a nobler cause, a person you thought you trusted more than any other. I've said before that I embrace this uncertainty, I do. And yet, as we approach the longest day of the year, when we should not be frightened, I am. I hold my children longer, embrace my friends more tightly, and plan when next we'll see each other. Each of these actions could be the last.

I'd like to say there's beauty in this fear. I am not so noble. I am, despite what is said, only human.

Something must change, and it will, and I understand that it will come at a great cost. Our bodies are not our own in this country: they belong to laws, to bosses, to landlords, to civility, and to other harsh loyalties that demand something terrible in return. I do not wish to be in this world, or to let my family alone in it. We must shatter it apart to build better, however terrifying this may seem.

I only hope the world left behind is kinder for my children. I only hope they knew how dearly they're loved as nothing less than their truest souls. If this country cannot love them, I will. Kill me for that insolence if you must. I'd rather we die proud than defeated.

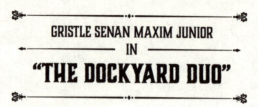

Something shocking out from Hien's hand had twisted up into Gristle's skull, had pulled everything into focus, had put his mind behind his eyes and his feet on the ground. It still hurt like hell had crawled up inside him. Gristle drank it in. This was happening to him, right now, right here, and he wasn't expected to go it alone.

I can face this, Gristle thought—Gristle *thinks*. He knows there's no going back to how it was. Gristle is grounded, and he hurts because of it, and with it, and for it. Reality hurts, he knows. It's no excuse not to face it. And so, with stunning clarity, he thinks:

It feels damn right to be in my own head. It's where I should be, should have always been. From here, maybe I can see things how they are.

When the world fades in, I'm sitting on a bed, with tin toys arrayed ahead of me in rows and swirls. Through the arch that separates this tiny bedroom, the kitchen is framed in the tugged-back curtains like a picture-show screen. The tulip-shaped bulbs of a spidery light fixture flick on above the table, shining across billows and rolls of cigar smoke. Within it, my daddy and aunt sit opposite each other at a table small enough their foreheads are nearly rested together as they lean over their work, like a person standing too close to a mirror. The differences are small: the gray in his hair, the pressed lines of her slacks, his bitten-down nails, her shined shoes. Between them, an open briefcase spills papers and files under the smoke dripping from their mouths.

Some part of me screams, wants to run for him while he sits so focused. But I know this is already over. This is a memory wrenched from the briefcase I keep them in.

We're in our dockyard apartment, with dried flowers and herbs pinned to the mottled plaster walls, Stregoni's misplaced hair ribbons hanging from the cupboards, Hàzell's typewriter balanced atop a trunk in the corner, and the air smelling like smoke and fish as the smudged windows rumble from the coal train passing too close. This was the last case they worked, before it all went wrong and was overwritten by the ending.

My daddy sighs and leans back in his chair until it tilts onto two legs. His fingers rattle on the table edge. "I just don't understand it."

"They had every street quartered off," my aunt says, picking up a file and standing with it, as if getting closer to the flickering light will force the answer out. This new electricity thing is a bust; I never saw one light that didn't crackle. "There's a good chance the sum's been squirreled away until the heat cools."

"I mean, I don't understand why you want us investigating a burglary in some little dirt-pile town." He starts shuffling the papers together. One sloughs off the table, sliding past the kitchen and into the bedroom. I shuffle forward onto my stomach to fish it up.

She keeps her eye on the file, voice flat with practiced patience. "I told you—the police won't work with us here, but this could get some favor back."

"I don't want favor from the folks who threw me in a cage for trying to feed us," he says, almost a snap. My shoulders tighten.

She looks to him quickly over the top of the page. "So you want another arrest warrant on you?" she asks. "Or for more family services folks to come knocking? You barely held on to Maxim the first time."

His nose crinkles. "I got friends working there," he mutters. He snubs his cigar in the tray and starts gnawing on his thumbnail with his back teeth. "They know I'm—"

"Can you stop chewing on your nails like an animal?"

He drops his hand and blinks hard. "They know I'm a better dad than all the folks above 14th."

"Friends can't stop someone from putting a bullet in you when they get tired of the legal route," she says, pragmatic and truthful. "So can we just try to keep things in order for a while?"

He grumbles.

My lips wrinkle. I look down at the paper. It's the front page of the *Hinterland Bugle*, talking about the burglary. I spin it in my hands, skating my eyes over the words and the pictures and advertisements in the margins. There's one for the Hinterland fayre, a drawing of all the pretty carousel ponies.

"We have to be realistic," she says, in a voice balanced between harsh and understanding. "Anyone with good standing to their name thinks you've got bad blood. Keeping your head in line is the fastest way to prove them wrong. And I don't care what you're hearing from other people about it."

Bad blood. A thing you can't escape 'cause it's in you. If my daddy's bad for what he's done, does that mean I am too? But she says we can prove otherwise, if we're helpful. I could be that.

My aunt stubs her cigar too and pockets it. Her eyes skate toward the door, to the stacks of pamphlets ready to go out and the posters collected like trophies. Strikes, rallies, manifestos. "Maybe you should come back to midtown. Not just for work," she mutters. Her cheeks run a bit pale, like even she knows it's a huge ask. "Bring some of your things and stay over for a while. It'll be like old times. We can put some proper air in you, some decent rest."

I squint, like that'll make things clearer for me too. The fayre was scheduled to leave town the very next day. There were checkpoints on every road, I know. But if it's a secret, something bad in your blood that you're hiding from everyone . . .

"Dad," I say, looking up. "What if the bad guys put the money in something for the carnival? That was leaving on a train, right?"

My daddy tenses, white-knuckled hands gripping the table edge. He gives a quick look around the apartment—he seems to look right at me and yet right past, expression all wide and squirrely.

He answers her, not me. "I'm not leaving Maxim," he finally says, like I'm not even there.

"Saints, of course not," she breathes, tossing the paper back onto the pile and trying to be casual again. "Bring the kids. We'll find room for them—it'll be like a holiday."

His jaw twitches. "And Hàzell?" She shuts her mouth, doesn't get a chance to answer before he looks away and whispers the next thought like a challenge. "You never liked Kitt, either."

I don't want to hear them talk about my mum. "Dad," I say, sliding off the bed and stepping forward into the archway. "What if—"

"I'm not bringing that up again," she says. She rakes the briefcase over and clasps it shut for now. "This isn't about Kitt, who, by the way, was paid to *teach* you, not knock you up—"

He presses his palms into the table, enough to screech up to his feet. "We were the same age—it's not like she was some predator," he hisses. "You know, she called it. She said you'll go after her every time I do something you don't agree with."

She pulls the case off the table. "I'm not going to stand here trying to kick a dead woman," she says. She grabs her hat off the chair back and fits it on at a careful, jaunty angle. "Call me when you want to be reasonable."

She steps toward the door. He jolts sideways so fast his chair topples over.

"I meant *Hàzell*. And you don't get to leave like I'm a kid with a tantrum that I gotta cry out," my daddy says, practically a snarl. "I don't understand why you two can't just get along."

Her eyes flash, lips start to curl, but she's always the reasonable one. Her voice comes out achingly even. "I had to open the paper to see my own name and face chumming with someone on a watch-list, right back in the same neighborhood I worked so hard to drag us out of. And then I find out you were seeing each other for *cycles* behind my back? Bringing Maxim? How do you think that made me feel?"

"I didn't know how to tell you," he tries to say. It's softer, maybe too soft to hear, because she doesn't back down.

"Fey are wired to be manipulators, everyone knows it. How many have we caught red-handed?" she asks him. "How can you be sure she isn't just using you for your connections? How can you be sure she won't . . . won't *blow up* and hurt you or Maxim or this entire block? You're playing with fire and you don't even notice!"

My stomach twists. His voice drops low. "And Stregoni Child?" he asks. His voice is like an angry animal, crouching ahead of the den. He blinks hard and twitches his jaw, all restless. "Is my eleven-cycle-old a manipulative genius too?"

She pauses. It's like I can see her hit a dead end. She backtracks to find something better. "We're twins, Second," she snaps, eyes as dark and wild as his. "I've been here for you, not Hàzell. Who got your life back on track after you got yourself arrested? Who took care of you and Maxim after Kitt died, huh? Do you know what it's like to watch yourself make the worst sorts of mistakes over and over when you can't do *anything*—"

"Then stop!" he finally says, like a gunshot. It rings while her eyebrows press in. He's grinning like a madman, shaking in all his atoms. I don't know what to do or feel. I'm scared of my daddy for the first time in my life. "I'm *so tired* of being the screwup anchor around your neck. If I'm such a disappointment, then just drop me. It's exhausting trying to figure out who you want me to be."

Her voice spikes. "Are you kidding me, Second—?"

"It's *Senan!*"

"Dad," I say again, a little louder as I walk closer, but neither of them turns to me. Like I'm a ghost. The lights snarl. "*Daddy.*"

"If you hate seeing the Maxim name get dragged in the paper..." he starts. Why is everyone so angry? Why can't they hear me? Nothing feels right or real and it all just hurts. He steps up to her, mirror image to mirror image. "Then maybe you oughta change yours. Because I'm not *ever* going to be a carbon-copy coward just to make you feel like some noble saviour—"

I rush forward and slam both hands and the newspaper on the table. Both of them jump, my daddy lurching backward so fast he nearly falls into the wall.

"Saints, Maxim!" he shouts. I flinch back and hold my hands up. He whirls his head around, like he's trying to see where I came from. "Don't sneak up like that!"

"I didn't," I cry. Am I dead? I feel dead sometimes, just a ghost looking back at myself. "I was sitting there the whole time. I was right there the whole time!"

Both their faces drain pale, but I don't even care about the fight.

"I was right there," I say. The light over the table flickers and sparks. "I was r-r-r-right th-th—"

"Oh, shh, hey," my daddy says. I'm supposed to be getting grown-up, but I feel like such a dumb kid when his posture's suddenly softer, and his face is open and warm, and he steps over to pick me up against his shoulder. I press my too-hot face into the rough wool of his waistcoat, clinging to him. "It's alright, Maxim. You just scared us. We were . . ."

"Adult stuff," my auntie says. She tries to laugh. "Siblings fight, but we all make up in the end."

"Yeah . . ." my daddy breathes.

I don't want to fight with Stregoni like that. I keep crying and I can't stop. Something bad is going to happen. I can feel it coming.

"Puff up, Ace," my auntie says, chipper enough over my daddy's shoulder. Her hand reaches for the top of my head. "No sense in tears over it. You know, when we were your age, we were already—"

I don't want to be like them. My stomach turns so sharp I think it's going to bust. I see lights, like a pattern in my mind.

When her fingers brush through my coarse hair, a static shock races up from my toes.

There's a white flash of light between us, a loud crack and a burst of heat. She snatches her hand away from the static shock.

"Saints," she hisses, shaking her hand out. I try to blubber an apology but it doesn't come. She looks back at me, wary.

For a second, while the coal train shrieks by to shake the lingering smoke apart, I don't think either of us trusts the other, even if we don't know why just yet.

◆

Hien's hand falls off my chest. Ebbs of exhaustion pulse into me, ringing against the weight at the core of my bones. My eyes are still closed. I know when I open them this will all be real. It won't be a memory. But something livid like a live wire is rushing up through me, tensing every ready muscle.

I have the answer. It's in there, and always has been. I'm my father's son, I can put the clues together, and I won't be afraid of how they pattern out.

Even when it hurts, I deserve to know the truth.

I open my eyes to the dark world where every shadow is an abyss, but I don't feel frightened. Ahead of me, Hien has leaned back into the crooked table, a blur that wobbles with heavy breaths while one hand lies steady between Quen's ears.

I turn from them to see Ashley still collapsed on the ground. He's breathing, and the wound isn't sucking air. He's stable, or stable enough. I'll leave it to fate. I've got this terrible suspicion that we're running out of time. That we have been since that day, even if we didn't know it then.

"Hien," I say, all severe with my back to them. Rory is unconscious too. I did that. "If I were fey . . ."

They send images and feelings into my head. Lights flickering; the lightning-like dome around us at the Dog; and then that moment where they didn't turn us invisible, but made the police's eyes scan right over us like we weren't there. Removed us from their brain, not their vision. It wasn't their idea, at least not from nowhere.

It would have . . . would have done no good to question your reality before you were ready to hear it, they struggle to say. Their voice begins to piece back together. *Some fey self-destruct outward, to get away from the hurt. And some fey implode into their own heads until the pain doesn't feel real.*

That twists into my stomach . . . a visceral recognition. But what if that isn't how things should be? What if the world is stranger than what we've been taught and told?

Hien's hand brushes faintly over my shoulder, just like that night at the Dog. I raise my fist ahead of me. The patterns in my head blink and spark, humming to themselves, building pressure surging into my fingertips. A flicker of vindication whispers up into the pulp of my teeth. I've spent so long hearing what I am—that I'm a mortal and I'm not like my daddy and that it's my job to watch my sister, and it's my job to be alright and never to stray off the path. That there's a right way to be, and I oughta be guilty if I'm not.

Come on, dickie, Hien says, grip tightening. It's both a comfort and a challenge. *Don't be a coward.*

I'm not.

I snap my fingers.

The connections in my head surge. Above us, the ceiling light burns up so bright I can see every shining claw and scale of Hien's fingers on my shoulder. I don't turn for them, but an ecstatic gasp rips from where it was sealed.

The light shatters sparks down over us, but I know what I am. And I know what I have to do to stitch this all up proper so Senan Maxim's son can finally win after all this hurt.

Welcome to the real world, Hien says. *Where to next, Detective?*

POLICE UNDER SCRUTINY AFTER CARNIVAL CLASH

HUNT FOR STILL-MISSING 2400R ENDS IN 13 BRUTAL HOSPITALIZATIONS

On the morning before Summer Solstice, and in the wake of 2400R stolen from a Hinterland bank last moon, the Puck's Port Police Department is under intense public scrutiny following a hasty night raid that resulted in nothing but cracked skulls and broken property.

Hinterland police and private detectives have been stumped since the money went missing from a bank vault. Blockades and searches were unsuccessful. The money was suspected to have been spent, leading authorities to question if the case could still be solved. That is, until Puck's Port's own infamous Maxim & Maxim, Private Detectives, suspected that the sum had been smuggled out on a carnival train, perhaps hidden within the equipment, and was heading right for the Fernnway Glenn park grounds for Puck's Port's Summer Fayre. While police had already been checking all train riders to ensure no illegal traveling, given the rise of "hobo" populations, they had not been closely inspecting any cargo. In an effort to "mend fences," Maxim & Maxim agreed to assist the police in their search. However, at that point, the dockyard duo became a solo.

"This line of work, it's dangerous. And carnival workers aren't exactly known for being accommodating folk, especially when you suspect them of grand larceny," Shona Maxim said. "My brother is a father of two who needs to get home safe, so we made the tough call to let him sit this one out."

After securing a warrant, Puck's Port P.D. officers were able to stop the incoming train and investigate, with the help of Shona Maxim. It was there that tensions escalated.

"To hear it from the folks in custody, it was a cage match," says investigative journalist Victory Eze, first to interview the 13 carnival employees handcuffed to hospital beds. "The police destroyed thousands of roundels worth of carnival equipment looking for the money, and when they couldn't find it, they rushed the sleeper cars. Imagine that: 13 carnival employees in one car, plus 30 police officers swinging batons at anything that moves."

While the Puck's Port P.D. has refuted these accusations, with Chief Dermott Ashley III stating that "the safety of this city is our top priority," known police critic Senan Maxim has stepped forward to speak in defense of the workers.

"This was a nonviolent crime, and the response was to crack heads and ask questions later. There was no definitive evidence that the money was even there in the first place," he claims. Maxim has not been shy about his feelings toward police, having called them "mad dogs" after a previous arrest. He is also the husband of known "radical fey," author Hàzell Stregoni. Senan Maxim went on to say that he did not sign off on handing the case to the police department. "This is not a Maxim & Maxim case," he made clear. "I'm not going to speak for my sister, and she can't speak for me. My name ought to be left out of it."

His sister has called this case a "tragic miscommunication" and has stated that she will speak no further on the matter until Maxim & Maxim can coordinate a proper statement following today's Solstice holiday. The carnival workers will remain in custody until further notice. Those with additional information about the robbery are urged to contact the police department. Miss Eze encourages anyone with information about the arrests to contact her through the *Puck's Port Herald* offices.

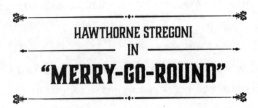

HAWTHORNE STREGONI
IN
"MERRY-GO-ROUND"

On the 51SC Summer Solstice, the air rang through Stregoni Child's pointed ears. The plod of horses, the rattling of wooden rides and flashes of thrilled screaming as coaster cars passed, barkers calling folks to their booths to play games for three pix a pop. The grease off popcorn and dust off animal hides turned to a film upon Stregoni's cheeks that sang like stars. Every song wanted an answer.

It was Maxim's palm slotted with theirs that kept them grounded.

"Stregoni!" The voice twisted through their cells, recognizable in the chaos. "*Dove stai andando?*"

Back down the path between the booths, Hàzell Stregoni's face blipped through the passing figures: golden-skinned, long-nosed, with dark eyebrows furrowed under the shadows cast by a lacy parasol that left her cheeks dotted with scales of light.

"The carousel," Stregoni and Maxim called in twin tempo. Stregoni gleefully squeezed Maxim's hand.

Under the parasol and his wide hat brim, Senan Maxim's face

was a somber-shadowed skull. His hand began to slip from his wife's arm; one dusty shoe stepped off to follow his children into the crowd. Because they were small, and Stregoni a fey, and the world was unsafe even under the summer sun.

Hàzell put her other hand upon his pale knuckles. There was something about her eyes in that moment, a taste Stregoni could nearly catch.

"*Bene*," she called simply.

The word was a starting gate: already Stregoni had turned on their heel. Maxim, tied up, was dragged to follow.

And they were off, through all the smells and sounds and feelings, as if flying upon them with their hands held tight. Ahead, the carousel loomed, its top speckled up with lights that made it look like a mystical mushroom cap. Stregoni could feel the drugged-up dirge of the calliope calling up through the soul. And all the while they ran, they saw the fey in the crowd. The ones with pointed ears sweeping popcorn bags away. The ones with ugly twists of horns barking for freak show tents. A fire-breather who was not a fey at all, spraying sparks above their heads to trickle into Stregoni's stomach and burn in harmony. Stregoni paused, gathering a heating hum in their belly.

"No way," Maxim was good to say, tugging them away from the fire-breather. Maxim wasn't a smiling sort, but their brown face was sincere and open. "It's not a competition."

"I'd win," Stregoni said.

Maxim rolled their eyes, but seemed to agree.

They tugged Stregoni along all the same, with their shoulders bumping warm against the other's. Maxim produced two tickets from the pocket of their dress (Stregoni would have lost them by then), and with that, they went stomping up the steps onto the ocean of polished wood and stared down each grinning carousel pony.

"I want the outside pony," Stregoni said, adjusting their short-sleeved shirt. They didn't want anything restricting their victory. "I'm getting the ring this year." Between the prancing steeds, they could see the candy-striped post that sprouted up about a foot from the carousel platform. Atop it, a pretty brass ring spun around and around like a planet. If you leaned out from your pony to catch that ring, you got a prize. After cycles of falling short (and a few cycles of falling *off*), Stregoni was going to win. "Pick me a good 'un, Maxim," they said, stretching out their long fingers.

"'Course," Maxim agreed. Maxim was a particular child, dragging their fingertips against each pony on the inner circle as if searching for something. As they went, Stregoni watched their two shapes twist long and strange on the center post's mirrors.

Maxim stopped, staring into the face of a milky white-blue pony with its face frozen in a gummy grimace. Stregoni suspected it was meant to be a whinny, perhaps even a grin, but something about its blood-red gums seemed more snarl-like. The outside pony was posed with its back arched into a buck, a wild challenge for a brave rider.

"Rain-right," Stregoni said. Maxim nodded, but looked a bit gray. "What?"

Maxim's lips pressed tight together. "Dunno," they said quietly. They looked off between the ponies to the crowd of parents. "I just . . . my dad's been kind of weird. Sort of fidgety."

"I'm fidgety," Stregoni said plainly.

"No, but . . ." Maxim took a deep breath. They looked more pensive than scared. "What if we aren't friends when we're older?"

Stregoni's heart flipped like a fish. They didn't even know what to say to that. And Maxim didn't elaborate, just stared off. They were such a quiet kid, and Stregoni not that at all. Sometimes it felt like they spoke two different languages. Stregoni could picture a world where they were older, and where their own voice was louder than Maxim's. Or else a world where Maxim, mortal, got every opportunity that Stregoni couldn't. It would be easy to resent the other then, wouldn't it?

Stregoni didn't want to say something to make everything better. The fear was real. So, while the other children raced for their rides and the gate of the fence clanged shut to say they'd be starting soon, Stregoni put their hand on Maxim's back.

Sympathy warmed in their fingers, singing to Maxim's pulse, to the insulted grimace of the pony, to the lights, the dirt, to everything. And that everything moved intently, but not violently. Their palm heated to a comforting glow like the sun beyond the cap of the carousel. They kept an eye in on themself, breathing like their mother taught them. The world grew louder, leaking back up through Stregoni's veins. The grass was dry beyond the carousel, humming in hopes of rain. The carousel was a series of sharp clicks and zips, electricity running through the wires.

Tzzt. Stregoni heard something deep within the bowels of the thing. They squinted to focus harder. *Tzzt.* A rhythmic click, and a smell that made them wrinkle their nose. *Tzzt.*

The carousel lurched suddenly.

A few errant sparks flew from Stregoni's palm to scorch the polished floor. Maxim wiped their eyes with one bare brown arm, the two exchanged a look that meant "thank you—I'm alright," and then Stregoni dove through the first pony's legs. By the time they'd scrambled up into the slippery-smooth saddle of the outside pony, they'd already missed the first rotation past the ring post. Stregoni cursed quietly, flicking one hand to get the frustration out. A few more sparks skittered away.

"Look, look," Maxim said from beside them, holding the pole of their horse as it churned up and down. "There's Daddy and Hàzell."

Stregoni looked off into the bright sunlight beyond the carousel's shadowy parade. In the crowd of parents, they weren't too hard to spot—both were stepped back from the rest, solitary pillars against the back of the nearest tent.

"Hey!" Maxim shouted, hands to their mouth. "*Dad!*"

Neither of them turned. Stregoni figured it was too far for quiet Maxim Child to be heard.

"I got it," they said. Stregoni put two fingers into their mouth to whistle sharp and then gathered all their breath back. "MA!" they shouted. An orange glow sang through their blood. "*Guardami!*"

A flicker of recognition tingled through the air, yet neither parent turned. Senan pinched the bridge of his tiny nose, staring at his shoes. The carousel was already rotating past them. Stregoni, curious now and always prone to eavesdropping, took stock of the tingling in their skin. They were alright, and dared to open their hearing a bit more.

Tzzt! Tzzt! It roared up from somewhere close, but Stregoni struggled past it to pinpoint their parents behind. Their mother's voice surged through all the noise, sure as always and yet wilting on the edges like a flower in the fall. "The fact that she even *suggested* taking my child from me should tell you everything you need to know. Are you really going to remove your spine because of one letter?"

Stregoni was already rotating past and yet could feel the letter in the grass between their feet, torn in two.

Tzzt! TZZT!

"I still should have gone to see her, just to make sure she's alright," Senan said. "There's gotta be some sort of middle ground here. I ain't totally innocent—"

Hàzell Stregoni, known fey radical, tightened her voice. "Saints, Senan," she hissed. "How many compromises will you make? You're not a doll for her to hold and dress and speak for."

"I know," he muttered. "But I've never been able to say that to her—she sounds like she's willing to talk about it—"

"Ring," Maxim prompted. Stregoni faced forward fast enough to see a kid two horses ahead lunge out for the ring post, but their fingers swiped far too high. *Sucker*, Stregoni thought, grinning and gauging the ring's rotations. It was only big enough to get one finger through—you had to be both quick *and* exact.

Stregoni hooked their toes into the stirrups, ready to lean out. But as they spun up closer, past all the linen collars and shining hair and flower crowns of the other children, they saw their parents as overexposed shapes in the burning sunlight. Their mother's hands were whipping faster, making the green grass sway at her feet. Stregoni kept an eye on the mortals nearest, but they were too distracted to be worried. And yet Hàzell's shoulders were shaking under her embroidered shawl, the words all fumbling into each other.

Tzzt! Tzzt!

"I can't just stop her from seeing the kids. She practically raised Maxim, and you know she cares about Stregoni just as much," Senan said through the crowd. "It wouldn't be right, for any of them."

The ring post came closer. Stregoni tensed their fingers—their nails were warming when they hadn't asked for that. They told the power to back off, but it just built up stronger to send rivulets of orange up along the veins in their hands. The more Stregoni tried to fight it, the higher it climbed. Like a disease.

TZZT, TZZT, TZZT!

"Senan, I need you to understand how desperately your sister craves control. I won't 'compromise' on my children," Hàzell said. From her forehead, two knobbly bones began to sprout, black as jet. "Maxim is proof of your first act against her, and Stregoni is everything she despises in me. At best, she'll use them against us. You mark my words: if you ever let her alone with them, she'll saddle them with the same pity she gives you. A person shouldn't make you feel guilty for existing."

Stregoni reached out into the sunshine, watching every aching semi-second of their hand surging through the air, of the ring glinting in its rotation, spinning closer to their reaching fingers.

"I know. Saints, *I know*," Senan said. "But she's my blood."

"I understand that," Hàzell said. Stregoni's longest finger hooked through the ring's eye at the same time their mother laid everything plain. "You must be your own body, or else you'll have no way to defend yourself when you realize the mistake you've made."

Stregoni tugged the ring free from its stand.

Tzzt, tzz—click.

They lurched back into the saddle, bringing the ring with them in a spray of confetti. Finally. Exactly as they'd planned.

"Mum!" Stregoni shouted, with a shriek of triumph that sent an orange glow beaming across their cheeks. Sparkles poured off them in a glittering haze far brighter than cheap paper, enough to make the kids behind gasp and the parents by the gate hesitate back. But Stregoni couldn't care. Their voice rang loud and true as they turned for their parents. "Mum, Senan, look!"

Stregoni had only a second to see Senan's hand on their mother's wrist, to see the grass dead in a great ring and Hàzell's antlers grown twisted and speckled with lights like stars.

And yet still, they both turned to Stregoni's shriek and their shattering of gleeful fey sparkles. Senan's face fell into wide panic, but Hàzell Stregoni began to smile. Her hands came up to clap.

Maybe that's what put her over the edge.

The tick-tick-ticking in the carousel ended in an electric and fiery hum, and then everything busted up orange.

◆

The memory played out, flames closing in and then replaced by nothing but dark. In it, Hawthorne Stregoni remembered some of her mother's last words, chasing themselves around and around the empty space of Hawthorne's body like hounds after hares.

Control. Pity. Guilt. Did Hawthorne deserve to have her own body carved out? Did Senan deserve the tight leash from his sister who called him foolish and reckless, considering how it ended?

Hawthorne was meant to believe that all this pain and guilt was justified, that it would move them forward, and yet nothing had gotten any easier. After so many cycles of spinning around and around, trying to get it right, was this moment on the office rug supposed to be her prize?

Hawthorne heard the doctors in the hall laughing. The room floated closer, smooshing together in smudgy shapes like a watercolor painting building itself before her eyes. *Be your own body. Be your own body.* Some of the last words before her mother busted up the fayre. The last words before a mad fey took the world down with her because she refused to let it break her. Was that selfish madness?

But Hawthorne had watched her mother's careful calm, funneled out harmlessly into the grass and antlers. Hàzell Stregoni was no rookie, was exact and specific, exercised the kind of power Hawthorne had been told couldn't exist. The kind of power that had to be ripped from her, to leave only the squirming, weak part inside that couldn't fight back.

Hawthorne had been guilty enough to let them take everything from her, and now there was no way to defend herself.

She was on her hands and knees in Doctor Sonder Secondchild's office. She felt like she was retching up something stuck in her stomach. She gagged on it, her spine pulling against her shirt, her limbs numb.

Mum's hands under mine. Antlers twining into the sky and sparkles off my hands—who did that hurt? No one. Their fear hurt them more than any fey could.

And fear was a hell of a drug. Fear turned to violence, and violence to pity, and pity to guilt strong enough to hand the keys over. Where there was guilt for mere existence, there was control.

She'd thought whoever had hired O'Taglio wanted to stir up fear. But maybe O'Taglio had always been meant to get caught, one way or another. Maybe this wasn't about fear, but pity.

In all this clarity, Hawthorne focused on the laughing doctors in the hallway, and struck matches in her galvanized stomach.

Scrape.

She thought of petals falling down around her mother. Those palms under her own, calling the sparks out with careful control, warming Gristle's back. Hien's power dripping down like clouds. Robin Goodfellow razing the Dog to ash? Her mother blowing up the fayre? But that wasn't Hawthorne. Why should she feel guilty for something she hadn't done, with no promise she would? And how could she pity Robin Goodfellow, who was only dealing back the violence given?

Scrape.

She knew if she stayed at the school, she was always going to be something to be saved, the tragic girl cut out of the bomb. There wasn't a girl inside, Hawthorne knew. There was just her, all of this her. This body was her body, and this body burned on purpose.

Light up, she thought. *Let's have a blast, Doc. The more I break myself, the worse I am. I could be powerful too.*

"Scrape," she whispered, closing her eyes to hear the spirit world whoop inside her. Let's make trees grow where you burned them.

In my head, there's something that bursts alive like a star. My neurons shout and laugh like horrible things heard in the woods. I don't wait for the flames to lash out toward me and pull me in when I ain't ready for them.

The more I fight myself, the worse it is. I'm not gonna fight anymore.

"Fwoosh," I whisper, and welcome the power proper.

In an instant, like gasoline and a match, the best sort of magic sprints through me. It swirls between my organs, runs up my veins, purrs out happily to hold me like waiting arms. When I open my eyes, the world is orange and red, the office warbling behind tongues of fire. I hold my arm up in kiddish wonderment to watch silver melt from my pores. It sparkles in there like strange freckles, catching all the light to blink into constellations.

I don't fight it, so it doesn't hurt. We're a hand-in-hand dance, me and the flames. My mind's clearer than ever, like someone's shut off all the radio jumble.

I wish it weren't true, but I've got a pretty little hunch about which folks got Rory to hire O'Taglio. I'm not their little damsel doll anymore.

It's time to get my own sort of justice.

Second,

I've just read the morning paper. I don't know what's gotten into you to challenge the police again. You will <u>never</u> get that curse off your back, and you've done a mighty fine job of publicly cutting yourself off from my help too. You'll lose everything for this: your career, your children. You might even lose me.

Your children deserve better than the chaos you and Hàzell are leading you all to. I deserve better than how you're treating me. I heard you before: I understand you've been feeling hurt, and we can work on that. You just need to talk to me and be honest instead of sneaking around with all these secrets.

You know I love you, even when it's hard. You know the fire and flood I'd go through to make sure you're safe—no one in this world is as important to me as you are. If you need me to make peace with Hàzell, then we can discuss that. I understand Hàzell wants you all to go to the fayre today, but if you have any love in your heart left for me, come to the office so we can make a proper statement to settle this. Bring the children, if you can, but I know Hàzell doesn't want them near me. You and I can talk, then we can meet them there and be a family properly.

Signed,

Your First and only, Shona Maxim

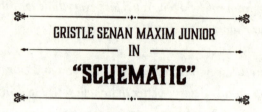

GRISTLE SENAN MAXIM JUNIOR IN
"SCHEMATIC"

My name is Gristle Senan Maxim Junior. I'm foy. Always have been, behind the corners in my head.

I don't care about solving the O'Taglio case anymore. I have a hunch that my world's just gotten a lot more complicated. It's terrifying, but it's real, and it won't stop unless I do something.

The Gattano brothers will handle Ashley one way or another—at the heart of their operations, they're hit men. As for us, Fionne's got our getaway vehicle waiting and ready, and I'm sure we'll need it soon once I collect my evidence.

I race back down the stairs two at a time and shoulder through the door into the garage. Before I even clunk the lever for the lights, the bulbs sear on overhead to match my screaming pulse. Each strobe cuts through the cement room across half-made cars and engines, tanks and tool shelves, pinups and the smell of oil and liquor and sweat, and there's usually a cat here but not right now—I think it's a few blocks over. I can hear it if I try.

Breathe, Mister Maxim, Hien says from behind me. I suck in half a mouthful. I need to focus—I can't get too carried away. This is just evidence collection, what I've always been good at. While Hien and Quen step in beside me, I pull out my camera.

Pop. Flash. The room snaps into proper place like the geometrics of inlaid floor.

My father, that day in the dockyard apartment, suns before it all went bad. His eyes glancing over at me, or every trolley driver doing the same, a person bumping my shoulder on the street. Something was there, but my mind didn't notice it. Maybe I did that to myself, or maybe I heard my aunt tell me the same thing so many times (I'm mortal, I need to watch Hawthorne, she loves me, and my daddy died because he didn't listen) that it rewrote things I knew were real.

The worst part is, I know she does love me, or a fraction of me.

I hear Hien writing and turn back to check, even if my eyes are wild under my hat and I'm breathing so hard I can't stand still. Their image flickers in and out behind their notepad.

What are you looking for?

I hardly have the time to fill them in. The end of this is over me like clouds closing in. I rush through the shop, heading for the cash register off to one side.

"My stepmother blew up the fayre," I say, even though I'm sure half the world knows that already. It's more that I have to say it all for myself, fill in the gaps. "At least that's what everyone thought. The only survivors were me and my sister because . . ." That dome at the Dog. I look over to Hien. The blur nods me on. "Because I protected us, I must have. But my memory was . . ." I wave my hand around, ducking behind the counter and hauling open drawers. Another photo for posterity. Patterns to make the chaos survivable. "Hazy. But I was told Hàzell self-destructed, from all the police and doctors and my aunt, so why would I question that?"

Hien hums. I find a heavy ledger and flip through, but it's just oil changes and engine tune-ups and tires. It's not what I'm looking for! I slam my palm against the counter; if not for a twitch of Hien's hand sending smooth warmth up my arm, I'm sure that would have hurt something fierce. I feel like I'm racing a clock. It's more than the idea of Rory waking up; it's that cosmic unbalance that says something will go wrong.

I shove my hands under my hat and grab my hair.

What else, Mister Maxim? Hien asks. The blur steps closer. Quen's looking around fast, like it's trying to gauge where the threat could come from. *I can't read your mind.*

"My aunt and my father were fighting," I breathe, staring up at the water-stained ceiling while the white lights burn too bright. "My daddy didn't want to work with the police anymore. She always said it was because Hàzell was tricking him." Because other people can't be trusted. People like the Dogfoot fey, who show us what freedom feels like. "But he was finally putting his foot down about it."

Hien tilts their head slowly up, half a nod. Quen's eyeing me. But I don't feel unhinged. I just need another clue, another moment of calm. Rory's passed out and could lie to me anyway. So just breathe, just talk. Make new patterns.

"The Gattanos are hit men," I say. Rory was a friend of my daddy and stepmum, their brothers respected them, from what I can remember, but everyone has a breaking point. "There was something off about that day, Hien. I just feel it. Hàzell was so . . ."

Hien's eyes flicker in the blur: eight, like a spider's, with thin pupils like a snake, blinding yellow in the grayscale until I shut my eyes. In that darkness, their thoughts come more as an idea: When you compare it to Robin Goodfellow razing the world to fantastic chaos, Hàzell's self-destruction was quick, brutal, exact, final, *planned.*

I go to snap my fingers to say they're on the money, but instead shut my hand tight before I accidentally break another light. I still don't know how to control this properly.

"Yes," I say instead. "My aunt had been investigating all the equipment, for a burglary. They never found the money but that doesn't mean it wasn't there." And she could have swiped it, paid enough to keep the rest plus the keys to the grounds. Even the cops can be bought. Because this city is what?

Shining with tears, built to be unfair, whispering and wrong. It's made of back alleys and dead ends, and people who don't jive slipping in the shadows. I learned it on my father's knee while he folded pamphlets, held me close, and said it would change if we were brave enough. All this time, I'd been told he was the reckless fool, and her a manipulative bomb waiting to go off.

I open my eyes and scan down to the dust mote, the faintest smell of oil and ash in the air. The toolboxes are all laid out on the tables and benches, the posters all look equally worn . . . Hang on.

Across the room, one toolbox sits suspiciously balanced all the way on top of a high tool cabinet. It's flanked by an old radio and clock, both covered in dust.

The box is clean.

I stride right to the cabinet and strain to grab hold. My fingers graze the top but can't catch the box's handle. Sweat drips into my eyes. My muscles tense.

I always thought it was convenient for the most well-known fey to break, Hien says as they march past me. The blur is a foot taller than me, which no one's ever been. And it's no trickery—an illusion couldn't grab the toolbox and place it in my hands.

With Quen hugged to their side, Hien flickers clear at a treacherous seven feet tall. They're wearing that long Hannochian snow leopard coat and dangling drop diamond earrings. But I still don't know if that's real. I don't know if they are. They raise a white eyebrow at my staring.

"Thank you," I say, my hands cold against the metal. "Hien, I don't want you wasting energy putting on what you think I want to see."

Is this your way of asking me to undress? they ask. It's the same cold insincerity and yet no beguiling grin.

"I wouldn't be frightened of the truth," I tell them.

I'd be, they say, one gram of honesty. They flick back to a mess of blurring shapes and colors. But at least I know it's not for me.

I'd rather have truth than blank loyalty.

"Alright," I say. I turn around and *thunk* the rusted box onto the table, flipping the latches. "Can you wave down Fionne?" I ask them. "If I'm right, I want to get out of here fast. Please, Hien."

They march off, Quen trotting after them. It leaves me alone with whatever I'm going to find. I need to know. I deserve to.

I open the toolbox in a flurry of papers, greasy with engine oil and whatever comes off slicked palms, slipped in by date. I thumb through, catching flashes of words like "bullet" and "no witnesses" and everything that makes my stomach churn.

I want to be wrong about this. I wasn't even on the hunt for what I've just walked into. I shuffle until my eyes skim over the right name. That fills in the gaps.

I was told only a fey could do something so awful, but everyone has a breaking point.

I lay the paper on the table. *Pop!*-flash. The camera doesn't lie.

Right here is the evidence that the collapse of Hàzell Stregoni was nothing more than a frame job, and that it happened only because my aunt refused to bend.

Date: 51SC/6S/30

CLIENT:

Maxim, Shona + Ashley, Dermott III

DESCRIPTION OF REPAIRS:

"An accident." 10-canister fertilizer bomb under fayre carousel, on brass ring detonation, Solstice, Fernnway Glenn. Keys to fayre handed off by Maxim for early entry.

PAYMENT:

2400R down + 7 cycles of immunity from cops

Rimetti a noi i nostri debiti. Camminare in pace.

DON'T TELL RORY

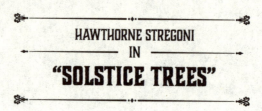

HAWTHORNE STREGONI IN
"SOLSTICE TREES"

The world is orange, like staring through a piece of colored sea glass. Heat wraps me up in a summery shine. I wonder if this is how mum felt when she was destructing—angry and peaceful and at home.

I still don't know if that makes us mad, or right, or what. But I can hear those doctors laughing outside, and they tried to break me. And they only got this 'cause of letting some sad mortal take the fall for them.

I don't think Doc Secondchild is smart enough to pull that sort of political conspiracy off alone. But I know who is:

My aunt and me are gonna be having a nice talk about it. Soon. Because I feel better than I ever have trying to be what she wanted.

In all the orange and red of the flames crackling around me, I focus on the door of the office and its wavy glass window. Through it, Doc Secondchild steps forward to meet another shadow and shake its hand. I'll bet those are the stress-test techs.

"Scrape," I whisper. I raise my hand up toward the door. *No more, Doc.* "Fwoosh."

The torrent of flame shoots forward, smooth and willful as when I was a kid. The door shatters open from the force. The doctors in the hall scream. I'm already running for the fractured gap, faster than I thought I could run, like a spark along a fuse.

Burnt hair and char and ash sear through the smoke. When I soar out into the bright hallway, there's two doctors thrown against the wall, dazed but alive in their padded tech armor. I see more of them stumbling back with their mortal eyes and ears and teeth. When Hien showed me their fancy hoity-toity Hannochian school, the teacher was a fey. Here, we're taught by mortals, because we're meant to become them.

"Stregoni," Doc gasps. I whip my head around to see him backing away, in a careful hunch. His lab coat and tacky tie singed, his face soot-blasted, everything swimming in my vision like lava. The polished floor and dark walls smear and roar in the light coming off me. The garlands burn with a smell like Mum's Old World offerings.

Secondchild holds his terrified ground while the other doctors race away. One of them hits the alarm—iron-reeking water shoots down from the sprinklers, but it fizzles up on my flames. I grin, fire licking up my tooth-lined throat and from my lips like tongues.

"S-Stregoni, take a deep breath," Doc says. He stumbles back through the rubble of the busted-out door. The sprinkler is wetting his hair, soaking his jacket. "We must have mis-measured the medicine. It's going to be alright."

"Sure is," I say. It rumbles and purrs, not really my voice. Or maybe it is, always has been. I kick a piece of smoldering rubble so it goes skidding down the hall. I snap my fingers on both hands—the flames roar hotter despite the water raining down, spraying him with sparks that flick through colors like the Dogfoot signs. I forgot how *fun* this is. And I'm all free now to see what I can really do when I light up those "evil" impulses rushing through me. "I feel real in-control, *Doc*, now that I'm not trying to stop what I am."

His shoes squeak—he collapses back over the sizzling remains of the door, landing flat on his ass and trying to scuttle backward like an overturned crab. "Stregoni—"

"I think you were all just scared of something stranger than you. Or maybe you were *jealous*."

I'm right over him and he stops trying to crawl back. Sweat beads down his raw-red skin. His eyes are huge, holding my image exactly how he sees me: my uniform incinerated right off but the flames turning to wings and robes, shining on those new silver specks that turn me to a glittering shine.

It's beautiful, I'm beautiful, enough to dim the rage. "I feel better than I have since I was eleven," I tell him, softer. I cool the flames to bathwater warmth. My body is mine. There are still carols playing from somewhere, still pretty bells and ribbons on the doors. I just want a nice Solstice, same as anyone else. "I won't burn anyone like this. You just gotta trust me."

He stares at me, gasping to breathe, twitching to stand. *Come on, Doc. You're a man of science, you've got logic. Just listen to me tell you that it shouldn't have ever been about going mortal. We could have all worked together. I mean that, really.*

"Maybe we were wrong," he mutters, his voice crackling. "This isn't a disorder, it's . . ."

Wonderful, I hear Mum say, a million cycles ago now. With my fey eyes, I swear I can see her, drifting on the edges where our plane meets the good path. *Powerful.*

"Demonic," Secondchild says, in the second where I'm distracted. I look down just fast enough to see him pull a syringe of that silver stuff from his coat pocket.

He swings to his feet. The flames roar back desperately, lunging to protect me in time. He staggers forward.

My incendiary arm goes through his chest like a hot poker through paper. The needle falls harmlessly to the ground. He sinks right up close to me, where his beard singes and his glasses crack from the heat.

I'm the Old World spirit who leads travelers astray. I'm retribution. His eyes dull, his skin blisters, his mouth drops open. My stomach lurches, because he's still the guy I've known since I was small.

"Madness," he breathes.

All science, no humanity. After cycles and cycles of his sort hurting mine, why should I feel guilty? I pull him closer, where my breath is so hot it burns his sweat to steam. "And don't you forget it."

I throw him down dead to the soaked floor with a hole through him, leaving him to gawk through his glasses at the burned rubble. I stare at my glowing hand and turn it like I'm lookin' at a ring prettier than carousel trash. I ain't the kind of fun Fionne wanted. I could steal kids, blight crops. If those stories are real, I wonder how far those fey were pushed before they snapped.

I'm not gonna feel guilty for protecting myself from a world that won't, not ever again.

"Gristle Senan Maxim Junior, I will *murder* you if you scratch this!" Hienne chups from the passenger seat as I haul around the few cars out so late, dipping into the slushy gutters and wrenching the wheels straight. "Where are we *going*?!"

"The school," I tell her. A head-on car honks at me just as I lurch back into our lane. Quen huffs. I lead-foot my way through an intersection while the traffic guard shouts. The buildings have turned from flat-faced warehouses to tidy stores all closed for Solstice.

Scribbling from the back seat. "Hien wants to know why the school," Fionne reads. "And *Fionne* wants to know why the hell you're driving—"

"Watch it, asshole!" someone shouts.

"—like you've got the devil on your tail!"

Garlands drape over the road, hung with flickering electric candles that muddle all the gray lights and shadows. The traffic's condensing down below it, all people trying to get home or to the still-open pubs in time for midnight. I whip my eyes across the lanes to find any sort of path.

"Look—"

Someone is too slow about moving forward so I haul half onto the sidewalk and duck back ahead of them.

"Look at this," I say. I hand her the paper scrap I took.

We're really not moving at all now. All I can hear is chugging engines and people honking. I can't see past the tall, boxy car ahead so I flip open the roof just enough to stand on the leather seat. The air sheers ice-cold against my feverish face.

Over the sea of cars, we're grille-to-bumper right up to the intersection, where the guards are ushering all the cars to redirect west.

They're clearing an eastbound path, down 8th. I don't like the look of this.

Fionne makes a strangled little squeak. I look down to see her gripping the paper so hard she creases it at the edges.

"Your aunt and Ashley paid to blow up the fayre," she whispers when she looks up to me. "Tell me I'm not reading that right. I know what Ashley got out of it, but your aunt?"

I know how you can justify things you don't agree with. Anything for family. "She thought Hàzell was ruining him. She kept saying Hàzell was an accident waiting to happen." And this? The proof that trusting the wrong people only ends in disaster. "She told my dad to come see her that day. I guess she never imagined he wouldn't."

Or accepted that he was better off dead than disloyal. And me? And Hawthorne? Were we just pawns in the game? Did she ever actually love me? Or am I only proof that my dad disobeyed.

She's been trying to make me everything he wasn't. But the sin was already set.

"Gristle, maybe we oughta tell someone. The cops or . . ." Fionne stops herself. She saw what happened at the Dog, and this right here proves that my aunt was making cop deals too. She closes her eyes and tries to breathe. "Then why the school and not her office?"

Because when my daddy was too dead to be her pitiable doll, who could she scoop from the ashes? Who could she save to ensure the Maxims would never be ruined by a fey again?

"We have to get to Hawthorne," I tell her. Maybe I don't really know who Hawthorne is, but I know I loved her before our aunt got in our heads, and I think I deserve to again. "My aunt put her in that school for a reason—I don't trust anything that's happening there."

The honking chorus is joined by a scream of sirens. I turn in time to see the police, and fire trucks, and ambulances race down 8th, ringing their bells and sirens so loud it sounds like Solstice came early. The electricity in my stomach comes sprinting up in response; the overhead lights blink and rattle as I shake the static from my hands. But we're still half-a-bell to midnight, and the traffic guards are holding us back.

I have an awful gut feeling that Hawthorne's the reason for that. "Come *on!*" I snap.

"We're only a few blocks out," Fionne says suddenly. She's already shuffling over on the bench, shoving my legs while I'm standing. "I'll bring the car around. You just go." Scribbling. Hien flips the notepad to her as they pop the back door open. Quen slips out onto the sidewalk. "Hien says to take Quen."

I drop back down into the car, already cracking the driver's door open too. "Is it an attack dog?"

Hien writes faster, pencil stabbing into the pages. They practically shove the notebook in my face, all frenetic annoyance.

Fire trucks?!?!?!

Fionne and I lock wide eyes. Maybe we'll need a familiar to calm down a fey getting too close to burning up. Quen pries its nose through the open driver door and grabs my pant leg between its teeth.

"Go," Fionne says, shoving her shoulder into mine to bully me out. "We'll meet you there."

I'm sweating through my suit now even as I slide out into the wintry street. "Fionne, if she's even a bit dangerous, they're going to arrest her for madness," I say. And I don't care—I'll get her out anyway. "This could be a getaway car."

She sets her shoe on the pedal, hands on the wheel. Part of her is still that girl who danced all night, and the kid who sat with us in the back booth of Cat's, but maybe with a bit of reality injected in. She knows what she's up against now.

We're not the same as our parents, but we're ready to fight all the same.

"I'm only doing this 'cause I'm counting on Hien to scrub this car outta people's heads before I write the article of the septennial," she says. Hien reaches a blurry hand forward to touch her shoulder as some acknowledgment. She doesn't even flinch. "And *you* can explain it to my parents, Maxim."

I'll have to trust them both.

"Come on, Quen," I say, and then we're both racing off onto the mostly clear sidewalk, dodging people who gasp and shout when we pass because they never saw me coming. The streetlamps flicker with every footfall. My duster tails whip behind me, my hat shoved back so brick-sharp air smears against every freckle and nerve.

I wonder if this is how my dad felt while trying to change this city. I'm not sure it matters. I'm only sure of myself.

We duck the corner onto 8th, racing down the intersection past a group of kids with Solstice sparklers, sidestepping a gaggle of drunk folks who try to pet Quen and get snapped at. The people in the still-open pubs press their faces to the frosty windows when another boxy police car races past. In the distance, around a bend in the street, the sky is more gray than black. The street's been completely cleared to let the crowd of emergency vehicles through. Even through that exhaust, I can smell burning.

There's a mess of emergency vehicles ahead, but the school is hidden around the tall buildings that border it. The sidewalk crams up with more and more people. Quen pries them apart with its pointed snout and hard shoulders. I follow in the wake. Fabric scrapes into my skin, arms and shoulders poke and jam and make my blood buzz. I put a hand on Quen's back, just enough to stay grounded.

Finally, I fight far enough into the mess of people shoved behind sawhorses and crowd-control police, and turn to see the school.

Four levels loom high above the street with flames soaring out from the third, licking char into the dark brick, the windows blown open and the street sparkling with shards of thrown glass. Emergency vehicles have blocked off an empty circle in front of the towering main gate. In terrible unison, the police wagon doors slam open. A thundering of boots hit the ground at once.

Usually iron's more an annoyance than a pain, but the smell is so thick that even I almost gag. If not for Quen sitting itself heavy on my shoes, I think I'd fade out of my body again to get away from the reek. Ahead, a dozen people in the crowd choose to wander off before this escalates, shaking out their hands to sprout small scales or crack the sidewalk pavement where no one will see.

Through the gaps they make, Quen drills us closer to the sawhorses in time to watch cops stream from four different vehicles, racing to the gates in metal armor and helmets, with silver and ash-wood batons on their belts and iron cuffs at the ready. They collide into divisions, funneling through the gate and right for the wide arch of the front doors. I lean like I'll somehow run to stop them. How can I?

Tires screech toward us from the other direction. They skid to a stop. Another door slams open.

"Madam President," a distant voice says.

Now there's someone I can handle.

Above the crowd, I turn to look. And there's my aunt, cutting through the streaming headlights with Hawthorne's iron jacket folded neatly over her shoulder. A doctor with burns all down their front stumbles from one of the ambulances, nearly collapsing in front of her.

"She went mad—lit up like a Solstice tree," they blubber as she catches them, like she's so benevolent and loving, a mother to everyone including two kids she stole. Is that love? "We misbalanced the solution—the stimulants overpowered the silver—she killed Secondchild!"

Silver? What the hell were they giving her?

The whole police mob has already disappeared into the inferno. Are they going to grab her like they did Robin? Or will Hawthorne be blamed when the building falls on all of them?

Nothing's changed since my daddy died, because the people calling the shots were already winning.

"Move," I tell the crowd, but no one does. They're all pushing toward the sawhorses, trying to see and hear. "Folks, I'm with Maxim & Maxim and I need you to—"

A sudden explosion rocks the street. The crowd screams. Glass and brick shower down onto the roofs of the cars and beam off my hat brim. In the firelight thrown down over us, I see a shadow. Almost a person, but with flickering gray shapes around them like wings or robes. The fey folk of legend and lore.

We all look up between our sheltering arms.

There's a disfigured gap in the wall of the school, leaking flames like a portal to the fey wilds, fire and sparks soaring out from a smoldering laboratory I can barely see through the churning embers. I smell silver so hot it's bubbling. And standing right on the edge of the building, looking down like a gargoyle?

"Hawthorne!" my aunt screams. She covers her mouth—I swear I see tears in her eyes. Three officers try to grab my aunt, to pull her back into the safety of the vehicle maze, but she roots her feet down hard.

"Auntie," Hawthorne says, so level I almost don't hear it over the sounds of the firefighters hauling out the hoses and trying to call the police back out of the building, and the crowd gasping and whispering, and the fire purring happily. But her voice vibrates from the ground.

Hawthorne stares from her third-story perch. I see the moment she decides what to do next. They'll call this madness, a fey gone too far, succumbing to the wicked impulses that can only be stopped with chemicals and shocks and padded walls.

My aunt knew exactly what she was doing when she ordered a bomb. And my sister knows exactly what she's doing when she leaps.

I have only a second to gather all the humming in my body and compress it properly.

"Everybody *MOVE!*"

My voice shocks out. White lines split from me to the next person to the next with audible cracks. The people yelp and dodge away, jolt again when they see me standing there as if I've only suddenly appeared.

Because, to them, I have. A wild fey who you never see until he's in front of you.

And that's not all I can do, I think.

Stay, Quen.

Yes, sir.

I rush through the sawhorse barrier, straight past the distracted guard. I don't know how to control this like Hien who can light up everything in me like telephone wires, or even like Hawthorne who soars down toward my aunt with fire racing behind her while the people below dive for cover. But my aunt doesn't move, even as she's deserted. She just looks up at Hawthorne like she's the world and not a comet racing down to burn all the shadows away. Does Hawthorne know our aunt orphaned us? That she would have rather we were killed than turned against her? Is that why her teeth are grit and her eyes are lava?

I know Hawthorne's figured out the game we've been trapped in.

I race toward my aunt standing alone, ducking through the people running away. She doesn't see me coming, but that's alright. It's all moving slowly now. I look up to see that white lightning knitting itself into a shimmering dome over our heads, just managing to catch Hawthorne in her descent. It's closing in the last of us:

The last of the Maxims and the Stregonis.

The dome seals us in even if I don't know how I made it. The screaming from beyond shuts off like a radio.

Hawthorne hits the ground so hard the pavement under her breaks and sends my aunt and me stumbling. The shock wave of fire rips aching across my ankles before it washes up the edges of the dome, flames crackling against the ripples of electricity. It's all so bright that the world looks like an ink sketch, stark black on searing white.

My feet simmer in my shoes, but I'm not afraid of what's to come.

Hawthorne stands slowly, turning her head to me amidst the crackling flames. Her eyes are pupil-less, just churning magma like when she punched me, with each grinning tooth an ember against the stove light down her throat that makes her voice rumble:

"Come to stop me, lug?"

I'm at an equal distance from her and from my aunt.

"Hawthorne," my aunt says again. "We just want to help." She reaches to me but doesn't turn her head.

"Yeah," I say. Hawthorne's whole body tenses. The heat rings louder, tightening my skin. I step for my sister, not my aunt, even when she whips angry eyes to me. "I found out something about the fayre," I tell her. "You oughta know. I oughta tell you. We—"

"Gristle," our aunt hisses. I don't look at her.

Hawthorne's flames pop with sparks. "Real good coincidence," she says, tilting her chin up at me like a boxer sizing their opponent. "'Cause I've got a damn good hunch about who hired O'Taglio."

The pattern lines up. I've lost every grain of trust for my aunt, but I'm willing to put them toward Hawthorne. And maybe to myself too, as I step up beside her. The flames don't hurt: they wrap warm around me like Summer Solstice sun.

"Saints," our aunt whispers.

We both turn to watch her wide-eyed with the iron jacket dropped at her feet. She stares back at us like we're strangers. Hawthorne keeps a smug grin, but I'm not the smiling sort. Maybe that's the fey in me.

"You look so much like your parents," she says.

HAWTHORNE STREGONI IS "IN THE RING"

I didn't expect Gristle to show up, especially looking so dragged out since the last time I saw him. He seems ten pounds thinner in no good way, back in his ugly old suit. But there's something about him with his hat pushed back, a strike of white through his hair now and a flicker under the deep brown of his eyes that used to be green and used to be hazel—I notice that now. Who's been changing him?

Outside the strange dome where only us three are crowded together, the firefighters and crowd-control police are looking around all confused, their eyes going right over us like we're not here. It's the same domed shield from the Dog. Part of me understands that it's what saved us as kids, and that it's Gristle making it.

My fey brother. I don't know anything about the jack, and I doubt he knows everything yet either, but after almost a septennial, we're on the same page. And now we're invisible in this secret ring beneath the lightning lines caging us together. It's the showdown we deserve.

"You look so much like your parents," my aunt breathes. She's statue-still, her clothes charred from me slamming down, her hat blown clean off to show her flushed cheeks, my iron coat reeking on the ground ahead of her like a snake ready to strike up.

"And you look like a murderer," I say. The pavement bleaches and dries under my feet. I wonder if I could learn to grow flowers there. "Tell me, what was the plan here? Get some sad patsy to kill a few innocent folks, turn her in to get some pity, get your school and make me mortal, then what? Were you just gonna keep me some drugged-up doll my whole life?"

"You're sick, Stregoni," she says, but not like Doc Secondchild. She says it with tears in her eyes, fumbling her hands and stepping forward like she'll rush up to me, even if I can see her skin turning red from the heat. "We never would have gotten this school without pulling strings. O'Taglio was just collat—"

"*Pah!*" I spit, all sparks. Maybe O'Taglio was a damn bigot, but she was some scared kid too.

My aunt backs off that trail real fast. "We needed new treatment. Secondchild told me that serum would help you."

"What if I don't want to be *helped*?" I ask her through my teeth, sending out more soaring flames. She flinches; I'm almost sorry. "You had to *kill* people for this. Secondchild tried to kill part of me—what if I could learn to control it instead?"

She shakes her head. "Think of your mother, the fayre," she says through building tears, "and killing that folk at the Dog. Is that what you want for yourself?"

Hien. Killing Doc Secondchild was to protect myself, but that wasn't. And am I worth more than three hundred dead, or however many else I might hurt? The pavement rumbles as some part of the school behind collapses, spraying dust and smoke around the dome as the police usher the crowd back further, but I don't look away from her. I feel the fire around me flicker, hear my head try to rush again. "I—"

"You're a good detective, one of the best," Gristle says to her, a scraping rumble when he steps even closer to me and doesn't burn. "I find it hard to believe that you weren't aware of Hien surviving."

Her eyes sharpen, mouth creases.

Hien's alive. I feel my fire bust up again and my heart stutter. I want to be pissed that Hien let me think they were dead... but then I just want to know how they managed it. Because I can see them on Gristle somehow if I really focus. Each of us tangling our roots into the next, straining up for the sun together like how our parents used to be.

Gristle's chin is up, eyes solid, body ready. "And should I fill Hawthorne in about your deal with Ashley and the Gattanos?"

Auntie Shona's jaw tightens. "I don't know what you mean," she starts. "If you've been hearing lies against me—"

Little white lightning lines zip between Gristle's freckles. "I found the paper," he says, in a voice booming like thunder. "You and Ashley ordered a bomb at the fayre. He got enough fear to take office, and you got what? A dead brother? A clean slate with his kids?"

My stomach snarls. My hands clench tight.

I want her to look sorry, but her posture is as firm as his. "It would have been quick," she says, voice trembling but sure. How many times has she told herself this? "Hàzell was set to hurt even more people with her reckless—"

"You don't know that!" Gristle snaps, louder than I've ever heard him. "Just because you can't control something doesn't make it dangerous. How can you still justify what you did?"

My mum didn't blow up the fayre?

"Gristle Second Maxim Junior," she says, pointing at him like a stern boss. The tears dry, because she never did bother to waste them on Gristle. Smoke whips around the dome like storm clouds. "Your father would have been dead before he was named if I wasn't there to clean up after him. Without me, you wouldn't even *exist*."

My mum didn't blow up the fayre.

"So he was just supposed to leave everyone else to get kicked like he was?" he shouts. "Nothing's actually gotten better in this city. We're just ignoring it—"

"YOU SAID I WAS DANGEROUS!" I scream, so loud flames race out from me and swirl up the dome, falling back down onto us like a meteor shower. My mum didn't blow up the fayre on purpose or by mad accident, because she was just as practiced and loving and stable as she said she was, and she could have taught us all how to do that too. "YOU HATED MY MOTHER BECAUSE SHE KNEW WHAT YOU'D DO TO US!"

Her hands jolt up to cover her head. "I did what I thought was best," she croaks, shaking like a child. "I know you know it. We can fix this now."

The pressure's let off. My voice tightens down. "My mum is *dead*," I say. The air squirms with heat lines. "How can you fix that?"

All the lights up and down the street are flickering on and off, on and off, on and—she straightens up in the silence, still trembling as she steps closer to me. So close, her jacket starts to smoke at the collar and hems. She's blinking hard to keep the dryness from her eyes.

"I see now," she cries, wiping a smudge of soot and tears away. Two star-shaped buttons fall from her sleeve, the threads charred. They sound like gongs as they hit the ground. "You're an adult now—things are different. We can compromise."

"Hawthorne . . ." Gristle warns, but I snap my arm out to block him.

I look at her, burning herself up for me 'cause she loves me so much. She made a school 'cause she loves me so much. She got herself into office 'cause she loves me so much. And I know it wasn't easy for her, none of it. Not surviving alone. Not watching her brother disappear into the madness. Not working with cops, and doctors, and spending long nights trying to fix her world. Can I blame her for not knowing any better than the dog-eat-dog dockyards? Was this the best she could do for me?

Can she change, even now?

"I don't want to be mortal," I tell her. I just want us to be together, for Solstice dinner at midnight. I wanted my family to come pick me up, but they burned up at the fayre, all of us. I can feel the flames around me dimming a bit. My throat's choking. "I want you to trust me, Auntie."

"I know—I understand now," she says with that breaking smile. The polish is melting off her shoes. Her face looks like a husk. "I do. I always have."

I want to believe her.

I can't, and here's the proof:

Her eyes dart over my shoulder. Through the crackling flames, I smell the iron reek of the police coming back from the building.

My aunt raises her raw-red hand to wave them over with their cuffs and batons. Because she still thinks that's best. And her pity will get me killed if she tries hard enough.

But they can't see us, because my fey brother's got my back.

Nice try, Gristle says from within this secret dome hiding us from the world. It's not words, but a deep rumbling up through the ground, low and loud. The gravel at our feet bounces.

Scratch. A voice like my mum's whispers from somewhere in my skull. I swear I see Shona Maxim flinch like she hears it too.

"You don't get to love me like that," I say. We're done negotiating.

Her posture shatters. Gristle puts his hand on my back. We don't burn like we were supposed to so many cycles ago. "I warned you."

"Hawthorne—" she tries to say, but we're done.

I don't know why she rushes toward me. I don't think I'm gonna *get* to know why. But I know as I see her getting closer, looking so old and worn down from trying to fix someone who didn't need fixing, that I won't get to hear her answer.

Before she can touch me, I bring my forearms up to block my face like a boxer. Some small part of me asks if I want to do this, and I know I do. I make the impulsive call.

Fwoosh.

Fire rushes out from around me like solar flares, burning with every color named and unnamed. It washes warm over Gristle and boils up past him as our aunt falls into it. She could just jump back, save herself, but she stands in all that squirming heat, rigid and still reaching for me. I watch her eyes while the heat eats up her wool jacket and blisters into her skin to incinerate muscle then bone while she doesn't even try to scream.

I wonder if she'd rather die like this than live in a mad world where she doesn't win.

Her hands crumble to ash before they can touch me, and Maxim and I are orphaned again.

◆

Gristle leads me out, with his duster wrapped around me and my bare feet stepping over the cold ground. I don't feel it. I don't much know what's happening. Nothing is orange and red anymore, cops and doctors and firefighters are shouting, but they're running right past us.

"It's alright, Hawthorne," Gristle says back to me. "Just don't . . . don't move too much. I don't know how it works yet."

Eyes can see us, but minds don't register it. Invisible.

Gristle leads me through the maze of cars and trucks and toward the empty street on the other side, while the school's burned-out windows stare after us, the crackling and crumbling calling out through the city streets. I don't know what'll happen to it with Secondchild dead. Or anyone, *us*, with President Shona Maxim burned to nothing but the memory of her eyes looking into mine and her hands reaching out to me.

Did she deserve it for crossing the one line I drew with fire? I'm too tired to know.

All I know is my hand is in my brother's like when we were small, and he takes me through the cars with the siren lights flashing around us like a good party. Some dog's beside me, walking with my hand drifting against its back. It's like it's tethering me down, its fur nice and rough between my fingers. Quen, yes, now I remember. Hien's familiar.

Hien's alive. I didn't kill them, and Mum didn't kill Senan or anyone else. I'm tired, but I've never felt more free.

I watch Gristle's broad back as we duck off the road between the lampposts dressed all pretty for Solstice. There's snow falling, shining in the gold light. We head down some alleys, weaving away, and then finally stop between two brick walls soaring high above us where the air smells like evergreen and spiced milk. Somewhere distant, carolers are singing. We huddle into the warm steam from a heating exhaust pipe that catches our colossal shadows.

Gristle looks to Quen, it blinks at him, and then goes trotting off for the street.

I can still smell the fire from here, but I think it's mostly a memory, cooked into our hair and clothes like when we were small. Gristle stares down at his scuffed-up shoes. We both lean our backs into the bricks. Despite it all, there's still a foot of distance between us.

I don't know what to say. Midnight must be soon. I just want to celebrate the Solstice, Gristle. Can we get some candles and some presents and some sparklers? Ring some bells, even if the sound hurts a bit? I'll tell you the Verdossi stories I remember. I'll try.

"What now," he asks. It doesn't sound like a question, just musing into the quiet snow and steam. When I look down, actually look, there's electricity humming around his tapping shoes, connecting pretty lightning lines between the embossing.

Well, howdee. I point down, so he knows I've seen. *I'm looking at you, Gristle.*

"Hmm," he grunts. "I'm . . . I'm not sure what to do with it."

Me neither.

In the space I've got now, I miss my mum. It's a hollow feeling, all deep in my stomach. I ain't never been allowed to miss her good and proper 'cause I was told she was nothing but a killer. So now that I know it was a frame up *because* Mum was so strong and so loved that she might have put this city on a new track, do I get that grief back? Am I allowed to hurt for my aunt, too?

It's Gristle who breaks the silence, loud like a door closing. "I miss my dad," he chokes. His hat's tilted back, so his face is wide and open like it was when we were small, real tears building up in his dark eyes. "I don't know what we've been d-doing since then. She had us at each other's throats. I've just been g-g-going in circles like she—like she wanted me—like she wanted me to *be her and not him.*" He swipes his arm over his eyes and keeps it there, dragging in breath. His knees buckle. Static ripples off of him. Suddenly he's that quiet, pensive kid I used to love, like Maxim Child was locked away all this time. Now he's here, gulping down the reek of this city and sobbing for his daddy.

Now I'm here, a fey again like when we met on that curb as mites.

Gristle, I think, like I can send it into his head. I keep my one palm tangled with his, but turn toward him. In that hidden spot between us, I hold my other hand out with the embroidered sleeve of his duster wide around my wrist. There are still little silver specks on my hand, twinkling like fresh snow. *Look.*

I open my palm, and the spirits give me a flame. It puffs a bit with my last reserve of energy.

He sniffs, chokes back a small sob, and then, in the shadowed space we make like a faerie ring, he holds his hand up next to mine. Our hands are so different, his huge and clay-brown and mine green-gold with spidery fingers. And yet, the same soot in the creases, and then a crack and flash in his palm; the slightest bit of electricity forces itself to light, dancing and twisting in tinsel-soft arcs. I know it's carving a path through his head that'll get stronger every time.

Go slow. Focus. Don't break the altar.

If we practice, don't rush or fight, just *be*, I wonder how powerful we can get. The fire and flash build brighter. They warm our faces, heat our clothes, dance in our strange eyes. He looks as blank-faced as always, and tired. I feel tired too while my senses sharpen in harmony with the world singing our song.

Not right now. He closes his fist. I close mine.

"Can we try?" he asks me. I don't think he means fire-and-flash, but just us loving each other again. I nod and wonder if I should hug him but don't know if I'm there yet. I know I want to be. I guess we really are all we've got now.

Well, not all the way.

Car tires slosh through the gutter beyond, just as claws click back to the alley entrance. Quen stares, a black silhouette with snow shimmering in its fur like stars. A clocktower bell rings in the distance. Midnight. The city coughs into a bust-up of bells and cheers, far enough that it isn't so loud. The darkest night is halfway finished. From here, longer days, sunnier skies. Something new.

"Happy Solstice, Hawthorne," Gristle says. A blast of fireworks in the sky paints color across his face.

I squeeze his hand to say it back, then we walk out after Quen. A powder-blue car is sitting at the silent curb, with Fionne leaning out the driver side to watch the colored sky reflecting in her glasses. She's not wearing her fancy coat, and her makeup ain't so young and party-girl like it was. Still, under all the popping colors painting across her cheeks, she's the girl I loved all my life, and still now.

Happy Solstice, Feenee, I think.

"Happy Solstice, H," she says when Gristle ducks into the back seat. I crouch by the door and put my chin on the rolled-down window.

"I start at *Dolly Day* tomorrow, like I said I would," she tells me, looking off for some distant place rather than at my face. "It's nice, my life. We should talk, if you wanna be in it. I figure that's more complicated now than it was."

That's for sure. Quen puts its heavy head on my shoulder, pulling me closer to the ground. It lets out a slow whine. I don't know where any of us go from here.

Hello again, Stregoni, I hear, from the smug bastard in the back of the car. My skin heats in response, but I'm too tired to do anything about it. *Would you like some guidance now, or are you content to keep fumbling in the dark?*

Puck's Port Herald

58SC, 1 Summer Moon, 1 Sun

"HISTORY REPEATS"
2 DEAD FROM MAD FEY, INCLUDING PRESIDENT MAXIM

Last night, at only a quarter-bell to Solstice, fey poster child Hawthorne Stregoni, 18, incited a mad blaze at the University of Stoutshire's Institution for Fey Re-Education on 8th Street, which resulted in the deaths of Doctor Sonder Secondchild and President Shona Maxim, Stregoni's aunt. Stregoni is the daughter of Hàzell Stregoni, infamous for the 51SC Summer Fayre Massacre. Stregoni had been sent to the school along with roughly 100 other fey children to learn how to control her Faerie Disorder. Now 2 are dead, and 12 injured.

"President Maxim was trying to calm her niece," said a still-stunned President Calligan Firstchild, who has found themself thrust quickly into office. "Maxim ran over with [Gristle Senan Maxim Junior], then Stregoni jumped down toward them from the third floor. I'm still unsure of what happened next."

Despite the presence of over 100 witnesses, no one was able to give an accurate report of the night's events. Doctors at the school have confirmed that Stregoni was given an experimental drug that may have led to this rampage, but aside from the murder of Secondchild and how she subsequently descended on her aunt, the story becomes muddled. Doctors have suggested that Stregoni's symptoms might have included the ability to influence others mentally, which would explain the apparent temporary memory loss in those observing the events.

Investigators at the scene found a crater with a pile of ash in the center, which they were able to identify, using dental records, as the remains of President Maxim. Gristle Senan Maxim Junior, 18, is currently missing. Investigators cannot confirm if he is another victim or perhaps acted as an accomplice, though those close to the family suggest he and Stregoni were estranged.

The Puck's Port P.D. urges citizens to stay alert as they search for Stregoni and for Maxim, and to report any suspicious activity. It is well-documented that most mad fey are caught within 48 bells as their behavior escalates. However, with 2 dead within only a few moons of operation, the public has begun to grow concerned by the University of Stoutshire's Institution for Fey Re-Education.

According to a staff whistleblower, Secondchild was aware that Stregoni's power constituted madness after several prior incidents, but the doctor had been given special permission to continue his study of this subject past her eighteenth birthday, when cases must be reported to higher authorities.

"We had been told that there was no risk of her reaching madness, that our methods had been successful. Much of our protocol for treatment of other fey is based on Stregoni's case study," the staff member continued. "It's gut-wrenching to see our work fail so spectacularly. We can't be certain if Stregoni is an outlier, or if our entire study is fatally flawed. We won't be sure unless we continue."

Due to damage to the building and the ongoing investigation, the school has been forced to pause enrollment, but it will continue to operate with its current students, and will cooperate with police investigations. Still, roughly 30 families have already removed their children from the program.

"We were promised this was best for [our child]," said one parent. "But I won't have them be a lab rat for untested procedures. I'm not sure what the alternative is, but it's not this."

If you or a loved one has Faerie Disorder, please consider seeking a stress-test for all those over 18. If you have any information regarding Hawthorne Stregoni, Gisele Senan Maxim Junior, Senator Dermott Ashley III (currently missing, more on page 8), or suspicious fey in your area, please call 777.

GRISTLE SENAN MAXIM JUNIOR
IN
"US MAD FOLK"

Even if Solstice was hell, I know I'm not going to check out again. I owe it to myself to stay sure, even when it's hard, and when it hurts, and when I don't know what will come next.

Ahead of me, the one-room apartment is too dark to parse, just a muddling of shadows. The window's boarded up, but through a small crack I see the coal-swept dockyard row where the sky is so dark you can't tell it's morning. Back home again, after so long away.

I take a slow breath and pull my camera up to my eye.

Pop!-flash.

Dark wooden walls and floor, the unlit and crooked stove, the sink dripping a moldy puddle. Someone in the building is practicing some brassy instrument, maybe a saxophone—it's leaking through the thin walls. Hawthorne's asleep on a bare cot with the dog curled up under her arm. She's still wrapped in my coat, asleep without conversation or complaint.

We're some ways from where we lived, more tucked into the southwest Hannochian quarter, but the air still smells like fish, and old water, and evening walks with my daddy and Hàzell and Hawthorne. I don't think we'll ever get to go back to the Ashwood Road office.

That's alright. Hawthorne and I got away.

I wonder if there's any sense in telling her that I killed our aunt. I pressed my thumb tight against my forefinger and sent a shock to root her in the blast so she couldn't tear away. Like my daddy couldn't run from the carousel explosion.

I let her burn before she could find a better way to trick us. I've got no regrets.

Pop!-flash.

"Gristle," Hawthorne mutters, half asleep. "Stop with the camera, lug."

I lean back against the wall with my camera in my lap.

Footsteps ring from the hallway. The thin streak of light under the flimsy wooden door shifts as shadows tear through it. I leave my camera and stand, ambling over. One voice reverberates through, in Hannochian made of round, warbling sounds like plucked strings. I wait until the conversation ends, and then another moment to hear the landlord head off, before I open the door to the dim hallway.

Hien stands ahead, blurry, hands braced on the railing overlooking the twist of stairs. I'm just in time to spot two small children crouched on the floor above us, moon-round faces peering down between the paper Solstice lanterns still hung from the banister. Hien snaps their head up, the children's eyes go wide, then they scramble off with gleefully frightened giggles to disappear through a door.

Hien stands for another moment. Their shape heaves in a few slow breaths. That brass music is louder out here, a tinny undercurrent to the fragile silence.

I close the door quietly behind. I can't hear anyone else moving outside their apartments.

"Do we have protection?" I ask.

I've called in a favor with my sister, Hien says. Their voice flickers, straining the air pressure into my eardrums. *The Hannochian Court is happy to keep your presence quiet, as long as you need it.*

Aside from old warnings that don't mean anything now, I have no reason not to trust them. I lean my back into the door.

"I'll wait for Hawthorne to wake up, and then we'll figure out next moves," I say. Do we head for the countryside? Maybe even out of Dale? But wherever we go, this growing cruelty is gonna catch up, like Hàzell always said. And I don't much know where I'd fit beyond Puck's Port.

It's a problem to consider later.

"You ought to sleep," I say. "Are you staying here too?"

The blur fizzes as Hien shakes their head.

My stomach sinks a bit. "Oh," I say, but I suppose it's understandable. I was hired, and then they felt guilty, and it doesn't have to be more than that.

They flicker. Suddenly they're facing me, smiling flat with shining gray eyes, hands in the pockets of their baggy trousers and no shirt to speak of. They're pretty, a raw sort of beauty. *Is that disappointment, Mister Maxim? What were you hoping to find?*

The horn warbles through a bad note. I narrow my eyes. "Be serious, Hien."

A whip of frustration sears through the room like an animal's lashing tail. They scoff and flicker back to the blur leaning on the railing, sinking even further now. *You're not frightened,* they say, somehow both a question and a statement.

I am. Frankly, I'm terrified of what's going to happen to us next. Can we stay here forever? Knowing that school is hurting kids the same way they hurt Hawthorne? Not knowing if Ashley'll drag himself from the Gattano garage to rain hell again? Not knowing if Calligan really is a better option? And whatever I have in me, is this madness? It races through me, burning in my veins. Yes, it's good to know my choices are my own, but that just makes them all the more frightening.

We're alone now. Again. I suppose I should have expected it.

"Go on, then," I say, because what else is there. "I suppose I'll see you or I won't."

But they don't move. I don't either. We just stand opposite the other like a dueling showdown. Finally, I hear them take a breath.

A deal then, yes? Hien says. Their image wanes, person-like then not, unreal and real.

"Hien—"

Close your eyes, they say, sharper. *I'll give you ten seconds of the truth, dickie. No messing with your head. And then you decide if I can be trusted near you.*

My skin starts to crawl. The wall sconces flicker once.

I still don't know what to make of them. Maybe this will stitch it up, or just leave me with more questions. Or maybe I will be too terrified to face them. At least I'll know what I'm dealing with.

"Fine, Hien," I say. I step up closer to them, in case they think to run away. "Ten seconds." I close my eyes, turning the world to only a diffused gray. They laugh, a tired rumble like an earthquake.

One second. There was this feeling, like the slightest ringing in my ears—I hadn't noticed it was there, but I notice when it stops. Ahead of me, they turn unearthly cold. It sends goosebumps all up my arms under my jacket, and every hair straight up like a spooked cat's.

Two seconds. The gray through my eyelids is now black and has always been so, as if something in front of me is blocking all the light. Taller than me was strange enough, but this feels taller than life.

Three seconds. I keep my eyes squeezed tight, feeling as if I couldn't open them if I tried, like a mental weight is sealing them shut. I raise my hand. It's shaking.

Four seconds. My reaching hand doesn't meet rough wool, or plush fur, or silk, or even bare skin. Instead, my fingers drag down the divots of something icy and metallic. Armor? Strange scales?

What the hell are you, Hien?

Five seconds. That current of music is still crooning when I reach my hand up higher, higher, and only then do I feel the warmth of skin when my hand falls against what I assume to be the side of a neck, though it would place them more than a foot taller than me.

Six seconds. My stomach is in knots, twisting and leaping. My fingers brush against long hair. I can reach no higher than the obvious point of an ear. I don't know what I'm doing, ever. I don't know what to expect of a life on the run, a life orphaned again, a life where my aunt built us up upon a lie burnt out from under us. Now we fall, spiraling like broken-winged birds. And who do I have in my corner? My sister, who I don't know, and this.

Seven seconds. *I wasn't meant to be tangled with you*, Hien says. I can feel their jaw flexing under my hand, their skin pulsing with feverish strain. *We shouldn't have crossed paths.*

What? Even at only eight seconds, I'm given a tentative, careful image, of stiff gold-brown hands shuffling through Dogfoot bills and letters, a few bells after O'Taglio tried to get into their office, a few bells before we were named, before Hawthorne lit up. I feel the still-shaken fear, Quen nudging my leg. The hands, each studded with scales that twist between gold and red and green, shift the papers until they come upon a business card tucked among them.

They stop. The scales flex carefully.

In the vision, I see a Maxim & Maxim business card. It's ordinary, except someone's penned more information in. I swallow. This was sent before I was named. It's the same card they flashed that morning in the Ashwood office.

Nine seconds. *You can't be certain who sent me to you*, Hien mutters. It couldn't have been my aunt—no one knew what name I was going to pick, not even me. *Whoever they are, they're powerful. I'm no stranger to fey squabbles, but you?*

Me. Someone knew me before I did. They made pawns of us. Did they expect me to follow through as I did? Do they expect me to run now, or stay?

Ten seconds. I don't open my eyes.

Hien's warning rattle snarls through the stairwell, chuckling against the lanterns, pulsing more strain from them.

You two may be fey, and your sister packs a wallop, but the sorts I tread with could eat you both, bones and all. Their face is lowered close—I can feel my breath gust back onto me. *So I'll ask again, Mister Maxim, for your informed and final opinion: Can you truly trust me?*

What the hell am I tangled into? What's the right call here?

I tighten my jaw.

"I just killed the president," I say. No more cowering. No more guessing. "Maybe you oughta be scared of *me*, Phong."

A surprised sound, somewhere between a snarl and a cackle, snaps between every dust particle in the air. My head's rushing like a grin.

I grab the back of their neck and yank them close until their lips crash against mine. For one second, then two, three. I don't open my eyes. Not when I fall back against the wall, not when my hands carve down the sides of that strange cold, not when I feel a wide belt on their waist and they're already yanking my tie away from my neck.

You're the strangest person, Hien says, equal parts compliment and insult. I don't care to respond. Screw the fear, and the doubt, and the guilt.

This is the mess we've fallen into. I don't know what world I've welcomed, but I'm ready to find out.

EPILOGUE

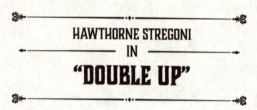

HAWTHORNE STREGONI IN
"DOUBLE UP"

The west side, dockyard smoke sits high this morning, enough to keep me hidden and turn the morning dark and damp while I crouch on the cornice of our hideout building. I want to bring fire into my palm, a smooth flame, but there's something off now. That slow I had on that serum's all dried up. Now I can feel the pyre spitting. Not like it's angry at me for keeping it in, but more like a newborn deer that don't understand where to put its feet just yet. It's a clumsy sort of energy. I hate knowing Hien was right about needing training.

But it's not to say nothing's different. Now, I ain't scared of calming myself the way Mum taught me. I sway a bit, just enough for some small smoke to leak out around my feet. I shake my hands and let some sparkles come off too. That helps.

I hear the access door close and immediately grab the cornice, getting ready to leap off and hope I can light up enough to save me, like when I jumped from that third floor. But when I look back over my shoulder, hair long and wild around my ears and my borrowed duster fluttering like a sail in the faint breeze, I know it's not anyone I gotta be worried about.

I lift my hand, almost a wave. Gristle just stares before he walks up.

"Can I sit?" he asks me.

I furrow my eyebrows at him. Why's he trying to be all polite? Still, I pat the smooth stone and even scoot over. He's a little more awkward than I am as he sits down, leaning all the way back so he won't fall. We sit just like that for a bit, looking down at all the dockyard people running their chores through the snowy streets. Somewhere distant, Fionne's starting her new job, because the world still turns. It's gotta.

"Someone hired me," Gristle says, quiet but sure. "I mean, someone told Hien to hire me. They must be fey—powerful, too."

How's he know that? I'm not sure how to get a question from my brain to my mouth. Before I can try, he rustles in his pocket and pulls out a card to hold between us.

"Hien got this a few days before we were named," he explains. And yet, right there's his name penned in. "*I* didn't even know what to call myself yet."

So someone wanted Gristle on the case. Maybe me, too. How much hand did they have in it all turning out like this? I swallow, thick and unsure. I poke at his name, then point to his forehead.

He squints at the gesture. "You think someone put the name in my head?" he asks.

I shrug.

He worries his still soot-stained fingernail across the card's corner. "I don't know," he says. "It's not like the word came from nowhere—I think I just made the jump between Dad's name and that." He squints a little longer, but just sighs. "And Hien's got mob family—"

I buzz my lips. Duh.

He shakes his head a bit, trying to sort his thoughts. "I just mean that staying here, with them and the sorts of people they know, now with everything *we* know, it's dangerous." The coal train roars over the elevated tracks in the distance, cutting a snaking line toward the countryside. We could hop a ride, try to start over. Gristle's breath blooms out like a smoke cloud. "But I don't think I'm ready to call it quits."

On Hien? But I see the way he's staring down at the streets. Kids are laughing there, along with the music of a penny-candy cart. It sounds like a calliope, like the last day when this city felt like we could truly make it better. How much has changed since Mum died? I know there are still fey scared out there, begging on the docks, hiding in their houses. But could we really make things better?

My eyes get all hot. I can feel my lip crinkle. I crush the business card in my hand.

"Hawthorne—" Gristle starts to say. I don't let him.

I tear sideways, right into his chest. My arms launch around him; his immediately wrap around my rib cage. I fall into his soft neck and he puts his chin into my bony shoulder and I wet his collar with my tears while I hold him so tight I can feel my whole body heating up.

"It's okay," he says, almost choking on the words. "We don't have to do anything about it now. I just wanted the cards on the table."

I hold him tighter. I want to know the whole story here, who hired us and why and what that means. Maybe I also want to stick around to make sure that school doesn't get any worse, even if I don't know what I can do about it. I just know that I want to do it with him. I want to fit my palm into his while we figure out who we are now. Not because we're all we got, but because I want to choose my brother.

I think he'll move, but he doesn't. "Hawthorne?" he says again. In the far distance, sirens scream, heading off for someone else they think is rotten. This city's always hurting. "I . . . I need you not to feel bad about . . . about what you did last night, with Auntie . . ."

My hands get even hotter behind him. I have to wiggle my toes to spark it all out. I don't feel too guilty, mostly because I haven't thought long on it yet.

"I helped," Gristle says. I want to be surprised, but I'm not. "If you start feeling like you did the wrong thing, then just remember that I think it was the right call, okay?"

I lean my forehead even harder into him. Alright, that's . . . that's fine, I guess. Maybe it'll feel worse tomorrow, or the sun after that, or in the middle of random nights when our guards are down. But for now, with the coal smoke heavy and the street loud, and him here with me, it's okay.

I sit back slowly, so I can look at him. He isn't wearing his hat, and his hair's all messed into windswept peaks with that new white strip so obvious. Even his tie is loose over one undone button. It's not much like him. Maybe the change is good.

I open my palm so I can get the card. But once my fingers are all unfurled, I flinch, mouth fumbling open and tears heating up again. All that's left in my palm is charcoal and ash. I look up to Gristle's face, ready to fumble an apology.

He only nods, the Maxim Child version of a smile. He holds up his camera. "I got a picture before," he says, and then adds, "I kinda figured you'd get clumsy like that."

I roll my eyes and actually laugh. It comes out in a mouthful of smoke and sparks, but it's still something brighter than it is heavy. I lean sideways into his shoulder and hold the handful over the neighborhoods that raised us, toward the port I came in on. I let the ash and charcoal fall from my hand, fluttering off into the breeze and taking all that hurt with it. The second my hands are clean, I shake them out and grab his palm in mine again. It fits perfect, even now.

"This filthy city," he mutters, sounding all at once like his daddy, and so very much like himself. "I'm glad we made it this far."

We watch the sun come up high over the city we thought we knew. I wonder what sort of other world's out there under the shining surface, what sorts of clues are waiting and enemies loading bullets and drawing up syringes. It's terrifying. But we're here together.

We can be a new dockyard duo, to build something better than we know.

ON NOIR, FEAR, AND HOPE

This book exists because of my partner, who has been a lifelong classic movie and film noir detective fan. When first asked to write a noir detective book, I shrugged it off—I didn't feel any connection to the genre. As a queer, trans, neurodivergent Italian guy, I'm closer to a mash-up of *The Maltese Falcon*'s villains than its hero. To me, noir was just a bunch of moody misogynists running around with guns until the screen faded to depressing black . . . I wasn't exactly wrong.

As a bit of history, the film noir and "hardboiled detective" genre came into popularity around the 1930s, in response to the mass disillusionment caused by WWI and the Great Depression. So many people had gone out to break their bodies for their country, perhaps hoping to bring back the "roaring 20s" they'd once known, and instead returned to the churning gears of industry, growing poverty, and very few chances to rise beyond it. Those filthy cities full of factory smoke aren't fiction.

And then came the hardboiled detective. He was dashing

enough for an audience of white American men to project upon, yet still jaded with the world around him, often on his way out of a respectable job or otherwise cast off by society, alienated from any detective duo partner, and never as rich or well-educated as his classic detective counterparts. Even if he did solve the case (which was never guaranteed), his ending wasn't happy, just resolved enough to close the curtain until a sequel called him back to the stage. He wasn't a hero for the beautiful future the audience wanted to live in, but one for the unfair, painful, disappointing, isolating present they saw every day.

Original noirs were clearly targeting cishet white American men, but marginalized authors and readers have even more reason to stick our fingers in a genre that's all about disenchantment and fear. Puck's Port is inherently queer, the fey encapsulate all the neurodiverse and mentally ill traits I live with, our heroes are fighting against ableism and government corruption and police violence... and yet, at the end of the story, despite their wins, Gristle and Hawthorne still contend with a world that feels only slightly better off. Whether they win, or lose, the filthy city still turns.

When you put it like that, it doesn't exactly sound hopeful. But there's something almost cathartic about sitting in our current terrifying reality instead of dreaming of a perfectly resolved future. It'd be tempting to give our heroes a utopic ending, but that's not the purpose of noir. I'm not sure it's the purpose of life either—believing it is will just set us up for failure. Whether we're falling for a new fad diet promising us the life of our dreams, or believing in a politician swearing to vanquish an enemy and bring about a new glorious day, or even hoping that just one more protest will surely send the empire into a tailspin, we're only going to be disappointed in the end. Nothing is ever so easy.

Noir is listless, and moody, but it reminds us that there will never be a world where we can lay down our fear completely. The problems we're all dealing with—capitalism, racism, transphobia, homophobia, colonialism, abortion access, ableism, and on and on . . . these are bigger than one silver solution. It might seem terrifying, and yet I offer you the alternative: if we're just one step away from total victory, it means we're only one step from total failure too. Instead, we have the opportunity to try again and again to build the world we want to see.

As I write this, I don't know if Gristle and Hawthorne's story will continue, and frankly I think that's the point. There will always be another barrier to break, another friend to help, another moment of fear. I'm not sure we'll ever stop feeling unsure, but I think that's part of being human. Instead of running from it, we can sit in those feelings together, and fight for a better future.

Even if we can't fight to win, we fight anyway, because that's part of being human. This filthy city may be tough to beat, but so are we.

In solidarity,
Matteo L. Cerilli

ACKNOWLEDGMENTS

Alright, let's do this.

First, to my little sister, Megan. If you know me IRL, you know I never shut up about how impressive she is, and how much I owe her for who I am today. Thank you for surviving childhood with me, and for agreeing to our adulthood peace treaty. Sorry for any accidental callouts in this—hopefully they're equally split between us. With similar apologies, thanks to my parents Wendy and Giuseppe for your work in raising two battle-dome brawlers. Thank you to my extended family too, and especially to the ancestral chorus of Italian anarchists that helped me write Hàzell.

Next, to my therapist! For privacy's sake, I'll leave your name out, but you know who you are and you hopefully know why you're in the acknowledgments. There are so many truths in this book that I couldn't have gotten to without your encouragement. Thank you for having my back during the hard parts.

To my early readers, Reanne Bast and Roxy Moldovanu, for being excited enough about this project to convince me to move forward.

To my phenomenal 5OL editor and "Matteo's Books Expert," Jess de Bruyn, for spinning an incredibly complicated story down into a perfect editorial letter. None of my rambling would ever make it to printed page without you. I owe just as much to my agent, Ali McDonald, for hyping me up since day one, and to Cassie Rodgers and Olga Filina for making up the rest of the awesome 5 Otter Literary team. Thank you also to my professors at York University for challenging me. I wrote the first draft of this in my third year at York, and couldn't have finished it without everything you've taught me.

To my editor, Peter Phillips, for scooping this up and giving me another run with the Tundra team. Thank you to Steph Ehmann for her publicity work with *Lockjaw*, and now to Graciela Colin for spearheading *Bad in the Blood*. Thank you also to Catherine Marjoribanks for the copy edits, Erin Kern for the proofread, and Matthew Flute for designing and arranging the typesetting and interiors and for directing the amazing cover by Evangeline Gallagher. And finally, to Nkechinyem Oduh for lending her eyes to Fionne to make sure I'm putting out the story I want to tell. A book is a group effort. Thank you to all the names I'm not aware of working the behind-the-scenes cogs to get this onto shelves.

To the communities that have held and loved me: friends, family, booksellers, librarians, readers, grocery store clerks, TTC drivers, and all the rest. Without you, this book wouldn't exist, and neither would I.

And finally, to my partner for being a weird little noir nerd. I would know literally nothing about the genre without you, so thank you for weighing in on all the aesthetics and themes, and challenging me where I need it. Hopefully this book is a fitting tribute that gives you much less second-hand embarrassment than *Something's Up with Arlo* did. I'm absolutely enamoured that I get to spend the rest of my strange little life making up strange little stories for you.